To Sian
with best wishes
from
Roger Thomas

Blue Tooth

Also by Bryce Thomas

Rhamin

Lucy Lockhart: The Awakening

Coming soon

The Last Spell

Blue Tooth

by
Bryce Thomas

THOMAS HAMILTON & CO.

This novel is entirely a work of fiction.
The names, characters and incidents portrayed in it are the work of the author's imagination. Any resemblance to actual persons, living or dead; events; organizations including companies and domains formed during or after the writing and publication of this book; or localities is entirely coincidental.

First published in Great Britain 2012
Thomas Hamilton & Co Publishers
80 Warham Road, Harrow HA3 7HZ

Copyright © Bryce Thomas 2011
Cover design by Helena Thomas © 2011
Cover artwork by Neil Booth

Bryce Thomas asserts the right under the Copyright, Designs and Patents Act 1988
to be identified as the author of this work

A CIP catalogue record of this book
is available from The British Library
ISBN: 978-1-907696-07-7

First Paperback Edition

Printed and bound in the UK
by CPI Group (UK) Ltd, Croydon, CR0 4YY

All rights reserved. No part of this publication may be reproduced, introduced to or stored in a retrieval system or transmitted in any form by any means, electronic, mechanical, photocopying, recording or otherwise, without the prior permission of the publisher, nor otherwise be circulated in any form of binding or cover other than that in which it is published and without a similar condition, including this condition, being imposed on the subsequent purchaser. Any unauthorized act in respect of this publication may be liable to criminal prosecution or civil claim for damages.

www.thomashamilton.co.uk

To my wife June

Whose love and support are my foundations

CHAPTER ONE

Rasci heard it first.

He heard it before Rhamin, before Yeltsa, even before Charka whose ears were the most sensitive of the pack. At first he thought that the sound was just a figment of his weary mind as he began to fall asleep, a memory of a noise he had heard in the past and which he was recalling as he began to dream. But then he suddenly realized that it wasn't a memory. The sound was coming to him from far, far away and he was hearing and feeling it right now.

But he didn't awake completely; not right away; not until his mind had travelled many miles into the distance to the iron bird; not before he had seen the people peering down at the ground looking though black tubes with shiny eye holes, searching the plain for something.

How Rasci knew it, he could not say, but he knew it all the same. These men were searching for a huge black wolf with white ears.

They were back again.

And they were hunting.

For Rhamin!

With his head on his front paws and his eyes still closed,

Rasci's ears suddenly stood up straight and began to rotate, first to one side, then to the other, homing in on the elusive waves that rumbled subsonically through the still warm air. His eyes flicked open as he lifted his chin from his paws. He sniffed the air, but the familiar smell of his comrades was all he could detect with his sensitive nose. He looked around the cave. Now Charka and Rhamin had sensed it too. They had opened their eyes and turned their heads towards Rasci. Neither spoke, but simply turned their ears toward the mouth of the cave and listened intently.

Then they heard it for certain. It was the same familiar sound of thrashing wings; first the remote, subsonic vibrations of compacted air, then the unmistakable beating of the rotor blades as they cut into the sky, whipping up the air currents as they carried the flying machine closer and closer.

Of any wolf, anywhere, Rhamin was the most fearless. If death were to come to him then it would come without his having worried about it for a single moment. Bigger, stronger predators feared and hated him simply because he had no fear of them.

He had no worries, no hang ups, and he took everything and every day in his stride.

Or he used to.

Now?

Well there were some things he would never have worried about. But in the last few months, things had changed for good, but not for the better. Now, there were some things that made his hackles rise and his blood run cold. And he could hear them from many miles away; the throbbing beat of their gigantic wings; the massive, rippling sound waves pushing relentlessly through the air, travelling to his ears as the rotors hammered through the sky. It was the sound of the men kind; the noise of their machines; the thrashing, thud, thud, thud of their helicopters.

The heavens had been peaceful since Rhamin's escape from the prison camp. His capture and incarceration with his mate Yeltsa were becoming fading memories, bad dreams that were to be pushed to the farthest recesses of his mind; experiences best forgotten so that life could return to normal. But the belief that everything would return to normal was, itself, just a dream, a wishful thought caught up in the moment of sheer relief after the spectacular and daring rescue that had led to Rhamin's escape back into the wild.

It was the day that the Rozalskis brought Lexa, the pack's wolf dog, back from the farm. Although she was marked with rippled scars that rucked the skin on her dark face and along her sleek and muscular body, landscaping her features like a rumpled piece of smooth tree bark, Lexa was now fully recovered from her injuries. And the celebrations that took place when she arrived had been so jubilant, so ecstatic that, tired, content and happy, every single wolf of the Rhamin pack had retired to the cool, dark recesses of the Darin, their cave, to rest and sleep. Until now, the only sound of movement was the steady rise and fall of so many weary chests as the pack slumbered peacefully.

But now the peace had ended. All the pack was awake and listening. Old Zelda sightlessly looked up at the roof of the cave, her bulging eyes seemingly seeing beyond the rock and into the open air above the Darin. She shook her head and groaned.

'No!' she whimpered. 'Oh, no.'

Lexa's floppy ears were forward and listening, now on full alert. The skin on her scarred and distorted brow wrinkled anxiously as she, too, listened with trepidation to the sound of the rotors beating closer and closer.

Then it was there; suddenly; louder and unsettling; so unsettling in fact that many of the wolves jumped up and spun around, looking up at the roof of the cave, just like Zelda, seeing in their minds beyond the rocks; seeing the machine that was coming upon them. The sound inside the cave increased tenfold as the rotor blades hammered and thrashed at the warm evening sky, forcing air and dust down into the gap between the cliff face and the rocky escarpment walls that hid the opening to the Darin.

Whoooosh!

Over it went, speeding away on its destined flight path. The threat had gone as suddenly as it had approached. The pounding din of the rotor blades was already fading behind the dense, rocky outcrop.

Men have many machines which they call helicopters, and just like someone or some wolf walking through a meadow, oblivious to the wildlife teaming beneath their feet, these flying machines go about their business, soaring above the landscape, to and from their various destinations, unaware of the living creatures on the plains and in the forests beneath them. And likewise, those creatures become accustomed to the sound of these monstrous birds, and simply ignore them as they do the machines on wheels that travel along the distant hardened tracks or roadways.

But not Rhamin. And not his pack.

Helicopters had changed their lives for ever. Hearing one of these metal birds again, and so close by, he would always remember how he and his mate Yeltsa had been captured and kidnapped. He would never forget how they had been shot with darts and pursued until they dropped from shear fatigue as some kind of sleeping sickness pumped through their bodies with every desperate heart beat and with every frantic stride they took.

Try as he may, not to think about that harrowing and traumatic experience, he would never be able to repress the memories that welled up in his mind even when he was resting quietly. So when, as now, one of those mechanical birds actually appeared, it was a hundred times worse. The mere sound of that dreadful machine in the sky was enough to set him panting anxiously and to make his heart thump wildly.

As silence returned to the plain, however, gradually his breathing calmed and he laid his chin back on his paws and relaxed again. Although these machines had never flown so near to the Darin before, this one appeared to have passed without incident.

Or so he thought.

The air had gone quiet once more inside the cave. The beat of the rotors had almost completely died away. But then, as suddenly as its sound had faded, the waning noise suddenly increased again. The machine had turned and once again the air was packed with turmoil as it roared up from behind the escarpment and hovered directly overhead. This time it was not travelling on its set course; it was balanced in the air like a hawk over its prey waiting for its quarry to move. That's what made Rhamin's blood run cold. This was not a flying machine going on its way from one place to another. This machine was looking for something. There was no doubt about it. He was convinced that the man-made predator was hunting once again.

'Look out!' Rasci yelped suddenly. 'Look out. They are looking for you Rhamin.'

'I'm safe here, Rasci,' Rhamin assured him calmly, although, inside himself, he did not feel so composed. His heart was hammering again as he fought hard to control his breathing, but he knew he must not let Rasci or any of the other wolves know how he really felt inside. He must remain their confident leader. If he stayed calm and composed then the rest of the pack would not panic. He peered out from the shadows, unable to see the hovering craft as it sent its trailing dust storm swirling into the mouth of the cave. He walked out of the darkness and stood assertively by the opening of the Darin.

'They are looking for you, Rhamin,' Zelda spoke up above the noise.

'They are definitely hunting for something, that's for sure,' replied Rhamin, now fully in control of his emotions.

'It's you they seek,' Rasci repeated gravely. 'I know that for a fact.'

Lexa was standing with old Zelda and Silvah. She shivered. 'It's starting all over again, isn't it?' she said, her voice shaking with trepidation. 'You escaped and now they are looking for you. They've come to take you back.' She forced down a deep sob that had welled up from inside her chest. 'I won't let them,' she cried, her voice cracking with emotion as she looked at her father. 'None of us will.'

'Surely they couldn't have known you'd had help to escape from them, Rhamin,' Silvah said, edging nervously to the opening where the dust storm from the thundering down-draft continued to churn outside.

'No, but they would expect me to make my way back home eventually,' Rhamin replied, still calm. 'They must reckon that I would have made it back here by now.'

'But they didn't know where *here* was,' Ramusan declared. 'They captured you over a day's travel away from the Darin. In all the wide open space out there, how do they come to be looking here?'

'Because they know where we are, young wolf,' old Zelda came in. 'They know we are here. They know our cave is here and they know we are in it.'

That's impossible,' Rhamin stated. 'The farmer wouldn't have told them. And he and his family are the only men kind that know the Darin is our main place of abode.' He shook his head. 'No, he wouldn't have told anyone.'

'No,' Rasci replied, joining Rhamin and peering cheerlessly out of the mouth of the cave, 'Ben and his family had nothing to do with it, I'm sure.'

'But something or someone has led them here,' Silvah asserted.

Just then, the sound above them changed again. The hovering metal bird had stood in the sky for ages, floating menacingly as if assessing its prey and working out how to get at it. Then, apparently concluding its calculations, it finally changed the beat of its wings, tilted to one side and thrashed off towards the eastern horizon from where it had originally come.

'Then we must move out to the forest,' Rhamin instructed, as the flying clouds of dust and sand began to settle outside. He breathed a sigh of relief that the danger had passed, at least for the time being. 'Nobody can tell them where we are when we are out there. Even we will not know where we will be tomorrow.'

He turned and looked at all his wolf pack gathered now around him. He smiled. Most of his wolves still had their hackles standing out like porcupine bristles. He knew then that not one of his pack would have stood by and allowed anyone to capture him again.

Not without a fight.

A fight to the death.

It was the end of a long day and dusk had already begun to pull in the cool night air. 'Darkness will be upon us soon,' Rhamin stated. 'I suspect that the metal bird has left for that reason and that reason alone. We must leave immediately if we are to make it deep into the mountain forests before that thing returns.'

CHAPTER TWO

There is nothing exciting about long plane journeys, except, perhaps, if it is the first time you have flown, and you are thirteen years old. But in Elsie's case, even though she had never flown before, there was not the merest particle of exhilaration running through her body. There was no thrill, no excitement; just a wretched sadness mixed with an inquisitive curiosity. The only reason her eyes looked out of the small, thick window at the side of her seat was to watch the terminal disappear below as the Boeing thundered up into the air. Her mother had taken her to the airport and seen her off, but Elsie knew she wouldn't be there watching as the plane accelerated along the runway, then lifted off and climbed. She would have left the terminal as soon as Elsie entered the boarding lounge, long before her daughter had embarked on the flight.

In seconds the runway and the terminal buildings were just toy town replicas disappearing through wisps of gossamer vapour. She was heading towards the distant tumbling clouds, alone, cheerless and with no real idea or explanation as to why she was travelling so far away from home.

When the plane had levelled out, the hostess came along

the aisle, leaned over the woman sitting next to Elsie and asked, 'Are you all right, Elsie?' She looked at the pale, young girl whose long straight hair ran over her shoulders like a cascade of sun filled, golden spring water. As Elsie turned her sapphire eyes towards the air-hostess, she nodded, then silently turned her head once again towards the window. The sudden rush of nervous adrenalin had dissipated. It had washed away, and in its place, a torrent of grief and resentment flooded into the empty cavity.

Holding tightly onto the book on her lap, she pursed her lips and thought how cruel life could be. Why had it happened to her? Why had her father died? 'You'll understand some day,' her mother had said with floods of tears welling up in her eyes. But Elsie understood already. She understood that while other children had a mother and father that made the family whole, she had only half a family. And that half was discarding her, sending her away.

'It's only for a short while,' her mother had said. 'Your uncle Raymond and Aunt Maria will look after you. It will be like a holiday.' A holiday for goodness sake! Since when do children go on a holiday when their father dies? Who on earth could expect a child to enjoy a holiday like that?

In Elsie's mind, it was a punishment, not a vacation. Was it because she hadn't been getting on with anybody lately? She certainly hadn't been getting on with her mother. Every day since her father had died, they would argue about something or other. The arguments were nearly always about Elsie's school work, or what she had done this time to upset the teachers.

Since the death of her father, Elsie had hated school; every single second of every single minute of every long hour of it. It wasn't that she didn't want to learn. Her appetite for knowledge was insatiable and had been since an early age. But since her very first clash with authority, she had found another means to learn, and it was Elsie's father who had furnished her with that means. It was quiet and solitary and it suited Elsie just fine. And since Elsie's father worked in a library, every other day he would bring home a book for his daughter to read, a novel one day, a factual book, the next time. Whatever the subject, Elsie would read it cover to cover.

Her favourite place to read was in her bedroom where, on her bed, with her legs crossed and leaning forward on her elbows, she would be absorbed into the text until, finally, she would turn the last page, sit upright, stretching her arms out to the ceiling, then close the book. A few hours would have passed, but her mother and father never disturbed her. Her mother was hardly ever at home anyway. Some high powered job in the local government, Elsie was told, but never did get a full job description. Her father worked in an office at the city library. An administrative position. He was the one who dropped Elsie off at school and picked her up later the same day. He made sure she was dressed smartly and saw to her meals. He, like his daughter, spent much of his time reading; sometimes books, but more often than not, papers and files from work.

With tear filled eyes, Elsie sighed. Her father had gone and wouldn't be coming back. The one person that really understood her had left her in a world full of people that didn't even like her. And equally, now, she detested the world and everybody in it. It was their fault her father had been killed. She hated being a child in a grown up's world governed by grown up's rules. Her father had been the only support in the bridge that spanned the years she would have to endure before she too, was old enough to argue back. Oh how she longed for that time to come. In the meantime, there was no way to soften the ache except to do what had always made her father so proud.

It all went back a long way

When Elsie was six, she had been watching her father as he read a novel. He was sitting next to his elderly mother. Grandma had come to live with them and her father would frequently sit and keep her company. His wife, Sally, was often still at work or when she was at home she would be busy doing something from which Elsie was banned. So Elsie would play quietly in the same room while her grandmother read a magazine and her father read his novel.

One day, Elsie had been standing facing her father. Suddenly, she begun to read aloud from a page of the book her father held open. She was reading the text upside down and as fast as her father was reading it the right way up. Turning another page, her father said to Grandma, 'Hey, mum, listen to this.' Asking Elsie to repeat what she had just done, once again the story rolled off her tongue. He had been so proud of her that day. But almost a year later the teacher's report came back saying that she was not only a poor reader, but that she was an unruly and destabilising influence on the rest of the class.

Does not concentrate...

Could do better...

Disruptive and insolent...

Argumentative...

POOR READER...

Poor Reader! 'What books are you reading?' her father asked the teacher at the school open day.

'The basic reading skills books, of course,' the teacher

replied. 'Pupils have got to master the basics, you know.'

'What, no proper stories then?' her father asked.

'The children have to learn to read first,' replied the teacher, curtly. 'Elsie could read if she tried a bit harder but, unfortunately, she's just lazy.'

It was then that he realized that his beloved Elsie was bored into a state of mummification. Of course she could read. The teacher was absolutely right, she wasn't trying. The teaching system had set the pupils a linear procedure and no child was expected to challenge it or move outside its constraining, boundaries. As a result, and despite the efforts of some of the very best teachers in the following years, Elsie had become a rebel and a trouble-maker.

Only her father understood her, and now he was gone for ever.

She would never forget her beloved Daddy.

Eventually, her eyes dipped to the book on her knee. With a deep sigh, she opened it. Absorbed in a novel, for a short while at least, she could travel to a land of make belief and forget the pain through which her whole mind and body was being hauled.

CHAPTER THREE

'Kill Zelda.'

'What? You are joking!'

'You sound like you have a soft spot for the scraggy old bitch.'

Solin stood up straight and faced Rhiana nose to nose. 'I don't have soft spots. You should know that.'

'Then Zelda must be killed.'

'What good will that do? She's a blind, decrepit, old bag of skin and fur. She'd be lucky to come out on top in a fight with a kitten, let alone a fully grown rabbit.' Solin sat down and then lowered his chest to the floor with a grunt. His ribs were still healing from the blow he had received fighting his last battle. 'I really am not comfortable with that idea.'

'You have to kill her.' Rhiana insisted.

'I can think of other ways of settling scores,' he growled dismissively.

'This isn't just about revenge, Solin. It's about…'

'It's about creeping up, and killing a helpless, blind old wolf. I would rather kill a worthier opponent.'

Rhiana sighed. 'Zelda might be blind, but she is a seer. Her eyes are sightless, but her mind sees beyond that cave.'

'And what? You think she wouldn't see me coming to kill her?' He shook his head and chuckled more at Rhiana than to himself. 'I'd have thought she would have seen that!'

'I've known that wolf since before you were born, Solin. She was old even then, but one thing I also know, she's proud, very proud. She won't be afraid to die because she has long outlived her allotted time on earth. She's been on borrowed time for years.' Rhiana thought for a moment and then added, 'And because she's proud, she won't go worrying her beloved Rhamin.'

Solin shook his head. 'I still can't see why we have to waste time on her.'

'Because killing her will prevent her from warning Rhamin. So he won't be expecting anything that we have planned. At the same time, killing her will draw him out of the Darin and into our trap.'

'Trap? What trap?' He looked at her curiously. He shook his head. 'All your traps seem to have ended in defeat up to now. And I don't mean defeat of our enemy.'

'We've had setbacks, that's all,' she sniffed.

But Solin continued. 'And why you should think that those stupid mountain cats could fight our war for us, I don't know,' he said, thinking back to the fight outside the boundary of the farm.

'That was Roxana's idea.'

'Yeah, well she's grown up funny anyway. Wolves for wolves and cats for cats, I say.'

'I think she's learnt her lesson, Solin. And anyway, the big cats have long gone.' Rhiana thought for a moment and then added, 'It was my fault really. It was I who made friends with them in the first place.' She thought back to when she left Rhamin's pack. She had left Solin behind, taking her other three cubs with her. One of those cubs, Brenlin, had befriended an orphaned mountain lion cub, and they had grown up knowing each other well. When Brenlin had a daughter, Roxana, she, too, had grown up and played with that mountain lion's young family.

'Where is Roxana, anyway?'

'With our vulture friends of course. They are keeping us informed at this very moment about the movements of Rhamin and his mangy pack, like they always do.'

'I don't know why they bother,' he said in disgust.

'Kara and Lutz have followed us for so long that they have become dependent on us. If they had to locate their own food they would find it very hard to compete with the other vultures and carrion eaters now.'

'They've become soft,' Solin muttered derisorily. 'Soft and fat.'

'And all the more dependent on us to hunt their food for them. And in return they go where we are unable to travel. It costs us nothing; absolutely nothing. We don't always eat everything we kill, yet they think we are leaving food just for them.' Rhiana licked her front paws and then said, 'They are our servants. They do our spying for us and we do little in return.'

'And what does Roxana think of your great scheme?'

Rhiana looked around warily. It was as if she were afraid Roxana would hear. She lowered her voice and said, so quietly that even Solin's sensitive but shredded ears could hardly make out the words, 'Roxana doesn't know about my scheme. It involves her but she shouldn't be aware of it or how she's involved.' She raised her eyebrow and, after a dramatic pause, she added, 'Yet!'

'How can that be? She's one of the leaders of our pack.'

'She *thinks* she is one of the leaders. She would like to be *the* leader.'

'Oh I don't think she feels like that, mother.'

'Open your eyes Solin. If you ever want your title, then open your eyes.' Rhiana suddenly realized that she was shouting. She sighed heavily and whispered once again. 'Roxana wants to be the leader; the one and only wolf at the head of our pack. We cannot allow that.'

Solin studied his mother for several minutes, turning things over in his mind; thinking of all the things that his brother Brenlin's daughter had said and done. He nodded slowly. 'Perhaps I have been a bit pre-occupied,' he said, keeping his voice low. 'I thought it was their intention to help *me*.'

'So did I to start with. But things are changing. I can feel it. There's an undertone and I don't like it one little bit. We must do what has to be done.'

'And just what is it you have on your devious mind then, mother?'

'You'll have to watch out for her. She is getting stronger every time we fail. The other wolves are starting to think that she's the leader of *your* pack. And she has become cocky with it, especially since that ill bred cur, Lexa, broke your ribs.'

'They're healing now,' Solin assured his mother. 'Another week or so and I'll be fighting fit again. And mentioning that dog, how about killing her instead? I don't want Lexa in my pack even if we depose Rhamin.'

'Fighting fit!' She paused and thought for a second. 'Fit to fight, eh?' Rhiana looked at her son with affectionate eyes. 'You'll need to be as fit as ever you were if you are to overthrow Rhamin and that illegitimate, psychologically challenged, idiot, dog lover he calls his brother.'

Solin nodded. 'We should have killed Rasci when we had he chance.' He studied what Rhiana had said for a minute and then said, 'Idiot? Yes he's a fool all right. A nut or two short of a squirrel's dinner, that's for sure. But, he is the dangerous one. He's not one to back down in a fight any more than Rhamin is. That is always dangerous when they don't recognise their betters. And that isn't the only problem. It is Rasci who somehow got Rhamin released. We still don't know how he did it. Idiot or not, I think he's the one to kill first. He travels alone more than any of the other wolves. We should be able to ambush him easily.'

'That's all well and good if we had all the time in the world to go looking for him. But we haven't. It is Rhamin we need to get alone and if we kill Zelda, his anger will overtake his logic. He won't wait for his pack to gather around him. He'll come looking for the killer alone and that's all we need.'

'And an army of wolves. We'll need that, don't forget,' Solin snapped. 'Rhamin is too big and powerful. Look what he did to our best hunters the last time we drew him out on his own.' He thought about what he was going to say next, and gave out a resigned sigh, reconciled to the truth. 'He hasn't exactly left me without scars either,' he said, thinking about the time Rhamin ripped his ears to shreds. 'Yet another failed plan.'

'We've made mistakes, I agree. We drew him out alone but we left Silvah alive. Remember? And he had help from that scrawny raven. This time he'll be completely alone.'

'But we'll still need our own best hunters there.'

'We won't need hunters or fighters. Trust me. We'll just need...' She paused.

'Just need what?'

'Not *what*. Who.' Rhiana thought for a moment. She knew what she was going to say but didn't know if Solin was ready for it. Eventually, in a very subdued tone, she whispered, 'Roxana.'

Solin looked at his mother, puzzled, waiting for her to continue, but Rhiana fell silent. She stood up and stepped closer to Solin. She just looked at him for a long minute and then eventually spoke. 'If my plan works, we will kill all those that stand in your way.'

Solin scowled. '*All those?* That sounds like you think there are others besides Rhamin.'

Rhiana sat down next to her son and curled her long tail around her paws. She leaned forward so close to his face that he could feel the tip of her nose touching lightly against his guard hairs. 'Just be careful of Roxana,' she whispered in his ear. 'She isn't going to do as we say much longer. If she takes a mate then she'll expect to take over the pack. And who knows who she will pick to do it with her. That's why we have to plan now and act quickly. Time is of the essence. You *must* kill Zelda, and do it soon.'

CHAPTER FOUR

'I don't know why Sally has sent Elsie to live with us,' Raymond said to Maria as they drove to the city airport. 'I'd have thought she would have been better off amongst the people she knows. I mean, think about the school for instance! She won't know anyone there.'

'For goodness sake, Ray, there is hardly anybody there, anyway,' Maria retorted.

'Well all the more absurd her coming to stay with us.'

'Look, don't you want Elsie to come here? If you don't, then why didn't you say something when Sally rang to ask you?'

'Of course I want her to come. I haven't seen her since she was five. But we are hardly the centre of the universe here, are we? I just don't get it. Why has she sent her *here*?'

'We're the centre of *our* universe and you've never complained about that.'

'Coming to live with us is not like just visiting. It isn't even like a vacation for her. We don't know when her mother will be taking her back home.'

'Her mother! Taking her back! You say it like she's a stranger or some piece of baggage that has just appeared in our lives, for goodness sake! Sally's your youngest sister, Ray, and she has nowhere else to send Elsie.'

'It all seems a bit strange, that's all,' he sighed.

Raymond drove on silently for several minutes whilst they both contemplated their own inner thoughts. 'I wonder what really happened,' Maria said slowly, half to herself as much as to her husband. She looked over her shoulder to the back seat of the station wagon where her own two children were fast asleep. She tried to visualise what Elsie would be like. The last time Maria or Raymond had seen her, Margo and Ben weren't even born. But Elsie wasn't like their own two children. Both had grown up in the wild countryside. Not only were they at one with the wildlife about them, but they had an uncanny ability to communicate with it. But Elsie? Well she was a city girl through and through. As far as children go, Ben and Margo were a world apart from their cousin. 'I hope they all get on together,' she said eventually.

'They will, don't worry.' Raymond glanced at her for a moment and placed his hand on hers to reassure her. He turned his face back to the road ahead and thought that, if they didn't, then they would have to work through the problem because they couldn't just send their little niece back home if things didn't seem to be working. There was no going back now. His sister Sally had made that clear right from the start. She had asked them if they would look after her daughter for as long as it took. They had both said yes. But as long as what took? They had never had a proper explanation as to why Sally couldn't still look after her. After all, there were plenty of single mothers around and many far worse off than Sally. And they had never had any explanation at all about what happened to Sally's husband,

Bill. Why wasn't Sally coming with her daughter, at least to accompany her on the flight and see her off into the capable hands of her aunt and uncle? That was just an enigma. Still, perhaps Elsie would be able to explain it all.

CHAPTER FIVE

No more could Rhamin let himself or his wolves wait for the one helicopter that was the harbinger of doom. A hundred such machines could pass now, but not a single one could be ignored, for that might be *the one*. All Rhamin knew was that now, whenever he or any of the pack heard a helicopter, they would have to hide.

Wolves have exceptional hearing, and if they are near the mountain forests, they have plenty of time to get to cover before the noisy, air-beating machines come into sight. These man-made birds cannot land amongst trees so, the wolves would feel safe under the canopy of branches.

But out on the open plain there is nowhere to hide. A single tree or even a small copse is not sufficient to conceal the whole pack even if they lay perfectly still. So, henceforth, whenever the wolves left the Darin, during daylight hours, they would have to avoid the wide open plains, and head towards the mountains and the forests. They could not afford to ignore the distant sounds, for if the men and the machines were hunting for wolves then being caught out in the open plain was not an option to contemplate ever again.

What was so different this particular day? Neither Rhamin

nor his pack could tell. Even moving slowly to ensure that Zelda was not left behind, they all had plenty of time to head to the deeply wooded foothills that ran up into the forests of the mountains. And there they rested under the thickest part of the canopy of foliage, waiting as usual for the sound of the helicopter to disappear as it continued on the remainder of its journey. But this time, once again, the machine didn't fly by. This time, as before, it headed straight towards the pack, flying low above the trees, sending down a vortex of turbulent air that shook the canopy and stirred up the loose leaves into eddies of miniature whirlwinds around them. The sound seemed to beat down on them too, thumping at the air, making everything that was not already shaking in the wind, vibrate from deep inside.

Somehow, this machine and its occupants seemed to know the wolves were there. It flew past and then circled around, as if searching for them, but not here and there, not far away and then flying close by. This predator hovered overhead with an uncanny and unnerving and accurate persistence. All the wolves looked to Rhamin. He sat down and, with his white ears pointing forward, he scratched behind his neck. Then, he lifted his head up to the waving canopy above their heads. 'We're safe here,' he said nonchalantly, though his insides were churning. He needed to reassure his wolves that the huge mechanical bird was never going to land where they were, even if they had been spotted.

He looked around, but still couldn't see how they could have given their position away. There were no gaps in the canopy. The wolves lay in deep, dark shadow with no sight of the sky. 'Stay exactly where you are,' he instructed as he noticed Lexa, his wolf dog, beginning to panic. He could tell she wanted to make a run for it. Like him, she knew what helicopters and their occupants could do. She had been there when the man called Petersen had hunted Rhamin and his mate, Yeltsa.

'They know we're here,' she shouted, her voice breaking up beneath the din. 'They're after us again!'

'It seems like it,' said Silvah, moving closer to her companion and, by pressing close to Lexa's side, reassured her slightly. Lexa had been there when Rhamin had been shot. She too thought her leader and his mate had been killed. Only Rasci had known they were alive, despite all he had been told. And, against all the odds, he had rescued them. Today, however, no one doubted at this moment that their captors had returned. Won't this man and his flying machine ever leave us in peace, she wondered? 'But Rhamin is right,' she assured Lexa. 'The machine cannot land here. As long as we remain in the forest we are safe.'

But, as they all watched the helicopter do a final pass overhead, before speeding off into the distance, she couldn't have known how wrong she was.

The wolves would wait until nightfall before venturing out of the forest. They had to move quickly and move they did. Without any fixed plan they decided to go back to the Darin; their secret cave, their fixed abode. Wolves have many dens and camping sites throughout their territory, but only one serves as a permanent base from which to rule their domain. The Darin was their head quarters, the sanctuary that the Rhamin pack used for most of the year. When times were good, then food was never far away. But, despite being hidden behind a ridge of rock at the side of an escarpment, the new predator seemed to know exactly where it was.

'I wonder what the men in that flying machine wanted,'

said Lexa, calmed a little now after her near panic. 'Were they really looking for us, father?' she asked Rhamin, still in need of reassurance, but knowing in her heart that she knew the answer already. And the answer terrified her.

Some fur had grown back over the twisted scars on Lexa's face and body. That fur had grown back but not black and dark brown, as was the rest of her coat. The scars were dressed with white hairs, as if marking out the crooked lines to emphasise her courage, her bravery. But she didn't feel brave today, and thinking about it, she never had done. Courage comes from determination to win. Bravery, in her eyes, was a creeping sickness that sapped a wolf's ability to think logically about the dire consequences of its actions. She looked at her leader and marvelled at the whiteness of his ears. They stood out starkly against the blackness of his coat. Those white ears had been the result of scars too, the result of her leader being hunted by men kind. But that was not when he was abducted. That was, as Zelda had told the story, years before, when he was a helpless pup.

'I don't know,' he replied, trying to play down the whole affair. 'But they were too close for comfort, that's for sure.' He looked up at the canopy one last time. It was still and calmed now. Then, followed by his comrades, he headed towards the edge of the forest. It was some time before any of the wolves spoke again. The sun was setting and, beneath the cover of the trees, daylight was beginning to fade quickly. Lost in their own thoughts, they meandered silently down the slopes towards the plain. As the tree cover thinned, the meagre light from a waning sun disappeared behind a grey carpet of sky. Soon the light from a bright half moon and pinpoints of light from the first stars to appear in the sky enveloped the undulating plain. Each irregular patch of trees, each roughly sculptured hollow and each rocky outcrop cast deep and dark jagged shadows across the grey patches of a landscape. Only in the darkness did they feel safe out in the open plain. Quietly following their leader, they opened their stride and loped towards home.

'Perhaps they were looking for those other men that were in the forest,' said Silvah, eventually, breaking the eerie silence. 'The ones Natan told us he had seen several days ago.'

'They won't be here now,' replied Rhamin. 'They will have been hunting.'

'Hmm, Natan thought they were searching for something,' said Silvah. 'But he didn't think they were hunting, not in that sense. If they had weapons they were not carrying them the way hunting men do. He said they seemed to be preoccupied with their search for something else.'

'I wonder if they found what they were looking for,' Lexa said, curiosity wrinkling her face. Her floppy ears and smooth coat gave her face an expressiveness that was less prominent with the other members of her wolf family. But none of the wolves seemed to notice all that much. To them, Lexa was just another wolf. She had been reared by them and hunted with them. Her wounds from the fight with the mountain lion were just about healed now, and soon, the fur would have completely grown back over the scars where the farmer, Raymond Rozalski, had stitched up her torn flesh. But the scars would always leave marks on her face and body. The disfigurement was nothing to be ashamed of. As with Rhamin's ears, the hair that grows back on scar tissue rarely grows back in the original colour. And because her body did not have a thick coat like that of her wolf companions, the fur above the scars would not be hidden.

The scar lines would be white like Rhamin's ears and she would carry them with pride. But there was no doubt in the minds of her companions. *They* knew how brave she was, despite her open fear of helicopters and the man Petersen.

'Natan gave those men a wide birth,' said Rhamin, thoughtfully. 'Perhaps he should have watched them for a while.'

'He was just following your orders, Rhamin,' Silvah insisted. 'Avoid the men kind at all costs, you said.'

'Well, old Zelda thinks there is still some danger. She warned us not to be complacent. And that flying machine has confirmed her suspicions. It has certainly convinced me!' As a cloud passed across the silver moon, he looked up at the darkening sky as if to reassure himself that the giant metallic predator had gone.

'And me,' Lexa grunted, trembling, unable to hide her feeling of foreboding. However courageous she was, those man-made birds from hell would always haunt and frighten her.

CHAPTER SIX

Rasci was already back at the Darin, sitting with Zelda, when Rhamin and his group arrived there. Rasci rarely hunted with the rest of the pack, preferring to go out alone. He spent much of his time thinking and sleeping, and since his brush with leadership, he was even more convinced that he was a loner. Saving Rhamin and Yeltsa had been the best thing he had ever done. He had used his courage, he had used his strength and he had used his cunning, but he had no desire to do anything like it again. In fact, only since the return of Rhamin, did he realize just what a rock the leader was for him to lean on. But he and Zelda knew there was still something very much amiss. They both had the same unsettling feeling of impending danger. The pack had celebrated his daring rescue and their escape to freedom. But he and Zelda knew it hadn't ended there. There was still a tangible and menacing cloud of danger hanging heavily over the pack. It was as if the kidnapping of Rhamin and his mate had started something much bigger. Indeed, it had. It had started a rescue mission that neither wolf nor man would have believed possible. But it had happened, and now, where safety and security should envelop the pack, there was the feeling of unease, an awareness of permanent menace and a sense of unfinished business.

Rasci watched as The Black Wolf settled near the mouth of the cave. He looked at his leader with admiration. Never did Rhamin ever show fear. It was as if he knew that he was a template for the shaping of all the other pack members. Whatever feelings Rhamin had inside him, his outer countenance was that of total confidence. Rhamin flicked the mosquitoes off his white ears and scratched himself nonchalantly while the others went to the water hole at the back of the cave. 'You heard it?' he asked Rasci, no emotion in his voice.

'We heard it,' Rasci replied. 'It was definitely looking for something. It wasn't just passing over on a journey to somewhere else.'

'It wasn't going anywhere else,' Rhamin said quietly. 'It was looking for us. I have no doubts about it. But the frightening thing is that it knew we were there, even though we had completely concealed ourselves beneath the undergrowth of the forest.' He sighed heavily. He was well recovered from his kidnapping ordeal, but the whole idea of it starting all over again tired him to the bone.

Rasci knew how he felt. He, too, was tired of the whole thing. Instead of being able to relax and enjoy their freedom, the threat seemed to be looming once again. Only this time, they knew what to expect. The problem was, they didn't know from what direction the threat was going to appear. He looked at Zelda, who instinctively knew he was looking towards her. Despite her blindness, the ancient old wolf had a remarkable awareness of what was going on around her.

'Yes?' she asked, waiting for Rasci to say what was on his mind.

'Oh, I was wondering what you thought Gran,' he stated plainly. 'If the men kind are looking for us then perhaps we are safer hiding in the cave.'

Zelda's response was unexpected. 'No!' she yelped, as if a hornet had stung her on the nose. And then, 'No,' she repeated, only more calmly this time.' She shook her head and grunted at her own outburst. She seemed to have surprised herself. She thought for a second or two and then said, 'I don't know.'

'You seemed pretty positive a moment ago,' Rhamin urged her.

She shook her head again. 'I... I don't know.'

Rhamin looked at Rasci, but he just shrugged. 'Perhaps I can try and see what the men are up to,' Rasci said, breaking the silence eventually. He hadn't used his psychic powers once since his return to normality. His normality was hunting, eating, sleeping and playing. He was happy again without the responsibility of leadership. He was happy to forget his recent experiences with Roxana, the female wolf that had betrayed him and his feelings. She had tempted him and used him and now that she was gone from his life, he never wanted to think about her again. He had been afraid to even attempt to meditate. If he did so, his ability to remote view could, perhaps, take him to places he didn't wish to go. But the needs of the pack were overtaking him once again. He knew it, and he knew that the pack, and Rhamin in particular, were going to rely on his abilities if he could use them to benefit them in any way. Yes, old Zelda had given some kind of forewarning, but her visions were never clear and precise. If anything, her predictions usually caused more anxiety than they would ease. Uncertainty is a breeding ground for suspicion and fear. The pack needed something more defined.

With a deep sigh of submission, Rasci headed towards the blackness at the back of the cave. Pressured by the need to find Rhamin, he had spent many hours there in the past months, clearing his mind of all other distractions and concentrating on seeing his beloved leader. Now Rhamin needed him again. But the motivation seemed so much weaker now; the danger was less imminent; Rhamin the leader was there to take care of the pack.

Gradually, Rasci lapsed into a fitful sleep, only awakening late into the night. He pricked up his ears. The gentle sound of some of the other wolves breathing shallowly as they slept, and the fluttering of a small bat somewhere in the dark cave behind him was all he could hear. But he had definitely heard something else. Was it in his sleep? Was it another dream? Had he really heard men talking? Gradually he began to recall. They had torches, but not the usual long, cylindrical sticks that men carried in their hands and which emitted a beam of sunlight that scythed through the darkness like a perpetual shaft of lightning. These light beams were attached to their heads, shining from their foreheads, cutting a swathe of visibility through a blanket of total blackness. Rasci closed his eyes and concentrated. Where was this blackness? Who were these men? He could see them in his mind's eye, slowly, silently searching, one man slightly ahead of the other. Both of them wore a similar kind of clothing, all one piece, all a bright orange colour and all tight fitting to their human form. Around their waists were black straps that had pouches and attachments. The lights on their heads were inserted into some kind of protective head covering. Rasci was engrossed in studying their form when, suddenly, one of the men spoke. As before, in all his visions, Rasci could understand what the man kind was saying.

'The sooner we find what we are looking for the sooner I'll be out of this death hole,' the shorter of the men said, kicking some dry bones as he shuffled his feet through the darkness beneath the light beam.

'They're long dead,' the leader said, a harshness in his voice lending an air of authority to his words. As the man turned his head, the light beam washed across a picture on the wall. It was hard to catch but as fleeting as it was, it looked like an image, an outline of a buffalo. Rasci had seen something similar before. He started suddenly, returning to complete consciousness in an instant. He looked around in the darkness and sniffed at the air. Nothing unusual; just the scent of the pack. He listened and waited for some sound to come from the blackness behind him. But nothing happened. The wolves were alone, he was sure of that. Gradually, he relaxed and slowly, the unseen tendrils of tiredness clutched at his mind and dragged him into sleep once more.

CHAPTER SEVEN

Spending a whole two hours in an airport terminal with two wide awake and adventurous children at 2.30 in the afternoon is not the easiest of tasks for any mother. The flight had been delayed by at least one and a half hours, but eventually, the screens above their heads flicked up the flight number and the arrival time.

Maria took the task of keeping Ben and Margo occupied whilst Raymond waited patiently for the passengers of flight 622 to disembark. Even then, there would be a long wait for passengers to collect their luggage.

Maria looked at Ben, her blond haired son who had caused her to worry so much when he began to talk to his invisible wolf friend. It seemed absurd now, how they had all been caught up in the lives of a pack of wolves all because of something that she, like most parents, would normally have put down to a child playing with imaginary friends. And Margo? Had it all really happened? She looked at the wispy hair that bounced in curls as Margo challenged Ben to a long jumping competition. She, of course was dictating the rules. She jumped from the seat whilst Ben had to jump from along side it. Well, it was only fair to set a handicap.

After all, she was only four and a half years old.

Had that little bouncy child really been able to communicate with the animals?

Maria shook her head in disbelief. Her husband had taken it all very seriously. Raymond had taken the children with him to steal a black wolf, the one that had white ears. Steal? Well, to his mind it was a rescue. But taking a captive wolf and releasing it back into the wild was not an act normally associated with being within the law of the land. In fact, since the whole business with the wolves had finished, it was hard to think that it had really happened and that it hadn't all been just some communal dream. Not one of the family had spoken of it since; not Ben, not Margo, not Raymond and definitely not Maria. Besides having broken the law by taking the wolves from the safari park, they would have been branded as eccentric goofballs by anyone that might get a whiff of the story. No, the whole irrational affair was better locked away in the recesses of their memories and never let out again. Perhaps with time, she at least could repress the memory such that the wolf thing never happened. Perhaps with time, the children would forget it too.

As the minutes and hours passed, the children seemed subdued, somehow. Perhaps they sensed that their cousin was on her way at last. Eventually, instead of playing, they stood next to their father, asking him questions about the unknown cousin from the big city in the east. But Raymond didn't seem to be able to tell them much. As they looked at the photograph of Elsie together, he explained that he had only met his niece once and that was when she was about five years old, and when asked what she was like, all he could reply was that she was like all other children, playful, chatty and always laughing; which was true of the five year old Elsie that he had met. What she was like now, he couldn't say. He knew what she looked like, of course. Elsie was the spitting image of her mother when she was thirteen years old, although the photograph didn't do either of them justice. Elsie looked far too serious to be Sally's daughter. Sally had always been a bubbly happy person. Raymond couldn't remember a time when she never had a smile on her face. Even now, after years of not seeing his sister, Sally's voice always sounded girlish and happy whenever they spoke on the telephone. Until recently, that is. In the frantic phone calls when she was pleading with them to take Elsie, her voice seemed altered somehow. But then, she had just lost her husband. No one could expect his sister to sound happy at a time like that.

Perhaps Elsie was the same. Perhaps the photograph had been taken after her father's death. After all, it was supposed to be up to date. It had been posted on to Raymond and Maria so that they could recognise and meet Elsie at the airport. His task was making sure he saw her and that she saw him when they passed each other. Otherwise, the day at the airport terminal might turn out to be a circus.

As it happened, Maria spotted the lonesome child through the crowd as she manoeuvred her way towards the exit gate. Elsie seemed in no hurry as she ambled towards them, pushing a trolley full of luggage and seemingly oblivious to anything and anyone around her. It seemed like airports were the most natural thing in the world to her; no awe, no curiosity. Her face wasn't even one of someone concentrating on what she was doing or where she was going. It was like when someone does something every day, the task becomes secondary to the soul. The body goes into an auto pilot mode whilst the mind gets on with something far more important. In fact, if Maria had to describe Elsie at that moment, she would have described the child as bored.

Raymond had, somehow, managed to miss seeing Elsie as he waded upstream through the torrent of bodies and trolleys. When he at last spotted her, he was looking back towards Maria. Elsie was almost at the spot where Maria was sitting with Ben and Margo. He cut across the large crowded floor, photo in hand, neck craning, so as not to lose sight of his niece. Elsie just kept walking towards the exit.

Then, in a brief second, Elsie glanced to her side, as if suddenly distracted from her thoughts. She had seen Ben and Margo. They had been looking at her for some time now. Somehow, they had recognised their cousin even before their mother had caught sight of her. Elsie stopped, pulled the heavy trolley to the side of Margo's seat and just stood there looking at them as if she had been with them all the time and had just wandered away for a moment before returning. She didn't speak. Instead, with her back to Maria, she stood there and waited.

'Elsie!' Maria said to catch the girl's attention.

Turning around, Elsie looked at Maria. Her face showed no sign of recognition. 'Aunty Maria,' she said, her voice flat and toneless. It wasn't a question; just a simple statement of fact, an acknowledgement. Still she stood there as if she was rejoining them; as if she had just stepped aside for a moment and then stepped back again. She looked around, scanning the crowd. Maria and the children just watched her.

'Goodness knows where your uncle Raymond has got to,' Maria said, to break the uneasy silence between them in the noisy terminal. Elsie's eyes fell on her uncle Raymond, waving the photographs as he pushed past the people that were blocking his way.

'Here he is now,' Elsie stated, still with a flat, matter of fact pitch in her voice, and then: 'There you are!' she said, as he came closer, in a way that made her uncle feel as if he had been the one for whom everyone had been waiting.

'Sorry,' he said, not knowing why he was apologising, and then, 'Elsie! Gosh you've grown!' He put his arms around Elsie and gave her an affectionate hug but Elsie barely responded, simply placing her hands lightly against his back until he broke the embrace.

'Hmm,' Elsie said as they stepped apart, and then, not unkindly: 'You look older.'

Raymond grinned. 'Fact of life, I'm afraid.' He took a hold of the trolley handle. 'Are you hungry?' he asked as he automatically began to lead the way to the exit.

Elsie shook her head as Margo and Ben each took hold of one of her hands and escorted their new cousin, gazing up at her in wonderment. Elsie smiled at them both in turn, squeezed their hands gently, changed her look to a frown and followed her uncle Raymond as Maria brought up the rear. They were heading towards the car park, before anyone spoke again. Elsie had just glanced down at Margo's upturned face.

'I like you too,' said Margo.

Elsie's smile returned. 'That's all right then.' She stopped, let go of Ben's and Margo's hands, bent her knees so that her face was level with Margo's and straightened the collar of the little girl's coat. Then, without a word, standing upright again and taking back hold of their hands, she marched on behind Raymond and Maria, once again silent in her own thoughts.

CHAPTER EIGHT

His past experiences had taught Rhamin that, with the one exception of the Rozalski family, he could not trust men kind. He thought back over his lifetime and tried to recollect just how the relationship between his pack and the farmer Rozalski had developed. How did it all start? It seemed as if they had always been friends, despite the fact that it was less than two years ago. During the worst drought he or any of his pack could remember, he and some of his hunters had raided Raymond Rozalski's farm in search of food. During that raid, two wolves were killed and the rest of his raiders had got away with not only a few dead sheep, less than they had planned to take, but with a dog pup of all things. The dog pup! Lexa. He smiled to himself, a wolfish smile made broader as he recalled how his half brother Solin had tried to kill Ben and Margo, the farmer's children, and how he had saved them by making Solin back down. That's when Rhamin stole Lexa as a diversion to prevent the farmer and his dog from killing any more of his pack.

And that's how it all began. Shortly after that, Solin became one of Rhamin's most dangerous enemies. He left the pack and plotted to use the farmer to kill Rhamin so that he could replace The Black Wolf as leader in that territory. Thank the heavens that the plot had been foiled, for if it hadn't been thwarted, then the farmer may never have prevented the man Petersen from shooting The Black Wolf that fateful day on the mountain. And then, Rhamin and his pack would not have been there to save the farmer and his companion from the attack by Bortag. Bortag! The huge starving bear and his family; the bear that had lost an eye fighting with the Rhamin pack during the drought. He wondered if the bear was still carrying a grudge. Wolves have few enemies apart from man, but Bortag was probably more dangerous than most men that came into the territory. Men have guns, but Bortag? Despite his immense size, he could run as fast as a wolf. He could weave in and out of trees and lope over the rock strewn ground as nimbly as an antelope. He had a muzzle that would crush a wolf with a single bite. And his claws were longer than a wolf's nose; a paw full of lethal cutting shafts of sharpened, hardened cartilage. Yes, bears were deadly enemies. The only consolation was that although the bears shared the same region as Rhamin's pack, bears didn't travel as far as wolves. But inevitably, their paths would cross again.

Of men, Petersen remained the most dangerous enemy of all, for he was a hunter of wolves. He was the man who had kidnapped Rhamin and his mate. It was from Petersen that Rasci and Raymond Rozalski had rescued them. Rhamin had no doubt that yesterday's persistent visit by the helicopter, whether the man was in it or not, was directly planned by Petersen. There was something Rhamin and his pack had overlooked. Wolves know all about tracking. There was something that, since his incarceration, had made Rhamin easier to track. The helicopter had not sought out any other group of wolves from his pack. It had headed straight for The Black Wolf; no hunting, no searching. It appeared as a speck in the distance and grew larger as, like a bee to a field of poppies, it made a straight line to Rhamin. It hovered over him and his comrades and, only because it was thwarted by the trees, did the metal bird turn and head in a straight line back from whence it came.

Normally, wolves know what is going on in their territory. But where men and their kind are concerned, often, wolves give the intruders a wide berth. There were men up in the mountain forests but Rhamin was sure they were not connected with Petersen. These men were looking for something, yes, but it wasn't wolves. A long talk with Rasci, who described what he had seen in his vision, confirmed that. But there was something happening in the mountains that warranted further investigation, and Rhamin planned to find out sooner rather than later.

It seemed an ordinary morning again after the frightening experience of the previous day. Everything outside the cave was calm. No beating sounds came to his ears from afar. It was time, perhaps to head back to the mountains and scrutinize the activities that Natan had reported. Along with Natan, Rhamin gathered an expeditionary force that was to accompany him on his reconnaissance. The remainder of the pack were to stay with Zelda and the three cubs, to hunt near and within the region of the Darin. With a promise that the outgoing team would return with food by the next day, they set off to the mountain forest.

Two hours or so later, led by Natan, they were heading

up the rocky mountain side. A hazy mist clung to the canopy above them as they entered the bottom of the tree line and headed upwards through the thick growth of trees, saplings, bracken, mulberry bushes and, fallen timber. There was little wind, but it was blowing from behind them. That didn't concern Rhamin too much, however. He knew that men kind relied very little on scent. Their noses can detect less than one five hundredth of that which a wolf's sensory glands can recognise. Unless the men had dogs with them, then approaching up wind would carry no warning to them. And if they had dogs, then the animals would bark a warning before the wolves got anywhere near. Dogs are notoriously bad at giving their masters' location away. For some reason they are reared and trained to bark at danger instead of circumventing it.

The thickening heavy air vapour deadened any sound they made, but gradually, and lead by Natan, as they made their way up the gently sloping mountain side, through the trees and around the rocky outcrops, the mist began to thin a little and soon they were able to see the brighter light of day above them. Now, treading carefully so as not to make any sound that would travel up towards their target, they made their way higher and higher, and eventually, they emerged from the mist into the clear, afternoon sunlight shining through the canopy of trees.

It was another good half hour before Natan stopped. He turned to his leader and whispered, 'We are nearly there now.'

Rhamin nodded. 'Go ahead,' he stated plainly. The rest of the pack remained silent as Natan turned his head back up the mountain and resumed his lead. Slowing down to sniff the air and listen for any tell tale signs of habitation, little by little he edged forward to the border of a small clearing. The ground was covered with crushed ferns as if there had been considerable activity there recently. Across the clearing, fifty wolf paces away or so, the forest continued its relentless journey up towards the sky. To their left there was a steep wall of damp, heavily weathered rock, coloured several shades of green by the mosses that competed to cover any surface that was exposed.

Rhamin led his pack to the right where there was a gap in the trees which looked like the start of a track of some kind and when he went closer to examine it, he saw that there was a vehicle with a covered space for the driver and passenger, but with an open back. A thing for carrying loads, he thought. It had been covered with branches and well hidden several paces off to the side of the track as if the people to whom it belonged were trying to avoid being seen there. But there was no sign of the men.

'Stay here,' Rhamin commanded. He stepped past Natan, broke into the clearing and stood there for a few moments. When he was sure that he was not being seen or watched by any men, he skirted to the right along the edge of the clearing. When he came back to the gap in the trees, he inspected the ground. First he sniffed it to see if there was any scent that he could recognise. There were definite traces of men kind, but not very recent. A damp atmosphere tends to hold smells in place for a while before they are dispersed by the sun and the wind. But the opening into the forest was on the south east side of the clearing and it would see little of the sun at ground level. He had been right, however. There was a track leading along the mountain side. He went along it for some way to try and understand who or what had made it and why it was there. The canopy overhead had closed in where trees had been removed to clear a passage. By his reckoning, the track had been cleared several years ago. There was growth of bracken that had pushed its underground root system well into the forest from the clearing. It would not have done that if there had been no daylight reaching the ground at some time. But now the passage beneath the canopy of trees was dark once again. The bracken that had once seen an opportunity to spread and grow, now stood brown and unregenerated. But the dead bracken was not completely trampled. To Rhamin this meant only one thing, the track was only used by a few men and then, only occasionally.

He headed back to the clearing and continued his examination of its borders. There was no other sign of man except for some large discarded items placed in a neat pile at the base of the cliff. He hadn't seen them when he first looked towards the rock face. The long square profiled objects were coloured to match their surroundings with stripes of green and brown and grey, blending them into the background so well that they were unlikely to reveal the presence of the man-made items either from a distance or from the air. Once again, he lifted his head and sniffed. When he was satisfied that the pack was alone, he looked towards the edge of the clearing where his wolves waited patiently. He yipped quietly to tell them to come over and join him. 'I suppose this is where you saw them?' he said to Natan.

'Yes, I'm sure,' the young wolf replied. 'Though I didn't hang about. I saw two men in strange clothing, and when one of them spotted me, that was enough to tell me I should disappear back into the forest. I didn't wait to have a friendship meeting.'

'You did right,' Rhamin said with a smile. 'Did they try

to follow you?'

Natan shrugged. 'I don't think so. They seemed to be busy over here. The problem is, I don't remember these things being here. As far as I can recall, there was a hole in the rock face where these things are stacked up now.'

'Really?'

Natan sniffed at the objects where their edges met the wall of rock. He tried to push his nose behind them, but they were heavier than they looked. He opened his mouth and tried to prize the edge of one of the objects away from the rock. The sound his teeth made against them told him something. 'They are hollow,' he stated as he sniffed at them again. 'But they are very heavy.'

Rhamin stepped back to look at them again. 'Well, there's no sign of the men now.'

'Nor what they are up to,' Rasci said, his body suddenly racked by a shudder that ran from the tip of his nose to the end of his tail.

'You all right?' asked Rhamin, seeing a distant look in Rasci's eyes.

'No, not really,' Rasci stated, suddenly focussing his eyes and looking beyond his leader at the cliff wall. 'I don't know what it is, but I don't like it. There's something not right here.'

'But nothing specific?'

Rasci shook his head as his eyes took on a glazed look. As he tilted his head, Rhamin stood and watched his companion. 'There's an opening behind there,' Rasci said, more to himself than to his leader. 'But I don't think we should go any further. I have a very bad feeling about the place.'

'We can't anyway,' Silvah said conclusively.

Rasci still remained deep in thought, his body rigid as if he had set to stone. 'They are in there,' he said eventually.

'Who? The men?' But Rasci didn't answer. Rhamin wanted to press Rasci harder, but it was obvious that the gifted wolf was trying to concentrate.

'They have sunlight in there. And things. Things for seeking other things. Things for finding something perhaps. I… I'm not sure. It's all a bit strange.' He paused and then said, 'They are a long way in there under the mountain.' He tilted his head as he concentrated. 'They are beyond the man-made passages.'

Man-made? Rhamin thought that strange, but remained totally silent.

'There's some kind of mechanical thing that makes a sound like the machines they ride over the plains.' Rasci continued. 'It's making light, carrying it in long creepers to many different points. Not in all the passages, though. Only the ones near the entrance.' He went silent and concentrated for a moment. 'I can see…'

'Are you sure you sealed the entrance?' the shorter of the two men asked his companion.

'Absolutely. No one will find the opening. What are you worrying about?'

'Oh, this place gives me the creeps. What with the bones and the wall paintings. It's as if they are watching us.'

'Yeah, they're watching all right,' the other one sniggered in a high pitched voice.

'I'm telling you, there is something watching us. I can feel it.' He swung around, the light beam on his helmet scouring every crevice, every tiny undulation in the walls of the tunnel, his eyes wide and fearful.

The wolf spirit watched him. He knew this man could sense his presence there. But the man couldn't see Rasci. As Rasci watched them, he sensed that the men were not what he had expected. There was something dangerous about them. In some way they looked and behaved differently to men he'd seen in his visions before. Or was it the place that gave Rasci that feeling? Or was it their voices? The voices seemed strange, but that could have been the resonance of the sound inside the tunnels the men were examining.

The man turned and carried on scanning the walls of the cavern with some kind of device in his hand that looked like a long, thick stick. Every now and again, a light on the stick flashed on and off again but it didn't seem to distract or influence the behaviour of the man as he swept his arm and the stick from side to side, in lines that covered the entire wall of the dark passageway.

The rest of the wolves stood and waited, watching the transcending wolf as his glazed eyes looked blankly at the stacked metal boxes that blocked the entrance to the passageway.

Then, suddenly, the statue that was Rasci's body shook itself back to full consciousness. He began panting as if he had been running to keep up with the pack.

'What is it Rasci?' Rhamin urged him gently.

'I think I can see… I think I have seen… I'm here,' he said shakily, looking around at all his friends. He paused and thought for a moment. 'It's an awful place,' he declared.

'You certainly are here,' Natan chuckled. 'Though your mind has been somewhere inside the mountain. We know that.'

Rasci still looked a bit unsteady. He sat down. 'I thought I saw myself in there,' he said. 'It was as black as death.' He shook himself again as if to make sure he was awake. 'But I was here. I was here all the time.'

Realizing for the first time what a stress it was for Rasci to use his special powers, Rhamin soothed him with a few kind words. 'You don't need to do this if you don't want to Rasci. We know there are men in there and so long as they are not bothering us, then we don't need to know anything about them.'

'They are looking for something. That's all I can tell you.'

'Then I think we should leave them to it,' Rhamin stated as he turned to face his pack. 'Come, we will follow that track to see where it leads us.' With that, leading his pack and sure that there were no men kind around to see them, he paced across the clearing and headed down the man-made trail. There was a sense of relief amongst the pack members. They all seemed delighted to be heading away from the clearing, so much so that they broke out in a chatter amongst themselves, no one saying anything in particular, just enjoying each other's company and companionship.

The tree cover seemed to form a tunnel over the track. It wasn't a road, but it was wide enough to get a man steered vehicle along it. There were indentations in the leaf covered ground that showed that such a vehicle had passed along the track at sometime, but the scent was cold. The parallel lines could have been couple of days or a week old. None of the wolves could tell. Silvah suggested that the tracks were not too old because there were few fallen leaves or twigs or other debris that falls from trees lying loose on the actual grooves that the man-made wheels had made. But still, despite the exceptional ability of wolves to pick up scents, there was little evidence that men had been there recently. The track followed the contour of the mountain side, cutting through trees and undergrowth where plant life had been cleared to build the make shift road. It wasn't long before the wolves noticed that the trail began to rise slightly, cutting beneath trees where, if the road had remained level, it would have been exposed and in the open. Clearly, whoever built the road wanted it to remain covered and a secret. For mile after mile, the pack loped along the mountain side, eastward, following the trail until, eventually, rising up again, it emerged once more into another clearing. But this clearing was different to the one in the west. This clearing had a barren rock surface formed by a level bed of rock that, as far as Rhamin could tell, hardly sloped in any direction. It was a strange alien area. No moss or vegetation hung onto the surface. It was as if it had been scrubbed clean.

Rhamin moved forward, signalling the rest of the pack to stay behind the cover of the trees while he examined the area. It was some thirty or so yards square, in wolf measurements about twenty five loping strides long and about the same in width. Rhamin sniffed the air and then at the rock surface. There were distinct traces of the smells of men kind. A burnt smell lingered on the hard rock surface, something similar to the scent left by a heavy road vehicle, Rhamin thought. But more than that, there were several different scents of two or more men, each one going to and from the middle of the clearing and heading through trees by way of the well camouflaged track.

The day passed quickly as they explored the rest of this mountain region, one that they had seldom visited before. With the investigation complete, however, and content that the men were no threat to himself or his pack, Rhamin decided that they would hunt a while, rest during the dark hours and return to the Darin early in the morning as the next day dawned.

CHAPTER NINE

Elsie sat silently looking out of the window from the back seat of the station wagon, next to Ben and Margo. Who were these strangers she had come to live with so far away from her real home? Yes, they were her uncle and aunt but she didn't know them any better than strangers in the city. The hard suspension of the station wagon made it rattle every time it went over the merest ripple in the road surface. Even that was alien to her, having been taken to school every day in her father's very much more up-to-date family saloon. But she had decided she was going to be polite. The silence of her hosts was probably a sign that they were just as uncomfortable with Elsie's visit as she was with appearing suddenly in their lives. And her father had always said that good manners and being polite cost nothing. Under the monotonous drone of the engine she would, at least, be able to reflect on her inner thoughts.

But the silence didn't last long. Both Ben and Margo had spent some time looking at their new cousin. Even Elsie was unable to ignore them, their excitement was so apparent. It was Margo who spoke first. She could tell Elsie was sad. Both Ben and Margo had been told about her father's departure from this world and even at her tender age, Margo knew that talking about it would just hurt their new cousin even more. 'Ben and I have got a dog,' she said to break the silence.

Elsie turned her head towards her little companion. Despite her determination to reflect her real inner feeling of deep complacency, she couldn't help but smile. Margo's cheery face was so disarming. 'Is that right?' she said, lifting one eyebrow to indicate that she was expecting more on the subject.

She wasn't mistaken.

'She's called *Smokey* and she's big. Really big!'

'Really big eh?'

Margo nodded.

'And she's fought with bears!'

Elsie gave out an involuntary chuckle. 'Yeah, right,' she said with a nod, her voice still flat.

'And wolves,' Margo continued. 'She's fought with *wolves*,' she repeated as if saying it once was not enough to emphasise the enormity of the deed.

'That's before she made friends with them,' Ben came in. 'We're all friends with them now.'

'Friends with the wolves eh? Interesting lives you live out here then?' Elsie's sarcasm was quite evident. These country folk must live their fairy tales, not just tell them.

'Oh yes!' Margo said with gusto, completely missing the irony in Elsie's voice. 'There's so many things we have to tell you. Daddy says that it's no good telling you because you wouldn't understand, but I know you will.'

'I understand most things,' Elsie said dryly. She was about to turn her head back to the window but Ben caught her eye and fixed her with another snippet of information.

'Smokey's daughter is a wolf.'

'Really.' Elsie's voice was still empty of any emotion.

'Well No. *Not* really,' Ben went on. He paused and thought for a moment.

Elsie raised her eyebrow again, a look of complete scepticism covering her face.

'Well, she is and she isn't.' Ben was struggling to explain whatever it was.

Elsie saw Raymond's head turn as he listened, but then he turned his face back to the windscreen and carried on driving without speaking. He would let the children find their own common ground with their new cousin. He and Maria would have plenty of time to get to know their young niece properly once they were back at the farm. He could tell that Maria was itching to join the conversation, but she, too, was holding back to see if the young ones could break the ice.

'Yes she is,' Margo argued, totally happy with the description and the way the conversation was flowing. 'Lexa *is* a wolf.'

'Lexa. That's the name of Smokey's puppy?' Elsie asked.

Margo nodded, her blue eyes wide with delight at parting with such valuable and revealing information.

'So your dog, Smokey, had a wolf for a puppy?' She would humour the children. They were remarkably polite for small children and despite her efforts not to grow to like either Uncle Raymond or any of his family, for some inexplicable reason, she was finding them totally disarming.

'Except that she's grown up now. She was a puppy but now she's a wolf.'

Maria realized that the conversation was heading in a direction that, at this early stage in their relationship, was likely to complicate matters rather than put Elsie at ease. 'Have you travelled a lot?' she asked, turning her head around so that she could see Elsie. 'On planes I mean.'

Elsie shook her head. 'Never on a plane, no.' She stiffened her jaw. 'I've only travelled out of the city a couple of times. With my father. We went on a river cruise once.'

'Did your mother not go as well?'

'Mother never went anywhere with us,' she replied bitterly. 'She was always working.' She paused and pursed her lips. 'Don't know why she ever bothered having me.' Elsie's voice cracked with emotion. She cleared her throat, swallowed and then added, 'I hate her.'

There was an uneasy silence. Maria didn't know what to say next. She thought for a second and realized that now wasn't the time to counsel her niece. She knew too little about Raymond's sister Sally or her husband, and talking about relationships without that knowledge would be strewn with pitfalls. She was careful to pick her words. 'Since you are staying for a while, perhaps you will tell us about your mother and father when you feel up to it.' She paused, searching Elsie's face for a response but it gave nothing away. 'After all, even though your mother and Raymond were brother and sister, we, neither of us, really knew much about your mum.'

'Snap.'

The response was unexpected. 'Oh, sweetheart, I know you're angry with her now, but I'm sure she has your best interests at heart.'

'Sending me here you mean?'

'Well, not just that.' Maria could feel that she was digging herself deeper into a self excavated pit. 'What does your mother do?' she asked, changing tack. 'You know, work-wise?'

'You tell me. I'm beggared if I know.'

That response was just as unexpected as the previous one.

'Well doesn't she ever discuss her job with you?'

'Some sort of public servant. That's all I know. Spends days away from home. Never discussed it with Daddy. Not that I know of, anyway. Just phone calls to say she would be late or that she had to travel here or there. Don't know why Daddy put up with her.'

'So that's why she asked us to look after you for a while?' Maria said awkwardly. 'I didn't know.'

'Your mother and I hadn't been in touch lately,' Raymond broke in to try and ease the tension he could sense building. 'But when she called to ask if we'd look after you for a while, I could tell she loved you. A mother's voice gives that much away.'

'Pity her voice never conveyed that when she was around me then.'

Another uncomfortable silence followed. Elsie turned her head once again and gazed out of the window at the passing traffic.

Maria thought it best not to break any more boundaries for the time being.

Raymond just drove, content that, at least while there was no talking going on, then the rift that was opening up between them and their young guest was not getting any wider.

Ben didn't notice any rift. He had just been absorbing what had been said with his usual impartial and open mind, an intellect uncluttered with awkward relationships and resentments.

Margo could feel Elsie's anguish. 'Don't be sad, Elsie. *We* all love you,' she said in her open and innocent manner. She put her tiny hand on Elsie's knee. 'I know you don't like us. Not yet. But you will. Honest.'

A tear welled up in Elsie's eye. She put her hand on little Margo's and squeezed it. But she kept looking out of the window.

It was a relief to arrive at the farm; not just for Elsie, but for Maria and Raymond too. The constraint of being in a motor vehicle was not conducive to giving each other the space they needed in order to build a relationship if, indeed, one was ever going to be constructed. After that, very little was said apart from, *Here we are*, and *Don't mind Smokey, she's harmless*, and *Come, we'll show you your room* and, *You can sit quietly if you wish*. Maria finished with, 'I'll make a few sandwiches and then we'll have an early night. It's been a long and busy day.'

Elsie responded perfunctorily with a nod.

And so Elsie spent her first night in a strange room in a strange house amongst total strangers. The place was remote, isolated and seemingly cut off from any form of civilisation. How much worse could it get, she thought? Out in the middle of nowhere, practically on her own, with two old codgers and a couple of loony kids for company. That *had* to be some kind of record.

The one consolation, it seemed, and it was quite a big prize in this no-win situation, was that Uncle Raymond and Aunt Maria liked books. There were two large stacking-shelves full of them in the spare bedroom. It would take a good while to work her way through those.

CHAPTER TEN

There are not many moments more pleasant than that precious time a few minutes after first light when, in the midst of a vast, green, towering forest on a lonely mountainside, under the heavy mists of dawn, all the birds are calling and announcing to everyone that the day is breaking and that, for all those that are there to hear it, their wake up call should be heeded, not only as the starting line for a new day with new spirit and resolution but, more than anything, this is the godly-created, marvellous and incredible opportunity to start the rest of your life.

And so it was for the pack. Despite the hardships of simply surviving the harshness of mother nature, overcoming the conflicts within the pack, or of even enduring the assaults of predators, there were moments when, all around them, with some soft and calming voice, nature was speaking to them, bringing them back to what they were and why they were ever there in the first place.

It was at times like this when, regardless of how worried you have been, how anxious about present or forthcoming events, you forget the dangers of the struggle to exist, and live the moment. And this must have been one of the pack's happiest.

The wolves had hunted into the night and, as they had descended the forested slopes, they had killed a deer. It was sufficient to feed them now and enough to take back with them to the Darin. Silvah and most of the other wolves just lay and slept. Before sleeping and, for the first time, feeling totally relaxed, Rasci meditated for a while, letting his mind wander to the farm. He was curious how Ben and his family were getting on, and he needed to know if they knew anything about the man, Petersen, returning to hunt for Rhamin. Ben didn't know anything, of course, but he would mention it to his father.

As daylight dawned, Rasci began play fighting with Bamar. Lexa and Ramusan were throwing a stiff branch in the air and racing and bumping into each other to see who could catch it before it landed. Rhamin and Yeltsa lay side by side, watching and at the same time feeling the pride they held within their souls for creating and holding together the finest group of wolves that could ever have been mixed and congealed into a single pack.

So, because of this moment of complete serenity, the distant sound of the predator, homing in on their location as easily as a bee seeks out its own hive, was all the more startling. Every wolf stood to attention. All had their ears pricked forward, twitching slightly as they homed in directionally on the resonating sound waves.

The men in their flying machines were back.

Then they realized what they were all thinking. Men in their flying *machines?* There was not just one this time. There were two if not more. The sound waves were blending together. It was hard to separate them. But there was definitely more than one. It wasn't long before they were able to tell that there were two metal birds and they were almost upon them.

'They still know where we are,' Lexa called over the din of the rotors.

Rhamin looked at her, puzzled. 'How can that be? We didn't even know we were going to be here until an hour ago.'

'They are tracking you, Rhamin,' Rasci stated, as Lexa took off into the trees. Rasci gazed up at the white patch of light that broke through the canopy of branches at the edge of a clearing. 'They have been able to track you since you left their prison camp. They just couldn't find you straight away.'

'How?' Rhamin needed answers.

'I really don't know,' Rasci replied as he turned away from the light and walked back to the other wolves under cover of the trees.

'Have you no idea Rasci?' Rhamin asked, still gazing out at the events that were unfurling over the clearing. 'You know men kind better than any of us. Haven't you any idea?'

Rasci shrugged and shook his head. 'If I had, I would…'

But Rasci didn't have time to finish what he was saying. As the two helicopters hovered over the clearing, several ropes coiled out of the machines, and hung, suspended like long feeler vines from an ancient fig tree. All the wolves seemed transfixed as they watched events unfold. First a man slipped expertly down one of the ropes and landed at the far side of the glade. The wolves watched on as he disconnected himself from the rope and then, lifting his arms above his shoulders, and pulling one of the firing stick devices from where it had been attached onto his back, he pointed it towards the watching wolves.

'Run into the thickest part of the forest,' Rhamin barked the order as he turned from the edge of the clearing.

The man was raising his gun, pointing it at Rhamin.

Steadying himself, he took aim, but he hadn't been prepared for what happened next. Lexa hit him from behind in the small of his back with the full force of her front feet. As he fell forward onto the soft ground, his gun made a faint cracking sound and something splattered through the leaves. The gun fell from his grasp and scuttered away from him over the thin, wispy grass. Lexa turned. She was inches away from the man's face before he had even lifted his head. Teeth barred, jowls slavering, Lexa was neither going to be taken by this man nor was she going to let him kidnap her leader again.

Reacting, the man lifted his arm to protect his face.

'I will kill you before I'll let you take any of us,' she growled as she clenched her iron jaws onto his forearm.

'Lexa!' Rhamin's voice was loud and authoritative. 'Leave him be! Come now!'

Reluctantly, Lexa let go of the man's arm. She backed away from him slowly, his face showing not fear but total shock. Whether it was because the prey he had hunted had retaliated or whether it was because he had been brought to the ground by a dog and not a wolf, no one could tell. Backing off slowly, Lexa snarled again and then turned to run. But she had only reached Rhamin's side when another man appeared in front of them. He must have abseiled into the forest behind the pack. He, too, had a gun.

But once again, this man had no chance to use it. Ramusan had hold of his wrist and, like a terrier with a rat, was shaking it from side to side so vigorously that his weapon was thrown from his grasp. It flew off, clattering against a solid tree trunk before disappearing in a patch of tall ferns. The man heard his forearm snap as the wolf's powerful jaws continued to clench shut. 'Come father,' Ramusan called as he let go. 'We will not let them take you again.'

As the wolves milled around, waiting for direction from their leader, another weapon was discharged somewhere. But this one made a completely different sound to the noise that had come from the first man's gun. This time the blast resounded through the whole forest and over the entire hillside, echoing as it rebounded from trees and rocky outcrops.

There was a yelp and then the sound of more running feet breaking through the brush and fern. Rhamin headed in the direction of the noise. There was no intention to flee. The pack would stand together to protect each other, or fall in battle.

Another two men were heading towards them. Each had a weapon, but the first man's firing stick looked so much unlike the one carried by his comrade that the wolves knew his weapon was to be used for killing. A wisp of smoke was still rising from the end of the evil looking tube. It had just been fired and it had sent a hot metal tooth into Charka's thigh. It was she who had yelped. She was dragging her hind leg behind her as she tried to run.

The second man raised his tranquilizer weapon in the direction of Rhamin, but, once again, the man's intended action was thwarted. Yeltsa, Rhamin's devoted mate, tackled him, but unlike the other men, at first, her opponent didn't go down. He was big and he was strong. As Yeltsa wrestled with the man's left arm, his right hand went down to his belt. He gripped a bone-handled knife that was sheathed in some kind of hardened animal skin, and drew it out.

Ramusan was in the centre of the mêlée once again. He grabbed the man's shoulder and, shaking it with all his weight, dragged the man to the forest floor.

'No!' Rhamin barked when he saw Ramusan turn his

teeth towards the man's throat. 'Let him live. Perhaps these men kind will learn that we are not going to give in to them.'

Ramusan growled, his anger almost too great to prevent his natural instinct to kill from taking over. He was finding it hard to obey his father. But, finally, finding control, and making sure that the man saw all his teeth close to his eye, Ramusan wheeled away. With his father and mother, he thrashed through the undergrowth and ran towards the thickest part of the forest just as another resounding report echoed through the trees.

A quick head count showed they were short of some wolves. Rasci, Silvah, Lexa, Bamar and Natan were missing now.

'Stop!' Rhamin barked. 'Listen!'

All the wolves did as they were ordered. Even with their heavy panting they could hear a fight going on in yet another location. Without another word, Rhamin set off in the direction of the noise. More men with weapons had formed a circle. In the centre were the missing wolves. Bamar lay on his side, chest heaving, and tongue dangling into the wet grass. At either side were Silvah and Natan. They were not allowing anyone to get near their wolf. Silvah stood, teeth barred, protecting Bamar from one side. The man she was facing had a damaged hand, blood running down it onto a limply held weapon. He didn't try to lift it or use it, but instead slowly let it drop to the ground as Rasci, hackles sticking out like the bristles of a porcupine and lips rolled back on his rows of white teeth, came up from behind and pushed his fangs against the man's good arm. His warning couldn't have been plainer.

The other three men were having trouble concentrating on their deadly work. Three black shadows had descended from above the trees, swooped down and, with flapping wings and raucous cries, had clawed at their faces before sweeping back up and over the canopy, away out of sight. Those men's eyes were on the sky, watching, waiting for another attack from the vicious birds. It was strange that carrion eaters would join an affray instead of waiting for the killing to run its course. It was as if they were on the wolves' side in the battle for their lives.

And of course, they were. The three ravens, Corvak, his son, Crufus and his daughter, Betrix had seen what was going on, and despite being naturally afraid of the huge spinning helicopter rotors, their fear dissipated when they saw their friends being attacked.

Although Bamar was wounded, he lifted his head when he saw the rest of the pack.

Another man, not noticed by Rhamin at first, was sitting on the ground, his back against a tree. He had dropped his weapon. Lexa had tackled him to the ground after he had been attacked and distracted by one of the ravens, and now she stood in front of him, hackles raised, teeth like razors barred next to his face. She had hurt the man but she knew that going any further would not benefit the pack. Kill a single man, and the whole pack could be wiped out in retribution. Zelda had taught the pack that much. None of them had forgotten the old wolf's ancient stories.

'Can you walk, Bamar,' Rhamin called.

The wounded wolf struggled to his feet. He was injured badly. Blood was dripping fast from his abdomen.

'Let's go, Boss,' he said to Rhamin. With that, wincing with every short stride, he and the pack disappeared into the trees.

Looking back behind them, the wolves heard the helicopters landing in the clearing. They were now no longer in pursuit. One at a time, each metal bird lowered itself noisily but slowly to the ground while the other one hovered nearby. They were collecting their wounded.

As the pack snaked through the trails, they spread out, until, as the trees thinned, they reassembled beneath a thicker patch of trees near the edge of the forest. Rhamin realized that there was no way either Bamar or Charka would be able to make a long journey. Bamar was already dropping behind. Urged on by Rasci and Silvah he struggled to walk.

'We'll head back to the Darin,' Rhamin instructed. Even in the forests there was no way to escape from the long reach of the predators. Until they discovered how the men in the metal birds could track and find them so easily, there were only two things they could do; run and hide.

Unless, somehow, they could stop the hunt for Rhamin.

And because of what had just happened, he had made up his mind what he was going to do to save his pack. It had taken him no time at all to formulate a plan. There was only one solution. But it meant a sacrifice.

Bamar never made it to the Darin. He slumped down on the ground on his belly, too weak to go any further. He lifted his head and looked out from the tree line of the great forest, letting his gaze span the plain that had been his home for the past four years. He looked at Rhamin. The face of his leader had changed somehow. Rhamin's jaw had clenched closed and his lips had curled back ever so slightly. The thin line of teeth showed his master's anger, his rage at what this group of men were doing to him and his beloved pack. 'Don't do what I think you are going to do,' Bamar said faintly.

Rhamin's jaw relaxed a little. He looked at his wounded wolf and licked him on the side of the face. 'I have no choice,' Rhamin whispered only loud enough for Bamar to hear. 'If I don't kill the man responsible...'

But he had no time to finish what he was going to say. Rolling sideways and resting his head on a bed of soft pine needles, Bamar passed out, breathed in deeply, exhaled, and with what seemed like a never ending breath outwards, he died.

For long seconds Rhamin just gazed at his fallen comrade. Bamar had died, not defending himself, but defending his leader. The thin grin of rage slowly worked its way along Rhamin's white teeth once again. He looked across at Rasci who was coming closer. Rasci had been with Charka. She didn't appear to be mortally wounded. Her leg had already stopped bleeding; the blood from the wound already thick and congealed around the tiny hole where the hot tooth of metal had entered the muscle and lodged in her thigh bone.

Licking Rhamin's ear, Rasci understood his leader's anger. 'We can get over this,' he said consolingly.

'Yes,' Rhamin replied. But his eyes did not reveal submission. They did not show Rhamin's acceptance that the pack would live through this tragedy and be stronger for it. For the first time in his life, Rasci saw a cold malevolent gaze fleet across his master's eyes.

Even now, as the pack made its way back to the Darin, every wolf knew that the men could and would trail them once again. These predators were relentless.

The wound in Charka's leg would fester. She needed help and Rhamin knew that the only creature or man that could do this was Raymond Rozalski. His was the only place they could go to ensure Charka's survival. But there seemed no way to summon that help. 'Is there anything you can do to call the farmer to help her?' he asked Rasci.

'I don't know,' Rasci answered truthfully. The farmer had his own life to live. There seemed no end to the wolves' need to draw this man into their lives. On top of that, apart from just keeping in touch with Ben as a friend and to learn more about men kind, Rasci had just wanted to get back to being an ordinary wolf, just doing wolf things. But the events of the last few days had sabotaged that dream. The easy life he had envisaged had unexpectedly and abruptly ended. And what had started like a perfect day had turned into the worst and most horrendous dawn, even before the sun had lifted fully off the long, undulating skyline.

CHAPTER ELEVEN

Elsie was awakened by voices in the next room. She lifted her head and peered at the alarm clock that stood next to her on the bedside table. It was two o'clock in the morning. She frowned. Perhaps she had been dreaming. But then she heard Ben's voice again. It was like he was having a conversation with somebody, but it seemed all one sided. It was a conversation with gaps where someone else should be speaking. She sighed, shaking her head and pulling the bedclothes over her. This was a weird family, where the children spent hours talking on the telephone in the middle of the night. What sort of family had she joined? The talking went on and on until, tiredness overcoming her, she sank back into a fitful slumber.

Breakfast was a good hour earlier than in the city. She woke to the sound of Ben and Margo squabbling over something or other. Nothing serious of course. Just the regular differences exacerbated by siblings. She smiled. This is what she had missed when her mother and father had produced an only child. It was obvious that Ben and Margo adored each other. Yet their arguments sounded to be on the verge of all out war.

'Hey, you two,' Maria's voice screeched up the stairs, and suddenly the two in conflict, united by the common enemy, chatted and chuckled as they ran down the stairs.

When breakfast was called fifteen minutes later, Elsie shuffled out of bed and pulled on her dressing gown. She opened the bedroom door and listened to the clamour of children chattering and their mother and father talking over the top of them; the sound of a family; a well balanced unit of children and adults. Where did she fit in to all this she wondered? She was the cuckoo in the nest for sure. She was a single child and as such she had been the focus of all the attention her father could lavish on her. She hadn't had to share him, except with her mother. That was just bearable. Only just. With a moist eye she trod heavily down the stairs.

'Good morning,' Raymond said cheerfully as Smokey rose from her basket and, with ears forward and a wrinkled brow, she went over and greeted their guest.

'Morning,' Elsie replied quietly but politely. She casually rested her hand lightly on the dog's huge, broad head and got a small wriggly movement from Smokey's stumpy tail in response as she walked on by. Maria waved her to the chair across the table from her two cousins. She sat down and calmly waited for life to continue around her.

'Rasci came to talk to me last night,' Ben stated excitedly, his little eyes wide with delight. 'He's a bit worried.' His conversation was directed at his father.

Raymond leaned forward across the table. 'Thought he'd have forgotten you by now,' he stated in a subdued half whisper as if there were some secret that the two men of the household shared.

'Rasci?' Elsie asked quietly.

'His wolf friend,' Raymond said, turning his face to Elsie.

His eyes crinkled as a self-amused grin spread across his face.

Wolf friend? That sounded strange. No doubt they would explain. 'I heard him talking to somebody,' Elsie said, nodding. 'I didn't think he would have a telephone in his room at his age!' She was wondering why her room didn't have one, although she couldn't think of anyone she'd want to call if it had.

'Telephone?' Raymond and Maria said in unison. They both looked at her momentarily and then burst out laughing.

'You have a lot to find out about this crazy family sweetheart,' Maria chuckled. 'And you *ain't* seen crazy yet!'

Elsie looked at her aunt quizzically.

'I wasn't on a phone, silly!' Ben said rather loudly as he realized he knew something that his older cousin could not possibly know. 'He comes to see me!'

Elsie just frowned. People visit children in their bedrooms at two o'clock in the morning? *Crazy* seemed a mild description of the goings on in the country. Would a townie ever know how the other half lived?

Raymond looked at his niece, his head tilted slightly as he tried to pick his words. 'Rasci is a wolf spirit of sorts.'

Elsie nodded. 'Right.'

The two adults could tell she was humouring them. 'We have some wolves around here that are friendly with us,' Maria stated. She was going to explain it all properly in a way that sounded a bit more logical. 'Only, our children have an ability to communicate with some of them.'

Elsie nodded. 'Right,' she said again in a monotone voice. Were these people trying to impress her or just amaze her? In either case it wasn't working.

'One of them can appear in front of me when he isn't really there,' Ben proclaimed.

Elsie nodded. 'Yeah.' An involuntary frown crumpled her brow. She was finding it hard to make eye contact with any of them. Looking straight at Maria, she said, 'This is a wind-up, right?'

None of the family answered that. Maria just looked at Raymond for his response.

'And Margo can talk to them without speaking,' Ben stated, ignoring Elsie's scepticism and looking at his little sister proudly. 'And they talk to her the same way!'

Margo nodded affirmatively as she stuffed a rather larger than chewing-sized lump of bread into her mouth.

'She can read their minds,' Raymond stated insanely.

They all seemed so normal when they met her at the airport, even if they were slightly less than bright-looking country folk.

'And they can read hers,' he continued, to explain Ben's comments.

Mind reading wolves. 'Yeah, yeah,' Elsie said appeasingly as she continued avoided eye contact and concentrated on positioning her knife and fork.

'We're quite a gifted family really!' Raymond continued.

Perhaps Uncle Raymond and his family were a bit eccentric. No, scratch that. This family was totally cuckoo. Living out in the middle of nowhere might cause that, she diagnosed silently.

'You wouldn't know by looking at us though,' Maria added.

Not by looking at you, Elsie thought. It's just when you open your mouths. She squeezed her fork and stopped herself from saying anything. They really *had* all seemed quite normal at the airport. But then they hadn't been talking so much. Yesterday seemed like an average sort of day compared with this one and it had only just begun. Yesterday there were adults on one level, children on another. But now the children were all on one side. What happened to the grown ups?

'Come,' Maria said, smiling, 'Let's not overdo it on her first day.' She placed a plate of mashed potato and grilled bacon in front of Elsie. 'Here you are sweetheart. Get tucked into that. You'll get to know us better as time goes on.'

Is that really necessary Elsie wondered? Perhaps she should just keep a polite distance in case whatever was ailing them was catching. Aunt Maria had said that she could start school when Ben and Margo went back after the half-term break. School, she thought. Perhaps the people there are similarly afflicted. But school in this part of the country can't be any worse than at home… Home? Why am I here in this place in the middle of nowhere, where no one in their right mind would want to spend more than a day or two, never mind a lifetime?

Everyone went quiet while they watched Elsie eat. Eventually, it was Raymond who spoke. 'So, tell us a bit about yourself, Elsie. We've done nothing but talk about ourselves since you got off the plane.'

Elsie swallowed what she was chewing and replied. 'Not a lot to tell really. Daddy died and Mum can't cope with me.' There was a hint of bitterness in her voice as she finished the sentence. She took another bite of bread, ripping it away from her mouth rather than biting it through. She chewed in silence while all four pairs of eyes watched her intently. As no one spoke, Elsie felt obliged to continue the conversation once she had swallowed what she was eating. 'I didn't want to come here.'

If she wanted to shock the farmer and his family then it wasn't working. Maria just smiled affectionately. 'No, I know you didn't, sweetheart.' She reached across the table and pressed the palm of her hand gently on Elsie's fist. 'We know it must be a wrench.' She squeezed Elsie's hand tenderly. 'To tell the truth, we weren't sure about it either.'

'That figures,' Elsie said bluntly, pulling her hand from beneath Maria's.

'Well, in a way it does,' Maria agreed. 'Neither I nor your uncle Ray have any grown up children.'

Elsie smiled. It was something her father used to tell her. She was grown up. He'd said that to her since she was seven. She warmed to Maria a little.

'And I'm a townie,' Elsie added. 'You'll soon find out that I can't even milk a cow or anything.'

'Well, you know, I'm not too good at that either,' Maria said, smiling. 'But life out here *is* different.'

'I suppose it's a bit lonely out here in the middle of nowhere?' Elsie couldn't help thinking that it had already affected their brains. 'Talking to animals and all.'

Raymond chuckled. 'Well, I see what you mean. But it's only lately that we discovered that Ben and Margo have a gift.'

Elsie looked at him quizzically. Were these people real or what?

'You'll see,' was all her uncle said on the subject. 'Come, eat your breakfast. We'll all take you on the grand tour when you've finished.'

'You three can,' Maria corrected, nodding at her husband and her two young children. 'I have to clear up here.'

As soon as Elsie had finished, Ben and Margo jumped up from their seats. 'Come on Elsie,' Ben shouted eagerly. He looked at his father with excited eyes. 'Are you ready, Daddy?'

Raymond put his hand on Ben's head, ruffled his hair and smiled. 'Come on then. Let the tour begin.'

Apart from being a vast expanse of not very great agricultural land plus some very large modern portal frame buildings forming the sides of a huge square yard, Raymond's farm was, to Elsie, quite unremarkable. All the cattle and sheep were out on the land somewhere, so there were none of those to be seen. The huge barns were, however, spotless. One contained farm equipment. A massive four wheel drive tractor, with a huge front-end loader and with wheels that were higher than Raymond's head, stood near the open end of the barn. One of the tyres looked brand new. 'I bet that tyre cost a pretty penny,' she remarked, thinking how much her father had complained about the cost of replacing tyres on his car.

'Oh, Mummy shot a hole in the old tyre,' Ben came in quickly. Then he realized what he had just said. 'It was a mistake. She thought Rasci was a bad wolf and shot at him and missed.'

Elsie couldn't help letting out a little chuckle. 'So, you aren't friendly with all wolves then?'

'Oh no, there are bad wolves and good wolves just as there are good and bad people,' Ben replied. Raymond just stood and listened. If Ben's conversation could make Elsie relax a little, perhaps she might begin to enjoy being in their company.

Eventually, Ben explained what had happened the night that a pack of wolves raided the farm during a drought. He explained that a bad wolf came into the house and was about to kill him and his little sister when Rhamin came to their aid.

'Rhamin?'

'That's The Black Wolf's real name,' Ben said proudly.

'And you gave him that name did you?'

'Oh, no. They all had names before we got to know them. They told us their names.'

Raymond winced. The conversation was heading back into the deep canyon that separated the land of the unbelievable from the land of the impossible. He knew how that looked to their young niece. 'And these are the farm implements,' he said by way of distraction. He waved his arm at the inside of the building to encompass all the equipment in the place.

Behind the tractor was an assortment of machinery, a long cattle trailer with flaps along the side that could be opened or shut to ventilate the interior, a huge steel sided tipping trailer, plus some tilling, ploughing and other machines that Elsie couldn't identify, nor did she really care. One thing caught her interest though. An old Jeep that Raymond had only recently reconditioned stood in a bay of the barn on its own. It appeared to have just recently been painted. In fact it looked like new.

'You've got a talent there,' Elsie said, rather less sarcastically than Raymond had come to expect. 'You should set up a business renovating old vehicles and then you could have time off, like every normal person.'

'Life on a farm *is* normal,' Raymond said crossly. 'The human race didn't evolve as a town dwelling, nine to five species.' He thought about what he had just said. 'Though I think that that kind of person is now a new branch of evolution,' he said dryly.

'Only joking,' Elsie appeased. 'I do know about The

Industrial Revolution.'

'Glad to hear it.'

Normal? Is that what Uncle Raymond really thought; that they were normal?

'So having wolves in your house is a normal farm activity?' Elsie quipped again. If everything the Rozalskis had said had any grain of truth, then it was a legitimate question.

'You'll learn, as life goes on, that circumstances change your life. You don't always control what happens. What happens, more than likely, controls you, Elsie.'

'I know that,' Elsie retorted bitterly as she thought about being sent to stay with Raymond and Maria in the first place. She'd had no control over that whatsoever.

CHAPTER TWELVE

Elsie was going to spend the rest of the day in her room, reading some of the books that filled the shelves. It was a good way to avoid awkward conversations with delusional people. She had no compunction to humour the Rozalskis. If they wanted to be, or pretend to exist in some kind of shaman community, then they weren't going to get praise or encouragement from her. The more she showed them how much she hated being there, the sooner they would tire of her and pack her back off home.

Home? She sighed as she contemplated that alternative. Her father was dead and she had a mother who didn't want her. She flopped tiredly back on her bed and covered her eyes with the palms of her hands. She wasn't going to cry. No, she wasn't going to cry.

It was Ben who knocked on Elsie's bedroom door.

'Elsie is very angry,' Margo had explained to him.

Ben had nodded his agreement. 'I don't think she likes any of us,' he'd responded. Something inside him told him that Elsie would rather be anywhere other than at the farm with them.

'Yes,' Elsie answered after the second rap on the door.

Ben turned the handle and opened the door slowly. 'Hello,' he said as he peeped around it. 'Can I come in?'

Elsie was lying across the bed, reading a book as usual. Pushing herself up onto her knees and laying the book down beside her, she nodded her head.

'Margo says you are very angry,' Ben began. 'Don't you like us?'

Elsie looked at him for quite a long moment before shaking her head. 'I don't know any of you,' she said quietly. 'And I don't understand any of you. I didn't want to come here, but it isn't you I don't like.'

'You don't like my mummy and daddy?'

Elsie shook her head again. 'I don't dislike them. I just don't know them.' She offered Ben her hand and he took hold of it. 'Come here,' she said and lifted him onto the edge of the bed beside her. 'I'm not used to having any brothers or sisters either,' she explained. 'You are very lucky having Margo to grow up and to play with.'

Ben nodded. 'She can be a bit of a bore sometimes, but she's very clever really.'

That made Elsie smile. Just by looking at Ben's face as he talked about his little sister, she could tell he was immensely proud of her.

If only she'd had an elder brother like that. But it wasn't the case and she had to fit her life, as it was, into the world as it was. The world spun around and travelled at thousands of miles per hour through space as it circled the sun, but everything on its surface depended on conformity.

'Do you read?' she asked her little cousin.

'Mummy has been teaching me,' Ben replied proudly. But I am learning more now that I have started school. Before Elsie could ask anything else, Ben carried on. 'I've even been teaching Rasci how to spell words,' he declared proudly.

'Rasci?'

'You know, the wolf?'

Elsie groaned inwardly. It came out as a sigh. She would humour him. After all, he had come to try and cheer her up. The olive branch had definitely been proffered, so the least she could do was try not to hurt this harmless and totally disarming child. She looked at him for a while, studying his little face. There was definitely a family resemblance. If anything, he looked remarkably like her mother, which probably meant that he looked a little like her because people often said she was the spitting image of her mother. If only she'd had a brother like him.

'So what exactly have you been teaching your wolf?'

'Come,' Ben said excitedly, jumping off the bed and heading to the door. He turned around and waited for Elsie to follow. With a resigned sigh and a spontaneous shrug of her shoulders, she got up off the bed and followed him.

Margo was playing in the back garden, though it wasn't so much a garden, more a wilderness of wispy grass with a few flowers struggling to decorate the perimeter of the house walls. A straight young tree, a seed dropped years ago by a bird, grew close to the wall of the farmhouse, and a rambling rose hung around the outside of the door forming a small archway under which Margo often passed as the princess greeting her subjects outside.

'Look,' Ben said excitedly, as he ran out to meet Margo. He found a dry, dusty patch of ground where the grass no longer grew because of the constant wear and tear of little playing footsteps. Easily locating a small stiff stick, he wrote his name *Ben*. Then, he wrote the words *Needs Help*.

'You need help?' Elsie queried.

'No.' Ben replied patiently. 'That is what I was trying to teach Rasci. *Ben needs help*. Only I could only spell my name then. I couldn't spell the rest of it.'

'And when did you start teaching him to write?' Elsie asked, smiling.

'When he came to see me at school. I wanted to show him more words but I couldn't spell them yet.' Then he added, 'Before we rescued Rhamin.'

Rasci had been watching Ben. Instructed to contact Raymond, he began to relax and meditate. He had travelled to see Ben with his mind so many times before, when he communicated with him to plan the rescue of Rhamin, that it had almost become a simple reflexive procedure. He watched as Ben explained what the words he had written meant.

'Will you ever need to tell me you need help?' he asked, suddenly startling Ben as he appeared as a vision in front of his small friend.

'Rasci!' You made me jump,' Ben said, crossly but ecstatic to see his friendly wolf's image. 'How long have you been there?'

'Oh, not long. But I saw what you have written. I am really impressed!'

'This is Elsie,' Ben stated, turning towards his cousin.

Elsie just watched the little boy playing his pretending game and tried to recall if she had ever imagined things just as clearly when she'd played alone as a small child.

Margo just stood nearby and grinned.

'The North American Indians use other signs,' Elsie said,

attempting to get back into a conversation with Ben rather than pretending to talk to a non-existent wolf.

'Indians?'

'They use stones to leave messages,' she explained. 'Or used to. They probably use mobile phones now!'

Ben and Margo chuckled.

'Tell her to explain them,' Rasci suggested.

'Rasci has asked if you can tell us what they are,' Ben said as a go-between.

'Right,' Elsie replied, smirking. She took the stick from Ben's hand and began to draw symbols in the dusty earth. 'They were done with stone's of course,' she explained, 'not with a stick. If it rains or if it's windy then the stones don't disappear.'

Ben and Margo nodded.

So did Rasci. He understood how easily dusty ground can become disturbed, not just by rain and wind, but even by the footprints of other creatures. No, stones sounded a great idea.

'This means *Help me*,' Elsie said as she drew a circle in the dirt and then drew two arrows pointing to it. 'And this means *We are going this way*, she said, drawing a simple arrow. She went through several other signs and symbols, not sure if she had remembered the right ones for the any of the messages she was explaining they carried, but as she drew the shapes and diagrams, they transfixed Ben and Margo. And unknown to Elsie, it spellbound Rasci also.

Thinking now that she was making progress at exorcising from these gullible little souls the belief in wolf spirits and talking, thinking animals, she began to play with them.

'I went this way,' she said, drawing an arrow and then placing the children's hands over their eyes. 'Count to fifty and then come find me!'

And off she ran.

'Forty nine... fifty. Right, we're coming!' And off the two children ran, following arrows drawn in the soil until, turning a corner, they faced the open fields. Stopping in the shade of a large oak tree, they looked at each other and shrugged. The trail had gone cold. Elsie had disappeared. For several minutes they searched the soil for more clues, but found none. They were about to retrace their steps when Maria came along and asked what they were looking for. When they explained, their mother frowned. She had come from the opposite direction along the fence and had not met or seen Elsie.

'I can't think where she must have got to,' she said to her children as she examined the signs drawn on the ground. For a minute, Maria began to be a little worried. Had Elsie run away? Had she got lost? Was she hurt or injured? All these thoughts and more began to track through her mind when suddenly, right in front of her face, a torso swung upside down in front of her face. Elsie had hooked her legs over a branch of the tree and simply swung down from it. Her smile looked strange in an upside down face whose head dangled loosely above a tangle of floating hair.

'Elsie!' Maria shouted. 'What on earth do you think you are doing?' She grabbed hold of Margo and Ben and moved them away from the tree as if they were in imminent danger of being squashed by a falling body. 'What on earth do they teach you in the city!'

Elsie didn't answer. She just swung back up, caught hold of the branch with her hands and, slipping her feet between her arms, dangled feet-down for a second before dropping lightly to the ground. Without uttering a single word, she shrugged and just walked off towards the house and the sanctuary of her room.

'Wow, did you see that?' Ben exclaimed to Rasci as their mother paced after Elsie.

'I thought your young friend was very agile,' Rasci said and then became a little more serious. 'Ben,' he began. 'Our pack is being hunted again.'

'Hunted?' asked Ben.

Rasci nodded. 'Yes. That man Petersen has been hunting Rhamin. He seems to be able to follow him wherever he goes.'

Suddenly Rasci disappeared. 'I've got to go!' he shouted as his image faded. 'I'll return as soon as I can!'

CHAPTER THIRTEEN

'Kara and Lutz have just told me that Rhamin is being hunted again by the man that captured him in the first place.' Roxana had waited until all the wolves in her pack had settled down after eating. The two vultures fed greedily on the remains of the deer carcass that had provided ample fare for all the wolves, and more. Their reward for being spies for Roxana.

'And have they captured him again?' Rhiana asked, her tone quite dismissive.

'Rhamin and his wolves are on the run. It seems like the men kind can follow him wherever he goes. They have tried to capture him again, but it seems like they failed.'

'He can hide in the forests,' Solin countered. 'They'll never find him there. We can find him because we can follow his trail. But men kind don't have our ability to...'

'Yes they *will* find him,' Roxana broke in. 'Kara has told me that the men can and are tracking every move he makes.'

'Impossible!' Solin's voice sounded angry. 'If he hides in the forests, then they'll never find him. We wolves can hear men approaching from miles away. If Rhamin decides to hide then they will not see him.'

'Kara tells me that they *can* find him. And they can see him wherever he is.'

'Those feathered snacks over there have only one good use as far as I can see. Why else are we fattening them up?'

'Quiet you fool,' Roxana answered crossly. 'How long do you think they will continue to be our spies if they hear you saying things like that?'

'They are telling you what they want you to hear, Roxana. In their case, no news is bad news. So they make it up as they go along. They are just scheming and inventing what to tell us so they can have their next meal. They are not interested in our plans to take over this territory. They don't see any further than our next kill. As long as we hunt to live, they are well satisfied. Battles for power are not what they are looking for; just a nice easy ride.'

'Sometimes I think you have inherited some of that idiot Rasci's mentality,' Roxana quipped. 'You can be totally stupid sometimes.'

Rhiana looked at Roxana and then at Solin. She had been right. Roxana was slowly but surely taking over the pack. She watched as the hair on Solin's back suddenly bristled.

Solin barred his teeth, as anger surged through his whole body. He stood up and faced his female adversary. 'You're forgetting just whose pack this is,' he stated, leaving no doubt as to what he meant. 'Call me a fool or stupid again and I'll kill you.' He turned towards the carcass where the vultures were feeding greedily. Without any warning he lunged at the nearest vulture. Lutz had just turned his head as he ripped at a strand of meat, otherwise he wouldn't have seen Solin, from the corner of his eye, bounding towards him. With a frantic flapping of his wings, and a squawk that sounded like the death throws of a hunted animal, the vulture narrowly avoided Solin's jaws. But he lost two tail feathers to the angry wolf's gnashing bite.

'Now calm down,' Rhiana shouted conciliatorily, trying to defuse the situation as Solin spat out the long tail feathers. Her plans involved Roxana, and Roxana relied on the vultures. However clever the young female wolf thought she was, Rhiana was soon to put her in her place. And that place was not as head of the Solin pack.

Roxana glared at Solin. She would have liked to take him on, fight him for leadership, but she knew she had neither the size nor the strength to beat him. The only way to depose him was to wait and let her own plan evolve.

'Killing our allies won't help our cause,' Rhiana reminded her son. She looked at the two vultures who had taken off and landed a good ten paced beyond their meal. With their beaks open with surprise and fear, and their wings held out to cool their agitated bodies, they just stood there and waited to see if they were ever going to be safe again with this pack.

Roxana went over to the vultures and talked quietly to them. No one else heard what was said, but eventually the two big birds reluctantly returned to the carcass, although it was quite clear that neither had an appetite for food any more; and neither took their eyes off Solin.

Roxana continued to glare at Solin. He just lay down with his chin on his paws and ignored her. He knew he had made his point, though his heart was still beating fast with the adrenalin that his anger had pumped into every fibre of his body.

'If we fight amongst ourselves then we will not be strong enough to accomplish what we want,' Rhiana said, still trying to calm them.

Solin lifted his head. 'Okay, mother, let's have it. What is your great scheme?'

Rhiana thought for a few moments and then said, 'If Rhamin isn't safe from those men anywhere…' She paused and gave Solin the *Let me finish* look. 'Then he'll return with his pack to the Darin.'

'And why would he do that?' Solin asked snidely.

'Because they are too vulnerable out in the open. I reckon he'll take his pack back to the Darin because it is defendable. Men kind can't get in through the entrance more than one, or at the most two, at a time.'

'Only if he's there.' Solin retorted. 'He and his wolves have to eat. They still have to hunt.'

'No, I reckon that he and his wolves will be safe so long as the men kind want Rhamin alive. If I know Rhamin, he'll only hunt at night. That will cut down the men kind's chances of capturing him. He'll only stay in the Darin during the day.'

'And he'll be trapped.'

'No.' Rhiana was emphatic. 'It will be a stand off. The men can't kill him because they want him alive. And if he stays with the pack, then they will not allow the men to take him like they did before.'

'And just how did they take him before?'

'Out in the open,' Roxana came in.

'And you know that for sure?'

'Yes I do know. I know because I was told what happened, remember? Rasci?' She looked at Solin for acknowledgement.

Solin knew full well how Roxana had duped Rasci into telling her all he knew. He smiled. 'Yes, you did that rather well, I must admit.'

'And I knew where he was so I could find him to get that

information because of my spies,' Roxana reminded him. She wanted to emphasise just how useful the two birds were.

'Hmm,' Solin reluctantly grunted his acknowledgement.

'Does this mean you two will stop arguing?' Rhiana asked crossly. She needed Roxana, and Solin wasn't helping things along by constantly challenging her.

Solin ignored the question. 'So you reckon that Rhamin will keep all of his pack close?'

'Yes,' Rhiana replied.

'And they will go out hunting for food at night,' Solin said, more to himself than to Rhiana or Roxana.

Rhiana nodded. 'He'll need all his able bodied wolves with him if he is to repel an attack by the men.'

Now Solin was following her train of thought. 'So we watch and wait.'

'Kara and Lutz can do that for us,' Roxana emphasised.

'They are not nocturnal,' Rhiana snapped a little too quickly. But she wanted to say it before Solin said anything. She took a breath and then, more calmly, she said, 'We can do our own watching from now on. We need to be ready to strike immediately as soon as they leave. It will be no good waiting for messengers the next morning.'

Roxana tilted her head, her brow creased, her expression one of confusion. 'Am I missing something here? Attack? If the pack is together, just who are we going to attack without Rhamin killing us first?'

'We kill his eyes,' Rhiana chortled, excitement welling up in her voice, her grin widening to reveal rows of strong, sharp teeth, and the whites of her own amber eyes widening as they lit up with the jagged flames of vengeance.

Roxana still looked perplexed. She tilted her head, waiting for an explanation.

'Zelda,' Solin said with a resigned sigh. 'We're going to kill the scrawny old pile of maggots.'

But Roxana didn't see in Solin's eyes the same excitement, the sheer joy that reflected in those of Rhiana.

CHAPTER FOURTEEN

In the afternoon Elsie watched as Ben played. Her little cousin was so disarming. He had been asking her questions about her life in the city, probing questions that, had they come from someone older, Elsie would have thought them impertinent and intrusive. But from Ben, the questions were totally innocent of any ulterior motive other than being fascinated by his newly found cousin who, in actual fact, seemed more like a big sister to him. He couldn't have explained why if he had been asked, but somehow, this stranger from the other side of the country had instantly bonded with him and his little sister Margo. He could tell she was angry of course. It showed in everything she said and did. She had been angry when she arrived. Now, she was even angrier. Ben and Margo's mother had shouted at Elsie and it hadn't seemed fair. All she was doing was playing with them. No, now she was very angry. Except when she was near Ben and Margo. In future, when she was with them, she would hold their hands and walk with them as they chatted and played. She would make up poems and stories that were sure to enthral them. She would tweak their collars or tidy their hair, or, with a bemused smile on her lips, she would just sit on the long wooden bench and watch them playing in the garden. But she wasn't going to play *with* them again. Not after this morning's fiasco.

Ben came over and sat beside her. 'What are you thinking?' he asked.

'She's thinking about that snail,' Margo answered before Elsie could reply. She pointed to a snail that had pitched its shell for the day on a piece of rock in the shadow cast by a tree.

Elsie scowled. 'How did you know that?' she asked and then shook her head. 'I must have been mumbling to myself,' she said and chuckled nervously to try and avoid any embarrassment.

'Tell us,' Ben prompted. 'What are you thinking?' He snuggled up close to his cousin and looked up at her face.

'I don't suppose it will hurt,' she said, smiling and leaning towards him. 'Do you like stories?'

Ben shrugged. 'Some,' he replied, curling up his little nose. 'It depends what they are about.'

'Let's find out,' Elsie whispered conspiratorially and then, sitting up straight, she began. 'Have you ever seen a fast snail?'

Ben's eyes widened. He shook his head as Margo came closer.

'Well, a snail has many hair-raising adventures if you watch them closely. For instance, when it is racing down a garden path, seeking the shelter of a broken plant pot after it has been spotted by a thrush.'

'Snails don't move very fast,' Margo declared. 'They can't race anywhere.'

'That's why they seem boring most of the time,' Elsie retorted. 'But if you see them going really fast then you'll need a high speed camera to catch them!'

Margo chuckled.

'The signs to look for are the tiny silver spots about a foot apart. You can often see the snail trail, dried like a silver ribbon on the paving slabs, but when you see the silver spots then you know the snail was in a hurry. That is when, like a kangaroo, it has used its powerful tail to spring off the floor and leap in huge hops to a place of sanctuary. When it does, it moves faster than a racing car. I've spent hours waiting to catch one on film, but up to now, my long vigils have been fruitless.'

'She's making it up,' Margo said, grinning ear to ear.

'Shhh,' Ben said. 'I want to hear all about snails.'

'Well this is the story of Shuffle, The Fast Snail,' Elsie explained. 'One day, on a bright sunny cloudless morning, Shuffle was meandering along the garden path, minding his own business, looking for a good leaf to eat. But the sun was very hot, so Shuffle decided to head for the shade of a big cabbage leaf. But something caught his attention. Something had, just for the shortest fraction of a second, passed in front of the sun, and fleetingly cast a shadow on the ground in front of him. He stopped and looked closely at the ground, but the shadow had vanished as quickly as it had appeared. At first he didn't see anything because the sun was shining so brightly. But, suddenly, the sun disappeared as a huge shadow enveloped him. And then, without any warning, from out of the sun, a bird loomed down upon him.'

'Wow,' Ben exclaimed.

'Shuffle had only a fraction of a second to react,' Elsie went on. 'But what could he do!?'

Both Ben and Margo shook their heads in amazement.

'Well, I'll tell you what he did. Without thinking, he

jumped. Then he jumped again, and then again. Shuffle headed straight for the cover of a broken plant pot, jumping faster than a flea. He knew that the bird couldn't get at him there.'

'Phew, that was a close thing! Good job Shuffle can move fast!' Ben said excitedly.

'And that's not all. When shuffle looked out from a hole in the side of the broken plant pot, he could see that the bird lay on its back, with its beak all crumpled where it had hit the hard ground. It wasn't very happy at all!'

Ben and Margo chuckled and looked at their cousin adoringly. They both knew she liked them. Elsie straightened Ben's collar and stood up to leave. He would have found it annoying if it had been his mother tidying his clothes like she did every school day before father drove him into school. But Elsie was different somehow. And not only did she seem to like being with him and his sister, Elsie didn't ignore him when he spoke to his invisible friend. As Elsie turned to go, his conversation with his cousin, for a moment or two, lapsed into silence and suddenly he was distracted.

Elsie turned and looked at the children again. 'Who's your friend this time?' she asked as she watched him playing his game.

Ben didn't answer. His eyes seemed focussed on some spot a few feet in front of him where a long wispy stalk of grass had headed and gone to seed.

'He's talking to Rasci again,' Margo answered for him.

'Rasci?' Ben and Margo were consistent at least with what they called their imaginary friend.

'He's the wolf Daddy has mentioned to you.' She paused for a moment while Elsie thought about what she had just said. Margo sensed that Elsie needed that moment. Then she continued. 'They can talk to us.' She paused again to consider her own words. 'Rasci is a real wolf. He can talk to me with his thoughts when he is with us. But when he's not here, he can talk to Ben.'

'Go on,' Elsie prompted. There had to be an explanation in there somewhere. At the very least it had the makings of another tall story.

'Daddy calls it *remote viewing* but Ben calls it talking to his wolf spirit.'

'And?'

'Ben can even see him.' She stopped and thought for a few seconds. 'I can't see him like Ben can when he isn't actually here. But when he's really here, he talks to me with his mind,' she said proudly. 'Because Ben can't understand what he's saying when Rasci is actually here. Only I can understand him then.'

Elsie smiled at her. 'I'm sure I'll understand you soon.'

Rasci was finding it easy to communicate with Ben in the presence of a stranger. Here he was, in front of Elsie who was watching his little man friend with interest, and he was communicating with Ben just as easily as he had done before. 'But she still doesn't know about us,' Rasci had surmised.

Ben shook his head. 'We've told her about you and the rest of the wolves, but she doesn't believe us.'

'Not yet. But perhaps later.'

Ben nodded.

'I don't know how to ask you this. Your father has been so good to us but...'

'Go on,' Ben prompted. 'Tell me.'

'Petersen is back.'

'Petersen!'

'Yes, and his men have killed one of our wolves.'

'They can't do that!'

'They already have. They've killed Bamar. And Charka is badly hurt.'

Ben paused for a long minute, contemplating the stalk of grass, or so it seemed to Elsie. 'She can come here. Daddy will help her,' he said.

Rasci shook his head. 'She can't walk. She has one of the men's bullets as you call them in her leg.'

'Then I'll get Daddy to come to her. Where is she?'

'In our cave, the one we call our Darin.'

'Where we brought Lexa?'

'That's right.'

'Daddy will come and help her.'

'I don't like to ask. He's been so good to us. It's such a long way to come.'

Ben shook his head. 'That doesn't matter.'

'It seems that wherever Rhamin is, Petersen can find him. He must have powers like we have. He can see things from afar.'

Ben shook his head. 'I don't think so.'

'But I'm telling you he knows exactly where to find him. He flies straight to him in his metal bird.'

'I've seen films about policemen that can track cars and things. Perhaps Petersen is using the same thing?'

'Films?'

Ben shook his head. 'I'll explain later.' He thought for a while and then said, 'I'll tell Daddy.'

Eventually Ben ended his conversation with Rasci. Elsie had been hanging on every word.

'So that was Rasci, I presume?' she said as casually as she could.

Ben was frowning. 'He needs our help,' he said eventually. 'Rasci says Charka is badly wounded. She's been shot.'

'Charka?'

'One of the other wolves in Rhamin's pack. They've killed Bamar.'

'They?'

'Petersen. He's the man who took Rhamin and his mate to a safari park. Daddy, Margo and I rescued them. Petersen's men have come back and killed Bamar and wounded Charka.'

Elsie studied Ben's features. His little pale face was flushed. His brow was creased with concern. He bit his bottom lip to stop it quivering. He really did believe he could talk to his wolf spirit. 'So one of the wolves really can talk to you?'

Ben nodded. 'He was in the garden when you showed us those signs. You remember?' He looked up at Elsie's sceptical face. 'You know, when I told you how I'd been teaching him to read, *Ben Needs Help?*'

Elsie nodded. 'And you really believe a wolf can be taught to read?' she asked, rather cynically.

'Yes,' Ben nodded. He pointed into the empty garden. 'He's still watching. He's still over there.'

Elsie glanced at the empty paddock and just nodded. 'Rasci says he really likes you.'

'Glad to hear it,' Elsie said with a broad smile. 'One thing I don't want is an angry wolf on my trail.'

'Our wolves never get angry with us,' Ben retorted. He paused for a moment as if listening and then said, 'But Rhamin is angry with the bad men. Rasci is worried that he has been pushed into such a rage. Rasci thinks Rhamin might go after Petersen and kill him. He's afraid his leader has lost all good reason.'

'Sounds like it would do more harm than good,' Elsie replied, seriously entering into the spirit of the conversation now. 'He just wouldn't be allowed to get away with it. In fact he would probably start a war where all men were going about killing every wolf they saw, just like it was only a few years ago.'

Ben nodded. 'I'll have to get Daddy to help. He will be able to stop Petersen killing our wolves.'

Elsie gave Ben another sceptical glance. She couldn't help thinking she had entered into a fantasy world of wolves, crazy farmers and their loopy children. But the whole thing did merit further investigation. As Sherlock Holmes said, *When you have eliminated the impossible, whatever remains, however improbable, must be the truth…* She was quite prepared to see it through to the very end.

CHAPTER FIFTEEN

Bears do not often stay together as a pair all year round. After mating, they go their separate ways. Bortag and Molem were no different. But they would meet up occasionally as, inevitably, their paths crossed. They would spend a little time together and then, as if tiring of each other's company, they would part again.

Bortag, the big male bear, weighing over sixteen hundred pounds when in full health, was Rhamin's arch enemy. His mate, Molem, was two thirds of his size, weighing in at a mere half a ton or so.

It was Fatz who saw the bear first. 'There's a bear approaching the Darin,' he barked, panting as he came over the rocky escarpment and emerged out of the sun.

'Is it alone?' asked Silvah, the first wolf that Fatz had come upon inside the mouth of the cave.

'No, she has her cub with her.'

'She? Yes I suppose it would be a female if it has a cub,' Silvah pondered. 'I meant, are there any other adult bears?'

'No sign of any.'

'Does she suspect that our Darin is here?' Silvah asked.

'Well she looked like she was just browsing until…'

'Until?'

'Until the men came. It looks like she was just wandering by. But the men-kind are back again too; this time in their ground travelling machines instead of the ones that fly. I think she's looking for somewhere to lie low until they have gone.' He paused and looked back behind him. The rocky slope was bare. For the time being.

'So the men are back and we have a bear wandering our way,' Rhamin said from the back of the cave. 'Marvellous!'

'I thought I'd better warn everyone about the men,' said Fatz apologetically. 'But it was then that I spotted the bear. I think she is just trying to avoid being seen by the men, that's all.'

'But that won't be all if she comes into our home, will it?' Rhamin stated crossly. 'You won't remember, but if it is who I think it is, we fought her and her mate Bortag when you were only a few days old. No, bears are not friends with wolves, and one thing I do know for sure; she's definitely not going to be friendly with us.'

'Then we'll remain in the cave until she and the men have gone,' Silvah stated to calm the situation.

'And if she finds the cave?' asked Lexa. 'Do we attack her and drive her off?'

'It's the men kind that we should be worried about,' Rhamin stated as he ventured closer to the mouth of the cave to see what was happening. He could hear the sound of the men's vehicles approaching.

Suddenly, Lexa spotted the bear coming down the escarpment to the flat shelf that ran across the mouth of the cave. 'She's heading this way,' she called. 'What shall we do father?'

'We move back into the cave. Give her room to hide if

she needs to. I doubt if she's looking for a fight with a cub at her side. Our real enemies, hers and ours, are the men that we can hear at the other side of the slope,' Rhamin said as the Jeeps engines were revved loudly and then went suddenly silent. 'Come, quickly.'

Silently and with a great sense of urgency, all the wolves loped into the dark shadows as they moved deeper into the blackness of the Darin. It was only with seconds to spare that they were all out of sight before Molem, with her young cub at her heels, sped, panting, into the cave complex. Snorting wildly, she nudged the young bear roughly to make it get further back into the shadows and then, with her own body between her cub and the enemy, she turned to face the opening.

From where he was watching, Rhamin could see past Molem and out of the mouth of the cave but his range of vision was so restricted by the huge bear that he could only see a small spot, a minute portion of the rocky slope.

It was enough.

As suddenly as Molem had appeared, so did a man. He was carrying some sort of device in his hand, turning it as if waiting for it to lead him. And lead him it did. He walked towards the mouth of the cave, waving the device from side to side, watching it with every sweep of his arm. Then, suddenly thinking better of his actions, he turned and shouted back up the slope to more of the men.

Within moments two other men kind slid down the rocky slope and stood alongside the first man just outside the cave. These men held firing sticks, or guns as Ben had described them to Rasci.

'He's in here somewhere,' the first man shouted, though none of the inhabitants of the Darin understood his words. 'Get some light in here!'

Although the entrance to the cave was only big enough for two men to walk through at the same time, the cave opened up on the inside where there was ample room for the three men to stand side by side.

The two armed men stepped forward first, each holding his gun at waist level, then slinging the weapons over their shoulders, they both reached into the other's back pack and drew out something that looked like a thick stick. They held them out in front of them and almost simultaneously two beams of light struck out into the darkness lighting up the whole interior of the cave like the morning sun on a rocky plain.

With the light from the torches shining directly into the cave, and in the vast shadow cast by the huge bear, it was impossible for Rhamin or his wolves to see from the back of the cave the expression on all three of the men's faces. In the sudden flash of light, the men saw what was standing on all four legs, only three paces in front of them. They were hunting wolves but they had found a big and angry bear.

Molem saw the astonishment on their faces, and she wasted no time waiting for them to react. Either she had seen men with guns before and knew how deadly they would be if they had chance to take them from their shoulders, or, Rhamin thought to himself, she was just frightened for herself and her cub, and reacted without any such reasoning.

With her body shaking with rage and fear, and before the first man could close his open mouth, Molem stood up to her full height on her hind legs and opened her own huge snout. She curled back her long rubbery nose, snarled, gave out a rock-shaking and blood curdling growl that echoed through the whole cave complex time and time again, and then, before the last echoes had faded, towering over the men, she rushed at the nearest man and closed her huge jaws on his shoulder. He dropped the device he had been carrying as she picked him up and, like a domestic dog takes a hold of a toy rag doll, she shook him from side to side. Then smashing the limp body to the ground, the huge bear let go of the man's shoulder, placed her heavy front paw on his chest, and looked only for a brief moment directly at the other two men. They had no chance to react. Protecting her young cub, and with intention of never letting these marauders get close to her baby, as if released from some magnetic force, Molem sprung forward at the arm and hand that held the dazzling torch beam.

In a jerk reaction, the nearest of the men lifted his arms in front of himself defensively before the enraged bear grabbed his arm and threw him up in the air. He hit the cave roof with a dull thud, screamed and landed, prostrate, at her feet. It gave the third man just enough time to turn and dive out of the mouth of the cave. Rolling forward toward the rocky incline, he shrieked to his colleagues and then fell prostrate in the gulley at its base. He knew that the only way to stop an enraged bear attacking was to pretend to be dead and then hope and pray that it lost interest in him.

One of the men on the ridge had already reached over his shoulder and, gripping the long handle of his rifle, he pulled it in front of him and took aim.

'No,' another commanded. 'The tranquilizer guns are no good.'

Hesitating only for a second while he contemplated what to do, the man dropped his rifle off his shoulder, drew out a small hand sized weapon from a holster by his hip, a weapon that looked nothing compared with the long firing sticks the wolves had seen before, and pointed it at Molem. With loud cracks that resounded with each shot into the mouth of the cave and echoed off the rocky cliff walls above it, once, twice and again he fired the small weapon repeatedly around Molem's feet and at the cliff wall above her head as he paced down the slope towards her.

At first the bullets from the man's automatic seemed to have little effect on the bear. She flinched and blinked as the bullets kicked up dust and splintered the rock but after eight or nine shots, she began to back away.

'Man down! Man down!' another armed man on the ridge of the escarpment shouted into a small attachment near his face as he, too, dropped his long weapon and drew out a hand gun.

Molem had already retreated several paces backwards into the mouth of the cave. Her growls seemed quieter somehow as if she were contemplating how to defend herself from these attackers. She dropped down onto all four feet again and, turning her huge, thick neck and looking around to make sure her baby was still there, said, 'Stay back inside the cave, Brunus.' To make sure the cub did as she was told, Molem reversed further into the caves, first pushing Brunus backwards with her huge backside, then turning and pushing her frantically with her muzzle.

The wolves watched, transfixed by what was happening. But none moved. They knew that all they could do was watch as the scene played out.

The first of the armed men bent down to see to his fallen comrade in the gulley, but apart from being badly shaken, he was unharmed. The armed man helped him to his feet and, with their hand guns at the ready, they advanced towards the cave together. The other man, still on the ridge, stood aiming his weapon at mouth of the cave.

With her cub secure, Molem turned back to the mouth of the cave and looked out. With her teeth barred, her voice boomed out towards the attackers as now, snarling even louder, as her roars were filled with such ferocity that the whole cave floor shook with the noise.

Slowly, and still aiming his weapon at Molem, the first armed man reached into his holster, pulled out a clip and reloaded his gun. He stepped forward until he was level with the nearest of the two fallen men. His colleague came alongside and grabbed the other fallen man's collar and together they began to drag their casualties back out into the open air.

But Molem was not appeased by the men's departure. The first shots from the men's pistols had been annoying but ineffectual. They had made her stop her charge forward and she had backed away, but now she was even more enraged and even more desperate to lead the men away from where her cub was hiding. Once again, and now following the men from the cave, Molem rushed forward and burst back out into the daylight.

More shots rang out from the men's pistols, but this time the men, in fear of their lives, and to stop the savage fangs of the enraged bear, aimed them at the huge predator. The pistols cracked, time and time again, hammering tiny missiles like stinging needles into Molem's body.

With saliva from her flashing fangs spraying onto the ground as her huge body lunged forward, she bounded up the escarpment and along the ridge. She followed the men with her eyes as, dragging their companions, they scuttled over the ridge, down the slope and back along the range of rocks towards their vehicle. Relentlessly now, with no other thought in mind now other than sheer rage, she bounded along the ridge and after the men. They had not only attacked her, they had hit her time and time again with their invisible teeth; burning, searing bullets that had torn through her chest cage and into her thorax. So now, all reason leaving her as her fury boiled, she attacked again, determined this time to strike down those who had hunted her and her cub so needlessly.

But she had little chance to reach the three men. Another man, this one with a long weapon, had appeared further along the rocky crest. His weapon had a red light beam already attached to it. Wherever he shone it, the invisible teeth would follow relentlessly. He pointed the spot of red light at her bleeding chest and discharged the weapon. The stick seemed to pound and hammer, striking again and again, spitting fire with hardly a split second between each discharge.

'Get to the Jeep,' the man shouted as Molem collapsed and rolled down the slope, leaving a bloody trail as she dropped off the ledge to the level ground.

With all her strength, she lifted her heavy body off the floor and, still moving forward, panting irregularly, and bellowing with rage as the pain soared through her body, she followed the retreating men along the foot of the escarpment. The men were already loading the first of the wounded men into a vehicle. Sensing her strength beginning to drain from her whole being, she bounded after them along the base of the rocky outcrop. But, falling forward, she rolled into a gulley and landed face down, between two big boulders, only a couple of paces from the killers' feet. She tried one more time to lift her body off the ground, raising her head, growling with barred teeth trying to grab at anything in her way. But finally the man fired another volley that drained the residue of life from the huge beast.

Now she felt no pain as more invisible teeth cut effortlessly through her body. Her last thought was not of anger, not of men and their deadly devices. In front of her closed eyes she could only see her young cub playing in the long, green summer grass. And she was there, rolling and tumbling with Brunus as her life-force drained from her and she lived and breathed no more.

Brunus went to the mouth of the cave. Seeing the way was clear, she climbed up the slope and peered over the top. It seemed like the men were not going to wait to see what they had done. Quickly they dealt with the wounded men, roughly dressed their wounds and then, with the sound of a revving engine, the vehicle in which the casualties were crumpled, departed even more quickly than they had arrived.

In the back of the cave, Rhamin and his pack waited and listened. Two of the wheeled vehicles had arrived. Only one had departed. 'Stay where you are,' Rhamin commanded. 'It isn't over yet. They are still out there.' He moved forward slowly and, seeing the entrance clear of men, he moved outside the cave and up slope. Determined to defend their leader and totally disregarding his orders, the other wolves padded out behind him. He looked around then nodded at his brave comrades to acknowledge their unwavering support. They were never going to leave him alone.

Without her mother Brunus had nowhere to go and no means of surviving. And even at this early age, she somehow understood that. As she looked down the slope of the escarpment, her eyes followed the trail of blood. Soon, she spotted her mother's body lying motionless at the bottom of the rocky slope. The men were still near, but seemed to be pre-occupied about thirty or forty yards away. She went down towards her mother and nudged her with her snout as if to wake her from her sleep. But there was no life in the body that lay before her and somehow, as all animals understand, she knew that. With a deep, deep sigh, she sat down beside her dead mother, nudged her a few more times and then began to sob.

'Petersen will want the hide,' a man shouted as he came back towards the slaughtered creature. 'We'd better not leave it for the wolves.' There was a silence for a minute and then he shouted, 'Jackson, you do the honours.'

Moments later, two men stepped towards the dead animal. 'Didn't expect a damned bear here,' one man said as he reached to his side and pulled a long knife from his belt. 'Petersen said we were tracking a wolf!'

'So we are,' another of the men retorted. 'He's in that cave somewhere, though how they come to be sharing it with a bear, I've no idea.'

Then, as they walked towards Molem's body they realized she hadn't been alone. It took a moment or two for them to appreciate that part of the furry mass that was wedged between two big boulders was not just the dead adult bear. Brunus was there snuggled close up to her dead mother's side. Her dark brown eyes shone in the bright sunlight as the men looked down upon their quarry.

'Well, well, well,' the first man said. 'Look what we have here.'

'Get the tranquilizer gun. We'll take this one back for the boss. At least we'll not go back empty handed.'

But Brunus had other ideas. Young as she was, she had no intention of being taken alive. She had seen her mother slaughtered in front of her eyes. Her fate, she reckoned, would fare no better. Without a warning, and as small as she was, she went for the man nearest to her. The man had a long knife in his hand, and as he lunged backwards to avoid the teeth of the young animal he slashed at the air in front of him to prevent the bear cub's jaws grabbing at his legs.

Somehow Brunus was afraid no more. She had seen her future. She had nothing to lose. It was one of the other men that drew out his hand weapon. Brunus watched as the man lifted it and levelled it her face.

But the man had no time to discharge the weapon.

From out of nowhere, Rhamin leaped down the slope, raced past Brunus and caught the man's hand with his long teeth. 'You've done enough killing today,' The Black Wolf snarled through a mouth full of flashing teeth. The hand gun rattled to the rocky ground. The rest of the men were taken totally by surprise by the appearance of the huge wolf. They knew they would earn no money if they killed this creature. But with the other wolves that were racing down the slope behind it, all with wide mouths, bristled coats and barred teeth, the men lost any will to fight on. They had faced this pack before. Now scrambling over the rock-strewn ground, they clambered towards their Jeep.

The wolves stopped at the base of the shallow escarpment, milling about excitedly. Then, hyped by the adrenalin-charged rush into battle, they fanned out into a well rehearsed attack formation. 'Leave them go,' Rhamin ordered. If the men hadn't got the message before, they carried one home with them now.

The pack watched as one man, clasping his wrist, and three other men clambered into their vehicle and sped away.

For a brief moment no-one took any notice of Brunus. She just stood there, next to her mother, waiting for the wolves to finish her off. She had seen her mother killed and, at the time, had believed that it was only a matter of minutes before the men would kill her. Until Rhamin came from behind her, she hadn't known that she was in a wolves' lair or anywhere near one. Now the men had gone, she knew the wolves would be no different. Her mother had told her that bears and wolves were enemies. Small as she was, she had already decided that she would fight to the death.

Turning to face the young intruder, the pack looked on as Brunus adopted a defensive posture. Like the wolves' coats had done when facing the men, Brunus's hair now bristled on her whole body, puffing her size up so that she would appear bigger and more fearsome. She curled back her long rubbery snout and revealed her rows of new, white, needle sharp teeth. The determined look in her eyes told it all. She was ready to fight to the death.

Surrounding the cub, the wolves just stood where they were and gazed at the phenomena. Never before had they had a bear in their cave. And had that been so, they would have fought to expel their mortal enemy. But it wasn't in their cave now and there was something about this small creature. It was the size of a full grown wolf, or even the size of Rhamin, but it was clearly just a young cub. Yet its courage and determination almost glowed as it backed away from the pack towards the greyness of the rocky incline. Backing up the slope, it made no move to attack until Rhamin stepped forward. Brunus snarled and lunged at him. Rhamin simply side stepped. He greatly admired any animal with courage, and if he wasn't going to kill it then he had to make room for it to pass. But, instead, and quite unexpectedly, the young bear turned and bounded up and over the slope. Not knowing that the cave was the wolves' home, the young creature was going to use the cave entrance to prevent its enemies surrounding it. In seconds she was already in the open mouth of the cave.

Rhamin was even more determined that he wasn't going to kill this brave and courageous little animal. But its reaction wasn't helping. Slowly, and leading his pack, one by one, the wolves all filed past the bear cub and entered the cave. Each wolf walked carefully and casually past Brunus who, not seeing the wolves show any aggression, feigned an attack on each and every one, but stopped short by inches as her teeth flashed at each of them.

But even as the mouth of the cave became clear and the young bear cub could exit safely, she did not attempt to leave. Brunus knew that she would never survive out there without her mother. To die fighting would be much quicker and less painful in the end. She turned and now facing into the cave she threatened and postured.

Still no wolves attacked. Instead, old Zelda, who had remained in the shadows of the cave, walked unsteadily towards the bear. Being blind, Zelda didn't need to be careful not to look the bear cub in the eyes. Totally oblivious to the snarling and lunging, she went close to Brunus, and just lay down beside her. Curious now, Brunus stopped snarling. She sniffed at Zelda. Then she looked up at the rest of the wolves. The pack was not attacking. The wolves were watching. They looked inquisitive with their ears erect and pointing forward. But most were sitting or lying down and they were definitely not attacking.

Zelda rested her chin on her paws and just lay there. Brunus could feel a sort of tranquillity overtaking her fear.

Her adrenaline was dissipating. It was being replaced by endorphins that made her feel relaxed. She sniffed at Zelda again and felt compelled to lie beside her.

Every wolf in the pack was transfixed. Somehow old Zelda had a way of mesmerizing other creatures. Amazingly, she had calmed the bear cub, relaxing her, making her feel safe. Brunus turned around a few times, waiting for an attack, looking for any possible danger. But there was none. All the wolves kept their distance further back in the cave. Like Zelda, now they were all lying down, and just watching and waiting.

For the best part of an hour the wolves just watched until, eventually, the bear cub was fast asleep with its chin lying across Zelda's shoulders.

CHAPTER SIXTEEN

In the morning, Rhamin had added another member to his pack. He had adopted a dog, why not a bear? He shrugged as he smiled inwardly to himself. He hated needless killing. Hunting for food, yes, but killing for the sake of it? Few wolves did that. Some men did. But Rhamin would never do it. His anger had almost driven him to take his revenge for Bamar's death out on the men kind. But today he saw the world differently. Bamar had died. He had been a brave wolf. But he had always been the first of the pack to say that revenge was not the answer. They had all shown compassion when Lexa joined the pack. Now they had done it once again. Without the coldness that men hold in their hearts Rhamin and his pack had felt the sympathy and concern for which wolves had once become renowned.

But the new day had begun and Charka still needed help. After a brief discussion with his pack, Rhamin instructed Lexa, to go to the Rozalski's farm and see if she could get Raymond to travel out to the Darin to help the wounded wolf.

Corvak had arrived. He had been back and forth the day before, circling high in the sky, watching the strange events unfold beneath him. Today, he too would travel with

Lexa as well as three more of the pack, Ramusan, Vela and Goma. None must travel alone and Corvak would warn them of any danger.

But it didn't happen like that. Just as the delegation was about to climb over the rocky escarpment, Charka called out. 'I can hear the men's vehicles again.' She was wounded but her hearing was still better than any other wolf in the pack.

Rhamin waited until the vehicle drew closer. This time it was only one vehicle. Fearing the worst, he climbed quickly to the top of the ridge and peered over. The single vehicle swerved and steered over the rock-strewn landscape. With a deep sigh of relief, instantly he recognised the station wagon. Raymond had arrived. It meant only on thing. Rasci's meditation and psychic visit to Ben must have worked after all.

The station wagon stopped at the base of the incline. First Raymond got out, then Ben and Margo. But there was someone else sitting in the back seat. Eventually and seemingly reluctantly, Elsie climbed out and gazed up at the rocky slope.

'Over here,' Ben shouted excitedly as he clambered up to the ridge. He saw Rhamin there and instantly his face cracked into a broad smile.

'This is Rhamin,' he shouted back to Elsie as Rhamin emerged fully over the top of the ridge.

Elsie didn't try to hide her astonishment as she watched her small cousin just clamber up to the big black wolf and, standing on tiptoe, he reached up and put his arm over Rhamin's shoulder. There they were, in the middle of a dusty plain and Uncle Raymond was allowing his young son to run up a rocky incline and not only stand next to the biggest wolf she had ever seen in her life, but her uncle was letting his son give the wolf a hug as if it were a big puppy dog. Ben called the wolf Rhamin. It had to be wild. Tame wolves don't exist!

Without the slightest concern for Ben's safety, Raymond turned back to the station wagon, opened the rear door and hunted inside for a brief moment. Leaving the door up, he emerged with a couple of LED stick torches and climbed up to join Ben. 'We can't see inside a dark cave as well as wolves,' he stated as he handed one torch to his son. Together with Rhamin, they disappeared over the top of the rocky ridge.

Elsie remained where she was, her arm around Margo. She was still trying to come to terms with the whole wolf business. 'They are quite safe,' Margo assured her, seeing Elsie's look of concern. 'Rhamin will look after them.'

A few minutes later the man and child returned with Rhamin and a dozen or so other wolves, one of which Raymond carried in his strong arms. It was Charka. She looked quite ill. The wound in her leg had already begun to fester. The leg hung limply as Raymond carried her. A dark liquid was discharging from the open wound. He rested her on the rocks for a moment at the top of the ridge while he caught his breath and then, scooping up the injured wolf in his arms once again, he carried her the rest of the way down the slope.

His face was serious. Frowning he said, 'They don't care one jot how many lives they take so long as they get what they want.' He paused while he negotiated the bottom and steepest part of the incline. 'Petersen will answer for all this.'

Gently, her uncle Raymond placed the injured wolf on a blanket inside the back of the vehicle. 'You wonder why we are friendly with these wolves?' he said to Elsie.

He paused and waited for her to respond, but she just watched, her mouth slightly open, her lips a little puckered.

'Well they saved my life.'

'And we saved Rhamin and Yeltsa his wife,' Ben added.

Elsie just nodded. She didn't know just what to say. The whole thing seemed to be hard to take in all at once. The size of the pack leader was equally dumfounding.

'We seem to have become part of one big family,' Raymond said as he made Charka comfortable by giving her another rolled up blanket to lean against.

Elsie nodded. 'You must admit, it did seem like a tall story.'

Raymond chuckled dryly. 'Well now you will have to admit that we aren't completely bonkers.'

'I can't say I would go that far,' Elsie answered. 'You are all still a bit weird.'

Raymond's face turned more serious. 'Petersen's men haven't just been here looking for Rhamin.' He was looking at the recent trail of rapidly drying blood.

'Rhamin? Is that really the wolf's name?' asked Elsie.

'It is,' Raymond replied and then his face hardened as he looked over to where there were several big boulders. Nodding to them he walked along the base of the escarpment towards the outcrop. 'Looks like they cornered a bear near the wolves' cave and killed it,' he growled angrily as he examined the work of Petersen's men. The bear had been shot repeatedly. By just glancing at the blood soaked corpse, he could tell she had been shot at least a dozen times.

'But why?' Elsie asked, dismayed. A deep frown creased her forehead.

Raymond's clenched his fist and tightened the muscles in his jaw. 'Because they don't have respect for any living creature,' he said through closed teeth. Then he added, 'I'm afraid that the bear had a young cub.'

'And?' Elsie asked, puzzled at the brevity of the statement.

'And the wolves have got it with them.'

'What, they're eating it?'

Raymond shook his head and chuckled.

'You mean it's alive?'

Raymond nodded, his face softening a little now. 'Looks like they are going to keep it here.'

'Keep it here? You mean they aren't going to kill it?'

Raymond shook his head. 'No. If I know *these* wolves, they'll adopt it.'

'You mean like Lexa?' Margo asked excitedly.

'Just like Lexa,' Raymond said, shaking his head in disbelief.

'So,' Elsie said with a tone of astonishment in her voice yet again, 'that conversation Ben had with a stalk of grass *really* was a discussion with a wolf spirit?'

'And that's the wolf,' Ben stated as he nodded and pointed to Rasci. 'And that's Yeltsa,' he said pointing to another wolf that watched everything that was going on with undivided interest. 'She was with Rhamin when we rescued him, wasn't she daddy? She's Rhamin's wife.'

'That's right,' Raymond confirmed.

Elsie just nodded and smiled. She still wasn't sure in just what scene of what play she was playing a walk on role.

'And that's Lexa,' Ben continued introducing the pack.

Lexa had come forward and was only three or four paces away from Elsie now. Elsie looked at the huge black and tan dog with the white, rumpled scars that distorted her face and the smooth coat on her shoulder rather fetchingly. The dog looked completely out of place with a milling pack of thick-coated wolves. Apart from the scars, Lexa looked exactly like the twin of her mother, Smokey. But the dog didn't behave like Smokey. She was, in every other respect, one of the wolves; friendly, but a little cautious and a little reserved whilst meeting another new member of the man's pack.

Elsie was trying to take it all in; the wolves, the huge dog that she had been told had been stolen as a puppy, the even bigger and jet-black leader of the pack with the white ears, Rhamin. She was coming to terms with the fact that all she had been told had not been some kind of rural, farmer-peasant legend. Somehow, her Uncle Raymond's family was not just communicating with a large pack of wolves. The pack was a part of his family. Or, even more bizarre, Raymond and his children were, it seemed, an extension of the Rhamin Pack. Whichever, there was no clear dividing line between the man's family and wolves' pack. Whether they were apart or whether they were together, it appeared that they all looked out for each other.

'Perhaps we should take Rasci with us just in case we need to communicate,' Raymond suggested, breaking into Elsie's thoughts.

'And Rhamin?' Margo asked. 'Petersen is after Rhamin. He'll be safe in our house,'

'Yes,' Ben agreed, jumping excitedly on the spot while he waited for his father to signal the two other passengers to get on board.

CHAPTER SEVENTEEN

The sixty mile trip seemed uneventful at first. Despite being wounded, however, it was Charka that heard the beating rotors before Rasci or Rhamin.

'The metal flying bird is coming back,' she stated matter of factly to her companions. Her voice was rather faint now. The trip and the festering wound were taking their toll on her depleting energy reserves.

'What? Now?' Rhamin asked.

'They are not far away. I can hear them.'

'Well they won't know I'm in this machine with Ben and his family,' Rhamin said as he lifted his head to the window and looked out at the clear blue sky.

But somehow, the occupants of the helicopter seemed to know exactly where he was. The machine didn't pass by the station wagon as he had expected. It passed over at first, heading towards the Darin, but the wolves' relief was only momentary. Within seconds of passing overhead, it had swung around in a wide arc and, retracing its path, began to hover above the moving vehicle. It was following them.

'They have been tracking Rhamin for days now,' Ben said without any hesitation. 'Rasci told me they know where he is all the time.'

'That's impossible,' Raymond answered.

'That's not what I heard,' Elsie joined in. I might have been sceptical at first but...'

'Sceptical!'

'Well,' Elsie said, subdued a little now, 'I thought you all belonged in a crazy home or something.' She had decided to be bluntly honest. She hesitated before carrying on with what she wanted to say. 'But when I heard Ben talking to thin air,' she continued eventually, 'I did happen to be listening. I was quite taken by the depth of his imagination. I thought it was all make-belief, you see.' She turned her head to Raymond who just nodded. 'But one thing I do recall clearly is that he did mention the fact that Petersen could track Rhamin.'

'Did he now?' Raymond asked, his face now deadly serious. 'And did they say how Petersen knows where Rhamin is? How does he know that we have Rhamin with us now?' Raymond looked in his rear-view mirror and caught Ben's eye. 'Did they explain that?'

Ben shrugged. 'I thought he must have some sort of tracking device. You know, like the ones the police use in the films to follow cars?'

'Tracking devices are big things. Wildlife reservations use tracking collars. Rhamin doesn't have anything like that attached to him. Tracking devices need a power source and batteries that last a long time. They are big and bulky.'

They all fell silent, contemplating what had been said. Apart from the quiet drone of the station wagon engine, the only other sound, clearly heard through the open windows, was the beating of rotor blades pounding at the air in the sky, high above them. The craft wasn't letting them out of its sight, but it was keeping a discreet distance behind them. Raymond was in no doubt that it was going to follow them all the way back to the farmstead.

Suddenly the sound of the rotors changed as the helicopter appeared in front of them, hovering over the plain about fifty yards ahead. It tried to land in the path of the station wagon but, at that point, the plain was flat and Raymond just swerved and went around the skids of the hovering machine.

Again, the helicopter tried to block his way, but again, Raymond just steered his way around it. He just kept on driving.

The plain across which they were travelling wasn't all flat. There were shallow gradients and long periods of rock-strewn and scrub-scattered land to cross. Travelling in a motor vehicle across such rough landscape was not fast. It wasn't like driving on a made road or across flat grassland. Progress was probably less than twenty miles per hour and in those areas, never at any stage did Raymond have more than a few hundred yards of straight track before having to swerve around rocks, gulleys or fallen trees. But the helicopter tracked them relentlessly until, suddenly ahead of them, Raymond spotted two Jeeps, one in front of the other, racing over the brush land towards them. One appeared to have just one driver. The other, when it came into view from behind the first, was open topped and had a driver and three passengers.

'If they think they can stop me then they have another thought coming,' Raymond growled through clenched teeth. As he drew closer to the two strangers' vehicles, they separated, one drawing towards the station wagon directly, the other pulling out to one side. Now they approached, about five or six yards apart and a hundred or so yards ahead. But the Jeeps, like Raymond's vehicle had to negotiate the stray rocks and hollows.

Raymond kept driving but slowed a little. 'Put your seat belts on,' he instructed the children. 'Make sure they are tight.' He scanned the landscape ahead, clenched his jaw tight, and, thrusting his foot down on the accelerator, drove straight towards the vehicle that contained the most people.

Charka saw nothing. She lay with her head on the floor of the station wagon, panting. Rasci didn't know whether to close his eyes or jump out of the open window. Rhamin just looked on, as calm as he ever was under pressure. No nerves, no fears. To Rhamin, whatever would be would be.

Elsie's eyes were wide with a mixture of fear and exhilaration. Margo watched events unfurl with her mouth open, but Ben's face showed the same determination as that of his father. 'You show 'em Daddy,' he said, as his knuckles went white with the pressure of gripping onto the seatbelt that ran across his chest.

'Hold tight,' Raymond shouted as they headed straight for the Jeep full of aggressors.

Rasci thought that the look on the driver's face in the vehicle that was hurtling directly towards them was more informative than the look on Margo's little face. His eyes were wide open and his jaw had dropped onto his chest. But the driver had been so intent on watching Raymond's apparent suicidal driving that he hadn't seen what was immediately in front of him. With fifty or so paces to go before hitting the station wagon the driver of that Jeep felt his steering wheel twisting from his grip as one of his front wheels ran into a small, rocky gulley. His vehicle veered off to the right, almost ejecting the passengers as the other front wheel hit a loose rock, causing it to zigzag out of control.

Raymond had seen the gulley and had deliberately headed towards it. Then, when the Jeep hit the hollow, he had already steered clear and, within seconds, had passed the Jeep with a good fifteen yards to spare.

Rhamin smiled inwardly. Ben's father was a worthy opponent. Raymond thought things out just like Rhamin did when the odds were against him.

Rasci was well impressed.

'Now they are behind us,' Raymond grunted, his jaw still firm with determination. 'Let's see if they know how to stop me now.'

But it didn't take long for the two Jeeps to resume their chase. Raymond skilfully dodged the rocks on the plain so that their followers had less chance of seeing them until they were upon them. A couple of times Rasci and Rhamin saw either one or the other Jeep bounce up and, on two wheels, struggle to stay upright. But they were not going to give up. Both wolves knew that the plain became much leveller as it neared the farm. The chasing vehicles would soon be able to overtake and head off the station wagon just as wolves overtake and close in on their prey with a pincer movement. The chase was certainly not over yet.

Raymond probably realized the same fact. Soon the plain would give way to flat smooth grassland. No tracks, no roads, but few rocks and even fewer channels and hollows to stop the hunters from pulling ahead.

Gradually, all could see the grassland up ahead. It looked like a green line on the horizon to begin with, inviting the travellers to an easy drive home for the rest of their journey. But it was the last thing Raymond or any of his passengers wanted to see. The ride home might be smoother, but with two vehicles in pursuit and a helicopter overhead, the chances of getting back to the farm without being overtaken were getting rather slim.

The green belt came slowly but surely, ever closer. Raymond looked in his rear view mirrors. He could see the Jeeps dropping back a little, biding their time. Their drivers, too, had realized that time was now on their side. As the thin shoots of green began to appear under the wheels of his station wagon, Raymond floored the accelerator. But the station wagon wasn't built for speed any more than the Jeeps. Slowly but surely the two chasing vehicles gained yard by yard, mile by mile. Ten or twelve minutes passed whilst Raymond drove as fast as the station wagon would go. A couple of more minutes and their pursuers would be drawing along side. A bead of perspiration trickled down Raymond's temple. They weren't going to make it. Petersen was going to get The Black Wolf once again. It was only a couple of miles to the farm gate but it was enough for their hunters to get what they wanted.

But then, with about a mile to go, and without any warning, the two Jeeps veered off and the helicopter banked away. In seconds they had all gone leaving Raymond and his party totally alone to drive home. Neither he nor any of his passengers could explain what had happened. For a minute or so, they drove on and then Ben shouted.

'Look,' he said, pointing to his left. 'Another one.'

Raymond, Elsie and Margo swung their heads around to see what it was that Ben had spotted. On a ridge, probably about a quarter of a mile away, a large, black SUV, an off-road vehicle with huge wheels, was parked facing the track that approached the farm. The sun glinted on its dark tinted glass and shiny black paintwork as Raymond drove closer. Rhamin and Rasci watched it too. Raymond made no effort to leave the dirt road to get closer but as he passed within a hundred yards or so if the sinister looking vehicle, it became clear that it would be impossible to see who was in it. The feeling of being watched suddenly hit all of the occupants of the station wagon including the wolves.

CHAPTER EIGHTEEN

'So Ben was right,' Maria said as Raymond opened up the back of the station wagon to reveal a wounded wolf and her two companions. 'Who on earth does that Petersen think he is?'

'He's a rich man with an even richer father. He thinks he's able to buy his way out of trouble.' Raymond shook his head and through clenched teeth he rasped, 'He's got it coming, that's for sure.'

'How badly hurt is she?' Maria asked, looking at the wolf she was later to learn was called Charka. Charka was looking quite ill. Her ears were laid back, her coat had begun to turn dull and starey. The fur on her face was already bristling out and her mouth drooled. She seemed not to have any compunction to lick the saliva from her lips.

'She's getting blood poisoning I think,' Raymond said as he lifted her up in his arms and brought her into the kitchen.

Smokey came to the door and greeted Rhamin and Rasci with her usual wriggling bottom and look of pleasure as Maria went through to the hallway to make a phone call.

Raymond placed Charka on the floor and began to clear the table.

'The vet is on her way,' Maria explained, coming back

into the room. 'She was on a call just a few miles away so she should be here any time now.' She looked at Raymond. 'Is there nothing you can do for her?' she asked, turning to look at Charka.

'Not without giving her an anaesthetic,' Raymond replied. 'She has a bullet lodged somewhere in her thigh.' He picked Charka up and gently laid her down on the big kitchen table. Maria brought a bowl of water over and Raymond began to wash the wound.

It wasn't long before they heard a car outside.

'She's here now,' Ben called moments later from the open door. 'The vet's here!'

'Come in Jo,' Raymond said, leaving Charka and going to the open door. 'We have another wild animal for you to look at.'

'Your definition of wild seems rather off the mark though,' Jo replied as she looked at the two wolves gathered by the entrance. She looked hard at Rhamin. 'So that big beast is the one I've heard so much about, is it?'

'He's a baby really,' Raymond said with a broad grin. 'Loves riding in the station wagon!'

'I bet!' Jo had got used to Raymond's dry sense of humour over the past years.

It took only a few minutes for her to assess Charka's condition. 'The first thing we have to do is get the bullet out of her leg. It's near the hip joint.' she proclaimed at the same time as opening a big case and taking out various pieces of equipment. 'I suppose she's got a name like the others?'

'Charka,' Ben said from the back of the room.

'Charka heh? Well, will you hold her head Ray while I inject her?'

Watched by Smokey, Rasci and Rhamin, Raymond did

as he was asked and held Charka's head firm so that she could not react to the stab of the needle. The vet took less than two seconds to inject her.

It took about two minutes for Charka to go to sleep. Jo put a tube in charka's mouth to hold her tongue down so she didn't choke, and then began to examine the wolf's rear leg.

Rasci now realized just how the bad men had taken Rhamin and Yeltsa from their home. Corvak had explained that the men had been putting the wolves to sleep and not really killing them with the invisible teeth of death that they spewed from their weapons called guns. And now he had seen how easily it was to make the target look dead. Charka was totally lifeless, yet, without even having it explained, he knew that the vet had only sedated her.

Rhamin stepped back a little when he saw what was happening. Few things could shake him but, strangely, Smokey's body, as she stood next to him, seemed to give out a welcome feeling of reassurance. The whole thing with needles and sleeping potions brought back memories, and they were not ones he wanted to recall.

With Charka asleep, Jo went to the task of removing the bullet from her leg. It was lodged in the bone and took quite an effort to remove it. Then she cleaned the wound with some strong smelling liquid, sewed it expertly and then injected Charka with a large dose of dark liquid, an antibiotic, which neither Rasci nor Rhamin understood.

'Ideally she needs another dose in two days time,' Jo stated.

'I think that can be arranged,' Raymond replied.

Jo filled another syringe with the same brown liquid and capped the needle with a plastic sheath. 'Here,' she said handing it to Raymond. 'I'm sure you can manage it. Under the skin on her neck.'

Raymond just nodded and took the syringe, placing it high up on a shelf out of harms way. Then he and the rest of his family watched as Jo gave Charka a final injection, one that brought her back to consciousness rather more slowly than she had gone to sleep.

'So what's this all about?' Jo asked as Raymond cleared the table.

'It's about a rich man taking wolves for his own enclosures and killing anything else that gets in his way.'

Raymond explained about the bear.

'And they killed Bamar,' Ben came in, saddened, but at the same time pleased to be able to impart his bit of information.

'Bamar?' asked Jo.

'One of the wolves in Rhamin's pack,' Raymond responded before Ben could give details. He went on to explain that he and his children, with the help of the large grey wolf that now stood in the doorway with Rhamin and Smokey, had actually stolen Rhamin and his mate Yeltsa back from Petersen's safari park. 'That was just before you came to patch up Lexa,' he explained. 'But they seem to be able to track Rhamin now. How they do it I can't tell. They didn't seem to be able to track him before.'

Jo looked at the two wolves that stood with Smokey, peacefully and curious, by the open door. 'That black wolf with the white ears is Rhamin I suppose?'

Raymond nodded.

'He's certainly a big guy. Don't get many of him to a pound.'

Rhamin sat down lazily and scratched behind his neck.

'Can I take a look at him?' Jo asked. She wasn't sure how close she could get to ordinary healthy wolves, and Rhamin's size was more than a little intimidating.

Raymond walked over to Rhamin. The wolf just sat there and let him stroke his broad head. Gingerly, Jo approached The Black Wolf and held out her hand. He simply licked it and remained as still as a statue, his amber eyes conveying total trust in his new friend.

Slowly the vet passed her hand over his head and then, after letting the wolf know she meant no harm, a fact that Rhamin knew already, she began to dig her fingers into the thick fur on the back of Rhamin's neck. Slowly she worked her fingers down to his skin and inch by inch felt and squeezed it. 'There's something irritating him,' Jo said, as she probed and prodded. 'At least twice now I've seen him scratching his neck. If it were parasites, then both the other wolves would be scratching. But the one here next to him,' she stated, nodding towards Rasci, 'seems quite content. And I didn't see anything on the poorly one.'

Raymond and his family just watched and listened.

'Got it!' Jo suddenly exclaimed. 'He has some kind of implant. Here,' she said, inviting Raymond to feel the tiny bump under Rhamin's skin at the base of his skull. 'We'll have to have it out,' she said matter of factly. 'But just how, I'm not so sure. It will mean making an incision.'

'What's an incision?' asked Margo.

'A small cut in the skin to get the implant out,' the vet explained with a smile.

Raymond turned to Ben. 'Can you tell him what we need to do?'

Ben looked at Rasci. Only when his wolf friend meditated could he talk to him. And Rasci wasn't meditating. He was absorbed in all the events of the last hour, watching, and understanding. But he turned his head to Rhamin and seemed to be sniffing at his leader.

'Rasci is telling Rhamin what you have to do,' Margo said suddenly. Raymond had quite forgotten how Margo had shown she could communicate with her mind when Rasci first came to visit the farm with Lexa.

Margo remained silent, looking at Rhamin and Rasci. Then Rasci turned his head towards Margo again and Margo said, 'Rasci says Rhamin will let you do it.' Then she added, 'But he doesn't want to be put to sleep like Charka. He wants you to just do it. Dig it out.'

'I can give him a local anaesthetic,' Jo explained. 'All that will do is numb the point where I cut the skin. He won't know I'm doing it.'

Margo looked at Rasci. 'Rasci already knows,' she said as she nodded at the grey wolf.

Rasci turned to Rhamin once again and then back to Margo.

'No, just dig it out,' Margo instructed. 'No injections. Rhamin doesn't trust injections. He won't let you go near him with a needle.'

Jo shrugged. 'Some day you'll tell me how you do that,' she said to Margo as she let go of the fur on the back of Rhamin's neck. She bent down to her case and took out a new scalpel blade. She took off the seal, and while she fitted the blade onto its handle, Rhamin just stepped forward and stood beside her, all the time looking at her with his big amber eyes.

Then she took out a small bottle of liquid, removed the lid and placed it beside the scalpel on the table. She pulled out another packet and withdrew a pair of tweezers, placing them on the packaging, and then took out another sealed tool. 'Open that for me when I'm ready,' she instructed Raymond.

Once again, parting the thick pelage with one hand, and with the other hand taking up a pair of curved scissors, she clipped off a small patch of the thick fur. Then, still holding down the fur around the site with one hand she picked up the small bottle and poured a few drops of liquid onto the bared skin. She replaced the bottle and picked up the scalpel and within a few seconds she had made an incision, put down the scalpel, picked up the tweezers and pulled out a small torpedo shaped object that was no longer than her little finger nail. As she held it up to the assembled audience, a thin wire, perhaps only a few inches long, could be seen dangling from the object.

'That's our tracker,' she said with a smile as she held it up to take a closer look at it.

'It doesn't look big enough. Are you sure that's it?' Raymond asked, now quite curious.

'Oh yes. See the wire? It's coated with some sort of plastic. But it's stiff enough to push under the skin like a needle. The actual tracker is just a miniature radio device.'

'And where's the battery?' asked Maria. 'Surely it needs a power source.'

The vet studied the object for a few more moments and then put it down on the table. 'Pass me the needle,' she said to Raymond.

Raymond unpacked the curved needle in which there was already threaded a cat-gut filament. Handing it to her, he tilted his head for an answer to his wife's question.

Jo looked at Maria and nodded. 'Some industrialists are developing new devices that can be implanted into the body and which don't need to be taken out again to fit new batteries or to renew the power source.' She bent over Rhamin and stitched as she talked. 'The medical profession has been developing ways to power heart pace-makers so that they can be installed once only. No battery changing, no maintenance. They contain a micro generator which either works off body heat or works off the energy generated by the body every time it moves. Simple stuff really. Just complicated getting it into a package so small,' she said nodding at the tiny torpedo on the table. 'What someone has done, and I suspect it is someone connected with the man you have told me about, is design a radio tracker instead of a pacemaker. It is definitely the man who took The Black Wolf that implanted this device...'

'His father has research facilities. He's a multi-millionaire and he's got all sorts of diverse companies,' Raymond stated.

'Well he simply made a miniature radio transmitter and applied the new technology to power it. Straight forward really. Of course, it would have a limited range. I suspect it was designed to locate escaped animals near or around the point of exit.'

'That would explain why they took their time coming after him again then,' Raymond suggested.

'I doubt if these gadgets were designed to track an animal that had travelled hundreds of miles away by car before the alarm was raised to say they had escaped,' Jo explained as Raymond described how Raymond, Ben and Margo had gone with Rasci, the other wolf, to the safari park and removed Rhamin and Yeltsa from right under the owner's nose.

'Well he won't be able to find Rhamin and his pack any more thanks to you.'

'Hmm. The problem is, he *does* know where to find him. He has been to his den. You said so just now.'

'Well Petersen won't find him when he's not at home then,' Raymond responded.

'It all sounds rather futuristic,' Maria proclaimed. 'Is this stuff with self charging trackers real or is it sci-fi? Goodness knows what they'll invent next!' She picked up the tiny device between her finger and thumb and, holding it up to the light, examined it closely. 'You'd never know what it was just by looking at it would you? Are you sure this is a real tracker?'

'Well it looks real to me,' stated the vet as she tied off the last stitch. 'And I might ask you the same about your wolf friends. If anyone had told me about these wolves, I would not have believed them to be real.'

'I didn't at first.' Elsie commented. She had just been watching and listening, totally fascinated with the goings on in her normally mundane life. Now, however, that had all changed. But just how much, she could never have guessed.

CHAPTER NINETEEN

Solin had gathered the seven trusted wolves that formed his pack to go with Rhiana, Roxana, and himself. These were dangerous times and there were men out hunting wolves. There was also his own pack hunting the same wolves. Rhamin and his curs would inevitably be on full guard. And because of what Solin had done before, if Rhamin or his pack saw Solin and his followers, then they wouldn't hesitate to either kill them or evict them from the Rhamin territory for ever.

Things were not made any easier by the fact that Rhamin and his pack had lapsed into silence. There were no communications; no calls to celebrate their kills; no calls to locate other pack members. Rhamin had forbidden any of the pack to howl whilst they were being hunted. This alone meant that the pack had congealed into a single entity, hunting, eating and sleeping together. Tracing the wolves would be easy if they were at the Darin. But being caught out in the open by the Rhamin pack was not an option to contemplate. Solin had to take every measure to ensure that his approach to the cave was not spotted by any of Rhamin's outlying guards.

They headed towards the Darin by day, keeping just inside the tree belt that ran along the rocky slopes several miles to the north. From there, it would be possible to spot any other wolves before they spotted Solin and his pack. Eventually, though, they would have to cross the plain and get nearer to Rhamin's cave. Solin and Rhiana knew the territory better than any other of their followers. That was one thing upon which Rhiana was relying. Roxana had never been to the Darin. When she had lured Rasci away from his pack in mind if not in body, she had done it well out of sight or sound of the Rhamin-Rasci pack. On the other hand, Solin and Rhiana had spent years there at the wolves' secret lair. Solin had been born there when Rhiana had been the alpha female to the then leader, Anval. Even after Rhiana had left, Solin remained as Rhamin's second in command until…

Solin tried to blot his own history from his mind. If things had been different he could have perhaps been leader of the pack from the Darin now, instead of trying to take it over by force.

But things *were* different! The past could not be unwound to change the present, and now they were on a mission. It seemed straight forward: Wait for Rhamin and his pack to leave the cave and then go in and kill Zelda and any other wolves left with her. He prayed that Lexa would be there. He hated that dog wolf with every drop of air he breathed. At least that would be a worthy kill.

But what they found was not what they had expected. It was late in the day and as they manoeuvred out from the protection of the tree line and closer to the cave, everything around them seemed very quiet. The pack followed Solin dutifully. He knew where they could stop and watch the rocky outcrop that hid the Darin, without being seen themselves should the Rhamin pack emerge and head in their direction. Presuming that Rhamin would hunt under cover of the trees, they settled on a rise, itself an outcrop of rocks that had at one time possibly formed part of the same escarpment that now hid the Darin. It was about a third of the distance from the den to the tree line, but not in a straight line between the cave and the foothills. It was close enough to watch but far enough away to be able to run for the cover of the trees if Rhamin headed their way, and if Rhamin and his pack headed straight to the trees in the foothills then they would be five or six hundred long paces away and would leave Solin and his wolves undetected as they passed them by.

What they didn't expect, was lots of vultures circling away to the left, above the base of the escarpment in a clump of broken boulders. But look as hard as he may Solin couldn't see around the rocks to identify on what food the birds were feasting. And search as he may, Kara and Lutz were not among them either.

As the daylight faded and the stars began to shine in the clear night sky like a pile of thousands of tiny shining rock crystals tossed in the air and scattered on the wind, Solin watched and waited. Still there was no sign of Rhamin or his pack.

'It's too quiet,' Roxana said, studying the landscape.

Rhiana's face, too, showed concern. She turned to him and asked, 'What do you think is going on?'

Solin Shrugged. He was about to go down to see what carrion the vultures were eating when a huge roar filled the darkening evening sky. The few remaining vultures scattered with flapping wings and loud screeches as Bortag, the big male bear emerged from behind the rock fall. He looked angry. He gave out several long whining growls and then stood with his snout in the air, shaking his head and repeating the call over and over again. Gradually the night cast the world into total darkness, swallowing up all the shadows on the landscape like a blanket of ferns over a shining pond. With one last tortured growl, and still shaking his head from side to side in a state of total anguish, Bortag bounded off towards the foothills and the forest.

'That's one angry bear,' Solin whispered more to himself than to his companions. 'I wouldn't want to face him even with the whole pack behind me when he's in that sort of mood.'

'We should have brought Kara and Lutz,' Roxana complained. 'They would have told us everything including what has got that bear so riled.'

'Your protest is noted,' Solin said dismissively. He smiled inwardly. He felt he was getting the better of Roxana now.

Roxana grimaced but remained quiet. She knew just how dangerous it was to be so close to the Darin. They were outnumbered, she knew that for sure. But neither did they have any advantage of knowing the territory as well as the Rhamin pack. To have an argument that might escalate to the normal snarling and gnashing of teeth between Roxana and Solin could be deadly. She would bide her time. But without her own pair of vulture spies, she had no way of wrong footing Solin and his mother. The problem was that Solin had ordered Kara and Lutz to remain out of sight. If they were seen in the air, he had said, then even from miles away, it would warn their enemy that he and his pack were somewhere nearby. And Roxana knew he was right. The birds could only spy during the daylight hours. Inevitably they would be seen, although, with the gathering they could see below them, with hindsight, Kara and Lutz would have been perfectly safe and undetected in the mêlée of feasting birds. But, alas, it was too late to go and fetch them now.

'Be patient,' Rhiana ordered. 'Bickering won't speed things up. If we are to see if the cave is occupied then we may have to wait all night and all day.'

'But what if the pack is away, hunting?' Roxana asked.

Solin shook his head. 'They are probably away now or sleeping off a meal. There's food down there. What do you think the vultures were doing, having a conference?'

'Then I expect they will appear before daybreak,' Rhiana snapped. 'We have already discussed this and our conclusion was that Rhamin would retreat to his cave if the metal birds could find him out in the open or in the forests.'

'*Your* conclusion,' Roxana corrected.

'Without a recent trail to follow then we have to wait and see,' Rhiana snapped 'They have been making no sound and it's too dangerous to even go around trying to pick up their recent scent.'

'But if they haven't left by now to go hunting then they can't be in the cave.'

'We cannot presume that they are out hunting. They may all be sleeping off a big meal. There's food down there. What do you think the vultures are eating?' she asked sarcastically. 'We haven't seen any wolves leave and until we do then if you want to go down and have a look then you go on your own.'

'Huh!' Roxana snapped back. 'At least we should get some sleep before we go down there. We'll still need all our senses about us.'

CHAPTER TWENTY

Elsie was restless. The night was warm and sticky and the farmhouse had no air conditioning. Even with the windows open she had to lie on her bed with the sheets strewn over the bottom bed rail. She wondered if the rest of the inhabitants of the farmstead had the same difficulty sleeping at night. She switched on the bedside lamp and picked up her watch from the bedside table. 1.00 am. It was going to be a long night.

Getting up off the bed, she walked over to the book shelves. There were plenty of books there that she hadn't already read. As she passed the open window she glanced out towards the paddock and beyond. The place was deafeningly quiet. There was no traffic going down the street in front of the house. There wasn't even the sound of distant traffic hammering along the big motorways. There was only one road and even that was more of a track than a road, and it led all the way to the farm from the little township miles from here.

So, if there was no major road, what was the faint light that she could see way beyond the line that the farm track took to the distant farm boundary? It was at times like this that she wished she had packed her field glasses. Although not very powerful, they would have made seeing further into the middle of nowhere much easier. Until tonight she wouldn't have cared. Until tonight what else would one see in the middle of this wilderness, but more nowhere? But now there was definitely something out in it, out in the blackness that people mistakenly described as the peace and tranquillity of the countryside. Apart from the stars it was eerily dark and despite the crickets, it was even more eerily quiet.

Forgetting all about the bookshelf, Elsie pulled on her jeans, reached into the corner and retrieved her socks and trainers and with only her nightdress as a top, she quietly opened the bedroom door and tiptoed down stairs. It was going well until, as she silently stepped towards the outer kitchen door, a cold wet nose pushed up against her hand. In total panic, she jerked her arm up in fright. Restraining herself from screaming, she sighed deeply and let her heart slow a little before lowering her hand and patting Smokey on her huge head. Her warm breath suddenly felt reassuringly comforting.

Taking a few more deep breaths, she stood there for a moment absorbing the safe feeling she was getting from touching Smokey and having her close by. Then, slowly, she tiptoed to the door, lifted the latch and stepped outside. Thinking Smokey would be happy to stay behind, she was surprised again when the dog brushed past her legs and started squeaking excitedly. Elsie had forgotten that Rhamin and Rasci were still outside, watching over Charka who'd had a bed made for her next to the rambling rose that grew up the side of the doorway.

'Right,' she whispered to herself, not sure if the wolves were going to make more than a few subdued greeting noises to Smokey if she were to walk past them and out of the farm gate. Quietly she retreated into the kitchen and located one of Raymond's Maglite torches and then stepped outside again. She quickly clicked on the torch. To her surprise, there was no sign of Smokey or the two fit wolves. Charka remained on the large blanket that was her resting place, looking up at Elsie with huge amber eyes. Elsie clicked off the torch again and headed for the gate. Her eyes were becoming accustomed to the starlight and as she walked nearer to the gate, the shadowy forms of Smokey, Rhamin and Rasci stood waiting for her. Somehow they had sensed that she was going to venture out into the darkness. They weren't going to let her go alone.

Elsie glanced over to the spot where she had seen the light. Perhaps she should have searched out Uncle Raymond's binoculars. But she had no idea where he kept them, even though she was convinced that he would have a pair somewhere.

But the light was still there so Elsie opened the gate, let her companions go through and, closing the gate as quietly as she could behind her, she followed them up the lane. As she trailed behind them she got the feeling that the wolves knew where she was going and that they knew she would need a body guard. She shivered. If the wolves were thinking that, then should she be going to see what this phenomenon out near the farm lane was? Now she wasn't so sure. But taking courage from her companions, she strode on, not using the torch apart from to flick it on and off once quickly to see if the road was clear when they approached the gateposts to the outer fence.

Gradually, and with every step, her apprehension grew as she drew closer to the light source. Now she could tell what the strange light was. It was the faint glow of the interior light of a vehicle. Suddenly, the light went out.

Elsie kept on walking along the lane. She would soon reach the farm boundary, but now, despite having the company of two wolves and a dog with her, she began to be really frightened. When Smokey growled, a growl that came from deep in her chest, Elsie nearly dropped the torch. Her hands were shaking and as she desperately fumbled to switch on the light, she sensed that both Rhamin and Rasci had already bounded ahead. Smokey stayed next to her ward. There was a sudden scuttering sound, something like a person's footsteps on dry ground. Fast footsteps. Eventually Elsie's torch came on and she swung the beam up and around, panning to see what it would disclose. The SUV that she had seen earlier that day was parked facing the farmstead. The driver's door was closing just as two dark, fast moving shadows, raced towards it. The vehicle's headlights suddenly broke through the night, an engine fired, the driver gunned it and spun the vehicle around wildly, causing Rhamin and Rasci to swerve out of its way. With headlights heading up the charge the SUV took off in the opposite direction and sped away, following its bouncing light beams into the blackness.

Elsie watched as the beam from the headlights eventually disappeared from view. The wolves ran around, picking up the scent of the man who had been on foot. In her torchlight she watched as they eventually came back over to her, joined Smokey with a lick on her nose, wagged their long brush tails and then waited until Elsie led them all the way back to the safety of the farmstead.

Rhamin and Rasci knew that the vehicle was out there. But they had no way of warning Elsie. All they could do was to go with her and make sure she was safe. Whoever the people were that were in the black, shiny, four-wheeled vehicle, they could no longer track Rhamin, the wolves were sure of that. But they weren't sure if the sinister vehicle had anything to do with Petersen. His crew in the Jeeps and in the flying machine had suddenly disappeared when the Black shiny vehicle had appeared. It was as if Petersen's men didn't want the occupiers of this new vehicle to see what they were doing.

Who were they, these people who were now watching the farm, Rhamin and Rasci had wondered? But the men certainly didn't want to be seen or identified. They kept their distance. They had dark glass around their big wheeled driving machine and they were not used to confronting wolves. Add to that the fact that they drove off faster than a hare with a scorpion on its tail when they thought *they* were being watched, made the whole thing very curious. Very curious indeed.

It wasn't surprising that Raymond was at the door waiting for Elsie when she returned. He had a deeply furrowed brow. His concern was quite evident, but when he saw Smokey and the two wolves with her, his face relaxed into a warm smile.

'I know,' Elsie said pre-emptively as she stepped past Raymond and headed for the stairs. 'I am confined to barracks!'

'Do you realize how worried we were when we saw the door open and Smokey and you had gone?'

'I had plenty of protection,' she retorted, waving at the wolves that were settling down next to Charka again. 'Anyway, you're not my father.'

'Would that have made any difference?' Maria said from

the back of the room as Raymond closed the door. 'What were you doing out there anyway?'

'I was seeing who the people were who were watching the house,' Elsie answered quite matter of factly. 'They obviously don't like me watching them watching you,' she added, smiling at the way it sounded.

'People?' asked Raymond.

'In that black SUV we saw yesterday on our way back with the wolves. You know, the one that caused Petersen and his bunch of bandits to suddenly disappear?'

'It was still there was it?' It was more a statement than a question. 'And how did you know?'

'I saw the light. They had the interior light on. I couldn't sleep, and when I looked out of my window I saw it.'

'So you thought that you would just go out alone and investigate?' asked Maria, crossly.

Elsie nodded. She already had her hand on the newel post ready to climb the stairs. 'Can we talk about it in the morning?' she said, dismissively. 'I'm rather tired now. The night air seems to have made me sleepy after all,' she lied, feeling more invigorated after her escapade than she had done all day. She marched up the stairs, determined not to lose the argument. 'And I wasn't alone, anyway,' she called back as she reached the landing, although she hadn't known she was going to have the three bodyguards with her when she decided to go out and investigate.

But nothing in the world would have made her admit it.

CHAPTER TWENTY ONE

Rhamin and Rasci had remained with Charka through the rest of the night. As dawn lifted the black sky off the horizon Raymond opened the kitchen door and stepped outside into the chilled morning air. It wasn't possible to tell what he was saying, but his gentle manner and his body language said it all. He was grateful that the wolves had accompanied Smokey to guard his adolescent niece on her midnight adventure. And it wasn't difficult to tell that, regardless of all the things he said to chastise her, Raymond was quite proud of Elsie despite her belligerence. No one knew better than Rhamin and Rasci that Elsie had courage. But Raymond knew it too.

He bent down and checked Charka. The swelling in her leg had subsided and her coat was no longer starey and dull. She was getting better. He put his hand in his jacket pocket and brought out the syringe that the vet had left with him. He uncapped the needle, held the syringe upright, pumped out the air bubble and then, gently holding Charka's fur on the back of her neck, pushed the needle under her skin. She jerked slightly but remained totally passive.

'He's already given you some of this stuff,' Rhamin said reassuringly. 'You were asleep but it didn't hurt you before so it won't harm you now.'

'I know,' Charka answered Rhamin with what sounded to Raymond like a soft whine. 'I know you trust him completely. That's good enough for me.'

After the short pricking sensation Charka felt a little discomfort as the antibiotic dissipated beneath her skin. But other than that, she felt no ill effects. She was already much better than she had been when Raymond came to collect her from the Darin, and that meant she was on the mend.

Raymond patted her gently on her shoulder, stood up and spoke to all the wolves. 'You'll be ready to go home now,' he said, with a tinge of sadness on his voice. 'I know Smokey will miss you,' he added as he turned and went back inside his home.

All the wolves sensed Raymond's sadness. Now that Rhamin was truly free from the clutches of that man Petersen, he couldn't help feeling events were drawing to an end of an era. But Charka wasn't ready to walk all the sixty or so miles back to the Darin. 'Can you talk to Ben and find out if it is okay for Charka to stay here until she is fit enough to return home to us?' he asked Rasci.

'He will let us know when we have outstayed our welcome,' Rasci replied. 'If last night was anything to go by then I imagine he'll be happy for us to stay and keep Smokey company.'

'Even so, we have wolf business to see to. Our pack is waiting for us to return.'

'I'll see what they have to say,' Rasci conceded. He went over to the far end of the little garden, lay down in the long wispy grass and cleared his mind.

'Daddy, Rasci wants to know how long Charka can stay. He's asking if she can remain here if he and Rhamin return to their pack.'

Raymond was sitting at the kitchen table, eating some toast and reading yesterday's newspaper. Ben was playing with his food, stirring it around on the plate with his fork. Elsie had joined them but neither she nor Raymond spoke of the events of that previous night. As far as Raymond was concerned it wouldn't do any good pretending to be angry when, in fact, he was quite proud of Elsie. Elsie thought it best to avoid another argument. After all, she had done what she wanted to do; she had scared herself half to death and, although she realized that it had been rather foolhardy in the first place, she knew now, after events had unfolded, that she had been perfectly safe with her three big bodyguards.

'Tell him that Charka has had all her treatment,' he instructed Ben. 'All she needs is rest. If they like, I'll drive them all back to their cave this afternoon. They should be quite safe now.'

As Ben relayed the message, Rasci couldn't help feeling that, unlike Rhamin, he believed that something, some event or occasion was inevitably going to change their lives once again.

As the sun rose to its highest point in the sky, Raymond brought the station wagon around to the front of the house. He left the back door open to let the hot air inside dissipate before loading up with wolves for his return journey to their Darin.

'Can we come too?' Ben asked for all the children.

Raymond smiled. 'I don't see why not. It's a long drive there and even longer coming back if there's nobody to talk to.'

'Well just you all be careful,' Maria said, frowning. 'Just because you have got rid of that tracker thing doesn't mean Petersen has given up on his ideas. Just you be careful, do you hear?'

'Yes Mummy, we will' Margo answered for all of them.

When all the passengers were in place, and all the windows were open to give full ventilation to the wolves who all lay facing the front, Raymond gave a short wave to Maria and set off down the farm lane. The children all waved as well. Everybody seemed relaxed now that Rhamin had had the tracker removed and Charka was getting well enough to return to her home. There was almost an air of celebration. Ben was singing. Elsie was smiling to herself, wondering what new phenomena she would discover in this mad world of her crazy Uncle; and Margo just sat and watched as the fencing and the trees flashed by. It wasn't long before they reached the outer perimeter of the farm. The easy driving was over. The rest of the way was rough terrain and still the happy atmosphere prevailed.

'So, just how did you find the wolves' lair?' Elsie asked, thinking to herself now that every time she discovered something new about this crazy family, it was going to make it easier to make up yet another of her imaginative tall stories. Or at least they would seem like tall stories because nobody on earth would believe there was even a grain of truth in them. They sounded like pure fiction. She had just somehow travelled into this new land of fairy-tale make-belief.

Raymond explained how he had been guided the first time by Corvak the raven. Ravens! It was yet another impossible story that, despite her common sense and logic telling her differently, Elsie forced herself to accept as a true account. When Raymond returned Lexa to the cave, of course, Corvak had led all the way until the pack met him a few miles east of the Darin. 'And since I'd been there before, it isn't so difficult to find a long, low escarpment almost exactly sixty miles due west of here. Can't really miss it. It's quite a feature compared with all the other rocky outcrops.' He turned his head and threw a glance back at the wolves. 'Rasci or Rhamin will show us how to get there if we get lost, I'm sure,' he said quite confidently. 'So you are in safe hands.'

He grinned. 'Or you're in safe paws,' he chuckled.

But his good humour wasn't to last long. No sooner had the farm boundaries receded into the far distance, than Elsie noticed a cloud of dust further ahead and off to the right. 'What's that?' she asked, thinking perhaps it was a small whirlwind, an eddy of warm air that was common on the hot dusty plains.

Raymond took a moment to focus his eyes. 'It looks like one of our friends again,' he said dryly. 'When will they ever learn?'

'Couldn't it be just someone out for a drive?' asked Elsie, not really believing that such a probability was even remotely likely.

'If they are then they are heading towards us,' Raymond replied angrily.

A moment or two later, as the wind changed direction, the dust cloud lifted for a few seconds. There was no mistaking the big black SUV. The sun roof was open and a man was standing looking out towards the station wagon. It wasn't clear at first what he was doing until seconds later they all saw that he was pointing a rifle towards them.

Nobody, except perhaps the wolves, heard the gun fire but the bullet ricocheted off the roof, just where the windscreen fitted into its socket. There was no hole, but a big crack slowly ran the full depth of the screen, dividing it in two just like the split screens on vintage cars.

'I don't believe this,' Raymond blurted. 'The man is obsessed!' he rasped as he swung the station wagon around and headed back in the direction from which they had come.

But the SUV had quickly closed the gap between them and was already drawing alongside. Its tinted windows gave it a sinister appearance. The man in the sun roof had disappeared inside. No one could see who he was or who was driving.

The noise of both vehicles became deafening as both raced at full revs, one in hot pursuit, and the other in desperate flight. When the man's head appeared, he was wearing dark sunglasses. Slowly, he rose up to full height again, appearing and disappearing in the flurries of dust that were being thrown up by the spinning wheels. The dust enveloped him again and then as it cleared, he lifted the rifle from inside the cab.

There was only a two or three feet gap between the racing vehicles. Side by side they bounced along over rocks and debris. Raymond, unable to see clearly ahead, simply drove towards the road that would lead them back to the farm. The trouble was, he had no idea if these mad men would stop when he reached the sanctuary of his own home. They seemed to be prepared to ignore all the laws of the land to get what they wanted.

As the man's gun levelled at Raymond, he braked the station wagon desperately. The gun discharged a bullet into the dusty ground ahead and to the right. Raymond slammed his foot down on the accelerator as the SUV braked. He was now slightly in front, but the SUV was much faster than the old station wagon.

Slowly, amidst the clouds of whirling dust, the black vehicle drew level again. The man raised his gun quickly this time. He wasn't going to give the escaping driver time to react. With the station wagon masked by a cloud of flying dirt, he squeezed the trigger and fired the gun blindly. The weapon fired rapidly and randomly in the direction of the station wagon, but as it did, a huge black form emerged from the dust cloud. Rhamin had leapt out of the open window and had landed with his huge front paws over the edge of the open sun roof. The momentum of his leap carried him forward as his teeth lashed at the man with the gun. The gun was still firing but the bullets went somewhere past Rhamin's shoulder. With the wolf alongside the long weapon, the man couldn't manoeuvre it to point either at Rhamin or at the passengers in the other vehicle. The aggressor had nowhere to turn it.

Rhamin could only see blood as he hit the man's face with his teeth. Once again, he could feel the cold hatred that had surged through him when men like this had shot Bamar. His anger was volcanic. There was going to be no appeasement today. All he could see before his eyes was Bamar dying in the long grass and Charka shot and wounded in the woodland. These men were not going to kill any more. They were not going to kill his wolves and they were not going to kill his friends.

The man screamed and the driver, seeing the jaws of lashing teeth above his head, swerved the SUV violently to the left away from Raymond's station wagon. He turned the steering wheel so fast that Rhamin really thought the SUV was going to turn over. It spun around and was balancing on two wheels as the driver swerved frantically to prevent it tipping over into a roll.

But the surface of the black vehicle was hard, shiny and slippery. There was no purchase for claws or teeth. The driver's twisting, jerking manoeuvre sent Rhamin flying through the air. He was somersaulting. He spun his tail like a gyroscope to try and stabilise his trajectory. It might have worked if he had been in the air much longer. But he was already dropping towards the ground. He hit it on his side, rolling over and over until he stopped moving. He waited a second or two to see if he felt any pain. The noise of the SUV was heading away from him. So was the sound of Raymond's station wagon - in the opposite direction.

Slowly, Rhamin stretched out his legs. They felt okay. He pulled them up underneath his body and stood up unsteadily, then, without thinking of shaking the dust off his coat, he began to run after Raymond and the rest of his friends. He was in a trail of flying dust and grit, desperately chasing the station wagon. Amongst the noise and clamour of a roaring engine and tyres ripping over the rough ground, he could hear the SUV behind. It suddenly appeared out of the dust cloud, its huge spinning wheels bouncing unaffected by the loose rocks and debris as it rebounded off everything in its path. It had turned around and was, once again, in hot pursuit. It was having no difficulty gaining on Raymond yet again.

In his mind, Rhamin wondered if its occupants were trying to kill him? Would they try again? He ran as fast as he could, but he couldn't shake off the SUV.

Just as the SUV came alongside, Rhamin swerved off to his left. They were going to have to twist and turn to catch him again.

But to his amazement, the SUV just carried on travelling past him. It didn't swerve, nor did the man in the roof even give Rhamin a second glance. His bloodied face just stared determinedly ahead, as the driver gunned the engine, hammering it to its limit, in hot pursuit, chasing the occupants of the station wagon.

Rhamin was tempted to slow a little. But he knew that if the men were not after him now, they would be hunting him down later. Somehow, Raymond and his children had become targets for this mad man's obsession. He didn't like that.

Realizing that he didn't need to follow the vehicles to catch them up, he leapt over the fence and began to cut across to the road that ran back to the house. The noise of the racing vehicles was still frenzied. Dust from Raymond's station wagon was hampering the SUV now but Rhamin didn't know if he would get to the road in time to stop the SUV catching up to Raymond yet again.

And then the noise changed. Suddenly the dust was flying up from the ground around Rhamin. Heavy rotors pounded the air down with every beat. The helicopter was back. A man was sitting inside with his legs out of the open door and his feet resting on the landing skids. In his hand he had one of the deadly weapons that had brought Rhamin down the first time they had shot at him on the plains. But then Rhamin had not expected their intention. He had not taken any evasive action. For a split second Rhamin's heart sank, but the feeling was soon overtaken by his anger, a blazing, flaming rage that fired his determination to bring these people to account. He swerved first to the left beneath the helicopter and then to the right, determined to make sure that anyone in the flying machine would not find an easy target this time.

But as quickly as it had appeared, the dust from the helicopter subsided and, ignoring Rhamin, the machine thrashed its way forward, past him and on towards the station wagon and its chasing predator. Within seconds it was over the SUV. The man with the bleeding face pointed his gun up at the machine and fired his weapon, but as he pulled the trigger the SUV lurched over another loose rock. As the gun jerked sideways, the tooth of death that it had discharged went harmlessly up into the sky. The man was about to aim his weapon again when, suddenly the helicopter bristled with more men all with weapons, all pointing them down through the sun roof of the SUV. The man beneath ducked down into his vehicle and shouted to the driver as it swerved to one side. Without further incident, it headed away from the farm road and disappeared over a ridge.

The helicopter hovered for a moment, its occupants clearly watching Rhamin. Then it tilted to one side, moved forward and escorted Raymond's station wagon back to the farm.

Rhamin had cut across the farm and was already at the farmhouse when the station wagon pulled up in the yard. Maria opened the door and Smokey rushed out to greet him.

'Oh. Never have I been so glad to see you,' Rhamin panted as he pushed past her into the sanctuary of the farmhouse kitchen. Smokey remained at the doorway looking out. She was the guard now.

Rhamin looked back past her and out of the door. The station wagon was speeding up the road towards the farmhouse. A moment or two later it screeched to a halt. Raymond was having difficulty opening his door. As he pushed against it, it creaked and then, amidst awkward scraping sounds, it opened reluctantly. He clung onto it as he pulled himself out of the seat. Rhamin could see that Raymond had been wounded. His right leg was bleeding badly and he was avoiding putting any weight on it. Maria rushed towards her husband and gave him her shoulder to lean on.

'Never mind me,' Raymond said between gritted teeth. 'Check the children.'

The helicopter had already landed and the rotors had wound to stop. A man jumped out and came rushing over to the station wagon. 'Are you all right?' he shouted to the children as he pulled the car door open. Margo just looked at him and nodded.

'That's Petersen,' Ben said, pointing at the man who had once been a hunting companion with his father.

'No we're not all right,' Elsie growled through her teeth, 'thanks to you and your gangsters. You'll pay for this,' she shouted.

The man went to the back of the vehicle and opened the back door. He looked at Rasci and Charka. Rasci snarled at him, barring all his teeth menacingly.

'Looking at your handiwork are you?' Elsie sneered. 'Another wolf you've shot. This one lived but the other one didn't.' Her voice was raised to a screech. 'You are the animal here! You should be the one imprisoned in a safari park for the rest of your life.'

Petersen just looked on and took it all very seriously. 'Those men had nothing to do with me,' he protested. 'If I hadn't turned up then they looked like they would have killed the lot of you.'

'Oh dear,' Maria said, a deep note of anxiety in her voice. 'What have you got us into?'

'Look, my men may have acted a bit heavy handed with the wolves, but we don't go about killing innocent men and their children.'

'Heavy handed?' Raymond spat and he leaned heavily

against the door frame. 'You've killed wolves for greed. You slaughtered a bear as well. In the name of what? Preservation of the species!'

Petersen held up his hands. 'Whoah! I came here in peace. If you hand over that wolf…' he said, pointing to Rhamin.

The Black Wolf was standing in the corner next to Smokey, his hackles bristling out his fur on his shoulder blades and along his back, his amber eyes boring into the man who had once captured and imprisoned him and his mate. Beside him, Smokey was watching the man's every move. Her muzzle was folded into ridges and her lips were curled back exposing her needle sharp canine teeth as she fought to control her urge to growl.

'Then I'll be out of here,' Petersen continued. 'No more conflict, no more injured wolves.'

'No more needless killing,' Elsie continued. 'But what if we don't hand him over? What if we tell you to get lost?' Her face reddened with anger. 'You'll carry on as before until you get your own way?'

Raymond turned and looked at his young niece. He smiled broadly as he thought that young Elsie certainly had courage and, at that moment, he couldn't help feeling very proud of her indeed.

'I don't have to listen to all this. I just saved all your lives. I came here offering to save more lives. I thought that you would appreciate what I'd just done.'

'You came here threatening to take lives,' Raymond shouted at Petersen. 'You have killed wildlife indiscriminately, and what for? Out of sheer greed, that's what you have been doing; killing and threatening to keep on slaughtering anything in your way until we, the wolves, or anyone else who stands up to you, capitulates. That is sheer open aggression.'

He sat down heavily on a nearby chair. 'Where was your appreciation when the wolves helped to save our lives up on the mountain you worthless hypocrite? What thanks did you give The Black Wolf for saving us from becoming bear food?'

'I see people like you all the time,' Elsie put in, angrily. 'You were obviously a bully at school.'

'Learnt your skill well,' Maria agreed.

'Some friend you turned out to be,' Petersen shouted back at Raymond, 'with a house full of mindless women. Thought you had some back bone. Seems like they've got you tied on a leash.'

'Raymond's jaw went taught. Get out!' he grated through clenched teeth. He pushed himself back up to a standing position and moved towards Petersen, reaching out towards him with his left hand whilst leaning on the table for support with his other. 'Get out or I'll throw you out.' At that moment, if he could have grabbed Petersen by the throat, Rhamin wasn't sure if Raymond wouldn't have squeezed the life out of him.

Petersen veered backwards to avoid Raymond's fist. With a shrug, he turned to leave.

'And don't think for one moment that I was ever your friend,' Raymond shouted after him as Petersen strode out of the open door and over to the helicopter. A hand popped out of the side of the machine and helped him climb on board. The rotors fired and began to turn. Half a minute later, Petersen and his men were soaring into the air and a moment or two after that the mechanical bird was just a black speck moving away at great speed and disappearing into the distant clear blue sky.

'The gall of the man!' Maria gasped as she watched the helicopter get smaller and smaller until it vanished. She turned to look at Raymond. 'That man thinks that he can bully people until they give him what he wants. Unbelievable!' she said, shaking her head angrily. 'What a nerve!'

'Well he's not having these wolves, that's for sure'. Raymond turned to look at Rhamin. The wolf's amber eyes watched Raymond's every move. He couldn't understand what was being said, but he knew that Raymond was making a stand for him and his pack.

'You'll have to get that leg seen to,' Maria stated as Raymond slumped down heavily on the chair. 'Can't do with you getting as bad as Charka there or whatever you call her. You'll have to go to hospital. The wound will have to have the bullet removed and be dressed.'

'Ring for a doctor,' Raymond said weakly. I won't be able to drive to his surgery.'

Maria frowned. 'You're right, you won't,' she said with a heavy sigh. 'You've lost enough blood already.' She paused and thought before adding, 'I'll drive you there myself.'

'No can do,' Raymond said firmly. 'We can't leave the children here on their own. We have a mad man or somebody out there, goodness knows who, if they have nothing to do with Petersen, shooting at us. And we can't risk having the children in the vehicle with us again if we come under the same kind of attack.' Then he added, 'Nor will I risk your life out there either.'

'Then I'll call the doctor.' She busied herself retrieving the first aid box from the cupboard and he watched as she opened it and rummaged through it.

'When did you last replenish this thing?' she asked, suddenly realizing it was difficult to find anything suitable for dressing even a small cut, never mind a bullet wound.

'Didn't think anybody was going to be shooting at me,'

Raymond answered coolly. 'Been doctoring a load of our own patients lately,' he said smiling and nodding towards Rhamin as Maria went over to the telephone.

'It does mean that the wolves will have to make their own way back home,' Raymond said with a sad note to his voice.

'Look Ray, as much as we like these creatures, your safety and that of all three of our youngsters comes first.' She picked up the receiver and listened for a second or two. Pressing the cradle a couple of times, she waited and then listened again.

'There's no dial tone,' she said, frowning as she looked at her husband.

'Give it here woman!' Raymond said fondly. He gave the children an askance look. 'It's a man thing' he said, grinning and then wincing as a pain shot through his leg.

'Serves you right!' Maria taunted. 'I didn't grow up into a big girl without knowing when a phone is out of order.' She offered him the hand piece.

'Use your mobile,' Elsie said, trying to be as helpful as she could.'

'Huh,' Maria scoffed. 'You're looking at the world's biggest technophobe. Mobile phone! What's that?'

'Not much use unless you want to talk to somebody else who's got one,' Raymond bounced back.

'Er. Like everyone hasn't got one!' Elsie exclaimed.

'Not everybody.' Raymond looked at Elsie. 'Have they?'

Ben and Margo looked at her. She raised an eyebrow and shrugged.

'Very diplomatic, young girl,' Raymond said, trying to dig himself out of a hole. 'We can use the radio. It's in the big barn.'

'Radio?' Elsie asked. 'You mean there are some ships about with doctors on them?'

'If you can just go and get it,' Raymond pleaded, ignoring Elsie's sarcasm. 'I'll show you the wonders of yesterday's modern technology.'

'What does it look like?' Elsie asked, now smiling. 'Anything like a mobile phone?'

'It's in a leather carrying case on top of the Jeep.'

CHAPTER TWENTY TWO

'Just who do they think they are, telling us where we can and can't go?'

'They are our friends.'

'We only have one friend there, Kara, and it isn't Rhiana.'

'Rhiana? What's wrong with her? She hasn't attacked us. She hasn't ripped out anybody's tail feathers.' He looked around at his backside. There was a noticeable gap in the spread of long stabilizer feathers. At the bottom of that gap his butt was still stinging.

'They treat us as if they own us.'

'Roxana doesn't,' Lutz protested.

'You don't see it, do you?'

'See what?'

'The power struggle. Solin, Rhiana, Roxana. Just who's running the show? Do you know?'

'Well, Rhiana is,' Lutz announced.

'And who is it that talks to us?'

'Roxana.'

'And you don't think it strange that the leader doesn't' even so much as nod a greeting to us?' Kara asked crossly. 'She understands our language as well as any wolf.'

'Perhaps she's too busy trying to get that mad dog Solin to do some proper leading.'

Kara grinned, her huge, curved beak wide as she chortled. 'Now you are sounding the right note. Now you see that there is no real leader. They all have something to gain by the others' demise. Which one will it be? To which one do we swear our allegiance? Rhiana? She rules the roost now but she's making way for Solin. Solin? He'll kill us even before he becomes leader if he has his way. And Roxana? She's our friend at the moment. Our only friend. But will she ever get to be leader while Solin and Rhiana are about?'

'We have to make sure she does then,' Lutz stated as if he knew just how he was going to make sure it happened.

CHAPTER TWENTY THREE

It was almost dark when the doctor eventually arrived at the farm. Raymond's leg was getting more painful with every aching throb as each hour passed.

'Looks like you've been having a bit of trouble,' the doctor said as he was let in through the door. He stopped and regarded the animals that were standing in the kitchen. Smokey and the big wolves almost filled half the room. 'Collecting wildlife,' he said, eyeing Rhamin up rather more seriously. 'One big animal, that.' he said seriously. 'Didn't think they grew that big nowadays.'

'Nowadays?' Raymond queried.

'Oh wolves used to be much bigger. Even bigger than your friend there, back in the stone age. Archaeologists have found their fossilised remains in tar pits. They have named them *Dire Wolves*. It means terrible wolves.'

'Really?' Ben asked, totally enthralled.

'Really,' the doctor confirmed with a nod and a friendly smile. He looked back up at the wolves. Eerily, they hadn't taken their eyes off him for a single moment. 'Dire Wolves were much bigger than wolves are today. Stockier as well and with shorter canines. It's thought they died out because they didn't or couldn't hunt like their smaller relatives. They were possibly just carrion eaters. Hundreds of them got caught in tar pits trying to get to animals that were already dead or dying in the sticky traps. Don't know why the rest of them disappeared though. It's quite probable that they couldn't move as fast as our friends here. It could have just been that the age of the really big animals had come to an end.' He shrugged. 'Who really knows?' He took another look at the wolves that were watching him with equal curiosity.

'Don't worry, they're totally friendly,' Raymond said, now wincing with every word. 'Don't let them put you off doing your job.'

'I won't,' the doctor replied, looking away from Rhamin's mesmerising stare and placing his bag on the kitchen table. 'You should be in a hospital.'

'Just get the bullet out will you,' Raymond said rather sharply. 'It's killing me.'

'Could well be,' the doctor replied bluntly. 'Gangrene will kill the strongest creature.'

'Gangrene? I haven't got Gangrene.'

'Soon will have,' the doctor said, going over to the sink to wash his hands, 'if you carry on avoiding hospitals.' He dried his hands on a clean towel and then took out a bottle of alcohol and some medical instruments. He put the instruments into a small stainless steel tray and poured the liquid onto them until they were submerged.

'Right,' he said, pulling on a pair of surgical gloves.

The operation wasn't a major one. An injection of local

anaesthetic and a good strong probe and he'd removed the bullet within minutes. 'I'll still have to file a police report. This is a serious gunshot wound.'

'What if I told you it was an accident,' Raymond said, looking for some latitude in the doctor's eyes.

'Your car is shot up. There are bullet holes in the roof and in the door. What sort of accident have you in mind?' His sarcasm was cutting. 'On top of that, I noticed at the end of your farm road that the end of your telephone line is dangling on the fence.'

'Cut?' Maria and Raymond's voices spoke as one.

'Yes, cut. I got out to examine it. You haven't upset someone lately, have you?'

'Yes, Petersen,' Ben called out. 'He's shooting at everything that walks. 'He shot at us.'

'No he didn't,' Raymond countered. 'It was his men in the helicopter that stopped the men in the SUV shooting at us.'

'And you say you want to report this as an accident!' the doctor exclaimed. 'Not in a thousand years.'

'Well, whatever,' Raymond said with a resigned sigh. 'Thanks for coming out anyway Doc.'

'You are welcome Raymond.' He turned to Maria. 'See that he takes both sets of tablets and make sure he doesn't drive or operate any machinery. Those painkillers will definitely make him drowsy. They will affect his ability to concentrate.'

'As if he needs tablets for that,' Maria said with a shake of her head, grinning.

'So Rhamin and Rasci are stranded here unless they make their way back home without Charka?' Elsie asked.

'They can stay here as long as they want,' Raymond answered.

'But they have wolves waiting for them,' Ben said, a frown creasing his little brow.

'Can't be helped, I'm afraid,' Raymond said wincing. 'Petersen knows that I won't be driving far. He saw my leg.'

Elsie was trying to piece things together. 'So he'll be waiting for Rhamin to break cover. He knows The Black Wolf's here and he'll have somebody watching,' she surmised. 'Rhamin's got to go from here when Petersen doesn't suspect he'll be going.'

'Seems like it,' Raymond agreed.

'But for the time being, he's marooned here?' asked Elsie.

'For the time being, I'm afraid so,' Raymond answered despondently as Maria helped him off the chair and, with her shoulder under his armpit, began to help her husband up the stairs to bed.

But the whole thing preyed on Elsie's mind.

CHAPTER TWENTY FOUR

Eleven o'clock passed; twelve o'clock passed; but still Elsie lay awake wondering how she could get Rhamin and his wolves to safety. At five o'clock she had decided what she was going to do. Quietly, she got out of bed, slipped on her jumper and jeans and slid her feet into her trainers. Then she got her small backpack, put several items into it from out of one of the drawers in her bedside cabinet, and tiptoed out of her bedroom and onto the landing. She paused there for a few moments, listening, waiting to see if she had disturbed anybody. All was quiet… except for the turning of a door handle on the door next to her room. In the dim light, Elsie strained to see what was happening. Gradually the door moved away from the jamb and Margo's little face peered around the door.

'Sshh…' Elsie said quietly, holding her finger to her lips. 'Where are you going?' she whispered even more softly.

'With you,' Margo whispered back. 'Ben and I knew you were going to go.'

'Ben and…' Elsie looked at the door of Ben's room. It was still closed. Then, quietly, Ben appeared. He was already dressed and waiting with his little sister. Silently, he opened Margos's bedroom door a little wider and together, Margo and Ben tiptoed out and down the stairs in front of Elsie.

'How did you know?' Elsie asked when they reached the kitchen.

'Margo knows lots of things,' Ben said, looking at his little sister proudly.

'We had better leave a note,' Elsie suggested. 'Better if they know where we are. At least then they won't worry.'

Margo and Ben agreed, and Ben ran over to the kitchen table, pulled out a big wide drawer and rifled through it until he had found what he was looking for. He handed a pencil and paper to his cousin.

Writing quickly, Elsie stated that she had gone to take the wolves back to their den and that she would be back later that day.

'So how are we going to get them there?' Ben asked.

'I'm going to drive them there,' Elsie said. 'And you, Ben, are going to show me the way.'

'In the station wagon?' Margo asked, surprised.

'Don't worry, my Dad...' she paused for a moment. 'My dad taught me to drive. We used to do dune buggy racing,' she said, biting her lip and trying to stop her voice trembling. 'Not a lot different really.'

She steadied her voice and then went on, 'I reckon that Petersen will expect all the wolves to leave together. He knows that one is injured so they aren't likely to leave until Charka is well enough to trot along with Rhamin and Rasci. He also knows that your father is too badly injured to drive. He won't be expecting the station wagon to be leaving today. If he does think Raymond will try it again, he certainly won't expect him to try it until he can drive.'

Quickly now, Elsie made a pile of cheese sandwiches and packed them into her backpack. With them she packed three bottles of water and three chocolate bars. 'That will keep us going until we get home,' she said, picking up her back-pack and going to the door. She didn't have to look for Rhamin and Rasci. They were already in the kitchen, sitting next to Smokey's basket. Rasci already knew what Ben and Margo knew. He'd been talking to Ben whilst they waited for Elsie to come out of her bedroom.

Smokey peered out from between them, her broad face wrinkled with curiosity, her ears forward; her face a picture of total concentration. Charka was in the other corner on her own blanket. She was sitting up. Her face was no less curious.

'Come on then,' Elsie said to the wolves. 'Let's get you home.'

Quietly, Ben coaxed Charka to stand up and come out of the open door. As she did, Rhamin walked beside her. Rasci and the children were next to follow. Then Smokey, too, went outside with them. It was her duty to guard the children. They were not going to leave without her.

They walked across to the big barn. It wasn't daylight yet, but despite the gathering clouds in the west, the rest of the sky to the east was clear. The stars were bright and dawn wasn't far away. They opened the pen gates slowly to reduce the disquieting peacock call of the hinges. Ben propped them open with some pieces of wood.

'Quietly now,' Elsie whispered as she opened the back of the station wagon and waved the wolves in. With a helping hand from Elsie, Charka managed to climb in first. Rhamin and Rasci jumped in beside her and Elsie closed the door and clicked it shut as quietly as she could.

Smokey waited patiently for Elsie to open the passenger door. She was used to riding up front with her master. Nothing was going to change now.

Ben and Margo got into the rear seats and, as usual, fastened their seat belts.

'Are you sure Petersen won't be waiting out there?' Ben asked, nervously.

'He will not be expecting anybody to drive anywhere. He's seen the doctor come and go. He'll presume no one else other than your mum can drive. And she won't leave your dad or you behind to take some wolves home. Her priority is looking after her own family, not a wolf's family.'

'And can you *really* drive?' Ben asked. 'Honestly?'

'Oh yes,' Elsie replied, a proud smile spreading across both cheeks. She pulled the driving seat forward and adjusted it to her height. 'You don't worry about a thing.' She re-set the odometer to show zero miles travelled, took out a few things from her pockets and put them within easy reach, fastened her seat belt and, with only a slight judder of the clutch, drove out of the yard.

Before first light the station wagon and its crew were already ten miles into their journey. Both Ben and Margo were impressed by her ability to drive such a big vehicle and it hadn't seemed to have suffered any mechanical defect despite the bullet holes.

Rasci and Rhamin were no less impressed.

But despite her confidence, Elsie was just hoping that her Uncle Raymond wasn't going to be up too early this day. He usually got up at dawn. Perhaps his pain-killers would keep him sleeping well into the morning. 'We'll be back by mid-morning,' she said nervously, several times over the next couple of hours as the driving became more difficult. She was only grateful that it was full daylight before the roughest part of the journey began.

Ben couldn't help thinking that Elsie was trying to convince herself as she steered around rocks and scrub trees. She was realizing that there was no real road to the wolves' lair. The going was difficult. 'What if I don't know where we are?' Ben asked nervously as they drove well into the second hour.

'Your father explained where we have to go, remember?'

'Where was that?'

'Due west. I have a compass,' she stated as she steered around another clump of scrub trees. She straightened up the steering as the station wagon entered another relatively flat part of the route and then pointed to the dashboard. Ben hadn't noticed before. Just off-set from the steering wheel, on the dashboard, there was a small box, about half the size of a jeweller's ring box, with its lid open. It seemed to be fixed by a suction device to the dashboard. Inside the open box was the top of a glass ball that floated around, seemingly effortlessly. Although it was not absolutely still, it was possible to see that, in the main, the letter "W" was facing into the cab. 'We're looking for a long, low escarpment. It's a long rocky outcrop.'

'That's right,' Ben said, his eyes lighting up quite excitedly when he realized that Elsie really did have a good idea where she was heading. 'We went there to collect Rhamin, Rasci and Charka.'

Elsie nodded. 'By my reckoning,' she said, looking at the dials in front of her, 'we have another eight to ten miles to go. And anyway,' she added, 'if we get somewhere near then the wolves will be able to get to their den easily enough. All we have to do is drive them as close as we can.'

Ben smiled. Elsie had definitely thought it all out. It was a relief really, to know that they were near finishing their adventure. He'd had quite enough excitement for one day. He sat back and relaxed. It was then that he saw Rasci's image sitting next to him. 'Oh, hi Rasci,' he exclaimed as he glanced over his shoulder to see the earthly form of the wolf lying next to Rhamin. Rhamin was wide awake and so was Charka. Their heads were up and their ears pointed forward as they looked around out of the windows. Rasci looked as if he was trying to go to sleep.

'Hello, Ben,' Rasci began, quite seriously. 'Charka thinks we have a problem. In fact, so do I. I've felt uneasy now for some time.'

'You're not feeling travel sick, are you?' Ben asked, a frown of concern creasing his forehead.

'No, nothing like that my young friend.' Rasci paused a second. 'You have to tell Elsie that we are in trouble.' The wolf spirit glanced to the back of the vehicle. 'Despite the noise of this machine, with the windows open, Charka reckons that she can hear another vehicle following us. I went into one of my trances and tried to see for myself. She's right. The same black machine that chased us yesterday is close behind.'

Ben's mouth dropped open. His throat was suddenly dry. 'Elsie,' he croaked. He cleared his throat and tried again. 'Elsie, they are following us again,' he said as he tried to moisten his lips with a dry tongue.

Elsie's head swung around. 'What?'

'The black SUV is behind us.'

Elsie glanced in her rear view mirror. 'I don't see anything,' she said, shaking her head. But a note of tension had already crept into her voice. 'What makes you think that?'

'Rasci has told me.'

Elsie was still coming to terms with Ben's and Margo's

ability to communicate with the wolves. 'And they know this for sure?' she asked, her own mouth feeling dry with apprehension now.

Ben listened to something, leaning his head towards the gap between himself and Margo. Then he nodded. 'Rasci says they are out of sight but they are definitely behind us, and they are catching us up.'

Elsie's face hardened. She had led a seasoned life in the city up till now, a life filled with risks of traffic and muggers and, well, goodness knows what. But in the quiet countryside she was finding that, contrary to her original opinion that life would be completely boring and meaningless, here, out in the middle of nowhere, the dangers to life were tenfold that of the city. And none of that danger related to the wildlife.

CHAPTER TWENTY FIVE

At last, as a curtain of daylight slowly replaced the black veil of night, Solin and his pack watched as more than a dozen wolves left the Darin. But instead of heading towards the boulders where the vultures had once again returned to feed, the wolves simply ignored the circling birds and headed towards the foothills.

The pack did not include Rhamin or Rasci. But Silvah was there and so was Lexa. It was just about what Rhiana had expected; most of the pack plus a few of this year's cubs. Except, what she did not expect was a bouncing playful bear cub. On leaving the Darin, it looked nervously towards the boulders where flocks of vultures hovered, took off and landed near some sort of carrion, but having moved past it with the rest of the wolves who seemed to ignore the big birds entirely, the bear cub began dodging and swerving along as it jousted with the young wolf cubs. They all trailed along beside the adult wolves of the Rhamin Pack, totally at ease with one another. The bear cub seemed to be completely integrated into the pack.

Rhiana and Roxana fully understood what was happening. Animals that are usually deadly enemies sometimes become friends. The mountain lions were a testament to that. But it didn't mean anything other than there was an extra cub for the pack to look after.

'Rhamin must be already out hunting somewhere. They are probably going to meet up with him now,' Rhiana put forward. 'And if Lexa and Silvah are in the hunting party then you can bet that the old wolf is left behind alone in the cave.'

'So where are Rhamin and Rasci?' Roxana asked. 'Are you going to go down to the cave and make sure they aren't there?'

'From that, I take it that *you* aren't going to go down and check,' Solin remarked snidely.

'It isn't my plan,' Roxana snapped back.

'We'll all go,' Rhiana commanded. 'There are ten of us altogether. If there are any guards left there, even Rhamin, then we have a good chance of overcoming them.' She paused and looked all the wolves in the eye. 'But if Rhamin isn't there, our target is the old wolf, remember.'

They waited for a good half hour and saw no further activity around the cave. The departing group had disappeared, probably already hunting in the foothills that led to the forests for their next meal. But Rhiana waited another while before signalling for her companions to work their way towards the rocky outcrop where the vultures were constantly feeding. It took no time at all to establish what the carrion was on which the birds were feeding.

'That explains the bear cub,' Solin announced dryly. 'Looks like the bear cub's mother was killed by men kind.'

'That's no problem of ours,' Rhiana snapped. 'Let's get on with our own business.' With that she led the wolves towards the escarpment that concealed the opening to the

Darin. Slowly heading up the team, she climbed the rocky incline and peered over the top. The mouth of the cave stared back at her like the mouth of an angry monster that had suddenly been startled by her appearance. But the mouth was empty.

'Come,' she commanded, looking back at her followers. 'Solin, Roxana and I will go inside. The rest of you spread out and keep guard. Call into the mouth of the cave if you see any other wolves approaching,' she called out to them.

Carefully, and making no sound, the three of them descended the slope and padded silently down towards the mouth of the cave. With their ears forward, listening for any movement, and their noses sniffing to pick up any trace of any of their enemy remaining there, Rhiana was first to step inside the opening.

'Come in,' a voice suddenly called from the blackness.

The three invaders suddenly stopped, their eyes wide, trying to get accustomed to the blackness; their coats bristled with anticipation of conflict. Should they retrace their steps while they still had a chance or should they carry out the plan that they had intended?

'Come in,' the voice repeated. 'What are you waiting for?'

'It's old Zelda,' Solin announced, his coat unbristling as he relaxed a little with the relief of recognising the old wolf's shaky voice.

'I'm quite alone,' the voice said, once again coaxing them further into the cave.

Slowly, still fully alerted, the three assassins stepped forward and advanced into the gloom.

'What do you mean?' Solin asked the voice. 'Why would you invite us into the cave if you are alone?'

'Why don't you come in and see?' the voice chuckled. The sound echoed eerily though the caverns.

The three assassins were still standing in the semi gloom of the daylight that found its way into the mouth of the cave. Despite their excellent visual ability, three more steps forward and they would be in total blackness with only their ears and their noses to guide them. They took those steps, their eyes adjusting a little more to the lack of light, though none were totally confident that their other senses were adequate to prevent a sudden attack from out of the blackness.

'How many of you are there?' the voice asked, still no nearer.

'Why do you ask?' asked Solin.

'Oh, I was just wondering how many of you it takes to kill one old wolf.'

'What makes you say that?'

'That's what you have come here for isn't it?' She chuckled again, causing another bout of strange, spine-chilling echoes.

None of the wolves answered, although Rhiana knew now that Solin had been right. The old wolf would see her killers coming even before they had set off on their campaign. The only problem was: was it a trap? Had the old wolf told the pack to disappear until the assassins arrived? Had she told the other wolves that had been in the cave that there was a pack of renegades on their way to kill her? She listened to see if any of the wolves outside had raised the alarm. Nothing. They were, as planned, alone in the cave with Zelda.

'Keep speaking so that I can find you,' Solin instructed. But despite stepping several paces forward, the sound of the voice seemed no closer. The three wolves slowly moved ahead, nose to tail, each following wolf lightly touching the leader with their chin. What seemed like ages passed while they sniffed at the damp air and felt their way forward, around upright pillars of rock and past hanging daggers dangling from the ceiling in the blackness. 'How are we going to do anything when we do find her?' Solin whispered but his silent whisper seemed to be amplified by the surrounding cavern.

'Don't worry,' Zelda's mocking voice seemed to answer immediately. 'Not far to go now.'

Another chuckle sent shivers down Rhiana's spine. Solin felt the shudder through the tips of the hair on his thick coat.

Roxana said nothing. Something inside her warned her that now wasn't the time to criticise either of her companions. She felt inclined to turn around and leave them to it but that would certainly be the end to her bid for leadership. Better to follow the whole plan through than be seen to be a coward.

The passage was getting narrower. Solin could feel the walls touching his coat on either side. He lifted his head as high as he could and sniffed. The ceiling to this cave seemed much higher as the walls got closer. Then, as suddenly as he had felt the narrowing of the passage, the walls receded again, giving a feeling of space again. Never before had he heard of any wolf travelling so far back into the cave complex where he was born. If anyone had said he would ever adventure into its blackness beyond the Darin he would have scoffed. What use was there in finding out what lay beyond the caves of the Darin anyway? It would contain no food. Even the resident bats, what few of them there remained after the long drought, didn't travel so far in.

In the open space now, they were getting close to their quarry. Solin could smell Zelda. He could feel the heat generated by her old body in this chilling hole. He could smell her coat on the walls where it had brushed by. Her footprints seemed to be everywhere. Come on, speak again, he thought, but he did not ask it. From now on, the old wolf would have to call out first. On and on the cavern seemed to go until, bumping into each other, they reached a blank wall.

As the three predators bunched up closer to each other and turned around trying to get their bearings, a heart spiking chuckle broke the deadly silence and echoed around the cave complex, repeating itself again and again until it was hard to tell which sound was an echo and which was a new and even more blood chilling laugh. They would have followed the sound of her voice, but the direction from which the noises came was from every wall, from every opening, every hanging pillar of rock.

CHAPTER TWENTY SIX

Driving faster now, Elsie felt danger with every turn of the steering wheel as she negotiated around rocks and trees. She glanced at the compass. The "W" had disappeared. The device showed "N" now. Trying not to panic, she steered back to the left until the "W" reappeared. Goodness knows how long I've been travelling north, she thought to herself. Her eyes had been fixed on the mirrors, trying to see what Ben and Rasci had told her was there.

As she straightened up on the line westward, from the corner of her eye, through the open passenger window, she glimpsed across the vast plain. Over to her left and still a long way off, she thought she glimpsed a rising cloud of dust. Whoever they were, they were slowly but surely catching them up. She looked at the speedometer. Her speed was only twenty miles per hour. The odometer said she had driven fifty four miles. She had to get the wolves to their den before their pursuers would inevitably see where she had dropped them off. She floored the accelerator and the station wagon lurched forward.

Ben and Margo gripped the door handles tightly. Their knuckles turned white as they squeezed hard to brace themselves as the station wagon careered over the uneven ground. The vehicle was bouncing about wildly, but the compass showed that she was travelling in the right direction. For a moment or two, she lost sight of the following SUV. She was getting away from whoever it was who was following them. But then, her steering wheel lurched to the right. The wheels had hit something big and it threw the steering wheel out of her hands as it spun around. The station wagon had turned at right angles in the space of a few yards. It was travelling sideways and showing no propensity to slow down. Then, she realized it had left the ground. It was sailing through the air. 'Brace yourselves!' she shouted and the wheels hit solid ground again and the momentum inevitably sent the station wagon tipping over and sliding onwards on it side as easily as if it were still on its wheels. Dust and grit filled the scraping vehicle as the open side windows ploughed along the sandy ground.

A big thump, a lurch to one side, Elsie wasn't sure which, and a creaking noise that told the story better than a thousand words, revealed to her and all her travellers that the station wagon had come to a standstill on its side in a hollow.

Elsie was shaken, but a lick from Rhamin's damp tongue, as the dust cleared, revived her. She coughed and shook her head to clear the dirt from her face and hair. Rasci had done the same with Ben. He licked his face, but Ben just pushed the big wolf's muzzle away.

'I'm okay,' he said, trying to release his seat belt.

Smokey was licking Margo's face as she dangled in her seat belt. Margo just put her arms around the huge dog's head and kissed her back.

Quickly, shaking her head to clear her vision, Elsie unclipped her seat belt and let her legs drop down beneath her. She was standing on the passenger door next to Smokey. 'We have to get out,' she said frantically as she saw Ben trying to release his seat belt. 'Here,' she said, pushing Ben's hand to one side. 'Let me do it.' But try as she may, the catch for Ben's safety belt wouldn't move. The belt was jammed. She reached for Margo's belt but Margo had already released hers and was lying awkwardly on the rear passenger door, the one next to which she had been sitting when the station wagon had been upright. Elsie lifted her up onto the edge of the open window. 'Jump down and run clear,' she ordered. 'Quickly!'

She turned back to Ben. He was trying to release the catch that held his belt secure, but it still wouldn't budge. Her backpack had fallen by her feet. She bent down to get it and, at the same time, scanned the debris inside the vehicle to see if there was anything with which she could cut the belt. When she looked up, Rasci had already chewed half way through the strap with his razor sharp teeth. 'You keep going, Rasci,' she said, not realizing that the wolf wouldn't understand her. She clambered out of the open window above her head and ran around to the back of the station wagon. Amidst the smell of spilling fuel, she unlatched the rear door, and prized it open, scraping it against the dry ground. Because the station wagon had tipped into a gulley, the rear door didn't move far, but the gap was wide enough for her to squeeze back inside. Rasci was seconds away from releasing Ben. Elsie caught her little cousin as the last thread of the belt gave way. Quickly, she pushed him out of the rear door.

'Come on.' she shouted to the wolves. 'Smokey, tell them!' she shouted, not really knowing why she thought Smokey could understand her any better than the wolves. But her gestures and frantic body language indicated only one thing. Get out! The fumes from the spilt fuel were almost overpowering. Within seconds, all the animals were outside, including Charka. Even she looked no worse for the tumble inside the turning vehicle. 'We have to get to the Wolves' den,' she stated, looking at Ben for some kind of help.

Ben just shrugged. He didn't know where he was nor in which direction they were facing. 'I'll get your compass,' he said, his eyes brightening with his brain wave. He turned to run back to the upturned vehicle.

'No!' Elsie's voice was loud and authoritative but she couldn't help feeling her own pangs of fear as she thought what she was going to say next. 'Stay there,' she said, catching him by the shoulder and spinning him around. 'Do you hear? Stay here.' Leaving go of Ben, she ran back to the station wagon. A thin, grey shaft of smoke was beginning to rise near the front of the engine. Quickly, she crawled back inside. A small flame appeared outside by the front wheel.

'Look out Elsie!' Ben shouted. 'It's on fire!'

The small flame at the front of the station wagon was growing, getting bigger as it crept towards the spilt petroleum from the fuel tank at the rear.

'Quickly, Elsie,' Ben called again frantically. The station wagon creaked as it slid a little further into the gulley, tipping more fuel from the tank. The petrol flowed more quickly now along the bottom of the gulley spreading both ways, some away from the broken vehicle, the rest flowed underneath it towards the engine and the front wheel.

Elsie couldn't find the compass; it had bounced off the dashboard and disappeared somewhere in the dirt and mess. Abandoning it now, she gathered her backpack and threw it out through the door window above her head. But now Ben could see she was having difficulty getting back out through the rear door. It had pushed closed as the vehicle had slumped lower in the narrow gulley.

Rhamin saw what was happening. He knew what smoke was and he knew that the flames that were spreading into the station wagon could burn Elsie the way he had been burned when he was a young cub. For the first time in his life he felt a pang of fear. The smell of smoke was triggering a reaction he had never expected. Visions of what happened to him when he was a small wolf cub crowded into his mind; the smoke, the flames, the pain… especially the pain. He hesitated, watching the smoke and the small flame. But his hesitation was only for a brief second. He shook himself to clear away the clutches of fear. Slowly his vision cleared and he was looking at the flames on the ground. They were spreading and the station wagon was starting to ignite.

Bounding towards the burning vehicle, and leaping onto the top of the upper door, he placed his huge paws on the edge of the open window. Quickly, he reached inside with his whole body, grabbed a hold of Elsie's collar and pulled her out through the window.

Pulling with her arms and pushing with her legs, she cleared the opening and rolled out and down onto the ground at Rhamin's feet.

The fire had only three inches to go now before it reached the fuel soaked ground. Two inches; one inch. As Elsie struggled to her feet and grabbed her backpack, Rhamin recalled how, when he was a pup and his pack was being hunted by men on horses, Silvah had grabbed him and carried him away from danger. He grabbed the belt of Elsie's jeans at the back, lifted her clear off the ground and, with Elsie dangling forward, and her toes dragging on the ground, he bounded towards Ben, Margo, Smokey and the other wolves. A split second later, the station wagon was engulfed in a ball of flames. A heat wave blasted against his hind legs as he sprinted away. There was a smell of singeing fur. It reminded him all too easily of the day he cheated the deadly flames once before. Then it had painfully singed the fur on his ears, but now, it was his guard hairs, his top thick coat that was insulating him from the fiery blast. And his body was between the blast and Elsie. She felt the heated air, but was saved from the flames. As Rhamin deposited her on the ground beside the others, Elsie, with her backpack in hand, turned and watched as black smoke billowed into the sky.

'Run!' Elsie shouted, struggling to her feet and putting her arms around Ben and Margo. Directing them along in front of her, she sprinted away from the blaze. As the tank ignited, a huge explosion, sent a scalding hot air wave thundering up to, over and past the fleeing passengers, pushing them to the ground and rolling them like tumbleweed in a deserted street. Rolling over and over, they came to a halt lying facing the wreckage. They all watched as the pall of black smoke rose into the heavy and rapidly darkening morning sky.

'If we had lost our pursuers before we crashed, they'll know where we are now,' Ben said, quite aware that they had not yet rid themselves of the people that had been chasing after them.

CHAPTER TWENTY SEVEN

'They are on their way back to the cave,' Kara said as she and Lutz soared a mile away from the wolves of the Rhamin pack. They were flying as high as they could to avoid being seen and recognised, but tumbling storm clouds were forcing them to fly lower and lower; much nearer to the ground than they would have liked. On a clear day, their eyes could locate a mouse from a mile high. But even now, no one on the ground could make out the two floating specks if they were even looking for them; they were staying well away to the south. Despite their lack of height, they were maintaining their distance.

Kara and Lutz watched, fascinated, as the pall of smoke travelled up towards them in a thermal vacuum caused as the fire drew in more and more air near the ground. As the smoke reached high into the sky, it spread out and thinned mingling with the thick, menacing blanket of storm clouds which seemed hardly darker than the rising black smoke. The day was just getting blacker.

From where they were, the two vultures could see the escarpment by the Darin. They could see the seven wolves on the ridge, waiting patiently for their leaders to emerge from the cave. Over to the east they could see the squad of wolves from the Rhamin Pack as they stopped. The two birds flew closer and watched as all the wolves gathered together. The young wolf cubs and the bear cub, along with two adult wolves, split off from the pack and carried on in a north easterly direction towards the tree line. The rest of the pack, headed by Silvah, turned and began to lope back towards the Darin. It wasn't too hard to work out what was happening. Their motives couldn't have been clearer. Having seen their young ones clear of the danger, ten mature wolves were heading for a battle.

With a single flap of their wings, and a tilt of their tail feathers, Kara and Lutz soared down towards the escarpment. All seven of the Solin wolves were still lying discretely out of view where they could see the opening to the cave. Any wolf emerging from the cave would have to have been looking purposefully to the top of the ridge to spot the waiting enemy wolves.

Closer and closer, the vultures sailed towards the wolves and then, as they soared overhead, at the top of their voices, they shouted, 'Run!' They flapped their wings and, circling back again, together they both squawked. 'Run for your lives!'

Although none of Solin's wolves understood the birds' language, they were under no misapprehension. A warning of danger from any animal is as alarming a note as any signal that can be relayed. The wolves stood up, watched the soaring vultures and, knowing the warning for what it was, they gathered together on the ridge. At first they turned in a north easterly direction and began to go down the slope heading towards the foothills, towards the forests and the safety of cover. They didn't know about the approaching enemy.

'This way,' called Kara, circling around and flying at them from the north east. Swooping over their heads, she called again.

'This way.' They called out again and again, their voices screeching with terror, as they circled and manoeuvred in the direction they wanted the wolves to follow.

The wolves hesitated but then picked up their pace and continued on their original course.

'This way,' Kara squawked again, circling around them and, this time, skimming so low that the wind from her flapping wings rushed against the wolves' thick coats.

The seven wolves stopped and turned to see Kara join Lutz circling low to the ground a hundred paces or so to the west.

'This way,' the two vultures shouted again. 'Come on you foolish animals!'

Without a word spoken between them the wolves turned and looked back at the opening to the cave, then, from their elevated position on the ridge, they looked out towards the west. Suddenly one of them took the lead and barked at the others. That wolf had understood. He had realized that the commotion by the vultures actually meant something more than just a warning to flee. He barked again then, breaking into a loping stride and followed by the others, he bounded away after the birds.

Now, with only an occasional call of their shrill voices, the vultures flapped their huge wings, gained height and circled above the escaping pack.

Kara had no intention of letting the remainder of Solin's pack run into any of the approaching enemy. After all, the wolves were still the providers of Kara and Lutz's meals. Just because Solin hated them, it didn't mean that the other wolves would, especially if the warnings saved their lives. Solin, Rhiana and Roxana were history. They had lost sight of what it was wolves do; hunt, eat, sleep. They had set out to start a war and vultures had no place in such a plan.

The pack of seven remaining wolves followed the two birds, loping as fast as they could away from the Darin. Soon they turned to the south. The vultures were taking them in exactly the opposite direction to that which their enemies were now returning. None thought to bark a warning into the mouth of the cave. None realized that it was exactly what Kara and Lutz had intended.

CHAPTER TWENTY EIGHT

'Run,' Elsie shouted to the wolves. She wanted to accomplish her mission. She was no doubt going to have retribution poured down on her from a great height when Uncle Raymond discovered she had burned out his station wagon. The least she could do now was finish what she had started and get the wolves to safety. 'They will not harm us.' She pointed westwards to try and make Rhamin, Rasci and Charka understand. 'Run!'

But the wolves and Smokey just stood there, not moving an even inch.

Elsie stooped forward and picked up Ben with one arm and Margo with the other. Leaving her backpack behind, she said, 'Come on then, we'll come with you.' She began to run, but her load was way too much for her.

'I know what you are saying,' Rasci said, still remaining where he was, 'although I can't understand a word of it.' He turned to Rhamin. 'Are we going to leave them here?'

'Not if I can do anything about it brother,' Rhamin said, looking at Rasci proudly. 'They have risked their lives for us. What sort of repayment would we be making if we abandoned them out here in the middle of nowhere? They are miles from their home. They have no means to get back there, and I am not so sure that the people in that machine are after us,' he stated, his ears forward as he listened to calculate just how close the following vehicle had come.

'I got that feeling too,' Rasci agreed. 'That vehicle is not the one that Petersen uses. It's the one that seems to have a different reason for seeing Petersen out of the way.'

'The same one that Petersen chased off with his mechanical flying bird,' said Rhamin.

Rasci nodded. 'Give me a minute,' he said, walking a few paces to one side.

Elsie had looked back and seen the wolves standing where she had left them. She strode heavily back to them and lowered the two younger children back to the ground.

Ben stood for a moment, relieved that he wasn't going to be carried by his elder cousin. For a moment he had been watching Rhamin but his head suddenly swivelled around from the wolves. Staring at a patch of clear air he began to nod and chat in a quiet voice.

'Rasci says we must all travel together. Those men are not after Rhamin. He thinks they are after us!'

'Nonsense!' Elsie gesticulated, waving her arms dismissively. 'What would they want with us?'

Ben turned away again and then nodded. Turning back to Elsie and Margo he said. 'Elsie, you get on Rhamin's back. I'll get on Smokey. Margo will ride on Rasci.' He didn't wait for any response from his older cousin. Smokey, Rhamin and Rasci had already laid down. Ben took Margo's hand, led her to Rasci and helped her climb onto Rasci's back. He made sure she had a firm grip of the wolf's thick coat. 'Don't leave go. Understand?'

Margo nodded and smiled. Out of the three of them she was actually enjoying the adventure.

Ben climbed onto Smokey's broad back. He grabbed a hold of the folds of skin on her neck and hung on tightly with his little clenched fists. 'Just hang on tight,' he instructed, 'and you'll be all right,' he added as Rasci stood up and, effortlessly it seemed, trotted over to Elsie.

Seeing just how strong these creatures were, surprised Elsie. They had weakly thin looking legs that didn't look like they could hold a wolf's weight, but then she remembered what she had read about them. They loped for miles, tirelessly. They brought down buffalo with their strength; they carried their prey when they had to in jaws of steel. She looked at Rhamin. He still lay on the ground, ears forward, looking at Elsie.

She shrugged. Picking up her backpack, she slipped her arms into the straps and swung it across her back. She stepped over to the giant wolf and began to get on his back.

Then, suddenly she leapt off and ran towards the gulley. Rhamin stood up and watched what she was doing. She was gone about a minute before returning to find that Rhamin had followed her. 'Come on then,' she shouted as she jumped up on Rhamin's back without waiting for him to lie down. Quickly, she sat astride his broad shoulders and latched firmly onto his thick coat with her fingers. 'What about Charka?' she asked suddenly aware that the injured wolf could not possible keep up with them.

'Rasci said she'll hide in a hollow. The men will be following us. She'll make her way home when the way is clear.' Ben looked at Elsie. 'She'll be okay, honest.'

Elsie frowned. Then looking beyond Ben and Margo, she spotted the cloud of dust thrown up by the SUV. It was racing towards them and would be there in less than a minute. Suddenly exhilarated by the whole adventure, her face became less serious. She smiled at first and then, contemplating the thrill of the chase, the smile broadened into a confident grin. 'Come on then,' she said with a new trill in her voice. 'What are we waiting for?'

The SUV only gained slowly on the fleeing wolves and their riders. The black clouds had turned to rain and were spotting the ground with heavy droplets of water. The windscreen of the SUV was coated in dust thrown up by the spinning wheels and the miles of dusty ground and, combined with a sparse scattering of rain drops, made a thick paste that coated the glass as the windscreen wipers tried to clear it.

Their pursuers were clearly in sight when Rhamin reached the base of the rocky slope, a few strides ahead of the others. He bounded over the steep bottom ledge and up the sloping rock face. Elsie struggled to hold on to his coat as she slid down his back. Realizing how difficult it was going to be for her to remain hanging onto his coat going down the other side of the slope, he stopped just before the ridge and lay down for his passenger to climb off. The other two, Rasci and Smokey had stopped at the bottom of the escarpment. Seeing Rhamin let Elsie climb down, they did the same and let Ben and Margo put their feet on the ground once again. Without needing to be told, and pulled along by holding onto Rasci's coat, Ben and Margo clambered up the wet, slippery slope and over the ridge. They looked back across the plain. The SUV was only a couple of hundred yards behind them. Despite having to keep washing the mud-streaked windscreen, its occupants had been able to keep their quarry clearly in sight. The wolves had not been able to shake them off. Quickly, and still clinging to Rasci for support, Ben and Margo slid and scrambled down to the mouth of the cave. Smokey followed by their sides. She too was making sure that the little children didn't slip or fall. As they looked at the opening of the Darin, more wolves emerged.

'Hello,' Lexa said as she stepped out into the open air. 'Fancy meeting you here!'

'We've got trouble,' Rasci stated hurriedly, breaking into Lexa's light-hearted mood.

'Well we have a little of the same,' Lexa said smiling. 'There are…'

'What?' Rasci broke in desperately. He needed to know what she was talking about but didn't have time to be playful.

'I'll explain later,' Lexa said, recognising Rasci's anguish. She tilted her head and pricked up her floppy ears. 'I presume what I hear is *your* trouble?' she asked.

The sound of the SUV roaring up to the bottom of the escarpment fixed everybody's attention.

'Quickly,' Rhamin commanded. 'All inside. As fast as you can.'

All the wolves bounded back inside the opening. Rhamin waited for the children to follow and then, with Smokey who had always considered it to be her role to protect the children, the big dog entered last, making sure that nothing or no one could reach the children without going through her first.

Smokey spun around and, with her head out of the mouth of the cave, sniffed the air. Slowly she backed inside and with her ears forward, her jaws slightly apart and her chest emitting a deep thundering growl she stood and guarded the entrance.

As Rhamin followed all the others into the dark cave, Elsie bent to pick something up.

'What's that?' Ben asked, his view obscured by the pack of milling wolves.

'A Maglite,' Elsie said, picking up a long black flashlight and testing it to see if it worked. A beam of light cut through the blackness.

'That's Daddy's,' Ben exclaimed. 'He must have left it here when he picked Charka up and carried her over the ridge.'

Elsie shone the beam of light around. The cave looked quite small at first. There was a cavern about twelve feet high and thirty feet long. At the back on the right, a small opening, perhaps two feet high led to another chamber which when Elsie shone the torch beam into it, turned out to be a space no bigger than small armchair. To the left of the cave a small spring filled a hollow and overflowed down a crack in the floor. Shining the beam around some more, she spotted something else in a corner by the side of the entrance. There, on the rocky floor of the cave, there was another torch and nearby, a rifle of some kind. 'So whose are these then?' she asked.

Ben shrugged. 'Must have belonged to the men who killed the bear,' he said, trying to piece together what had happened. He picked up the second torch and clicked it on. He scythed through the blackness with a thin shaft of light. 'This one works too.'

'Save it for now' Elsie instructed. 'Goodness knows how long we'll have to hide in here.' She clicked off her torch and Ben followed suit. Silently, they all stood where they were, staring at the daylight at the cave entrance.

But they weren't hiding and they all knew it. They were trapped. The people who had been chasing them knew exactly where the wolves, the dog and the children had gone. They were all refugees and they had all disappeared over a ridge in a rocky outcrop that broke the surface of the plain like so many other rocky outcrops in the miles and miles of wilderness. They had entered the cave, but there was nowhere to hide.

CHAPTER TWENTY NINE

'I can't believe it,' Raymond exclaimed as he read Elsie's note. He looked out of the window and saw that the station wagon had gone. 'She's only gone and driven off in the station wagon,' he shouted angrily. 'I didn't expect kidnapping and auto theft to be on this girl's CV when we agreed to look after her!'

'This girl? She's flesh and blood Ray, not somebody who we've taken on as an odd jobber.'

'Well I'm not bothered what she is. She's back home on the next plane when we catch up to her.'

'Now just calm down Raymond,' Maria said firmly. 'Getting worked up isn't going to solve the problem, is it?'

'Worked up! I'm not worked up Maria, I'm absolutely livid!' He limped over to the dining chair and sat down heavily. 'Not only has she stolen our vehicle, she has taken our two children with her on her mindless escapade.' He looked around. 'Where's Smokey?'

Maria shrugged, trying to be less frantic than she felt. 'She's probably gone with them. You know what she's like.'

'Oh great!' Raymond still gesticulated, shaking his head. 'She knows that there are people out there who don't care who they hurt. She saw me get shot in the leg. What is she thinking?'

'We've done everything to convince her that we can communicate with wolves, Ray. All she's doing is trying to do what you failed to do; get them back home.'

'And just how does she reckon she can do any better?'

'Look, what's done is done. She's got the station wagon. We are stuck here. You'll just have to call the police.'

'Oh great. Then all hell will be let loose.' He thought for a moment. 'I'll go after her,' he said eventually. 'But I'm going armed.'

'And just how do you reckon you'll do that? It's a long walk!'

'I'll go in the Jeep,' Raymond grunted.

'Since you did it up you haven't even let it see daylight. *Can't take it out. It hasn't to get a speck of dirt on it,* you said.'

'This is different now Maria. They're in danger.'

'Yes, you're absolutely right,' Maria conceded. 'But are you up to driving all that way and back?'

Raymond looked at her for a second. 'I reckon you'll be doing the driving.'

'Me! I haven't even been allowed to sit in it!'

'All right,' Raymond shouted. 'It was my special pet project. Now are we going or not?'

Maria nodded. 'I'll get your gun. If they shoot at us again, then you shoot back. Do you hear?'

CHAPTER THIRTY

Rhamin was looking at all his wolves. Most of them seemed to be there, but then he noticed that one in particular was missing; one that rarely ventured far from the cave. 'Where's Zelda?' he asked, looking at Lexa.

'That's what I was going to tell you about,' Lexa answered. 'She said she knew that some wolves were going to come and kill her when we all left to go hunting.'

'Some wolves?'

'Solin. But she was rather strange. She said he was coming to kill her but it wouldn't be him.'

'It wouldn't? Then who did she say it would be?'

'She didn't actually say.'

'So what are you telling me here?'

'She's telling you that Zelda had a plan,' Yeltsa came in.

'And?'

'And we carried it out,' Yeltsa continued. 'We all left the Darin and went as if we were heading north to go hunting in the foothills. Then we were to turn around when we got there and come back.'

'And the assassins would come inside the Darin and try to find her,' Silvah continued. 'But of course, once they were inside the cave then we would have *them* trapped.'

Rhamin sighed. 'So what are you telling me? Have they come inside our home?'

'Oh yes,' said Lexa enthusiastically.

'And, getting back to my first question, where is Zelda?'

'She's, well she's…'

'She's led them deep into the caves, Rhamin,' Yeltsa explained. 'Zelda has been exploring them for ages now. Not with her eyes of course, but with her other senses; smell; touch; even hearing.'

'And Zelda is somewhere in there with some of our enemies between her and safety?' Rhamin asked incredulously.

Yeltsa shook her head. 'Zelda was confident they would not catch her.'

'And you believed that?'

'Solin and his gang were going to strike sometime when we left the Darin. And you know what all creatures that are threatened say: *Attack is the best means of defence*. You know that to be true, Rhamin. We never try to bring down a buffalo that charges at us do we? And without you here, we had to decide how to handle the situation.'

Before Rhamin could take the discussion further, Rasci rushed from the mouth of the cave. 'The men are coming over the ridge,' he barked so that every wolf could hear.

Elsie didn't hear the words of course. All she heard was the warning bark. 'Right,' she said, determined to end this situation of men chasing wolves once and for all. She marched over to the mouth of the cave and stood there, with her hands on her hips, watching as the first of the men slid down the incoming slope.

The man was tall and spindly but seemed fit and agile as

he descended. He seemed rather surprised that Elsie was standing there confronting him. As he reached the bottom of the incline he planted his feet firmly on the ground and, standing less than two paces from Elsie, stood up straight and said, 'Where are your parents?'

Of course! They must think that a grown up drove us here, she thought quickly. 'Protecting the wolves,' she snapped back as another man reached the top of the escarpment and sat on the ridge with a gun on his lap.

The first man took a stride forward but Elsie stood her ground. Suddenly, he reached out quickly. 'Gotcha,' he shouted as he grabbed hold of Elsie's shoulder.

Rhamin saw what had happened and instantly bounded forward but, at the same time, a shot rang out from the gun of the man up on the ridge. Rhamin felt the warm air move his coat as the hot invisible tooth sped past his face and hit the rock by his feet, making him spin off to the left. The bullet ricocheted off the hard floor and whined as it travelled back up past his side and bounced off the cliff face behind him. Suddenly he remembered vividly the hot metal tooth that had nicked Silvah's face as she was carrying him to safety when he was a small pup. He looked up at the man who had fired the weapon. He was sliding something back on the gun. A piece of hot shiny metal ejected and spun into the air. Knowing he had only a second to reach his target, Rhamin spun back to face the rocky incline and raced up the slope towards him. The ejected cartridge was still coming down, seemingly in slow motion as Rhamin flashed past it. As it rattled onto the rocks by Rhamin's side, the man had already pushed part of the weapon forward, latched it down and was lifting the gun to his shoulder again. His actions were fast but Rhamin was faster. Astonished by the sheer size and speed of the wolf and startled by his blackness and the white ears that pointed forward as it sprung upwards at him with a mouth full of long, deadly fangs, he lost his balance and fell backwards just as Rhamin's jaws lashed out at him. The slope had no hand or foot holds to stop the fall. The man somersaulted and tumbled all the way to the bottom, sprawling awkwardly onto the ground as he dropped off the bottom ledge and hit the floor with a breath-snatching thud. Rhamin only watched the fall for an instant, making sure he knew where the man was and then bounded back down the slope towards Elsie. But he needn't have worried about the man who had attacked her.

Incredibly Elsie had taken hold of the man's hand and not only lifted it off her shoulder but had somehow twisted it so that the man was bent over with his face level with Elsie's waist. He had reached into a leather pouch on his hip with his free hand and had drawn out a small hand weapon but he'd had no time to lift it up to use it before Smokey had savaged his arm. Now on his knees with Elsie holding one arm and the heavy weight of Smokey pulling down on the other, the man was cursing and shouting for help from his comrades.

'Leave him,' Rhamin ordered. 'Everybody back in the cave.'

'But I have him,' Smokey protested.

'There are more of them over the ridge and the next time they'll come with weapons. All of them.'

Knowing that Elsie was in as much danger as the wolves, Rhamin grabbed the arm that Elsie had twisted. Looking into her eyes, he tugged it to tell her to leave go. The man yelled again with the pain of Rhamin's iron grip as the wolf's teeth pierced his forearm, but somehow Elsie understood what he wanted. Breathing heavily and trying to regain her breath from the exertion, she let go and scampered into the cave.

They weren't in the sanctuary of the Darin more than a couple of seconds before two shots rang out from the ridge, sending more hot teeth of death down at the disappearing animals. The invisible missiles bounced off the cliff face, narrowly missing Rhamin's back legs as he bounded into the opening and disappeared from sight.

'We can't fight them,' Rasci barked. 'They will kill us all.'

'Then we join Zelda,' Rhamin decided. 'We go deeper into the caves.'

CHAPTER THIRTY ONE

Elsie was shaken. What was the man's intention when he grabbed her? And if he was after the wolves then shooting at Rhamin seemed to totally defeat the whole object of trying to capture him. She had already decided to look at the back of the cave. Unless she could find some way out of this trap or at least somewhere to hide then, inevitably, the men would find her or Ben or Margo, or any of the wolves that they wanted. She clicked on the Maglite and walked past the milling wolves.

It was the first time Rasci, or indeed any of the inhabitants of the Darin had ever seen the inside of their home so clearly. When the torch was switched on, every facet of the surrounding rock stood out in all its magnificence. Wavy wings of creamy rock decorated the ceiling in the far corner of the cave. The hole where Yeltsa had her babies glistened with tiny white crystals where the constant rubbing of her and the cubs' fur had polished the rock as smooth as still pond water. But what caught his attention was a picture on the cavern wall. It showed a man with a long pointed stick, facing a long horned antelope. He didn't recognize the type of antelope but the painting looked so real that the man and the creature seemed to be leaping out of the cave wall. Even more remarkable was that the painting clearly depicted several wolves at the man's side. They were not hunting him, they were hunting *with* him.

At the back of the cave there was a narrow gorge, perhaps wide enough for even Rhamin to squeeze through, but so far back that neither he nor any of the sighted wolves had ever gone through it to see what lay beyond. He knew now why Zelda had gone there. She could not see inside the Darin, the place that all the wolves called their home. Travelling a few yards further into another unknown cavern or passageway would have been no challenge to blind old Zelda.

Rasci took the lead. He wanted to be in front of Elsie. He knew there were other wolves in the blackness that could be a danger to the young adventurer. Ben and Margo kept close to Elsie's back, Ben clinging onto her loose shirt tail and Margo holding onto Ben's free hand. Smokey followed next, brushing against the legs of her wards as she constantly tried to make sure that she was right where she needed to be if any danger approached from the front. Lexa followed Smokey after giving her a quick lick on the nose, a swift greeting that she had not had chance to give in the turmoil of the events that were unfolding. The other wolves followed on in a thin line, at the rump of which Rhamin held the rear guard. He turned and watched the opening to the Darin until his wolves had made their way some distance along the passage. The light from Elsie's distant torch faded as it bounced around the twisted gorge and reflected off the glimmering cave walls. Before he lost the light completely, but not before he saw the men approaching the mouth of the cave, all carrying their deadly weapons, Rhamin turned and bounded after the line of wolves.

The narrow gorge sloped downwards as it twisted to the right and then to the left. Then, when the roof of the passage seemed like it was going to get too low for Rhamin to pass through, the floor dropped down gradually again and the tunnel suddenly opened out into another large cave.

Despite the danger behind, and the dire sense of urgency to keep going forward, the wolves and children alike could not help pausing to take in what they were seeing. Elsie had adjusted the light beam to pan out rather than shine in a narrow pencil beam. There were giant pillars of cream coloured rock rising from the floor to the ceiling which was some twenty or so feet above their heads. There were long walls of rock that seemed to be of the same construction only they waved like hedges of a maze through the whole cavern. Stalactites hung down like huge icicles of water hanging from the cliffs during the harsh winter and, pointing up towards them, stalagmites reached up like arms grasping to touch the formations that hung from the ceiling.

'Keep going,' Rhamin barked from the rear as he finally moved from the narrow passage into the newly discovered cave. But even he paused momentarily to see the magnificence of this magic underworld.

Elsie, Ben and Margo knew they had to keep pushing forward without understanding Rhamin's commands. She shone the torch around to find some way through, some exit that would take them out of the cavern but away from the men who, even now, she knew were still hunting them. Pacing around the cavern, she realized there was no exit. There were no passage ways heading out except for the one at the point of entry. A waterfall fell into a pool at one side of the cave, but its access was a mere crack a few inches high above a slab of solid rock. She sighed. 'Dead end,' she groaned, pushing her hair back from her face and putting her arm around Margo's shoulder.

Ben clicked on his own torch. There had to be somewhere to hide, even if they could go no further. 'Over there,' he shouted suddenly as he panned his torch beam around the cavern. Holding it steady, he pointed it high up onto the rock wall above the cascade of water. His sharp eyes had spotted something quite extraordinary. There, behind a curve in the cave wall that had originally cast a dark shadow over it as Elsie swung her torch beam around, was a magnificent picture of a buffalo. 'Wow,' he exclaimed. 'Look at that!' Then he added, 'I wonder who painted these pictures.' Then after another moment's thought he said, 'I wonder how they got up there.'

'Ben, you're a genius,' Elsie exclaimed. She ran over to the wall and stood beneath the painting. Behind a huge barrier of calcined rock and to the right of the waterfall, a crudely carved stairway led up the side of the wall. From the outside of the stairway the small waterfall sprang from its crack in the rock face and tumbled down in a glass sheet to a hollow where the water gathered in a dip and then spilled over and disappeared down another narrow crack in the floor. 'People have lived here in these caves,' Elsie cried out. 'I've read about cave paintings somewhere,' she commented as she peered upwards. 'But they have made a way to an upper cavern, look!'

At the top of the stone carved stairway, another hole in the rock led out of the cavern. Elsie ran to go up the steps when Smokey's deep growling bark stopped her in her tracks. There, at the top of the carved steps, and peering out into the cave was the face of a wolf Smokey would recognise any day. She had seen it when she had joined in the fight with the mountain lions. This wolf had ears that had been torn to shreds.

Hearing Smokey bark, Rasci and Lexa bounded forward. Solin just stood there, not aggressive, not submissive. He turned his head and said something to somebody behind him. Slowly, Rhiana and Roxana appeared beside him.

'So these are the assassins,' Lexa called for all to hear. 'These are the cowardly wolves that entered our home when we were away. They came here with the sole purpose of killing a helpless old wolf.'

'Rubbish,' Solin countered. 'Old, yes. Helpless! She's as cunning and deadly as she ever was. She's a snake in a tattered wolf's coat.'

A wicked chuckle echoed around the caves. 'Zelda!' Rasci called out, his voice heavy with relief. 'Is that you?'

'It is, my lovely young protégé,' the same voice answered from somewhere, but just from where, it was impossible to tell.

'Well, what is your sentence, Rhamin?' Solin demanded. 'I don't want to be hanging around in this damp hole all day. We saw and had enough of it with the light out.'

'Kill them,' Lexa growled, lunging forward. 'I'll do it.'

Solin bared his teeth and stood his ground.

'Stop!' Rhamin commanded. 'Zelda is safe.' He turned to all his pack. 'And we need all the wolves we've got. At the end of this day we may be a lot fewer than we are now. We are up against a deadly foe. At the moment we are running for our lives, but if we are cornered or trapped, then we will be *fighting* for our lives.'

He turned to face the renegade wolves at the top of the stairway. 'Join us today and if we are still alive when this is over then you may go free. You have my word.'

Everyone knew that when Rhamin swore an oath then

he never went back on it.

'Well, what will it be?' he demanded.

'We were just on our way out,' Solin said, a wicked grin flashing on his teeth in the meagre light. 'But I suppose we can stay and help you out if you can't manage without us.'

'Help us out! You...'

But Rhamin stopped Lexa from finishing. 'Quiet!' he barked. 'I'll have no dissent.' He looked back up at Solin and his companions. 'I haven't forgotten what you did or even now what you have been plotting. And Lexa bears the scars to remind everybody of your treachery. But I take your answer as being that you are joining us. You leave when we know all who remain alive are safe. Double cross me and the sentence is death. And that is my oath. We will all make it our life's ambition to hunt you down and kill you, all three of you.'

'Well we've mooched around up here for long enough now, and this way doesn't offer any way forward,' Solin announced. Neither Rhiana nor Roxana spoke. 'I reckon you'll...' He paused. '*We'll* be fighting our way out anyway.'

Rhamin tilted his head to Ramusan. 'Go and have a look,' he said, looking at Elsie. She understood what was happening. She saw the big young wolf head up the rocky steps and, with her torch in her hand and following Ramusan, she climbed up past Solin. The renegade just stepped aside to let them pass. A minute or so later, Elsie returned to the top of the stairs and, with a look of total dismay and resignation on her face, she shook her head. Ramusan called from behind her. 'Total dead end,' he barked.

Rhamin blew out a heavy sigh. He knew how everybody felt. His heart had sunk and so must those of all his companions. For a minute they were all silent, contemplating the battle that was to ensue. Rhamin turned to look back along the passage that had led them there. He could clearly hear the men talking as they followed along the same route.

'Try this way,' Zelda's voice broke the silence and echoed once again around the cavern. But her voice didn't come from behind Elsie or the wolves at the top of the steps.

Every set of eyes scanned the cavern. Then, slowly a white-grey muzzle poked out through the falling sheet of water. Unhurriedly, a head appeared as the water separated around her neck and rejoined again to continue as if it had never been interrupted, giving her head the appearance of being disembodied and mounted on a glass panel. 'Looking for me?' Zelda asked, sniffing at the air and glancing around with her sightless eyes.

Rasci was the first to greet her. 'I've been worried about you Gran,' he said, giving her a reassuring lick on the side of her head as she stepped through the cascade. Her thick water repellent coat seemed as dry as ever it was.

'Oh, I can look after myself, young wolf. You don't have to worry about me.'

'I can see that,' Rasci agreed, giving her another affectionate lick. He had remained unduly quiet for the last few minutes, trying to get his thoughts together about these insurgents who had double crossed and betrayed the pack more than once before. From now on he was going to stay next to his Gran. He had no qualms about killing any of the three renegades if they came anywhere near her again.

Elsie lost no time examining the hole behind the sheet of water. 'There's another passageway,' she called as, totally disregarding the water, she stepped through it and disappeared with the light. Her torch threw out an eerie glow from behind and through the cascade of water, making its glittering light spread out around the whole cavern in shimmering patterns and shadows.

Ben switched his torch back on for more light as Margo stepped through the water helped by a hand that appeared and then disappeared through the wet veil. Then, as Ben held the light, Smokey followed, and without any instruction all the other wolves trailed in line. The renegades went last except for Rhamin who followed the troupe with Ben who still kept his torch switched on.

Rhamin had told Solin that he was welcome to go back the way they had come. But he, Rhiana and Roxana would have no lights to see their way back and, most certainly, they would encounter the enemy from whom they were all fleeing. None of them had taken up the offer.

Eventually, Rhamin and Ben joined his sister and his cousin. The floor of the pothole had risen and fallen a few times as they scrambled along and over it, but after a few minutes the floor levelled, the walls widened out and a fork appeared in the passageway up ahead. Slowly, the group gathered behind Elsie.

Elsie took the route of the biggest passage which looked the most promising but she soon turned and shouted back to Ben. 'No room to get through here,' she called out as she came to a steep incline which had a row of flat and narrow crevices where the floor met the ceiling. 'I doubt if Margo could even get through this gap.' As her torch beam shone back over the top of the wolves, they all turned and went back the way they had come. Disappointed, she indicated to all that she was retracing her steps and doing so, and with a heavy heart and fearing the worst, she then proceeded to follow the smaller narrower fork in the passage. Her heart sank even more as the ceiling became lower and lower until she was walking bent over at the waist. The passage went on and on but didn't seem to change much in size. The floor of the passage had a groove on it as if water had at some time worn it away. But other than that, the route seemed endless. Neither she nor any of her companions knew how long they had been walking along this never-ending hole in the ground.

Elsie was beginning to wish she had brought her watch but she had left it behind in her urgent attempt to get the wolves out and away from the farm. She couldn't help feeling the pangs of fear that were slowly seeping into her soul. She had no idea how long she had been in this narrow pothole; ten minutes? An hour? But she soldiered on, keeping her nerve only because she needed to reassure Ben and Margo that she would get them out of this mess. She had got them into all this. Now she felt responsible for getting them out. Without that responsibility, she would have curled up in a ball and cried long before now. She wondered whether, if they retraced their steps, the men would have gone by now. But that thought was abruptly ended when she heard men's voices echoing around the cavern with the wall paintings. They were only at the rear end of this never-ending passage. She hoped and prayed that they didn't find the pothole behind the waterfall. She was thankful that, somehow, all the wolves, the dogs, as well as Ben and Margo, all knew they had to be totally silent. Any noise they made would surely travel back along the passage like a message in a telephone wire. With nowhere else to go, the sound would reverberate and echo backwards into the cavern the same way that Zelda's startling bark had done.

She was just beginning to question the wisdom of ever entering the cave in the first place. But where could they have hidden in the open plain. Their pursuers could and would have followed them anywhere. With a resigned sigh and realizing that the position they were all in could possibly have been worse, though how much worse, she had no idea, she plodded on. No, it could have been much worse, she muttered to herself as the ceiling of the passageway became high enough for her to walk upright once again. But the relief of being in a bigger space was soon overtaken when she realized that the floor of the passage had become much wetter.

CHAPTER THIRTY TWO

At first the water was just on the surface of the rocky floor but, gradually it got deeper until they were all splashing along, ankle deep in water. Perhaps it couldn't have been much worse, she was deciding, when, suddenly, the hole, along which they were all trudging, opened up, slightly at first and then, began to widen out into yet another cavern. She kept on walking. Still, the water washed around her ankles, even deeper now. Eventually, shining the torch downwards to see where she was going, she realized that, somehow, the light beam was spreading wider. She was able to see more and more as she went further into the cave.

A few paces later and she gazed upon a huge cavern. Its roof, as high as the inside of any church, became lighter and lighter even though she kept the torch beam pointed downwards to see where she was walking. She had read too many stories about people falling into bottomless pits inside tunnels and caves. She was going to make sure that such an event did not happen to her. Suddenly, as she moved forward, the floor of this cave began to rise and once again, with squelching trainers, she was heading the troupe back up onto dry ground. The floor seemed to shine more than the floors of the other caves. But the light it was reflecting was coming not from her torch, but from high above. As she reached halfway across the cavern, she turned around and then, clicking off her flash light for a moment, and still facing the oncoming assembly, she gazed back towards them. She could still see.

The dogs and wolves and her little cousins were eventually emerging in single file from the shallow water and joining her on the dry rock floor. When they got to her they turned and faced the rest of the oncoming wolves. But then, averting their eyes to the right, they gazed into the cavern in astonishment. It wasn't just the fact that there was light somewhere in this underground vault, light emanating from somewhere other than either her or Ben's torches, but the whole shape of the place was unsettling. Elsie saw the expressions on Ben's and Margo's faces as they stood beside her. Looking up from the floor now properly for the first time, and seeing what they were seeing, she gazed in wonder.

Off to the right of the entrance through which they had arrived, was a smaller cavern, a cave that was perhaps the height of a double-decker bus. But it was no ordinary cave.

They were all looking at a remarkable work of art.

Elsie hadn't seen it until she had turned back around. But now, it was all she could see. From the roof of the bigger cavern a huge rock form protruded and pointed downwards towards them and as she considered it, more and more it looked like the giant muzzle of a wolf. Between the top of the protrusion and the roof, part of the formation looked like it had formed, or had even been carved, to look like a wolf's face. Below the muzzle was a gaping wide mouth.

The roof of the mouth was part of the roof of the cavern,

or so it seemed. It was lit, as was the roof of the rest of the cavern, by thousands of tiny pin-point lights except, that inside this huge mouth, the lights all gathered along ridges that crossed from one side to the other, ridges like those on the roof of a wolf's mouth. At the front of the muzzle, a fan of stalactites formed the top front teeth and rows of similar fan-like features formed the upper back teeth. Two huge stalactites formed the two upper canines, pointing down to two stalagmites which in turn formed the upward pointing bottom, long teeth of the wolf's jaw. The bottom jaw mirrored the one above. More rock formations that seemed as if they could only have been carved rather than formed by the drip-drop of thousands of years of mineral laden water formed the bottom jaw and all its teeth.

'Wow,' Margo gasped. Of all the youngsters, throughout the whole ordeal, she had shown less fear than any. 'What a fantastic cave!'

'Are you okay?' asked Elsie.

Margo smiled and nodded happily as if she were on a day out at an amusement park. 'What are all those lights?' she asked, pointing upwards.

'Some kind of firefly, perhaps,' Elsie pondered. 'Or some kind of luminous bacteria. There are lots of luminous things in the world. Most of them live in the darkest depths of the ocean. You'd be able to read a book by the light of a single deep sea angler fish.'

'Gosh!' Margo said as she went closer to her cousin.

Elsie could see that Margo had something else on her mind.

'How did you do that thing with the man's hand?' she asked. The whole movement had been flitting through her mind ever since it had happened.

'Ju-jitsu,' Elsie replied, as she examined one of the upright, bottom canine teeth.

'Your daddy showed you that!'

'My mother taught me that when I wasn't much older than you are now.' Still she examined the tooth. It must have been six feet high.

'Your mummy. Wow!' Margo exclaimed in awe. 'Your mummy taught you all that!'

Then suddenly Ben noticed what had caught Elsie's attention. The huge canine teeth of the massive wolf's head were not the same as the other light, creamy coloured calcium based rock formations. The canines were much darker in the dim light. They were a bluish colour. Clicking on her torch again, Elsie walked closer to one of the upright teeth. She could see as the light passed through the rock pillar that it was not just one but various shades of blue. She put her face close up to it and passed the torch around to the opposite side. She marvelled as the torch-light shone through what seemed like an artificial stalagmite, refracting and dispersing, making it look truly magnificent as the light bounced and echoed within it from crystal to crystal. She felt it. It was as hard but not as smooth and as cold as all the other rock formations in the cavern. It seemed to be made up of hundreds of interlocking crystals but how they were formed she could not tell. Had they been put there, she wondered? There were no signs of dripping water. She switched off her torch again. There seemed no point in wasting the batteries.

Rhamin and Rasci gazed up at the awesome mouth. It looked so real. Even the curled, arched tongue seemed to be the right shape in a snarling wolf's mouth. Somehow, the muzzle hung from the top of the cavern, so realistically that the head looked like it had poked, like Zelda's, through a veil of water. But what welded all the wolves to the spot were the eyes; wild eyes; deep yellow eyes wide with anger.

CHAPTER THIRTY THREE

Despite standing on one leg and having to hold onto the Jeep with one hand, it only took a few minutes for Raymond to connect the battery onto the Jeep and start it up. Every few minutes though, he had to stop to catch his breath. The pain killers he had taken were definitely not helping him concentrate on his work. Unless he was lying down, the tablets made him feel sick. They would wear off soon, he thought, determined to take no more until he had recovered his family.

With his hunting rifle safely stowed behind him, he sat back in the passenger seat and, with a wave of his hand, he indicated to Maria that they should start their long drive to the wolves' lair.

But they hadn't gone far when they discovered that the doctor had called the police. Their car was heading up the farm road as Maria drove towards the boundary.

It took a few minutes to explain what had been going on. He told the two officers that he and the children had been shot at by some men in a black SUV. He explained that a man called Petersen, although trying to steal live wolves was managing to kill everything else around him. But he did explain that, had it not been for Petersen and his men in the helicopter, then Raymond and his family might have all been killed. He explained what Elsie had done, keeping the reason for her taking the station wagon brief. There was no time to explain too much to the policemen, although, no doubt, they had been given some details about the mad family that had wolves in their house.

After a few more minutes explaining where they were heading, and declining a ride with the police officers, the police car fell in line and began to follow the Jeep across the dry, dusty plain and on towards the cave that was the home of the wolves.

CHAPTER THIRTY FOUR

'We need to know where the men are,' Rhamin stated plainly as he spoke quietly into Rasci's ear. 'This cavern is huge, and even if we find another way out, it may be a dead end like before. We have to find the right way forward, but we can't afford to be trapped. If they are coming behind us then we have to move on.'

Finding it difficult to drag his eyes off the massive blue toothed wolf, Rasci turned his head and walked to a quiet part of the cave. Within seconds he was meditating. For a long while he studied what he was seeing in his mind. The two men who he had seen before with protective head gear and with lights that shone from that headwear, were up to their waists in water, wading along a passage not unlike the one along which Rasci and the whole of the Rhamin pack had just travelled. He shook his head to try and clear his thoughts. Surely, these men had nothing to do with what was happening at the moment in this cave complex.

Gradually his mind focussed on the Darin, the first cave in this chain of caverns which all the wolves had called their home. It was empty. No men, No wolves. But there was light coming from the back of the cave. There were men with torches in the narrow gorge that had carried Rhamin, his pack and the children out of harms way. They were coming back, getting close to the cave now. Then they emerged, three of them. They walked across the cave floor to the entrance. It was then that Rasci noticed a fourth man sitting in the opening to the cave, looking outside, just watching the rain. He had bandages on both arms. One of the men called to him. What was he saying? Rasci concentrated harder.

'The caves are flooding.' His voice was clear now.

'Told you they would if these storm clouds reached here,' the man at the entrance stated. 'This outcrop of limestone is part of a broken chain of outcrops that form an escarpment running all the way to those foothills to the north.'

'And?'

'And the water doesn't appear to run off into any rivers around here, does it?'

'Meaning,' the other man still queried.

'Meaning that it goes down sink holes and runs underground.'

'So your conclusion is?'

'We wait and see what happens. When the passage ways beyond this cave are flooded to the top then I reckon that the flood waters will have done our job for us.'

The other man smiled and nodded.

Rasci snapped back to consciousness. Focussing his eyes and swinging his head around to see where Rhamin was, he found him standing with his back to him, looking at and studying the giant blue teeth.

'We have to get out!' Rasci exclaimed.

'I think we are all very aware of that,' Rhamin replied, turning back to face his brother.

'Urgently,' Rasci added.

Rhamin just continued to look at Rasci. He knew an explanation was coming.

'The caves are flooding. It is raining outside and the water we went through to get here is already filling up the passageway. It will soon be too late to go back out.'

'It has always been too late to go back out that way,' Rhamin said with emphasis. He thought for a moment. 'That means the men can't get to us now either,' he said, a pensive look crossing his face. 'We are safe for the time being.'

'But we don't know if there is another way out.'

'Then we wait for the water to go down again. It won't rain forever.'

'And what if the men are still there with their deadly weapons? What then?'

'Hmm.' Rhamin pondered the remarks. 'Back to plan A then. We fight until either they are all dead or we are all dead. Simple really'

Quickly Rhamin gathered his wolves around him. Lexa had always been a wolf. Smokey was honorary wolf until they resumed their normal lives. And the same applied to Elsie. Ben and Margo were already honorary wolves and part of his pack. Now Elsie had been bestowed with that title too.

'It's up to you Rasci to tell Ben what is going on. We must find an exit and we must do it sooner rather than later. Tell all the wolves to spread out. Even Zelda. Don't leave a single part of this huge cavern undiscovered. Although subdued, there's plenty of light for our eyes and it seems like Ben and his family are able to see quite well. As a last resort they can use their light sticks if they can't see so well.'

Leaving Rasci to convey the message to Ben, the rest of the wolves spread out to every corner of the cavern.

Solin watched and listened as Ben talked to an imaginary friend. 'I understand, Rasci,' Ben said nodding his head. 'I'll tell Elsie and Margo.'

Solin glanced at Rasci who, instead of hunting in a corner or a crevice, was lying with his head on his paws, eyes open, but seeing nothing as he stared blankly at the cave wall. He grunted to himself but said nothing to Rasci. Solin decided he wouldn't say anything to his fellow insurgents, Rhiana and Roxana either.

As Rasci came out of his trance, he lifted his head and listened. Something had changed. The wolves squeaked odd comments to themselves, relaying what they had found, or in particular what they hadn't found. Ben was chatting to Elsie whilst Margo was following Smokey about. Ben didn't want to worry his little sister with what he had to tell Elsie.

But the background noise seemed different. In fact Rasci hadn't really noticed any background noise earlier. Now there was a definite deep rumble. No place specific. It was as if the whole cavern was making the sound.

'Rhamin,' he called as his leader turned to look at him.

Rhamin tilted his head in acknowledgement. 'Yes?'

'Do you notice the sound?'

Rhamin thought for a moment, shook his head and concentrated. 'Hmm. Yes I can hear it now you've mentioned it. What is it?'

Rasci shrugged and shook his head. 'I think it may be the rainwater.'

Rhamin looked around. 'Where's Zelda?'

'Over there,' Vela replied, facing to where Zelda was following the base line of the cavern with her nose.

Rhamin went over to the old wolf and stood next to her. Without his speaking, she knew he was there. 'Yes, my young wolf?' she said, lifting her head and gazing sightlessly at him.

'The noise. Have you any ideas?'

Zelda knew exactly to what Rhamin was referring. 'It's water. The caves are flooding. The rain is here to stay.'

'How far did you get when you explored these caves before?'

'Not as far as this, that's for sure. That passageway that we've just come up went on so long that I gave up and I turned around. I thought I'd never get back for dinner!'

Despite the seriousness of their predicament, Rhamin chuckled.

'There is a way out,' Zelda continued. I've seen it in my mind. But I'm afraid I don't know where it is and…' She broke off and cleared her throat.

'And?'

'Oh it doesn't matter. It isn't important.' Her voice was shaking; only slightly, but Rhamin noticed the slight quaver.

'Are you all right Zelda?' he asked, pushing his nose against her grey muzzle.

She was silent for a second before she answered. 'I'm fine,' she said and turned her head away.

'What were you going to say old girl?'

'As I said, it wasn't important.'

'Everything is important at the moment, Zelda. Any

information. Anything at all.'

Zelda looked down at the floor. 'I'll tell you anything you need to know. You know you can trust me on that.' She thought for a while. Rhamin was still there, waiting, listening. She knew. 'Is there anything unusual about this cave? There have been a few sounds of astonishment?'

Rhamin explained the shape of the huge rock formation and the colour of its teeth.

'That is very interesting.' She thought again for a few seconds and then went on, 'You've noticed that we have been going uphill for quite a while now as we've been travelling through this big cave?' she asked.

'It slopes up to the back there, yes.'

'And which way does the rock formation face?'

'Up to the back.'

'And what is facing towards it?'

'The back of the cave. There's a solid wall of rock which has steps leading up to it, long steep ledges more than steps.'

'And the wall is like the rest of the cave?'

Rhamin thought for a moment. He shook his head. 'No, it is straight up, not curved like most cave walls.' He looked at it some more. 'The ledges are all squared off as if they were steps but leading nowhere. Nothing looks like it. The rest of the caves haven't got a flat edge anywhere.'

'Then your way out is towards the top of the steps. There is no doubt about it.'

Rhamin knew better than to argue. Straight away he bounced up the incline and joined Yeltsa and Silvah who were already there. 'Anything here?' he asked as he reached them.

'Yeltsa shook her head. 'Doesn't seem like it.'

'Wait!' Lexa barked. She stood there stiller than the blue toothed rock image. 'There is air moving past us,' she declared suddenly.

She ran down the slope, barked and jumped on all fours in front of Elsie.

'We need you up here,' she barked and looked towards the higher ground.

It was the first time any of them had barked loudly. Elsie knew that Lexa was trying to tell her something.

As Lexa ran back towards Rhamin and Yeltsa, Elsie presumed she was to follow. At the top of the slope, Lexa just stood, floppy ears forward, willing Elsie to understand. She whined a little, trying to explain in her own language. But Elsie just shook her head.

'She's trying to tell you that she can feel a breeze,' Margo called from half way inside the huge wolf cavern.

Elsie licked her finger and held it in the air. Sure enough, one side felt colder than the rest of her finger. 'There's air moving towards that rock there,' she said pointing. 'It's the rising water,' she continued. 'It has already filled and blocked the passage. Air can't get out back that way so as the rising water fills the spaces it is causing the air in the cavern to compress and blow out through some other opening.'

The wolves watched her. Her antics with her finger had impressed Rasci but now he was looking at Margo. Somehow, he understood what Margo was thinking as she listened to Elsie.

But search as they may, the only place air was passing out of the chamber was through a long crack at the base of the top ledge.

Elsie shone her torch at the crack but it was too narrow for even a mouse to pass under it. She could see nothing. But the speed by which the air was pushing through the gap, seemed to be getting faster. Where she had first felt a slight draught, now there seemed to be a definite breeze. It meant only one thing; the water behind them was rising even faster.

CHAPTER THIRTY FIVE

'Where's Margo?' Elsie called to Ben. She scanned the huge cave. It was as wide as it was long. 'Have you seen where she's gone?'

Ben looked around. 'Last time I saw her she was sitting on Blue Tooth's tongue.'

'Blue Tooth?' Elsie smiled. 'Yes, of course.' She ran down the slope towards the blue stalagmites. Jumping over the front teeth she climbed up onto the curved tongue. The mouth sloped back down from the top of the tongue, twelve or fifteen feet into the back of its throat. The tongue was rough, just as a real one would be, full of tiny fleshy teeth that rasp at food when the tongue is licking it.

Margo was there looking at the walls. They were smooth and yet when Elsie looked again, at one time there had been some kind of characters carved onto them. They were not carved into the walls; they protruded from the walls in relief.

'What does it say?' Margo asked, walking along and looking closely at every character.

Elsie shrugged. 'I've never seen any writing like it before,' she said honestly.

'Not even in any of those thousands of books you told me

you had read?'

'Not even in one of them.'

'Wow!'

Rasci had followed Elsie over the tongue and into the wolf cavern. He noticed the characters and, remembering what Ben had said about being able to convey your messages without actually being there, he wondered what this writing said. But he could see Elsie studying it closely and he also noticed her shaking her head. Perhaps we will never know, he thought to himself and turned to go back out.

As he climbed over the tongue again, and walked past the enormous blue teeth, he glanced around to see what everyone was doing and where they were. But the cavern was vast and because it had huge, wavy, curtain-like walls running down from the ceiling to the floor, it wasn't possible to see more than two or three wolves at any one time. He did spot Solin, however, huddled in a corner, discussing something with Rhiana. Rasci didn't expect Roxana to be far from them. He trotted over to them. 'Planning your escape?' he growled. 'Only to be expected.'

Solin lifted his head suddenly as if he were uncomfortable being seen with his mother. 'We'll let you know when we find it,' he jousted back as he licked his lips and moved away from Rhiana slowly. 'It looks like there's no way out of here,' he commented more seriously. 'Unless we go back the way we came.'

'That's not an option now.' Rasci replied. 'Unless you're a good swimmer,' he added. He explained that the tunnel had already filled with water.

'What about that lake,' Solin said, pointing his nose to the very furthest corner of the cavern. 'That hasn't got any higher.'

Rasci just shrugged. As far as he was concerned Solin could head back if he wanted. His heart now heavy with despair, he walked some way across the cavern floor and found Rhamin. 'What do you reckon?'

'It's not looking good,' Rhamin said with a noticeable sigh of fatigue. 'There's got to be a way out if Zelda says there is. The trouble is, finding it.'

There was something playing on Rasci's mind. The lake. What had Solin said? The water in the lake wasn't getting any higher. Yet all the signs were that the water was rising rapidly everywhere else. 'Come with me Rhamin.' he said, heading to the far side of the cavern. There, as Solin had said, was a small lake nestling up against the furthest cave wall. From high in the wall a thin stream of water fell from a collection of small potholes and cascaded over rocks and crevices and finally, stirring and mixing with the water of the lake, travelled no more. 'I wonder how deep it is?' he pondered.

Rhamin looked at Rasci, puzzled. 'Not very deep I suppose. Why do you mention that?'

'Well, all the water in these caves is fed from streams that are filling up with the rain. Except this patch of water. It has a small stream falling into it but look,' he said, pointing with his nose to the rusty red tide mark along the rocks and across a small shingle beach. 'The water level looks like it has remained constant for ever. There's no stream or river taking the water away. Why isn't the lake getting higher? Why isn't it overflowing? Why?'

'I'm sure you are going to tell me,' Rhamin said, quite honestly believing Rasci was the most brilliant of wolves even though he was a fool in his spare time, at his meal times and at almost any other time as well.

Rasci just looked at his brother. 'If you wait a minute, I'll perhaps be able to tell you,' he said as he dived headlong into the crystal clear water and, breaking it into waves and ripples, he disappeared from view as his feet paddled vigorously.

Despite their dire situation, Rhamin couldn't help letting a smile trickle up the side of his long face. Rasci would always have something in his head to take a wolf's mind off its worries. He stood and waited. Then he waited some more. Then he fidgeted from one foot to another. Rasci had been down under that water now for over a minute. Another minute passed as Rhamin's face began to show grave concern. Lexa had joined him when she heard him give out a low whine. 'Come back brother,' he was saying quietly under his breath.

'What's the matter?' asked Lexa.

'It's Rasci. He dived in there and has drowned I think. He's been under the water for far too long to survive.'

Lexa squealed and ran to the side of the lake. She was about to dive in when Rhamin shouted. 'No! If Rasci has died, then we are not going to lose another wolf.'

'We are going to die anyway,' Lexa said philosophically. 'Perhaps today or tomorrow, if we are trapped in here. What have I got to lose?'

Rhamin felt defeated. How could he argue with that? He stood by Lexa a gazed down on the rippling water. They both stood there for a long time, watching and waiting. The surface of the water had become still again before they turned to leave.

Solin had wandered nearer to see what was going on, but he had kept a safe distance. He had no intention of getting in anybody's way, especially Rhamin's. He stood further down near a sandy bank and watched for a while before saying, 'His body is coming up. I can see it rising.'

Rhamin and Rasci spun around. Rhamin turned on Solin angrily. 'Keep your humour to yourself,' he barked, almost unable to stop himself from attacking him.

But Solin had been telling the truth. 'See for yourself,' he said as he looked towards a dim grey shadow rising from the depths of the water.

Rhamin put his face closer to the surface so that he could see if it was Rasci or just some illusion caused by the moving water and the twinkling light high up above. Then suddenly, right in the front of Rhamin's nose, Rasci's head broke through the surface of the water, lifted a good half of the length of his body into the air and, gulping in a lung full of air, splashed back down under the water. A second later he bobbed back up again, panting heavily, his eyes wide with excitement. 'I think we may have a way out,' he panted, paddling to the sand bank and pulling himself out. He shook himself vigorously, so much that he nearly lost his balance, and then, recovering his foothold on firm land, he turned to Solin. 'Sometimes I think you could have made it as a leader after all,' he said, and then, 'if you hadn't been such a fool.'

Solin grunted. He was in the firing line at the moment so he wasn't going to exchange insults.

'So are you going to explain why you've just shortened all our lives whatever day our end is due?' Rhamin said, anger in his voice, but utterly relieved.

'It was Solin's idea,' he said, shaking himself thoroughly again.

'Yeah, blame me won't you?' Solin responded, as if he fully expected any mishap to be put down to his interference.

Rhamin looked at Solin. 'I doubt if you forced him into the water. I was with him.'

'Okay, don't blame me then!'

Rasci smiled. 'There's another way out of here,' he began. 'But I couldn't tell if it went out of the ground or just out of this cavern. He tilted his head. 'Is it me or is that humming sound getting louder?'

They all stood and listened for a second or two and then Rhamin said, 'It's louder.'

'Thought so,' Rasci said, shaking his head to clear the last drops of water from his ears. 'The other problem is, it is impossible to tell if the tunnels are flooding at that side as well, so if we are going to try going that way, we had better get started.'

'But what about Elsie and Ben and little Margo?' asked Lexa.

'I'm going to explain it to them now,' Rasci said, and went a few yards up the side of the lake where the bank was steeper.

CHAPTER THIRTY SIX

'I can swim,' Ben said as Rasci explained what he had discovered.

'You'll have to hold your breath mind,' Rasci explained, though he didn't say for how long.

'But Margo can't swim,' Ben went on. 'Not under water.'

'Try and explain what we have to do,' Rasci instructed. 'Tell Elsie and tell Margo.'

Ben lost no time running to find Elsie. He told her about the discovery.

'We can't leave Margo behind,' Elsie said to Ben, as they went back to the Blue Tooth cavern to find his little sister.

Margo was just where she had last seen her, studying the writing on the walls.

Ben concentrated on a blank piece of air for a moment or two. Rasci's wolf spirit was still with him. 'Rasci says it's essential that the wolves go soon.'

'Then you go with them, Ben and I'll stay here with Margo until you get help.'

'But what if we don't get out?'

'Then Margo and I are no worse off.' Elsie took a hold of Ben's hand and led him to where Rasci was sitting. 'You must go now, Ben because the water is rising all the time.'

'We can't leave those two alone,' Rhamin stated, once all the messages had been relayed. 'One of us must remain with them.'

'That won't be a problem,' Smokey said. 'I will not leave them.'

'And I'll stay,' said Zelda. She had no intention of testing out her lungs at her age. She knew how much air she could take in when she tried to hold her breath. It wasn't very much.

Within less than six minutes, all the wolves had followed Rasci. He led the way with Ben holding his breath and hanging onto the thick fur on Rasci's neck with one hand and onto his torch with the other. Ben was coughing and spluttering when Rhamin arrived on the sandy bank where he was recovering. He had held his breath as long as he could and felt compelled to breath in seconds before Rasci bobbed up from the surface of the water in another cavern. He gasped for air as Rasci broke the surface of the water and, dropping the torch, he scrambled onto the wolf's back as he walked into the shallows. He knew then that little Margo would surely have drowned if she had followed.

He was surprised that this cavern, too, had the same little creatures, whatever they were, clinging to the ceiling and throwing a dim light down into the cave. But he realized he would need his torch at some stage. Knowing that he had dropped it only yards from the edge of the lake, and still soaking wet, he went to dive back in and retrieve it, but Yeltsa had seen it. She saw what Ben was about to do, and pushed past him and dived to get it. She came back to the surface but hadn't found it, so taking a few more good deep breaths, she dived down again. Ben waited, confident that he could find it, but after about half a minute, this time

Yeltsa surfaced with the torch in her mouth, she swam to the shallows and walking up to Ben she offered it to him as he patted her on the head.

Ben quickly took of his jacket and his shirt and wrung as much water out of them as he could. Although it was warm underground, he knew he would lose his body heat much faster if he wore his clothes soaking wet. For the time being, he would carry his shirt and jacket.

Rasci hated having left Elsie and Margo behind. He was trying to work out whether he would have been better staying behind to keep Zelda company, but time was of the essence. If there was a way out, then they had to find it before the passage way to the exit was closed off by flood water. If the water rose in the Blue Tooth cavern then the cave was high enough to perhaps ensure they did not drown before Ben could summon help. Getting Ben safely back to his mother and father was crucial to saving his sister and his cousin.

As all the wolves gathered ready to go, Ben stood up and slung his wet shirt and jacket over his shoulder. He clicked on his torch to make sure it still worked, and a beam of white light shone across the cave. But he switched it off again. At the moment there was light, and although greyer than the torch light, like Elsie, Ben knew the importance of conserving the torch batteries.

Rasci bounded across the cave, dodging around pillars of rock until he came to another opening. It was lower than the passages they has been through before, but Ben, being small, only had to stoop forward a little to be able to walk easily along it. He switched on his torch and led the way. Unlike the other passages, however, this one was not so long. Within minutes they had reached a fork in the pathway.

They took the right hand one. For about five minutes they travelled along this pot hole until Ben came to a rock wall. The passage was much higher here, but there was no way forward. Up near the top of the rock wall there was a small hole, but too small to get through even if any of them could have reached it. Below it on the floor of the passage a pile of sandy grit where water had run out and spilled onto the floor. It was dry now. For the time being.

Disheartened, they all turned back and returned to the fork in the passage. One more chance, Rhamin whispered to himself as, once again, Ben took the lead.

The roof of this passage was even lower than the last one. Rhamin was almost on his belly at one point and Ben just clung onto Rhamin's coat as he bent forward so that he did not lose his balance. But soon the tunnel widened again and it was definitely going upwards, as the floor tilted first to one side and then the other. To Rhamin heading up hill felt like a good thing. The sooner he got to the surface the better.

At times, Ben found it hard to stand up and walk on the slanting floor without leaning against the slope with his right hand as the floor tilted to one side and with his left hand as it tilted in the opposite direction. The rumbling sound of the water had faded into the distance for a while, but now, suddenly he could hear it again, getting louder the further they went and the higher they climbed. Gradually, the passage floor levelled out again, until it was as flat as his father's farm road. But it was rougher than before and so were the walls. They were going past darker rock and, as they walked on, perhaps for another ten minutes or so, it began to look as if someone had hacked away at the sides of the tunnel to make it bigger. The roughest sides had seams of shiny substances that looked like distant streams seen from a mountain as the late evening sun shone on and reflected off them. Ben fingered them inquisitively as he walked past them. And still the rumbling got louder.

Suddenly the mark of man appeared once again. Not paintings or even writing this time, but now there were occasional big pieces of wood, each one supporting a cross beam. Rhamin thought he knew what they were for. Ben definitely knew. There were occasional tunnels running off at right angles, but no one even thought of seeing if any offered an alternative way out. They just kept walking straight on.

Instead of being damp, now the passage was dusty and dry, and it still sloped upwards, though not as steeply as it had earlier. Ben coughed as their footsteps stirred the dust. He could hear some of the wolves at the rear sneezing and coughing like himself. But still there seemed no end to the passageway as they trudged on and on.

Some of the wooden posts were rotting away. Rotted remains of others lay on the ground, already past their usefulness. Even with Ben's torch shining forward through the dust, the whole place was dark and oppressive. It was impossible to see who was just behind and who had dropped further back. Rhamin hoped everyone was still there, following closely. But whoever was there, some would never be seen again.

CHAPTER THIRTY SEVEN

Elsie was scared. Scared for herself; scared for Margo. She was even scared for Smokey and old Zelda because if she and Margo had to climb up high onto a rock or a ledge, that would be an impossible task for a nine stone dog and a blind and lame old wolf.

She walked around the huge cavern, checking every possible corner and crevice. Apart from diving into the lake and emerging at the other side of the cave wall, there was no way out. Demoralised and tired, she joined Margo who was, again, inside Blue Tooth's mouth, sitting happily and patiently on the top of the bunched up tongue. 'We'll be okay,' Elsie said to her as she and Smokey went over and sat beside her.

'*I* know,' Margo said cheerily as she glanced once more around the walls of Blue Tooth. 'I wonder what it says,' she said, looking at the inscriptions. 'Is it some sort of message?' she said pensively, more to herself than to anybody that might be listening.

'There will definitely be a message there somewhere,' Elsie explained. 'All writing carries a message. This probably tells the story of some tribe that once lived in or used these caves.' She thought about it for a moment and then continued. 'They certainly knew how to draw and paint. Their pictures are much more detailed than the famous cave paintings that we all read about.'

'*I* haven't read about them,' Margo said, her voice rising at the end of the sentence, the tone in her voice marking a question.

'You will,' said Elsie,' trying to boost her own confidence. She needed to keep talking. As long as she was thinking about other things, then the walls of this dire situation would not close in on her already growing feeling of hopelessness. 'When you start reading books.' She paused and thought about what she had seen in these caves. 'Most of the famous cave paintings are in France and Spain,' she went on.

'Where's that?'

'They are countries far away from here. And there are several caves that have drawings of hunters and the animals they are chasing. But although they are very good paintings, they are nothing like the ones we can see here. And I don't recall reading anything about there being writing in any of the caves.' She spoke more pensively now, talking more to herself than to Margo as she continued to look at the walls. 'This civilization used proper writing, not hieroglyphics. They were quite advanced.'

'What are *Hairy Griffinks*?' asked Margo.

'Hairy Griffinks?' Elsie laughed. For the first time since this whole dreadful escapade had started, her spirits had been lifted, not by hope or success, but simply by her little cousin who, with her innocence and total belief in Elsie and the wolves, had shown not one particle of fear, not one grain of despair. She looked at Margo and considered how she was so much like Rhamin. Although Elsie couldn't communicate with the wolves like Ben and Margo, she had still been able to detect that Rhamin went through life totally oblivious to threats and danger. He was a true leader; an inspiration to all who accompanied him. And Margo's fearlessness had now lifted Elsie's spirits from dropping into a hole of despair.

But, resigned, now, to the fact that there was no way out of the caves, she was determined to keep Margo entertained. At least she was not going to discover just how hopeless the situation was. Gently, Elsie put her arm around her and snuggled her into her side. 'The Hairy Griffink,' she began and then paused to think. 'The Hairy Griffink was an unfortunate little creature used as a paint brush or as a pen to do writing by people in ancient civilizations.'

'Really? Wow!'

Elsie chuckled. 'It had a hairless, rigid body and a bushy tail.'

Margo listened, her eyes wide, watching every expression on Elsie's face.

'It is for that reason that Hairy Griffink was the original name for writing done in pictures.' She watched Margo's awestricken expression as she continued. 'This later got misspelt over the years and became *hieroglyphics*.'

Margo was still spell-bound.

'Sadly for them, it was discovered that they were very handy for ancient writers to pick up and dip in their inks and paints to use as a pen or paintbrush. The Egyptians used them a lot. A Chinese traveller discovered them, and much, much later, when they had died out in the Middle East, the Chinese bred them to use for writing their alphabetical characters and later still for painting delicate patterns and pictures on their porcelain.'

Elsie looked down at Margo's upturned face and squeezed

her a little tighter while she thought of a suitable ending to her tale.

'After being used as a paintbrush,' she continued after a moment's thought, 'the Hairy Griffinks would jump into the nearest pot or bowl of water and bathe themselves. Unlike many animals, they were not very good swimmers. Many of them drowned. They died out completely in the early twentieth century.'

Margo was enthralled, her mind conjuring up a picture of some unfortunate little creature that was picked up and used as a paintbrush and when let go, set about dunking itself in water to wash itself clean.

Elsie chuckled. If she had only had a baby brother and sister, she could have made up hundreds of silly stories to keep them and herself amused. Now she was doing it because, deep down, she was really frightened. She had found something in these farmer's children, something she had craved for, not knowingly, but craved for, nevertheless, and she knew now she was so close to losing it forever.

CHAPTER THIRTY EIGHT

Rasci was in the middle of the line of wolves. He had lots on his mind. Gradually, the long, hopeless journey was sapping all his resolve. Minute by minute, he was getting more and more depressed as the tunnel went on and on relentlessly. He felt responsible somehow. He'd allowed three children to join them and they were possibly dead or dying by now. He thought about his knowledge of the human race; what he had gained from that knowledge and what he had lost. He thought about Margo, the helpless and innocent little girl who had been caught up in all this. And he had been thinking about Zelda and Smokey and Elsie trapped with little Margo. And Ben? He was with this train of wolves but he was just as likely to die if they never found their way out from under the ground. The light beam from Ben's torch was already looking dimmed and if it went out all together, what were their chances of survival then? No, he wasn't really thinking about anything to do with escaping. He was to blame for bringing these children into all this and so he was to blame for getting the wolves into it as well. It was his entire fault. He wished he'd stayed behind in the Blue Tooth cave. He deserved no better.

When the roar came it took every wolf by surprise. Ben had heard something and turned around to shine his torch back down the passage. But even before the torch beam had swung all the way around, a thunderous, grinding roar shook every particle of his body. A cloud of dust hit him and knocked him backwards. Wolves seemed to be rolling over and over and then yelping and then running. They were all running. Ben found himself hanging at an unusual angle and holding onto Rhamin's coat with his left hand. His feet were dragging over the ground, hardly landing a single step on the dusty floor. The dust was choking. Huge jaws just held him about his waist in a vice like grip as Rhamin thrust him forward through the fog of powdery dust. The roof of the tunnel was caving in and the only way to survive was to outrun it. Ben had managed to keep a hold of his torch in his right hand, but the beam waved and shook about as Rhamin galloped for their lives, racing past collapsing wooden props and jumping over rocks that had already left the ceiling. But the roar seemed to be chasing them, getting louder as more and more dust blasted past them. The whole tunnel was imploding as each of the worm-riddled, rotten, wooden pit posts gave way under the ever increasing strain.

Then suddenly the thundering noise died. But Rhamin kept on running for his life.

When Rhamin eventually stopped the dust was already settling. Miraculously Ben had not only been able to cling onto Rhamin's coat, he had still been able to cling onto the torch whilst he had been bounced along. Rhamin opened his jaws and slowly released his grip on Ben's waist. Unsteadily, Ben stood up and regained his footing on the ground. They carried on walking forward making sure that the roof of the tunnel was not going to collapse on them again, but when Ben turned around and levelled the torch beam, his heart sank. The only wolves with him were Silvah, Ramusan, Lexa, Yeltsa, Natan, Goma, and the one who had saved his life, Rhamin. They all stood there, coughing and sneezing, black mucous dripping from their jowls and their noses as they waited for more wolves to appear out of the smog.

A minute; ten minutes. The dust was slowly thinning as it settled, particle by particle in a thick layer around their feet and on their coats. The torch beam cut heavily into the dusty air but even the wolves' keen eyes could see no further than a few paces in any direction. 'I'm going back to look for Rasci,' Ben coughed as he broke into a trot, running back along the tunnel. But he didn't get far. The falling rocks in the collapsing tunnel had chased them even further than he or any of the wolves had thought. All he found was a huge pile of boulders and dust blocking his way. There was no way back now.

Solin had been hanging back, following the light beam that Ben carried fifty or so paces ahead. Rhiana and Roxana were hanging back too, perhaps ten paces ahead of Solin. Rasci had been ahead of them. Then it all happened. Rhiana was arguing with Roxana. Solin had decided to leave them to it. He could hear them barking and growling at each other in subdued tones as they followed in line but he couldn't hear exactly what they were saying. Whatever it was, it was causing them to growl louder and snarl at each other. Then they started a fight. Roxana went for Rhiana and Rhiana bounced away, showing Roxana a full set of fangs. It was a normal joust, the sort of thing that happens in all packs when one wolf tries to exert its authority over another. It was all part of the hierarchy of pack life. But as Rhiana bounced backwards, she landed square against one of the upright posts. The post was rotten and, crumbling into chips of soft mulch, it gave way immediately. The job it had been doing for hundreds of years had finally been terminated. The tiny residual upward force it had maintained on the horizontal prop that held the roof of the tunnel had suddenly gone. The falling support was still wedged on top of a second, firmer prop at the other side of the tunnel. As one end dropped and still with the other end on top of the upright prop, it formed a lever against the roof. The rocks in the roof shook at first as the free end of the horizontal prop dropped to the floor. Rocks began to fall where the point of the lever prized at the ceiling. Then, as several slabs of stone fell away from the point of the lever, both remaining pieces of timber folded together and collapsed into the tunnel.

A few seconds passed as a rumbling noise grew into a roar. Then the dust cloud came; nothing but dust, ramming along the tunnel like a tornado, blanking out everything that was happening behind it. Solin couldn't see it, but the tunnel was giving way, as if retaliating, piling tons of rock on top of the offending wolf that had disturbed its status quo. But it didn't end there. The weight of the roof falling in and the vibration from the horrendous thundering noise, brought the next set of props down and then the next until the whole tunnel was collapsing inwards. Solin turned and ran for his life, falling rocks clipping at his heels as he sprinted blindly onwards, crashing into more posts in the total blackness, loosening them and causing even more of the ceiling to cave in. But all he could do, as he bounced from one after another, was to keep galloping blindly back into the black void.

A thunderous roar filled the cavern as something, somewhere collapsed. The sound sent Zelda into a fit of anguish as it drowned out the roar of the rushing, hidden water. It wasn't in the cavern. It could have been just outside, where the rest of the wolves had gone. It could have been miles away and the sound could have travelled unimpeded through the caves and passageways. Nobody knew. Then the noise settled again giving way to the unrelenting noise of the rising waters.

Calmed by Margo, as she stroked the old wolf' shoulders, eventually Zelda lay silently just inside Blue Tooth while Smokey watched over her and the children from up on the summit of the arched tongue. But soon her body began to twitch and jerk as she dreamt. She had always had visions in dreams, but over the years as she grew older and blinder, her gift had faded. She had been so happy when Rasci had shown her that he could do all the things she had once been able to do. Perhaps he was even better at seeing with his mind that she had ever been. She couldn't remember. But she had seen that there was a way out of the caves. The problem was, she hadn't told Rhamin everything. How could she tell him that some of the wolves with him would not survive? He may never have left with them in the first place. And how could she tell him that she wasn't going to be with him when he did reach the cool, fresh, clean air of the outside world? She grunted in her sleep. Why couldn't she have foreseen all this and worked out some way of making sure it never happened?

Because fate is determined long before you take your first step, however long ago that may have been, her inner soul called back to her. *What will be will be. All you can do is bend the future, moulding its path slightly, improving the journey but never changing its design or destination; never changing its final purpose, its ultimate intention.*

So are we all to die?

But before the question could be answered, her mind turned to the Blue Tooth cave. Rasci had explained how men kind use writing to convey messages and information. The writing in the cave must say something! But what? She grunted again as she turned to take the pressure off her aching hips.

Regardless of what it says, it tells you something.

Heh?

You are looking at the writing.

Zelda groaned. Her mind was as tired as her aching old body. Of course I'm looking at the writing! What does it say?

Stop looking at the writing. Forget what it says.

I never knew!

Then don't think about its translation.

Translation? Her mind began to clear.

It tells you…?

It tells me that…

That?

That men kind came here.

And?

And that means they didn't swim through or dive into a silly lake to get in here!

At last!

So where did they come in?

You tell me.

There's a crack where the air is exiting?

Hmm. Could be.

Could be? Yes, it could be where the ancient men kind came in. But Elsie looked at it. Only her kind can use tools to prize it open. It looked such a heavy rock.

You are losing track again!

Heh?

Go back.

Go back? To… *Could be?*

Keep going.

Look somewhere else?

Hooray! As you used to say when you used to teach and prompt Rasci.

Used to? What do you…?

Suddenly Zelda jerked awake. She was panting heavily. Smokey was licking her face to sooth her. Elsie and Margo were knelt beside her, stroking her thick coat. She lifted her head and looked around.

'Are you all right?' asked Smokey.

'All right?' She paused and thought about where she was. Then she saw the ancient characters that were inscribed on the inner cheeks of Blue Tooth. 'Oh, I was dreaming.'

She couldn't help recalling how she and Silvah had awakened Rasci when he had been having bad dreams. But was hers such a bad dream? She tried to recall what it was about. The writing on the walls, as Rasci had described it, was not just a fancy pattern. It conveyed words. But the dream was about ignoring the writing. Suddenly she realized what it had been about. 'Smokey?' she called.

'Yes?'

'Did you know that Rasci could see things with his mind when he wasn't actually there?'

'*Could* see things? You speak as if…'

'I speak as if he used to do it,' Zelda snapped. 'I meant nothing by it.'

'Okay!' Smokey said to sooth away Zelda's anger. 'Well, yes, I came to understand that he has a gift.'

'I have that gift as well. Or I used to have it. Things fade as you get older.'

'I'll take your word for that,' said Smokey confidently. 'Use it or lose it I say.'

'Hmm, well the time comes when using it takes so much more effort than it did when you were young and fit.'

'Yes, well I have been told that you aren't just old.'

'Not just old?' Zelda's voice rose at the end of the sentence. It was definitely a question. What had Smokey been told? And by whom? She was insane? Going mad? She shuffled her front paws underneath her chest, moving to push herself up off her belly.

'You are *very, very* old,' Smokey said, unable to stop herself from chuckling as she watched and heard Zelda's reaction. 'In fact you are anciently old.'

'Right, *young* wolf dog,' Zelda said firmly and emphasising the age difference markedly. 'Listen to me. There are sometimes several answers to a single question.'

Smokey sighed and shook her head. 'If you say so, old wolf.'

Zelda shook her own head. 'Sometimes I think you must be related to Rasci. Be serious, do you hear, wolf dog!'

Somehow Smokey liked that title. It was the same one Rasci used for Lexa. 'Okay,' she said, trying to suppress the fermenting bubble of laughter that had germinated somewhere in her tummy. Though, why she felt a tiny tremor of elation in the first place, she couldn't tell. It was so good, though, to laugh even under extreme circumstances. Somehow it helped to clear the mind; to unclog all the cluttering white light of information that can sometimes overload the brain when it is under great stress. And they *were* under great stress, all of them.

'What I am saying is that there's another way out of here.'

Smokey looked at her, her head tilted and her ears forward with curiosity. Zelda had sensed that she was waiting for instructions. 'Where haven't we looked?'

Smokey shook her head. 'I think every wolf and even Elsie, Ben and Margo have searched every corner a dozen times.'

'There must be somewhere. There must be an entrance that men kind used to come in here. Look at it Smokey. The mark of man is all over it. I might not be able to see it, but I can touch it. I can feel it.'

Smokey whined a brief acknowledgement and then jumped up on her toes. Suddenly a light of determination flashed into her eyes.

Margo had been watching Smokey and Zelda talk to each other in their dulcet tones. Her eyes met Smokey's but Smokey saw it first. She saw that Margo had seen what was in *her* mind, even before the spark of recognition had flashed across the little girls own eyes.

Margo stood there, her lips slightly parted as she thought about what was now in her own mind. Almost in a trance, herself, she pushed a fallen tress of hair off her now grimy face with even grubbier hands. 'Zelda has told Smokey that there is another way out!' she shouted, suddenly and excitedly as she looked up at the face of her bigger cousin. 'Elsie, do you hear?'

Elsie stood there bemused. Dogs and wolves talking to

each other. One telling the other something that no one could possibly know. She shook her head; not because she didn't believe Margo. She was well past that stage. But she didn't know whether to believe that this was just some long, awkward and terrible dream of her own. Any moment now, would she wake up and find herself back home in her father's arms?

'Elsie!' Margo shouted to bring her cousin back to reality. She danced about excitedly and tugged at her arm 'We must keep looking.'

CHAPTER THIRTY NINE

With the police car right behind them, it was mid-afternoon when, with about four miles to go, Maria finally drove towards the rocky escarpment that fronted the Darin. The driving had been hard in lashing rain and with a squally blustery wind battering the occupants of the canvass-topped Jeep. They hadn't been able to see more than twenty or thirty yards in front of the windscreen and progress had been even slower than they had anticipated. But Raymond and Maria were happy they had refused to accept a lift from the policemen. While Maria drove around rocks and gulleys, it gave them chance to talk and discuss what had happened and what they not only intended to do, but what they intended to say.

Now, for a short while at least, the rain and the wind had abated a little and visibility was much clearer. 'Not far now,' Raymond said as he pointed westward. The outcrop wasn't in sight yet, but Raymond knew the landscape well enough to know where he was.

But then, as they travelled a little nearer to the Darin, Raymond spotted something about half a mile off to the right. Despite a period of heavy rain, a column of wispy blue smoke was still rising into the blackened clouds. Something was burning.

As they steered off course and headed towards the smoke, Raymond and Maria's hearts sank. They could see the station wagon, or what was left of it, lying on its side in a shallow gulley, still smouldering inside where the combustible materials had been sheltered from the rain by the vehicle's metal body, and still smoking after being burned out. The policemen were out of their car before Maria or Raymond could get out of the Jeep. By the time Maria, with her shoulder under Raymond's armpit, had helped him walk the ten paces or so to the gulley, one of the policemen was already turning towards them.

'No bodies inside,' the sergeant stated, a look of relief on his face telling that, for a short moment, they too had feared the worst.

The other police constable was still examining the wreckage. Eventually he joined the sergeant and said, 'It's hard to tell what happened. And with the rain, there's no trail to follow to see where the children went.'

Raymond looked around desperately. All he could see was the top of the escarpment rising above the horizon a few miles away. Limping back to the Jeep, the police constable helped him back into the passenger seat. He looked around for Maria, but she hadn't followed. She was inspecting the ground near to the burned out station wagon. There were no tracks but there was a pile of stones. It was not a natural pile formed by nature's wind and weather. It was constructed. It formed a line of about eight stones and a point made up of another four smaller pebbles. It was an arrow and it pointed towards the escarpment and the caves.

CHAPTER FORTY

Ben sobbed. He loved all the wolves, but Rasci had been special. Rasci wasn't just a friend. He was someone with whom Ben had planned to discuss everything in the world.

Rhamin was silent. Once again fate had taken arms against him. First, men had kidnapped him and his mate Yeltsa. Then they had killed Bamar and injured Charka. Now men had driven them deep into the caves and, even if the wolves with him survived, once again, men had killed more wolves and possibly even some of the children. He remembered what Bamar had said. They should not retaliate. But once again, the seething, thin grin of rage ran along The Black Wolf's lips.

'We had better keep moving,' Yeltsa said as she tried to break Rhamin out of his venomous mood of hatred and fury.

'You go ahead,' he snapped. He needed some time to remember his lost friends.

'We don't have a lot of time,' Lexa put in. 'Ben's light stick is getting dim. We must keep going.'

Yeltsa tried once again. 'Come, Rhamin. We have others to try and save. If we take the wrong steps now then they will surely perish too.'

Rhamin snapped out of his ire. Thinking for a moment, he lay down next to Ben and gently pulled at his arm with his teeth. Ben understood immediately. He was to get on Rhamin's back and ride as he had done on Smokey's back out on the plain. 'We can't be far from the entrance,' Rhamin explained. These are tunnels made by men, not water. They enter from the open air. We must arrive at that opening soon. From now on we run until the light goes out.'

Standing back up, he looked behind him. 'Are you all ready?' Without waiting for a reply he set off at a fast lope. There was no time to lose and with Ben's light losing strength with every minute that passed and with every stride they took, they were all in a race against time.

CHAPTER FORTY ONE

The caves were rumbling louder yet again. The whole cave complex seemed to be vibrating with the same resonating sound. Zelda lay in the mouth of Blue Tooth and tried to work out what it was that she was missing. She had thought the opening had got to be opposite the mouth of the Wolf cave.

Margo stayed close to Elsie. She felt that Elsie was getting close to solving their problems.

Elsie looked at the sheer wall of rock facing Blue Tooth. The steps that ran up to the first ledge turned and continued up to the top one. Perhaps that wasn't where they came in. Perhaps the men of ancient times sat up there. Perhaps they sat and watched people enter. Perhaps the cave was a vast auditorium with the shelves as rows of seats, not steps. And perhaps the entrance to this vast theatre was behind the stage, inside Blue Tooth.

Elsie frantically searched the giant mouth. It was like a huge theatre. If it were designed for a grand entrance then the people would walk up the throat and over the rough tongue to emerge with their heads rising out of nowhere until they stood at the top. She tried to remember what the stage at the local theatre was like where the school she had attended did their school plays. There were side entrances. She looked along the walls at the writing that stood out so clearly in relief. Looking at it more closely, the characters that formed the writing appeared to be in vertical columns rather than horizontal lines. She followed the columns of writing until, on a flat platform in the very deepest part of the throat, the writing ended. She felt every row where the bare rock began. There was no seam between one or the other; no opening, no doorway.

She contemplated what the use of this theatre was. Why was it underground? How far underground was it? What civilization used it and transformed it into the shape it was now? How much of it was natural? How much was carved by or added to it by people? Why was it a wolf's head? She had all the questions, but none of the answers. And would any of the answers give her a clue as to where any opening was, even if she found them?

The water was still rising. The slope up from the tunnel was already covered with water. Another thunderous sound roared through the cavern as, once again, something gave way and collapsed. It must have been something close, for now, instead of rising steadily, the water was raging so fast up the tunnel that the pressure pushed it up through the water surface like a huge frothing fountain before the force of gravity dragged it back into the unsettled, stirring water and then levelled out. For a moment Elsie had feared that the water was actually boiling, and now it was calmed again she let out an audible sigh of relief.

She glanced across to the lake in the far corner of the cavern. It was still well above the rising water. It looked unmoved, its surface as flat and calm as ever. But it wouldn't be long before the rising flood waters engulfed it. She reckoned that the lake was about on the same level as Blue Tooth's bottom jaw. Soon there would be nowhere to go.

CHAPTER FORTY TWO

The blackness gradually ended as the light from the dimly lit cavern emanated up the darkened tunnel. Without slowing, and now only vaguely able to see what was in front of him because of the dust that coated his eyes, Solin kept on running until he was as far away from the pursuing, falling death trap as he could go. Panting desperately, his lungs were burning with the dust that he'd had to inhale. But the dust cloud was settling now, getting thinner, as he still ran as fast as he could for his life. Eventually, more weary and bruised than he thought he had ever been, he found himself heading towards the lake. Its calm surface and air of tranquillity seemed to be, somehow, reassuring. Without stopping, he waded into the water by the shingle bank and submerged himself completely. He couldn't hold his breath for long. With a gasp, he broke from the surface, letting the water run off him, washing the dust and muck from his eyes. Again he ducked under the water and broke back out through the surface, this time clearing the dirt from his nostrils and mouth. He swam and rolled in the shallows, watching as the black mists of dirt that washed from his coat gradually darkened the water around him. Then, still in the water, he paddled along the edge of the lake to where the water was clearer, and drank and drank.

He stood there panting for some time, water lapping against his belly, still watching the clouds of dirt off his coat dissipate in the calm water while he contemplated what to do. As he looked at the huge cave, and as his movement in the water sent huge ripples coursing around the surface, he noticed that where the water lapped against the far wall there was a submerged ledge running around the edge of the lake. It disappeared between two big columns of rock which, themselves, were standing majestically in the water; columns not unlike any others he had seen recently in the huge caves and caverns. He looked at them for several minutes and then, feeling his body temperature finally coming under control, eventually, he waded out until his feet no longer touched the ground and began to swim to the far wall of the cave.

Slowly, he pulled himself onto the ledge and shook himself vigorously, spattering the creamy-grey rocks with black splodges of water as it continued to clean the dirt out of his thick coat. Careful not to step off the ledge which was only a couple of inches beneath the surface of the water, he followed it round until he reached the two pillars. Between them was a narrow gorge, stretching as high as the cave ceiling but only just wide enough for him to squeeze through. The ceiling continued at the same height and, as luck would have it, the phenomena that lit the cave that he was leaving behind continued to the other side of the gorge as the floor began to rise steeply upwards.

CHAPTER FORTY THREE

As Ben's torch battery depleted, the light beam became weaker and weaker. The wolves seemed to still be able to see by the dimmest of lights long after the place seemed to be cast in total blackness to Ben's eyes. To him, the torch light was barely visible, but the wolves ran on as if there was still ample light. But eventually, the light did completely fail as they joined a bigger tunnel now, where there were long metal rails fixed to huge slabs of wood. Rhamin had seen rails like this before. He'd seen the contraptions that travelled along them. The tunnel wasn't big enough for such creatures, but he knew that the rails would lead to the open air and safety. Carefully and forming a chain by resting their chins on each other's back, they followed Rhamin as he felt his way along the metal rails.

The dull light of day, when it appeared as the tunnel bent slowly to the left, made all their hearts jump. It seemed so far away at first but it took no more than a minute to reach the opening as they quickened their pace. It wasn't what they had expected. At one time the hole in the rock face must have been on level ground, but where the tunnel emerged, now the land had collapsed and slipped away leaving a drop the length of several wolves down to a scree of broken rocks that spread out like a fan towards a deep river bank. Rhamin and Ben looked over the edge and watched the raging water. The skies were still dark and rain lashed down the side of the cliff face above them, cascading the water over their heads as it gathered speed. Where a bird or squirrel had dropped a seed, a scrub tree had taken root in a crack on the cliff face and one of its branches hung near the side of the opening.

Ben dropped lightly down from Rhamin's back and stood there beside him, letting the rain splash against his face. He opened his mouth and let the raindrops wash the dirt and dust from his tongue before even attempting to swallow any. When he did, his throat was still loaded with dust.

Rhamin looked at Ben and then, trying to coax him to follow, carefully, and supporting himself with his front paws the best he could against the steep rock face, he let himself slide down as far as he could before hopping down to the scree. On the loose and broken gravel he couldn't get a foothold and, unable to stop his descent, he slid down to the river bank. Yeltsa came and stood next to Ben and watched as Rhamin slid away. She would not follow Rhamin until she knew that Ben was not going to be left stranded in the mouth of the tunnel.

Ben knew what was required of him. He stretched out with his finger tips for the branch of the tree, but it was just out of reach. He wished now that Elsie was here. She'd have reached it easily. But thinking of Elsie made his mind turn to his little sister. Margo was still somewhere far underground and there was no way back to find her. With a heavy heart, and really caring little now for his own safety, he sat on the edge of the opening, turned around and let himself down the steep cliff wall by hanging onto the ledge and dangling there for a minute or so at arms length. The drop wasn't very far, perhaps ten feet. On a normal day he would have been too scared to do it. But now, and thinking how brave Elsie was and that she would have no problems with such a task, he simply let go. His feet hit the scree and as they slid away down the shingle slope, his body dropped forward onto the bank of shattered rock. Rhamin stopped him from rolling any further as he scuttered down the shale covered slope, finally landing on level ground at the bottom, against the wolf's front legs.

Without much hesitation at all, all the other wolves and Lexa followed Rhamin's example, putting their feet on the wall below the opening and then, with a slight hop, dropping onto the scree. The fear of staying in those deadly tunnels and caves outweighed any fear of the drop. The fine shingle did an excellent job of breaking their fall and slowing them down as they each slid, amidst a small avalanche of wet rock and gravel, towards Ben and Rhamin.

As Rhamin looked around, he realized that he knew the river. It was not a big affair but it was running as violently as he had ever seen it. It was swollen now with the torrential rain water as it emptied its contents down the mountain, through the forest and across onto the plain. He knew if they followed it they would not be far from home. The problem was, they had been driven from their home and there wasn't any good reason to return there for a considerable time. He called out to see if any members of the rest of his pack were nearby. Powla, Vela and the cubs could be somewhere near. But the call was deadened by the trees, the deep river gauge and the raging river. They didn't answer or if they did, it wasn't heard.

He looked at the sky. It was probably still some time before nightfall, but it was hard to tell with the dark sky blocking out the sun. Leading the way, Rhamin took Ben and his remaining wolves to the shallows at the edge of a curve in the river, where the current was not so strong and where they could wade into the water and wash the dirt from their nostrils and eyes. They all drank greedily, even Ben. He washed his face by scooping up water in his hands and sloshing it over his face. It took a while, but eventually he began to feel that he could see and breathe much more clearly. It was well worth taking the time to clean up a little. Unlike the wolves, however, he didn't wade into the water. He had no thick coat to protect him from the cold. He had lost all but his shoes, vest and trousers. Already, he was drenched and was feeling the chill from the lashing rain.

As Rhamin emerged from the water, shaking his coat vigorously to shed the cleansing liquid, once again he lay next to Ben and tugged at his arm. They were all hungry, but they had no time to hunt. Time was of the essence. They had to get Ben to warmth and safety, but more than that, Ben had to get help for his sister and Elsie. They, along with Zelda, and Smokey were still trapped underground and the rain showed no inclination to be stopping or even abating. He knew that it was only a matter of time before the caves and tunnels would be completely flooded to their ceilings.

Once again, Rhamin lifted his head in the air and howled. He wanted all the wolves that were around to know that he was safe. The wolves that Silvah and Lexa had left in the forest would be somewhere within earshot. But still the heavy squally rain and thundering water drowned out the sound of his calls.

There was only one thing he could do. With Ben on his

back, snuggled deeply into his thick coat, and accompanied by his companions, Rhamin prepared to set off towards the farm. He would have Ben home and safe before the sun rose in morning.

But Rhamin had covered less than fifty strides when he heard the cry of a single wolf. Charka's sharp ears had picked up Rhamin's signal. Faint as it was, and with the wind carrying her call towards Rhamin, Charka's response told him that the injured wolf was near to the Darin. He took only a moment to reply to his companion, and then, setting off slowly at first, making sure that Ben had a firm hold on his coat, Rhamin's legs began to move faster and faster as he headed towards Charka, his own home and the caves.

CHAPTER FORTY FOUR

Their inspection of the cave revealed no wolves, no children. And although they hadn't known about the men that had chased the station wagon, there was no sign of any other vehicle nearby, or any sign that any had been there. The rain had obliterated all the tracks. The SUV had gone and so had the men who had been in it. Raymond and the policemen were none the wiser. All they could do was drive around and see whether they could see any sign of the children or the wolves.

The call from Charka stopped them before they could drive off. They hadn't heard Rhamin's call, for humans have poor hearing compared with wolves, but Charka was somewhere nearby. Despite being up-wind, her call clearly indicated that she was close. When she called again, Raymond hoisted himself back into the Jeep. 'Drive that way,' he instructed as he pointed in the direction of the foothills and the forests.

Maria didn't need telling. She was in the Jeep and starting the engine before Raymond could say another word. Swinging the front of the vehicle around, she stamped on the accelerator and sped off to the north.

Two minutes, that was all it took before Raymond and Maria spotted a lone wolf. 'It's the one you had the vet come and patch up,' Maria said, noticing the dirty, mud-stained dressing on the wolf's thigh.

'Well so it is!' Raymond exclaimed, not having noticed the dirty grey dressing against the grey wolf's coat. 'That means they are around here somewhere. It was that wolf that needed the ride home!'

'So why is she alone?' Maria asked, deeply concerned. 'Why aren't the other wolves with her? Where are our children?' Her voice was full of trepidation.

Raymond didn't have any answers for her. The problem was as perplexing to him as it was to Maria. Only one wolf, and that the injured one, was around after the vehicle in which they had all been travelling had turned over and caught fire. There were no bodies near the wreckage so they must have all got clear. But where were their children? Where were Smokey and the rest of the wolves?

Charka couldn't tell them. Not only had she no way of communicating with these men kind, but she hadn't been there when the children and the wolves had ventured into the deepest darkest depths of the Darin. No, all she knew was that they had all been chased by bad men in an evil looking black, big wheeled machine. All but she had fled to the Darin, and now, Rhamin had called to say that he was safe and on his way down from the forest and the foothills. She had no way of telling Raymond or Maria any of this.

CHAPTER FORTY FIVE

As Solin climbed up the rough rocky slope, the light began to fade again. For some reason, the creatures, whatever they were, that so welcomely gave off light, didn't seem to thrive in the tunnels and potholes. The sound of the water thundering away in the background made him shiver as he climbed further on. The slope, he noticed was actually a gradient of shallow steps. Now it was at least three wolves wide, and appeared to spiral upwards to the left and then flatten out on a higher level. But, although much leveller now, it was still pitch black. He sniffed around, hoping that he would pick up a scent that he could use to direct him out of this hell hole. Following the wall to the left he kept his shoulder against the rock. It was useless. The only thing he could think of was to get a mankind's light stick from somewhere. But to return to the lake, to swim under the rock partition, and to go and persuade Elsie to leave the little girl behind and lead him out to safety with her torch was purely wishful thinking. No, he had to keep going and hope that he got lucky.

Luck! He stopped and thought about that word for a moment. How lucky had his life been? He had been born second heir to the title of pack leader, he had failed at luring Rhamin into a trap, he had miserably fallen short when it came to employing the likes of Roxana to help him reach his required status, he had been forced to join Rhamin's pack again, even if only temporarily, after another of Rhiana's cockeyed plans had gone wrong, and now he was buried alive. Quite an impressive list of failure and defeats. Still, the consoling thought was that a lesser wolf would have been killed long ago. At least he was a survivor. Up to now!

Realizing that he was depressing himself, he concluded that he must still be alive for a reason. Why else would Rhamin have spared him not just once but several times since his defection from the pack? Why else was he still alive when Rhiana, Roxana and a big part of Rhamin's pack, including the leader himself, had all perished? He coughed brutally, shook himself out of his sombre mood and moved forward again slowly but surely. The air was clean, he'd taken on plenty of water and he could last for days.

He fumbled on again for a few minutes before realizing what he had just concluded in his thoughts. *The air is clean*.

So where is it coming from? He held his nose upwards and sniffed. Nothing there. Normally, with his acute senses, he could have detected from which direction the air was flowing by pointing his nose upwards and sniffing, but despite washing in the lake, his nose was still caked with the dust he had been breathing and eating. Then he remembered what the girl Elsie had done. She had licked her finger and held it in the air. Somehow she could tell which way the air was moving. He licked his nose so that it was really wet and then stuck it up in the air. Sure enough, one side of his nose felt ever so slightly chilled. The air was coming towards him, he was sure of it. He sniffed at it for a moment to no avail, but the idea of finding its source lifted his spirits. Following that direction now, and testing it every few minutes by licking and re-wetting his nose, it wasn't very long before he came to a crack in the floor of the cave. He sniffed at the rush of air that was squeezing through the gap. He could see a dim light at the other side. Perhaps this was the door to freedom, to the outside world, to the foothills and the trees and the plains...

He stopped himself hallucinating. Light from outside would not, under any circumstances that he could think of, come from beneath him. Not unless he had somehow taken to suddenly being able to walk on the ceiling. Shaking his head he followed the gap round. It was as if there was a large slab of rock, and not a thick one at that, barring his way. He scratched at the gap trying to get a purchase on the edge of it with his sharp claws. It seemed hopeless, but it was the only idea he could come up with at that particular moment. He scratched and pulled at it with his claws again and again...

If it hadn't been for the fine sprinkling of dust that was wafting down to the floor, Margo wouldn't have noticed the scraping noise. The thundering clamour of the water filling the cavern below had made hearing anything other than another booming noise impossible to hear. 'Elsie,' she shouted, above the noise. 'Look.' She pointed up to the back of Blue Tooth's throat.

Elsie ran over and watched. There was definitely something or some one trying to get through. But the ceiling was way above their heads. Even with a long pole, she would have needed a scaffold to stand on to reach it.

Then Smokey barked. Not at the dust; not at the scraping noise. She was lying fifty feet away by the front fangs of the sculpture. She barked again and Elsie ran over towards her. One of the wolf's blue fangs was wobbling slightly. Elsie looked at it; it was perfectly still and solid. Then, yes, a slight movement. They hadn't imagined it. Then it was perfectly still again. She looked back towards Margo. The dust had gone. Then another sprinkle as the tooth shook once more. Elsie thought for a moment. There was some kind of opening and the tooth must operate it, she thought. Quickly, she ran over the back of the tongue to Margo, picked her up and brought her back to the front of Blue Tooth's mouth. If there was a door, she didn't want Margo anywhere near it when it opened. Whatever was moving it and making the scraping sound, Elsie wanted Margo and herself to be as far away as possible when they found out what it was. She put Margo down by Smokey's side and grabbed the top of the tooth. With all her strength she heaved it first towards her and then away. It moved a little. Again, this time putting all her weight against it with her shoulder, she pushed, but it didn't move. She went to the other side and, once again, putting her whole weight behind it, she pushed once more. The tooth moved slightly at first, but then, as Elsie jerked it again and pushed hard with her shoulder against it, it gave way, bending almost at forty five degrees before stopping dead.

It was the squeal and the growl together that turned everybody's heads. At the back of Blue Tooth's throat, a long, thin flat platform had tippled backwards and forwards for a moment as if balanced, then with the weight of a wolf on one side of the balance it dropped slowly down until its end had come to rest on the rising up-slope of the rear of the tongue. The movement of the platform was remarkably smooth and silent. But it was the rolling, tumbling, growling wolf that was making the noise.

Solin had landed.

Shaking himself as he planted his feet well apart to steady his balance, Solin stood up on his toes and said, 'At last! I thought you were never going to open it.' His head was just visible above the rise of Blue Tooth's tongue.

Smokey had never forgiven Solin. While Rhamin was about, she had been prepared to let him join the pack for a short time, so long as he kept out of her way. Now he was in her way. She bounded up the rise of the tongue and down what remained of the opposite side of the slope towards her arch enemy.

'No!' Elsie shouted, but Smokey was taking no notice. 'Down!' she commanded, remembering some of the orders she had heard Raymond using. 'Down!' she shouted again.

At the second shout, Smokey slid to a halt, only inches away from Solin's barred teeth. Neither she nor Solin moved for several seconds.

'Solin! Smokey! Save it till you are out of this tomb.' Zelda's voice broke the impasse. She had barked her command. She stood up shakily and slowly walked up to the crest of the rock wolf's tongue. Solin and Smokey were still barring their teeth, though Smokey had turned slightly to one side to see what orders she was to be given next.

Elsie strode up to both of them. Fearlessly, she stood between them, looking first at Smokey then at Solin. 'Now listen here,' she shouted, her voice firm with authority. '*I* am leader now. Don't you forget it,' she said, pointing to her own chest.

Neither wolf nor dog understood the words, but they understood the body language and the tone of her voice. They both backed away from each other as Elsie walked away with her hands on her hips and her lips compressed. To Margo it looked like her lips were compressed with anger. Only Elsie knew that she was really suppressing a broad grin. She didn't know how this renegade wolf had reappeared back in the Blue Tooth cavern, but she knew one thing for sure; without him they would still be waiting and watching the rising water.

CHAPTER FORTY SIX

There was no point in hanging about but if they were to move on then Margo came first. Elsie picked up her backpack and took out a cheese sandwich which she handed to her little cousin. Margo devoured it eagerly. Then, after taking out a bar of chocolate for Margo and one for herself, Elsie slung the bag over her shoulders. Margo quickly stuffed the chocolate into her coat pocket and then waited for Elsie to eat hers.

Solin, although not knowing how they worked, was relieved that Elsie had the use of a flashlight. He had no wish to carry on, blindly stumbling along in total darkness. With the Maglite in her left hand and Margo's little hand grasped firmly in her right, Elsie led the way. Following on, Smokey escorted Zelda up the ramp and Solin tracked on at the back, content to keep out of the big dog's way.

After climbing the ramp, they found themselves standing where Solin had scratched at the floor, in a small, low topped cave. Its floor seemed flat, but as they walked away from the opening, the floor dropped away suddenly, sloping down once again for some considerable distance until they eventually arrived on a level plain which had pillars of rock from ceiling to floor. Whether these were columns that had formed when stalactites reached down and met the stalagmites that were stretching upwards, or whether they were manufactured in some way, as she believed was the case with Blue Tooth, the columns definitely looked as if they were supporting the roof. And if that were the case, then, by Elsie's reckoning, they were not very far from the surface.

She panned the light beam, looking in every direction. The cavern was so big that the light did not reach the furthest walls. All they could do was walk around its perimeter and see if there were any other stairways or tunnels that might take them higher and to safety. She was convinced that they were only a very short distance from the surface and freedom. The floor was smooth and flat. The ceiling was the same. Even the pillars, as she passed them, looked identical. This was not a cave, she was sure of it. But just what it was, she had no idea. It reminded her of the underground car parks that are built in the cities. But out in the middle of nowhere?

The roaring sound was still there. It hadn't abated even a little bit.

They had wandered on this featureless plain for longer than Elsie could estimate. She was beginning to think that this was another dead end, but there was no use going back. They all knew there was no way out, back there. Or if there was, they had failed to find it. Their only hope was to keep moving forward. The problem was that where the floor had been perfectly dry when they first descended into this place, now the floor seemed to be covered with a thin film of water and five minutes later, the water was ankle deep and getting deeper with every stride. Elsie's worst fear had just materialised. The water had filled all the caverns below them. Now, it was slowly but surely heading towards the ceiling.

Elsie didn't know how long her torch light would last. Every stride forward seemed to bring the water further up her legs. But when she turned and took some steps back the way she had come, the water was deeper still. It was rising fast. She bent down and, holding Margo under her armpits, she swung her up to her chest. The water was too deep for the little girl to wade through now. It had already reached Elsie's knees. It would soon be above Margo's waist.

Eventually, as Elsie stopped and adjusted Margo's weight on her arm, she paused to take a breath and listened. While they had been wading through the water, the roaring sound had faded, but in their effort to move on, she hadn't noticed. There seemed to be a tranquil silence now. From now on, the only sound would be the sloshing of all their feet as they moved relentlessly through the water.

For a moment she put Margo down but to keep her dry she seated her on Smokey's back. They rested for a short while and then she licked her finger and held it above her head. The air was passing them, coming from behind and disappearing up ahead. But the floor was rising slowly, closing the space beneath the roof so that now her finger was only inches from the ceiling. It was no use; they had to keep going. Once again she lifted Margo in her arms and waded onwards, following the stream of air. She quickened her pace, but it was hard carrying Margo. Her arms were tired but so too was her whole body. And behind, the old wolf Zelda was almost swimming now, struggling to keep up.

Smokey, and Solin were doing the same, partly walking on tiptoe keeping their bodies as high out of the water as possible, partly swimming as they relaxed every few moments, and mainly bounding forward over the water to avoid its dragging resistance. Smokey moved ahead, trying to urge Elsie onwards. The two wolves stayed close on Elsie's heels but Zelda was now in serious trouble. She had no strength left in her withered body. Soon she would have to let the rising water take her.

Suddenly, Smokey bounded once again through the water, jumping to clear it with every leap. She had spotted something and was a good ten yards ahead when she barked. The sound coming from deep within her chest and echoing through the water filled chamber. Without another sound, she rose up and cleared the water. She had found some steps, not ordinary steps, but a series of high ledges that rose towards the ceiling. As Elsie shone her torch, by the fading light beam, she could make out an opening in the roof. Pushing harder through the water now, she went after Smokey, striding out to reach the ledges. Solin and Zelda followed.

Elsie lifted Margo and placed her on the first shoulder-high ledge next to Smokey. She jumped up and pulled herself onto it alongside her little cousin. Solin bounded up to join them. Once again they were clear of the water, but Zelda was still standing below, shoulder deep in water. She was noticeably weaker now. She stood panting, her face blindly looking up at the rest of the group on the ledge. Solin and Smokey just shook their bodies to rid themselves of as much water from their coats as they could as they waited patiently for Elsie to lead the way once more. Zelda began to shiver.

As they all looked up ahead they were certain they had not a lot further to go. There were thick, deep stone steps now, almost as high as Elsie's shoulder, leading to a grill way above their heads. Was it freedom?

Elsie thought she could see a star twinkling through the

bars, like a beacon leading them home. Desperately now, and with Margo still in her arms, she climbed the huge steps, placing Margo on each and then jumping up and pulling herself onto the next one before picking Margo up again only to repeat the process time after time. She was right; there was fresh air and freedom at the other side of the grate. The opening was about eight feet square with heavy stone bars that criss-crossed at right angles. But it was huge. Each piece of the grill was over four inches deep and two inches wide. It must have weighed many tons. Someone at some time had meticulously carved the grill out of a single piece of solid rock. It looked old and weather worn. The edges on the centre arms of the grill were rounded much more than those at the edge, it appeared, where the weathering process had taken less toll. The grill was ancient, but it was big. And worst of all, it was unmovable. Frantically, Elsie shone the weak beam of her torch around. There were four round, stone-lined tunnels, each about five feet in diameter, heading away like spokes in a wheel.

Smokey and Solin had been right at Elsie's heels, leaping up each step behind her. But Zelda was still standing down below, in the rising water, struggling to climb onto the first of the high stone ledges. Her painful hips did not permit her to jump like a young wolf.

Leaving Margo at the top, Elsie jumped down the steps and joined Zelda. Putting her hands under the old wolf's chest, she heaved Zelda's front paws onto the next step. But before she could get behind her, the old wolf's back legs had collapsed under the weight of her body. Zelda was too tired and too weak to carry on.

CHAPTER FORTY SEVEN

Raymond and Maria were as surprised as the police officers when they saw Rhamin loping over the plain with a passenger on his back. They had waited in the Jeep and parked close to the police car so that they could converse through the open windows. They watched Charka as she lay on the ground, and, with her ears forward, and her nose pointing in the direction from which she expected her leader to return, she just patiently watched and waited.

Charka's patience did little to abate Raymond and Maria's apprehension. For nearly twenty minutes they sat and fidgeted, hardly talking apart from Raymond saying, *Come on, where are you?* more times that Maria cared to count. But eventually Rhamin returned. The biggest shock was that Rhamin had returned with some of his wolves, but with only one child: Ben.

Elsie, Margo and his dog, Smokey were nowhere to be seen.

Maria jumped out of the Jeep, mindless of the battering rain, and ran towards The Black Wolf. Wincing, Raymond struggled to get out at his side of the Jeep, and began to wish he's taken a couple more of the pain-killer tablets that the doctor had prescribed. But ignoring the knives of pain as best he could, he joined Ben and Maria.

Ben was black with rain-soaked dust that had caked his whole body. His dirty, streaked face, although he had washed it in the river, looked like a grubby pale mask on his little shoulders.

'Margo and Elsie are trapped in the caves,' Ben uttered, wretchedly. His eyes were wide with fear. 'And the caves are flooding!' he blurted desperately.

Maria suddenly found it hard to breath. Raymond ran his hands through rain-soaked hair, a feeling of despair coursing through his whole body.

Once the policemen had recovered from the shock of seeing not only a wolf carrying a young boy on its back, but seeing that it was the biggest wolf they had ever seen in their lives, the sergeant said to his companion, 'Get a cave rescue team. Tell them where we are and tell them that children are trapped. Tell them anything! Get help. Get... get a helicopter out here!'

His partner didn't seem to be so panicked. Calmly, he radioed in to his Head Quarters and explained the situation clearly and precisely. 'They're onto it,' he said quite reassuringly. 'Don't get too worried.'

Raymond and Maria, however, couldn't have been more worried if they, themselves, had been dangling, suspended by a single hair over a bottomless pit. Their insides were racked with anguish. Holding Ben close to them, warming him in a blanket supplied to them from the police car was, perhaps, the only thing that, at that moment, made life bearable.

Raymond could stand it no more. And looking into Maria's face, he knew she felt exactly the same. Grabbing his spare torch from behind the seat, he told Maria to drive towards the caves. He shouted his intentions to the policemen and, Maria, relieved to be doing something, anything, started the Jeep's engine, spun it around and sped back the way they had come.

CHAPTER FORTY EIGHT

Suddenly, Solin was there at the bottom of the steps with Elsie too. 'Come on old wolf. You're going to be the death of us all,' he said to Zelda, jumping down into the water and nudging her roughly with his muzzle.

'Leave me and go,' Zelda said, knowing that Elsie couldn't help her any more. But Elsie didn't understand the whining noises coming from the old wolf. They sounded like calls of despair.

'What are we going to do?' Margo shouted down to Elsie. 'Which tunnel do we take now?'

Elsie shook her head. 'I don't know.' Never had she felt so desperate. Never, since the death of her father, had she felt so lost and helpless.

Smokey had gone up each of the pipes a few yards and was trying to help make a choice.

Quickly, Elsie jumped up the steps one at a time again and joined Margo. The torch beam was turning from white to yellow. There was no light coming from the other side of the stone grill except a splash of star light from a small patch of clear sky between the dark but broken rain clouds. Desperately she shone the light beam into each of the round tunnels.

With the others well out of earshot, Zelda turned to Solin. 'You came here to kill me,' Zelda said to Solin. 'Do it and let them get on.'

'Stupid old wolf. How long do you think it would be before that big ugly dog took her revenge and tried to kill me? She's been waiting for an excuse to attack me and you'd give it to her.'

'Call Smokey down here. I'll explain.'

'Right, and you think she'll let me kill you? You are stupider than I thought.'

'I'll ask you both to do it.'

'Well it looks to me like we might all be joining you anyway. We are all still trapped. You might as well just stay here and do it on your own.'

'It won't work.'

'What won't work? You reckon you can't manage to die. You're telling me you won't depart this world unless somebody kills you? You're really are an old fool!'

'No, I'll die, but too late to help you.'

'Help me? Don't make me laugh. I'm the last wolf you'd want to help.'

'Then think about the two girls. You're the children's only hope. Someone has to guide them when the light she carries goes out. The water is still rising. I can feel it still rising, still getting deeper. You must take the right tunnel now or it will be too late to turn back and try another one.'

'And your dying will help her make the right choice? Yeah, that will be a fat lot of use.'

'Listen to me just for once in your life,' Zelda scolded crossly. 'My mind is not as agile as it used to be. I can't see with it what I could. But it isn't because I have lost the ability, it's because I have lost the strength. I use too much of my life force staying alive. If I am dead, then my mind can be released from that burden. Without my body holding me back and sapping my strength, I can travel up each of these tunnels. I can do it faster than you can climb back up these steps to the children. By the time you get to them, then I will know which way you have to go.'

'And you can miraculously come back and tell us. Great idea! I don't think! You get stupider every time I see you.' Solin shook his head and turned away. 'Goodness knows how you have survived so long,' he muttered, to himself beneath the sound of the lapping water, rather than making himself heard to the old wolf. 'Why on earth Rhiana wanted to kill you I just can't fathom.' He turned back to her. 'You're a liability,' he said so that she could hear him. 'But you can die on your own. Don't expect me to do anything to help you.'

But Zelda was adamant. 'I can help you by telling your mind, Solin. Listen to me. It's your only hope. It's the children's only hope. I'm going to die here anyway. Kill me now while no one is watching.'

Solin gave out a heavy sigh. For a brief moment, he thought about what Zelda had said. Then, resigned to what he must do, and without another word, he barred his teeth and grabbed hold of Zelda's fur on the back of her neck. Using all his strength, he lifted her clear of the water and, shaking her to one side, threw her into the air. The weak old wolf gave off no sound. A moment later she landed squarely but weakly on her feet. Shaking herself unsteadily, she realized that she had landed on the next ledge.

'I'm not listening to any more of your rubbish you old pile of offal. You either climb the steps or I throw you up them,' Solin growled. 'Which is it going to be?'

'You always were brainless,' Zelda grunted as Solin jumped up on the ledge and moved to grab her again. This time Zelda sniffed at the wall of rock in front of her and reached up and put her front paws on the next ledge, which, like all the others, was at about head height when she stood on her hind legs. She was not a heavy wolf, but the years had bowed her legs and eaten away at her muscles. With her back legs gradually sagging under her meagre weight, the claws of her front paws slowly began to relinquish their grip on the ledge. But when Solin noticed her legs giving way he shoved his head in between her back legs and, jumping up himself, lifted the old wolf, this time smoothly, onto the next stone step.

'Don't tell me you are going soft on me,' Zelda jibed.

'Shut up you old fool,' Solin ordered as once again they repeated the procedure that elevated her yet another step upwards. 'You'll die soon enough, believe me.'

'Rhiana isn't going to like this. Solin, her great son, gone soft!'

'Say what you like, it will make no difference.'

'Where is the scheming traitor, by the way?'

'You don't need to know.'

'Need to know?' Zelda wrinkled her nose. 'Am I missing something here?' She pondered on the remark. 'You returned alone. What happened to the rest of my wolves? What happened to Ben?'

Solin was quiet for a moment. But when he spoke, it wasn't with any pleasure in his voice. 'Rhiana's dead if you must know. They all are.'

'All these holes lead to more water,' Smokey said as Zelda and Solin reached the top step. 'See? Although it is only trickling, water is coming in from them, not running away. That grill is the only exit.'

Smokey tried to bite the stone bars but, despite being worn and flaky, they were still solid. At some time somebody or something had tirelessly carved the grill out of solid rock.

'That's no use,' Solin commented as he pushed past her. 'Nothing will move that.'

'And have you any better suggestions?' Smokey demanded.

Without acknowledging the question, Solin put his nose through one of the holes in the grill and emitted from his throat a long and protracted howl.

'And that's your pathetic answer, is it?' Smokey leered. 'You really think that if any wolves can hear you, they will come here and be able to lift this thing off our tomb?'

Ignoring Smokey completely, once more, Solin pushed his nose through the stone grill and sent his voice echoing into the blustery wind with a strange and most peculiar howl.

CHAPTER FORTY NINE

Darkness isn't always the same.

Dark cloud covered night skies cast the world in darkness, but not dark enough to prevent the keen eyes of wolves and other nocturnal predators from seeing clearly. Then there is the darkness at the back of the Darin where little light reaches out from the mouth of the cave at night, but where there is still light enough to see the shadowy form of Zelda.

And then there is total darkness. Darkness of a tunnel beneath the ground. Darkness unbreached by a single particle of light; a darkness that convinces you that you are dead and buried. Or if not *dead*, then buried alive.

Rasci couldn't tell if it was total darkness or if he was blind. For what seemed like hours he lay motionless, contemplating where he was and what had happened to him. He sniffed the stale air. The acrid dust stirred as he lifted his head.

'Hello,' he whispered, not knowing what to expect. He was answered by complete silence.

He cleared his throat and tried again, his voice stronger this time. 'Hello,' he called. Still silence. Then he tried to move. There was some rubble around him but little of it lying across his body. Slowly he moved his front legs. They seemed to be working. Now his back legs. No pain. Slowly, pulling with his front paws and pushing with his hind legs, he crawled forward. The silence was almost unbearable as he listened to his own breathing. Still, he knew not whether he was dead and buried and was merely the remaining element of his spirit form moving from the grave, or whether he was still alive. Should it be this hard to tell one from the other?

He tried to think back to what had happened last. They were all together in the caves; Rhamin, Ben and Margo and… no, just Ben. They had left Margo and Elsie behind. But most of the other wolves were with them. What had happened? They were in some tunnels and… and Rhiana and Roxana were quarrelling. They were just behind him. They began to fight. Then he remembered. Rhiana had knocked the mouldering wooden prop and the roof had fallen in on all of them. Wolves ahead were disappearing in the dust as they ran. Ahead, the light that Ben carried had disappeared behind the avalanche of falling rocks. The roof behind him was already filling the passage. Rasci had stumbled sideways into one of the tunnels that led off at right angles to the one in which they were walking. Then the falling roof had followed him. The first thing that hit him, probably some of the rotten, mulched wood supports, seemed soft, knocking him over and rolling him sideways as it glanced off his rear end. He thought his thick fur must have perhaps cushioned him from the first impact since the rocks that followed were sharp and heavy and shook every bone in his body as he scrambled to his feet and attempted to get out of their way. In the blackness, more rocks had hit him, knocking him to the ground again. They seemed to follow him each time he scrambled forward but he was disorientated by the first blow and bouncing off one wall at one side and then the next as, each time he fell, he struggled to get back onto his feet. He went down again and again under the weight of more falling earth and rocks but struggled to get back up and keep pushing himself forward with every remaining particle of strength. Things rolled against him pushing him forward, others rolled past him, he couldn't tell what, and he just staggered on as fast as he could, tripping and stumbling in a direction away from the collapsing roof. Something hit him on the head and time seemed to stop. Was the roof still caving in? There seemed to be a scraping, scratching sound as if he were digging with his paws, and needles of rock, as sharp as teeth, seemed to be digging into the thick fur at the back of his neck. That's the last he remembered

He sighed. How long had he been there? What should he do? If he were dead then his spirit should be able to travel out of this place. He concentrated, and sure enough, he could see Rhamin. His leader was with Ben at the mouth of the Darin. They were with Ben's mother and father and two other men kind. They were entering the caves, and Yeltsa and Lexa were with them.

He concentrated again. Zelda and Smokey were looking up at an early evening sky. Dark storm clouds were parting and a single star twinkled through the clouds upon some kind of criss-cross, man-made grate. He looked down at them, but they couldn't see him. He was a ghost. Then he noticed that they were not alone. Solin was behind them. So were Margo and Elsie. With relief, he realized that, although he was dead, they were still alive. But they were trapped and the water was still rising behind them relentlessly.

He glanced around. They were in a forest but all was not well. His companions were trapped on one side of the stone grill but there was no freedom at the other side. Half a mile away, Rasci could see Bortag. He had always been an angry bear. But if he knew about the death of Molem, Bortag's temper would, by now, have turned to rage. And he was heading towards Rasci's trapped friends as if he could smell them; it was as if he knew where they were. Then he heard Solin call out. He was placing his nose through the stone grill and howling. A strange kind of call considering he was crying for help. But then Rasci realized Solin wasn't calling for help. Solin was calling his enemy, their enemy. He was calling out to Bortag. He must have perhaps recognised where they were and where the big bear might have been. Perhaps Solin had seen the grill before. Perhaps he knew Bortag often frequented that area. Perhaps he had befriended Bortag the same as he has befriended the mountain lions. But no, that wasn't what Rasci could see. Solin wasn't calling to Bortag for help. He was insulting their enemy, telling Bortag he had fed on the remains of the bear's dead mate. He was baiting him; he was challenging him. No, he wasn't calling for help; instead, he was drawing in the deadly danger and with every step he took closer to the sound of Solin's voice, the bear was getting angrier and angrier.

CHAPTER FIFTY

Zelda said nothing. She knew what Solin was doing, but she had no strength to stop him and neither had she the will to dissuade him. Water was already lapping only a few feet below the ledge on which they were all trapped and more was coming in now from the huge shafts that surrounded them. The pipes were not draining the water away; they were inlets pipes, channels that brought water to the opening, not away from it. Like the spring inside the Darin which was an overflow point where water escaped from beneath the rocks, here, the grill, she realized, was where the water escaped when the underground chamber beneath them became full.

Smokey wasn't sure who Solin was calling. To her, he sounded demented. Instead of calling for help, he was trying to get some creature called Bortag to come and kill him! Not a solution she had in mind. She was about to grab Solin by his thick fur and drag him away from the grill, but Zelda poked her with her nose and quietly instructed her to let him carry on. She knew what Solin was planning. If he was right, and she wasn't sure how he could be, Bortag would hear him and come to the grill. Only Bortag would have the strength to move the cage lid that entrapped them. And when he had removed it, then Solin would sacrifice the old wolf while he, at least, escaped to safety. She smiled inwardly. Rasci had been right, Solin was no fool. He had strength, he had cunning. He could have been a good leader if he hadn't taken the wrong path in life.

And turning back was useless. The water level had already risen up the huge steps. Soon it would reach their feet. There was no escape. If Solin's calls brought wolves, then they would still perish. Zelda silently hoped that Bortag was, as Solin firmly believed, somewhere near enough to hear him calling out. At this moment, if there were any survivors of the Rhamin pack, she fervently hoped that the pack did not arrive first.

CHAPTER FIFTY ONE

'Rasci?' Ben asked the question silently but Maria heard his whisper.

'Yes, it's me Ben.'

'You're alive!' Ben shouted, unable to contain his excitement.

'Er, no, Ben. I can see you and I can see Elsie and Margo. But I'm afraid I exist no longer.'

'But I can see you. You are sitting in front of me like you always do when you come to talk to me.'

'That might be the case, but I'm afraid you'll have to forget about me.'

'No! I couldn't ever do that!'

'What I mean is that you must help me to help the others. I can explain where they are. Margo and Elsie have survived - so far, but they are in grave danger. They are up at the north side of the forest, but they are trapped. They are in a hole that faces up to the sky. The water is rising behind them and there is some kind of cage on top of them. They cannot get out. And there is even more danger facing them when and if they do escape.'

'But Daddy can get them out,' Ben said eagerly.

'I think your daddy is injured. He'll not be able to get up

to the forest in time. You must try and get the people with him to go up there.'

'But how will they find it. Where is the hole?'

Rasci's spirit vision shook his head. 'I'm not sure. I think I could guide you.'

'How?'

'Just follow what you see.'

'You mean you are going to walk with me?'

'No, go in the mechanical things first. Go directly towards the foothills and the forest.'

'In the Jeep, you mean?'

'If that is what you call the one you want to travel in. But you must go now.'

Ben turned to his father. 'Daddy…'

'I heard,' his father said, stroking Ben's head affectionately. 'I heard enough to know that Rasci is going to help us find Margo and Elsie. Quickly now, back to the Jeep.'

Limping badly, but helped by Maria, Raymond clambered back into the Jeep. He shouted to the two police officers and explained that he thought he knew where the children were, and, not venturing to explain any further, he, Ben and Maria set off, steering the Jeep once more around rocks and gulleys, heading towards the foothills.

As they drove up closer to the tree line, sure enough, Ben spotted Rasci's spirit form. 'He's there!' Ben exclaimed, pointing at what was just a patch of thin, spindly trees. But he could see Rasci even if nobody else could. The wolf spirit was sitting waiting for them. As they drove nearer, Rasci's form stood up, turned around and loped forward taking a path that the Jeep could follow easily.

'That way,' Ben shouted excitedly.

'No, stop,' Raymond ordered suddenly. He let the police

car catch up and then asked the officers if they would get into the Jeep. The terrain was not one for an ordinary two-wheel-drive car. The police officers did as he suggested and squeezed into the back of the Jeep with Ben squashed between them. Then, guided by Ben, Maria drove on, following the trail, taking directions from her son if and when they were needed.

CHAPTER FIFTY TWO

A gap in the black clouds had halted the rain but the respite looked ominously short. The heavy breath of the huge bear could be heard over the sound of the shuffling branches that were being whipped up by the wind. His was a panting, grunting kind of noise as if he had run a long way and was keeping up his speed to get to his destination sooner rather than later. But Zelda knew it was his normal savage, aggressive sound. He was scared of nothing. He liked to let every creature in the forest know the fact. It was a sound he had made so often and for so long that it had become his normal noise. It was Bortag's sound.

'Come on you festering old runt,' Solin baited. 'I can hear you,' he shouted into the darkening night air as loud as his sore, dust-filled lungs could call. 'I can smell you.' He coughed and sneezed to clear his throat and nose. 'Who killed your mate?' he called, not expecting any answer. But he wanted to get this bear, the arch enemy of all wolves, angry.

If any animal had the luck to have their prey call out and give them directions to find them, it was only because that prey was either crazy or had another motive in mind. And Bortag knew of Solin. The tales of the forests went everywhere. The fight that the wolves had with the bears three years ago had become folklore; Solin's attack on the farm, his contests with Rhamin. But Bortag had never forgotten the fight he'd had with the Rhamin pack.

'I know you saw Molem's remains down by Rhamin's cave,' Solin shouted. 'Good riddance! That's one less ugly bear in our territory.'

'I make my own territory,' Bortag snarled back, suddenly revealing his presence as his huge head came into view above the grate. 'Remember? It's you wolves that keep out of my way, not the other way round.'

'That didn't help Molem did it, you big bowel full of waste?'

Bortag roared. 'You want to die! I might just help you do it!'

'No chance!' Solin snapped back. 'Look at yourself! What are you compared with a sleek wolf?'

'You are trapped!' Bortag snarled, with a heavy accent as he looked at the covered hole. 'Nothing you say to me will alter the fact. You are going to die!'

'Looks like it,' Solin said resigned now to wait till Bortag decided what he was going to do. He knew the bear was not dim-witted. 'But you won't have the pleasure of finishing us off. We can say what we like to you and you can't do a thing about it!'

'So why call me? You were calling me, weren't you?'

'Calling you? Yes, I was calling you, Bortag. Before I died, I wanted to let you know how ill thought of you are by all the creatures in this land.'

'You never were much of a jester from what I've heard,' Bortag replied in a gruff and gravelly voice. 'You called out to me because you are trapped. So what's the deal?'

So the old bear was no fool after all.

'Plenty of food here if you open it up. Some of the prey

can't even understand what we're talking about.'

'I understand you well enough,' Smokey growled.

'You aren't the easy pickings,' Solin barked back and turned to Smokey with barred teeth. 'Keep quiet you foolish flop-eared dog,' he growled through clenched jaws.

'Flop eared! Seen yourself lately?' Smokey retorted, but she realized what Solin was doing and said no more. With the grill removed, some of them might have a chance to escape. As they were, they would all die if the water continued to rise any further. Then, with what seemed like a resigned growl, she said, 'Huh, well the old wolf is dead meat walking, anyway!'

Bortag pushed his long snout against the grill. He could smell old Zelda. And he could smell the children. These were the offspring of the species that killed his mate. Growling, he paced slowly around the grate. He snorted and poked his long rubbery nose through the grill again. Then he lifted his head, turned and began to walk away. He wasn't really hungry. Letting his enemies die where they were was good enough.

Smokey moved up beside Solin as they saw the big bear disappear from view. 'Great plan that was,' she snarled. 'Now what have you in mind? Anything else to pass the time?'

'It's your turn next,' Solin countered. 'It's your turn to think of an escape plan.'

'It wasn't much of a plan anyway…'

But Smokey had no time to finish what she was saying. Solin shouted once more. 'Tasty meat, bear meat. Molem's body was a bit tough though.'

Suddenly, and without warning, the bear's enormous head appeared over the edge of the grill. He was still there and, roaring with rage, he pushed his huge paw through one of the gaps to try and reach Solin. He pulled and rived and jerked at the grill, every part of his thick fur rippling as the effort shook his whole body. But the huge stone didn't move. A small wisp of dust sprinkled into the water that was now lapping around the captives' feet.

Elsie drew Margo close to her as they peered up at the fearsome creature.

'Is that the best you can do then?' Solin snarled, nipping at the bear's paw as Bortag withdrew his foot and began to use his claws, scraping beneath the edge of the grill. But the huge stone still didn't move.

Bortag lifted his head and sniffed at the cold evening air. There was danger heading his way, he could sense it. It was probably the men kind looking for their young ones. But they would be too late to save them. He hated men more than he hated Solin. At that moment, and blinded by rage, his only intention was to reek revenge on the species that killed his mate. Suddenly he stood over the grill. His one good, cold eye stared down at the wolves and children.

The opaque, damaged eye, the one blinded in his fight with the Rhamin pack, was even more startling, Elsie thought. It had a look of death about it. She shivered and clutched Margo even closer to her as the bear's good eye examined her.

Margo seemed enthralled, her little face gazing up at the bear's face. Her lips were parted as she studied the big eye.

Solin stared back at the huge face, saying nothing now. A noticeable hatred was passing between him and the massive predator as he waited for the inevitable.

Then, roaring in a frenzied fury, Bortag reared up to his full height above the grill, blacking out most of the dim light that remained in the late evening sky.

Elsie squeezed Margo close to her side, cowering in the mouth of one of the off-shooting tunnels. Smokey was quivering not with fright but with nervous tension. Her adrenaline-packed body was ready to fight. She backed inside the tunnel in front of the children. She would guard them with her life. But, if they had to run, the tunnel was not the route that led to freedom. Like all the other offshoots, it could run for miles and there could be a grill at the end of it just the same as the one above their heads. And anyway, the bear could probably get up it easily on all fours.

Zelda remained out of the way, her head facing out of one of the opposing pipes.

Elsie couldn't understand why old Zelda and Solin seemed so calm, so unaffected by the stress that had overcome Smokey and herself.

Margo looked up at Elsie and gave her a reassuring smile. She didn't say anything. It was as if she didn't comprehend the terrible and imminent danger. As she turned her fascinated gaze back to Bortag, she looked like she expected the marauding bear to lift them out of the hole one by one and wave them off safely down the mountain.

The huge bear hovered over the grill as if working something out and then, hesitating just for another second, with all his weight, brought his front paws down on the edge of the grill.

Thump! The ground shook around them. Dust and grit splashed into the water by their feet but the grill remained intact.

The water was still rising.

Bortag stopped and contemplated for a moment, once again, exchanging a malevolent stare with Solin. Solin still remained silent. His hackles were bristling, but he seemed calm. Elsie noticed that Smokey's hackles bristled not only all the way along her backbone but around her neck and face as well.

It was hard to tell what the old wolf Zelda was thinking. She appeared to be calmly awaiting her fate. Her head was tilted slightly to one side. She seemed to be listening to and sightlessly watching everything with great interest.

Again the bear reared up and once again, as if assessing the situation, paused for a fraction of a second before bringing his entire weight down on the grill with his front paws. Once again the ground shook, powdery dust fell but the grill remained in one piece. Venting all his anger and pent up rage, again Bortag rose to full height and again, this time without pausing, the bear brought down his entire weight and his strength. He did it again and again, all the time, his one good eye locked on Solin's eyes with a venomous hatred. Again he rose up and again he thumped down with all his weight until the ground shook for what seemed the hundredth time. Then, as if he knew it would happen, a powdery crack appeared in one of the stone sections of the grill. It was beginning to break.

Solin saw it too. In the gloom of the tunnel, the bear didn't notice that Solin had spread his back legs and had braced himself against the solid floor ready to leap out. He was going to be first out of the hole. He would escape before the bear had chance to realize the gap had opened up. Just one more hammering thud and the grate would cave in.

Thump. Down came Bortag. Crash went the grill, scattering fragments of stone off Solin's thick coat and splashing into the water all around his feet.

Solin was like a coiled spring. As soon as a corner section of the grill collapsed inwards, he catapulted out of the hole, past Bortag's face and was already gone before the bear could lift his weight from where it hung, in the neck of the hole where the grill had collapsed. Bortag stood up and looked around. Solin had gone, but it mattered little. The hole was there.

For the captives, the route to freedom had been opened. It had been cleared by a vicious and relentless predator, a killer who could run as fast as any healthy wolf. Some of them, the children in particular, would never escape. They could neither run fast enough nor fight such a huge and vicious creature. Smokey would try to defend them, both Margo and Elsie knew that, but it wouldn't be enough. One dog against Bortag was no contest.

Elsie reckoned that Zelda had not got the faintest chance of even climbing out of the pit alive. The bear would reach in and kill her or she would remain down there and die in one of the four useless tunnels. As for herself and Margo? Well, without something to distract the bear, then she and her little cousin had no better chance of survival.

Smokey still stood guard in front of her wards, bristled, growling and tensed, ready to attack, ready to defend her children to the end, preventing the huge bear from sticking his paw or his face into the opening. The bear wouldn't risk injury, particularly to his one good eye. He would reach in with his huge paw or just simply wait till his prey came out into the open.

Zelda moved forward from her tunnel retreat and, pushing past Smokey, stood up in the opening with her face only inches from Bortag's huge snout. The bear would take her first. At least that would give the others some kind of chance.

Bortag lowered his face and sniffed at the old wolf. Their noses touched but he suddenly withdrew his face, lifted his head and snarled as something hit him from behind.

Spinning around, Bortag faced Solin. The wolf had not escaped to freedom. He was free, but he was circling the bear, waiting to attack as wolves do; hit and run; lunge in, tear and retreat. Solin had hit the bear with his front paws and bounced away, not attacking, not biting, not even making a sound. He was just getting a response, trying to distract the bear from his immediate intention.

Seeing what was happening, and while Bortag was turned towards Solin, Smokey bounded past Zelda's shoulder and leapt out onto the fern-covered ground. She, like Solin, began to circle the huge bear, knowing that one bite, one swipe with the creature's huge claws could, would kill her.

And then, as Elsie, standing on tiptoe, peered over the edge of the opening to see what was happening, the bear just growled something to its adversaries and, without so much as a glance backwards towards the hole, began to walk away. She couldn't tell what had happened or why the huge predator had just turned and casually walked off up the tree-covered slope. Why had the bear gone to all that trouble and then simply abandoned the hunt?

Margo knew, as did old Zelda.

Ignoring Solin and Smokey as if they were two pestering flies around him on a hot, sunny day, Bortag turned back. He stepped up to the broken grill and, once again, put his face through the hole. As Elsie backed away into the sanctuary of her tunnel, he poked his nose close to old Zelda. Zelda didn't step back. She pushed her face closer to Bortag; so close that he could easily take her head in his huge mouth.

'That's for saving my daughter, old wolf,' the bear growled to her with a heavy accent but with a lighter tone in his voice. 'And I know who really killed Molem.' An unusual grin crept up the side of his mouth towards the dead and disfigured eye, making Bortag's face look even more frightening. 'That useless wolf Solin really ought to do something for himself so that he can truly claim credit for it. If he killed Molem then I'm a rabbit!' He lifted his face away from the hole. 'No, I know exactly who killed my mate.' He shook his head and growled as he contemplated what he had just said. For a moment he had seemed calmer, but now, his anger seemed to boil again. 'Trust me, they'll pay!' he roared and then, almost casually and totally disregarding Solin and Smokey as they bounced against his thick coat, he turned away once again.

Without so much as a glance back, he walked off uphill, further into the forest and disappeared behind the wall of trees. 'But it won't always be like this,' he called behind him. 'Keep your distance Solin you pathetic gad fly. You're no friend of mine.'

And with that last warning he was gone.

CHAPTER FIFTY THREE

With Bortag departed, Solin took charge. Even Smokey had no objections. Somehow, her enemy had turned comrade, if only for a short while. He had, by some sheer fluke, managed to get them safely out of the ground. And more importantly, he knew his way about the forests as well as any wolf in the Rhamin pack. The least she could do at the moment was let him be the leader and guide them back to safety.

With a little help from Elsie, Zelda struggled out of the pit. Then Elsie lifted Margo out into the open. Finally, she climbed out herself and watched as Margo looked at Solin.

'He thinks that Mummy and Daddy are on their way,' Margo told her. 'He has heard a car or something.'

'And you know that how?' Elsie asked, frowning.

Margo just shrugged. 'You'll have to believe us some time, Elsie. Ben and I can talk to wolves. *I* can hear their thoughts.'

'So what's happening now?'

'Solin is considering if he should leave us here. Zelda has told him that she'll take us back if he wants to leave. He has kept his bargain, she is thinking.'

'What bargain?'

Margo shrugged again and remained silent. She hadn't been taking a lot of notice what was being said or thought by the wolves when Rhamin and his pack caught up with Solin and his renegades.

'Solin says he'll stay a while. He says Smokey is about as good a guide as a dead sheep and he says that unlike Zelda, he isn't blind!'

'Is that so?' Elsie questioned with a wry smile.

'And he knows the forest around here.'

'Glad somebody does,' Elsie countered. 'Better tell him to lead the way.'

Margo didn't say anything, but Solin began to weave his way through the trees and walk slowly away down the fern-covered slope. They all followed, tired and silent.

Zelda walked unsteadily beside Smokey, following Solin's scent, sniffing her way around tree trunks and rocky obstacles. The children followed. The heavy rain had stopped for the time being but there was still a fine driven rain forced through the trees by a strong wind. What remained of the evening light had disappeared once again behind thick black storm clouds. It had been a gloomy light when the clouds had separated for a brief period, but it had been enough to aid their escape. It hadn't lasted long enough, however, for them to get down the mountain side. Eventually they had to stop despite the wolves' ability to see. Zelda made some unusual noises which Margo seemed to be able to translate.

Elsie searched in her backpack and brought out the last sandwich. She offered it to Margo but it was all wet and quite unappealing. She handed it to Solin who promptly turned his head away in disgust as if he realized that the sandwich was inedible. Zelda seemed the only one of the group who was happy to eat it. It was soft and easy to chew and suited her toothless mouth.

For a long time, they sat and waited, eating the last chocolate bar and drinking the rest of the water that Elsie had packed. Eventually, however, listening to the sound of the jeep climbing through the forest, they saw the first flashes of light from the vehicle's headlights. Then the engine went silent as the Jeep could proceed no further. Again the children, Smokey and the wolves waited until, after another long wait, they saw the first light from the torches of the search party that was heading up towards them.

CHAPTER FIFTY FOUR

Rasci had done his job. He had led Ben and his friends up the mountain and through the forest until they found Elsie, Margo and Smokey. Zelda was safe and Solin moved away into the cover of the trees so that the humans and their offspring could reunite without Maria seeing the wolf that had once attacked her and her children.

It wasn't just Smokey that went wild with excitement when she saw Maria. Elsie and Margo ran towards her and hugged her tightly. Maria rocked them from side to side as her relief gave way to tears. 'Oh, my children,' she sobbed. 'My precious children.'

Raymond had had to stay behind in the Jeep. The pain in his leg was unbearable now. But Maria had carried on climbing the slope with the two police officers following Ben, who constantly carried on talking and changing direction as, quite unbelievably, he followed the path of his imaginary friend.

Now Rasci could rest in peace. His job was done. The children were all safe once more.

He would miss them all. Ben had changed his life and that of all the wolves in the Rhamin pack, but knowing Ben's father and mother had been a real privilege as well. And as for Elsie, she had suddenly become a real leader herself.

As he faded from Ben's view, Rasci returned to where he lay, in the black tomb that was to be forever his resting place. He sighed and wondered what would happen next. He was used to leaving his body and remotely seeing things far away. Would he leave his body forever now, he wondered? Quietly, locked in his own thoughts, he just waited to see.

It was a sneeze that made him jump. In a dark, black, lightless tomb, a sneeze is not just unusual, it is impossible. But he definitely heard it. He turned his ears to listen more carefully. His ears! Though he couldn't see anything, not even his body, he felt his ears move. He moved his eyes. He could feel the grit and dust in them. He lifted his head and sniffed at the warm air. Then he sneezed; and he sneezed and again he sneezed. His throat felt dry and sore. His chest felt raw on the inside. Why was he feeling like this? He should be past feeling physical pain.

Gradually he sat up and tested his limbs. They were all working as far as he could tell. Slowly he hoisted himself onto all four legs. He ached but felt no sharp pains but one. When he moved his head, a pain cut into his neck like the claw of a mountain lion.

'Huh,' he said to himself, not sure that being alive was a viable alternative. He would soon be dead that was certain.

Walking straight ahead, he stepped into a wall. He turned at right angles and stepped that way. Now he was stumbling over rubble and eventually found that the tunnel was blocked to the roof. Once again he turned and this time tried stepping directly away from the rubble. Apart from a few stray pieces of rock on the floor, the route seemed clear. This was the rest of the tunnel, the one to the right up which he had dived when the roof of the main tunnel fell in. Most likely it would be a dead end, but he decided he had nothing to lose by following it.

He had only gone six or seven paces when he stumbled over something soft. As his nose wasn't working very well with all the dust up it, he prodded whatever was at his feet. It sneezed. It was another wolf. Fantastic! He wasn't alone. At least he had somebody to talk to; but then he realized it was just someone else trapped, another ill-fated creature like himself. No, he wasn't alone; he had someone to die with.

He tried to sniff at the wolf's fur to see who it was and if he recognised it, but his nose was so inflamed with mucous that it was impossible to tell anything about it.

'Hello,' he croaked, his voice hoarse, his throat burning. Whoever the wolf was, it would not recognise his hoarse and rasping voice any more than he was to be able to tell which wolf was trapped underground with him.

The figure at his feet stirred. A few moments passed and then, 'You're awake then.'

'Heh?'

'You're awake. You've been unconscious for ages.'

That voice, like his, was raucous and throaty. No doubt this wolf was feeling just as bad as Rasci and in his dust-filled ears it sounded worse. But it was definitely a female voice.

'Who is it?' Rasci asked, shaking his head to try and clear some of the dust from his ears. But he stopped almost immediately when he felt the sharp pain at the base of his skull. His head still hurt even to move it. He realized he must have been knocked senseless by the rock fall.

The other wolf remained silent.

'Have you been unconscious too?' he asked.

'No.'

Rasci's heart sank. If this wolf had been wide awake then surely it would have made an effort to find a way out. 'So there's no way out of here then?' he asked despondently.

There was a pause and then the voice said, 'Possibly.'

'You mean?'

'I mean possibly,' the voice scratched through the black, dust-laden air.

'Have you looked?' His voice sounded no better. In fact every time he spoke, his voice became drier and more painful. It sounded strange in his own ears

'I've felt around if that counts.' The wolf gurgled a long and painful cough as she cleared the dirt from her lungs.

'And what have you found?' Rasci's was curious as to why this wolf had remained where she was if she had explored the tunnel. Now he coughed horribly.

'It's a long tunnel.' There was an awkward silence. 'Look, are you all right to come now?' she asked.

'Never felt better,' Rasci tried to joke. He wasn't getting any laughs. 'Are you going to lead the way?'

There was no answer, but Rasci heard the wolf stand up, turn around and begin to walk slowly along the black tunnel. He kept his chin near her hip so that he didn't have to feel his way forward.

'Be careful you don't crash into any walls or anything,' Rasci cautioned.

'Don't worry, it's as straight as a light beam.'

'Which we haven't got, remember. I ache enough without crashing into you or anything else.'

'Don't worry, you'll be fine. For a while, anyway.'

Rasci thought for a moment before speaking. 'Roxana?'

'Yes?'

'So it is you?'

She sighed. 'I know. You'd rather it had been anybody else. But you've got me. All right?'

There was another long and awkward silence as they padded forward. 'All right,' he said eventually with an air of caution. He knew that this wolf could never be trusted. In fact he couldn't trust himself not to leave her to find her own way out, only, at this moment, she seemed not only to be the one who knew where she was going, but she was taking the only route available to either of them. He would bide his time, he thought.

Rasci's head was throbbing; his mind was racing. What had this evil wolf in mind to do? What was his plan to act before she could do anything? She had come to kill Zelda. He mustn't forget that. Even choked with dust her voice was luring him into some form of trap. He could feel it. They carried on walking in total silence.

Once again, Roxana's sneeze broke through the silence like a sharp thorn piercing his skin. The pain stabbed at his neck as he jerked his head upwards. It broke him out of his reverie instantly. He felt he needed to talk.

'So how did you end up in front of me? When the roof fell in, I mean? As far as I remember, you and Rhiana were behind me.' He stopped for a second before carrying on and catching up with Roxana as quickly as he could. If she knew where she was going then he wasn't going to let her out of his reach. 'Where is Rhiana, anyway?' he asked as his nose contacted with the warm fur on Roxana's rump.

'Dead.'

It didn't come as a surprise. Rasci knew that the rock fall

had been started by Roxana and Rhiana being unable to stop themselves from quarrelling. He had heard the first prop disintegrate and the movement of the other props that once held up the ceiling. Yes, he had a pretty good idea what had happened behind him. 'And Solin?' he asked eventually, not revealing that he knew that Solin had somehow survived and by some means had managed to join Margo and Elsie.

'Neither of them got out. As the very last glow from the boy's light stick disappeared behind the rock fall, I saw you dodge into this tunnel. It seemed like the best place to go so, in total blackness, I followed you. Then I knocked you down and fell over you and rolled ahead just as the roof came down on you.'

'And why were you still there when I came round?'

Again there was silence. She didn't want to explain. As far as she knew, Rasci was the only other survivor after the rock-fall, and being alive and alone in a black tomb… even now, with Rasci by her side, she was finding it hard to suppress the fear she'd had… the fear that she still felt. But she would never tell him how she had waited in the blackness, shivering with fright, waiting to see if he would survive, nor how afraid she still was. She would not reveal to him her weakness. And if he didn't remember, then she would never tell him how, in her panic of being trapped underground, alone, in that alien place, she had dug the debris off his chest and, sinking her teeth deep into his fur and skin, had dragged him by the scruff of his neck from under the fallen rubble.

They walked more slowly now as Roxana sensed she was nearing some obstacle.

'What are we approaching?' Rasci asked, breaking the uncomfortable silence.

'You'll see.'

Suddenly Roxana stopped. She had been slowing down with every stride, as if she'd been counting the number of paces but now she began to feel her way forward, prodding the air with her nose. Rasci just waited, hearing her sniffing, feeling her fur against his chin as she cast about in the blackness. And then she backed back a little, shoving Rasci backwards with her backside. A few seconds passed before she lunged forward, rearing up and hitting something with her front feet.

Rasci heard something give. It was wooden for as Roxana hit it, a small crack appeared where the rotten wood began to split; a crack through which a narrow shaft of light cut like lightning into the utter blackness. It was only a thin blade of light, not very bright, but its suddenness made them turn their eyes away until they got used to seeing again.

'I heard men's voices,' Roxana stated. 'They were nowhere near this wood wall, but they were somewhere underground like we are. I could hear their voices a long way away. I didn't want to make any sound that drew them to me because they might well be the men that pursued Rhamin into the caves. I listened and waited until they went away.'

'And what did you need me for?' Rasci asked seriously. 'You could have broken through on your own. You obviously knew you could.' He paused and then, after considering their situation, he said, 'Or were you afraid; afraid of the men; afraid of the darkness; afraid of being alone?' His voice was bitter but the words seemed to catch in his throat.

Ignoring Rasci's last question, she replied, 'I thought I could break through. That's different to knowing.'

'So you could have tried instead of returning to the other end of that black tunnel.'

'I've seen you meditating. I realize now how you did the things with that young man kind when you saved Rhamin and Yeltsa.'

'Boy, they are called boys.'

'You can see him in your mind and he sees you. I was watching when you were talking to him in the cave.'

'So?'

'So you can use your mind to see whether there is any way from these caves. There have been men in them and I don't want to meet up with them. We seem to be having a lot of trouble with men and their fire sticks. I wanted you here to tell me… us what they were up to.'

Rasci went quiet for a minute. 'You're right, there have been men in some of these tunnels but they aren't the ones that chased us and they aren't there now,' he said after concentrating. 'But I have seen them before and I don't think they are friendly.'

'What, you've met them?'

Rasci shook his head. 'Only in my visions. But one of them must be gifted. He can tell when I am watching him.'

'Gifted? You mean he sees things like you do?'

Rasci nodded again, but his neck was still hurting. He moved his head from side to side to try and ease the pain.

'Do you know why they are down in the caves?'

'Huh,' Rasci grunted. 'They are looking for something. That's all I know.'

'Well, if they can get in then we can get out.' With that, Roxana lunged at the old door again, splintering the cracked, dry wood where one rotten board joined another. 'Right,' she said, as she poked her head into the light void beyond. 'Let's go.'

They were back in the cave complex. The calcined,

water-mined cavern was a stark contrast to the man-made tunnel they were leaving behind. Where the man-made tunnels were straighter and had level floors, they were weak and usually shorn up by rotten wooden posts, except for the last tunnel which although straight, seemed to be cut through solid rock rather than crumbling clay and shales.

Now they were back in the caves, once again, the firefly or bacterial light, whatever it was, dimly lit their way. Rasci marvelled at how such a dim light seemed so bright when Roxana first broke back out of the tunnel. Now it seemed more than adequate by which to travel, though in which direction, they still didn't have any idea.

'Which way?' Roxana asked.

Rasci remained silent. He concentrated on finding the men he had seen in his vision, the men who Natan had originally seen in the forest. But finding them didn't mean that he had a map in his head. Locating them in his mind didn't mean he knew in which direction his mind had travelled. Unlike his remote body travelling through the forest with Ben to lead him to Elsie, underground there were no familiar landmarks, no up and down hills, no sun or stars that helped him recognise where he was or where and in which direction he had to go.

'To the left,' Rasci stated eventually after working out that he'd turned right from the collapsing main shaft and therefore, by turning left now, it would keep them going in a similar direction to that which they were travelling before the roof caved in. 'I think it is to the left,' he stated as he turned to head that way. 'The other direction…' He paused before saying, 'that must lead back down to the caves.' As his mind focussed on Blue Tooth he added, 'And… and the water. There is much water. And it is still rising.'

His heart felt lighter as he considered what had happened to his friends, the ones they had left behind in Blue Tooth. They, at least, were alive now. Somehow they had escaped from the ground while he was leading Ben towards them, though he didn't know how. Somehow they had removed the big grill that he'd seen over the point of escape. And somehow, they had miraculously avoided Bortag.

But he knew the children and Smokey were reunited with the farmer and his wife, and he knew that Zelda was, once again, with Rhamin. That was what really mattered, and now he didn't want to concentrate, anymore, on seeing them in his mind. He had been able to help them but nobody was there to help him now.

Except Roxana. And he knew that she could only be trusted to help herself.

CHAPTER FIFTY FIVE

Rhamin, Yeltsa, Lexa and Silvah had followed Raymond's Jeep to the foothills and up the mountain. It wasn't difficult to keep up. Although somewhat puzzled by the way that Raymond had managed to locate his family, somehow he and his wolves had known that they were heading the right way to find them.

His feeling of grief for the loss of some of his dearest wolves was abated a little by the sight of old Zelda and the children they had left behind in the flooding caves. The night had fallen on them quickly. It was black and the squally rain still attacked in sharp bursts before relenting and leaving calm periods that seemed like there had been no wind at all.

With Margo on Elsie's knee and Ben on his father's knee and two policemen plus the driver, Maria, there was no room in the Jeep for Smokey. But Smokey, with some words from Raymond, was happy to follow the vehicle until the occupants found more room. She felt good to be free and, for the first time, she was beginning to realize just how liberated her wolf companions were.

But, as Zelda wasn't strong enough to keep up with the Jeep, Smokey said her farewells.

She looked at Zelda and licked her face. 'Goodbye,' she said.

'Goodbye,' Zelda replied, licking her on her nose affectionately.

Then Smokey looked at Solin. For a brief moment she saw the quietness in his eyes that she had only ever seen once before, the time he had forced Zelda to climb the huge steps up to the grill. 'Well, I'll see you again, no doubt,' she said awkwardly.

Solin averted his eyes. 'Not if I see you first,' he said, turning away.

'You can stay with us if you wish,' Rhamin said to Solin as they all watched the children depart with Raymond, Maria and Smokey.

But Solin declined the invitation. It was as if he sensed it was not the time to rejoin the Rhamin Pack. 'Things to do,' Solin called back over his shoulder as he loped off into the night, his tattered ears flapping against his face in the stiff wind. 'You kept your word so I'll not bother you anymore.' Solin had seen his mother and Roxana disappear in the rock fall underground. With Roxana out of the way he would seek out the rest of the wolves that they had collected together and take over his own pack at last without the overbearing obsession of the two females.

Or so he thought.

CHAPTER FIFTY SIX

After dropping off the policemen at their car and taking Smokey on board, Maria drove through the night. The children all slept huddled together with Smokey in the back of the Jeep.

Although he was grateful to the wolves, Raymond's priority was to get his children home to safety. He gave Maria rough directions, but in the dark, cloud-blackened night the landmarks were hard to see with just the headlight beams. It was an arduous drive, but eventually, and followed by the police car, the family pulled into the farmyard.

Raymond's first action was to go to the kitchen cupboard and take out some painkillers. His whole body was racked with pain. The desperate hunt to find the children had distracted his mind from the condition of his own body. But since reuniting with his children and Smokey, and gathering down the slope by the police vehicle, the pain had become crippling. He needed to take the pills and lie down.

Maria set to the task of getting the children out of the Jeep. The police officers helped carry Ben and Margo into the house. Elsie slept on until, being shaken gently by Maria, she realized she had arrived safely back at the farm.

CHAPTER FIFTY SEVEN

Rhamin couldn't help feeling a sense of relief when Solin declined his offer. They had never got on well and, inevitably, Solin would have disrupted the pack again as he had done before he left. It would start, as before, as a simple disagreement and, eventually, it would grow into an all out war. Their sibling rivalry was just too strong.

All his wolves were hungry, but Rhamin had needed to get them all back to the Darin to rest. Slowly, he led them home.

For the first time in the last two days, the area around the entrance of the Darin seemed to be peaceful and calm. There were no enemy wolves. There were no men with their sinister black vehicle or their deadly weapons. Wearily, the wolves, led by Rhamin, went into the shelter of their cave and, tired beyond fatigue, they all lay down to rest, sleep and recover.

But Rhamin had one more thing to do.

After a few minutes of contemplation he went over to an outcrop of rocks and climbed up on top. Raising his head into the air, he called the rest of his pack. As if they had been waiting for his call, the sound of several wolves howling their return message sounded faintly on the night wind. They were returning with food. Thank goodness he had sent that part of his pack away from the Darin before the terrible events that had followed with the hunting men. He had to somehow break the news that some of his dearest friends and family had died.

Rhamin's mind kept returning to the men that had chased him and the children. He knew that the man who had captured him before could no longer track him since the doctor had removed whatever it was from under his fur that had led Petersen to him. But Rhamin had felt there was still something or someone out there that was hunting not the wolves but the children. Everything that had happened with the men in the caves had been because of the children, he was convinced of that. Without Rasci, however, he had no way of finding out what was happening.

Rasci? Solin said he was dead and Rhamin had no reason to disbelieve him. When Rhamin followed the Jeep and Ben up the mountain, he had no idea that Rasci had helped Ben and the farmer to find Zelda, Smokey, Solin and the other two children.

Rhamin thought of asking Zelda if she could see what the bad men were up to, but she was too tired and too weak to do anything but rest.

He knew, however, that the men who had hunted him and the children into the caves were still a threat. He could feel it; he could sense the imminent danger. His ordeal might be over. But deep down in his stomach, Rhamin knew the farmer and his family were still in grave danger. Whatever their motives, the bad men were unlikely to stop until they had finished what they had started.

Unless Rhamin finished it first.

CHAPTER FIFTY EIGHT

The lights inside the tunnels were not made by nature. It took little time at all to leave the cave complex and arrive inside the man-made tunnels again. As the luminous light from the caves disappeared behind them another light emerged. Long black cables that looked like tree vines stretched along one wall and every hundred paces or so a small globe of some kind gave out an orange glow. 'The men are in the passage up ahead,' Rasci stated as the two wolves trotted onwards. They stopped and listened. Sure enough, they could hear the men's voices faintly reaching towards them.

'The old map was wrong,' the first one was saying.

'That plan was drawn by people hundreds of years ago,' the second voice proclaimed. 'I took the rubbing from an engraving on a rock inside the Caves of Dorius. The carvings are more than four thousand years old, thousands of years before this land was supposed to be inhabited by man.'

'And the carvings told you that there was a fortune in gold and diamonds in these caves. Yes, you've told me a thousand times. But we have searched now for two years. We have discovered mines that were worked by men hundreds of years ago. Do you think that, possibly, they might have been looking for the same thing as us? Or perhaps they found what we are looking for so it just doesn't exist anymore!'

'These are old gold mining shafts. They found what they were looking for. There is no sign that they ever ventured into the caves and found what we are seeking.'

'They'd have seen the cave paintings.'

'Yes, but none of them indicate that there is a cave somewhere, a tomb, something built thousands of years ago and which was some kind of altar. Somewhere down here I am convinced there is the place we are looking for. Somewhere, there is a cave called the *Arena of the Wolf.* It is on the map. It is here. I know it.

'And we have failed to find it. The whole mountain is honeycombed with mine tunnels. And after that the mountain is a labyrinth of caves, some totally inaccessible and all out of bounds when it is raining like it is at the moment.' He paused and then added. 'Look Brad, we've been in here now for two days. I'm tired and I need to see daylight again.'

'Then we'll come back again when the water levels have fallen,' Brad replied. 'But we'll have to stay until morning. It's pitch black outside.'

'Another night in this death hole,' the smaller man retorted. 'God, I hate this place.'

'It's only a few hours to morning. Another night on a camp bed won't hurt. Then we'll go. We'll turn off our generator, seal the tunnel and come back when the weather dries up or when we have more pumping equipment.'

'I don't know if I want to come back. The whole place gives me the creeps.'

'You're just a wuss.'

'I'm telling you, there is something, some being down here with us. I can sense it.'

'I don't know what has got into you. You never carried on like this until this last visit.'

'It wasn't in here the last time we continued our search. But it has changed somehow. I can feel it in my bones.'

'Look little brother…'

'Don't call me that. I'm two years older than you.'

'So what? You are smaller than me as well,' the voice said with a chuckle. 'We aren't supposed to be on government property. But the government don't even know these old mines exist. When I enquired about them, they had no record of mining in this area. It's as if the mines were made by people hundreds of years before modern man was supposed to have occupied this land.'

'That would be five or six hundred years ago. Who would have done mining then?'

'How would I know? But then, thousands of years ago someone had an amphitheatre somewhere underground near here as well. My map shows…'

'I'm sick of hearing about your map. Come on, let's get some sleep and then we can get out of here. That presence is getting closer, I can feel it.'

Rasci and Roxana had no choice but to rest as well. For several hours and a few hundred paces away from the men, they lay silently with their own thoughts, waiting for the men to lead them from the underground tunnels and caves.

Fatigue and stress from the last days and hours had taken its toll. Apart from when he had been unconscious, Rasci had had no rest. Perhaps Roxana had rested while she waited for him to come round, but he didn't ask. He had no interest in the wolf that, at the moment, was keeping closer than his shadow. Sheer tiredness overtaking him, he slept like a corpse.

'They are leaving,' Roxana stated suddenly, breaking Rasci from his slumber. 'I can hear them. They have awakened and are walking away from us.'

'Then we need to keep up with them,' Rasci croaked as he tried to stir himself to full consciousness. 'They will lead us out of this death trap.'

'Death trap? Yes, you are right.'

'I don't ever want to go underground ever again,' Rasci said, as he stretched and stood tall on all his toes.

'You live in a cave!'

'A cave with an opening and light that shines in from outside. This underground is not our Darin.'

'Your Darin is the same death trap,' Roxana argued. 'You've discovered that. Once you are inside it then you are cornered. You are trapped. Your predators can starve you out by just sitting outside and waiting for you to come out. You have no means to flee.'

'We did though.'

'And most of your pack has died.'

Rasci shrugged. He didn't want to tell Roxana what he knew. He was about to tell her to shut up when the tunnel was thrown into total darkness. 'The men have stopped their light. They are leaving. Quickly, we must catch up to them.'

'Not so easy in the dark.'

'The tunnel is straight. It just rises upwards. Just keep going. Follow me if you like but I'm not waiting for you.'

'Wouldn't expect you to,' Roxana snapped as she loped past his shoulder in the blackness. Up ahead, there was some kind of faint light. There was a hole and... 'Quickly, they are sealing the opening,' Rasci exclaimed as he saw the last of the big metal containers close against the entrance. 'Hurry or we will be trapped forever!'

CHAPTER FIFTY NINE

It was the noise of the wolf barking behind the big steel container that made the man turn back towards the barricade they had built across the opening to the ancient mineshaft. The man listened for a while and called his partner over.

'There's an animal trapped inside,' the man said. 'It must have wandered in when we were in there.'

'I can't see how,' the other man stated. 'We keep the entrance closed.'

But the barking sound still continued to come from inside the shaft at the other side of the big metal containers.

'Here, get that bar and give me a hand to shift this crate to one side again.'

'But what if they are wild animals?'

'Well, that's it, isn't it? They or it or whatever it is, isn't likely to be a pet budgerigar! Come on, help me here.'

Together they lifted the heavy barricade away.

The wolves looked nothing like the animals they were. Two creatures, both a dull grey colour, with starey bristled coats, both covered head to foot in a layer of thick dust and grime, stared out at the two men who stared back in total amazement. The shorter of the two men held a metal bar in his hand, keeping it across his body in a defensive stance. The taller of the two tilted his head, put his hands on his hips and just stared back at the two pairs of vivid amber eyes.

'What do we do now?' Roxana asked Rasci. She stood side by side with him, unsure what he was going to do. He had been the one to call out to the men. He seemed to know that they would return to release them.

'Just walk past them casually,' Rasci instructed. 'Don't look them straight in the eyes. They may take that as being a threat.' He shook himself and threw off a cloud of black-grey dust and then, as casually as he could, he walked past the two men. At that moment, being set free from that dreadful underground grave sent the most intense feeling of relief coursing through Rasci. He had never felt that fresh air could taste so good.

Roxana followed. She controlled her trepidation well, for she had never encountered men kind so closely before. She, too, shook herself and wandered as casually past the men as she could, all the time, keeping the one with the bar visible in the corner of her eye.

Five or six paces past the men, Rasci turned towards them. He studied the two men as closely as they were studying him. Slowly, he sat down and showed that he was neither afraid nor a threat. Somehow, he felt that the smaller of the two men was able to sense what he was feeling. 'You are the one who could see me,' Rasci said with his mind.

The shorter man put his hand to his forehead and stared into the wolf's eyes. 'This is it!' he said quietly to his brother. 'This is the presence I could feel.'

'Presence? What do you mean?'

'This wolf. He's the one I could feel watching us. I'm sure of it!'

'Watching us. from where? They haven't been anywhere where we've been until they appeared here just now.'

'I can't explain it,' the short man said. But this wolf,' and he pointed to Rasci as he said it, 'this wolf can do what I can do.'

'What, talk to the spirits?' the taller of the two scoffed. 'You are as bad as our mother. You must have got it from her.'

'I'm telling you it can communicate with people. I can sense it. It's as if it is able to talk to me.'

'Yeah, right. Well tell it to beggar off so that we can get on and leave this place wrapped up. We can't afford to let anyone else start exploring what we have discovered.'

'What have we discovered though? We've an ancient map that you dug out of an old derelict building. We've discovered a load of ancient mine shafts, mines that were dug out before man was supposed to have been here. And we are looking for something even older, something thousands of years old that dates back to a time before men were not even supposed to be anything more that savages in bear skins.'

'We haven't even scratched the surface. There must be a hundred miles of passages we haven't yet explored.'

'And none of then have led to anything other than some old worked out gold seams.'

Rasci couldn't understand what the men were talking about, but he felt that the smaller of the two men was not only able to sense his presence of thought, but was the one who had accompanied his companion more in a manner of support than in a spirit of adventure and discovery. He stood up, turned away and tried to close out of his mind the fact that the men were so close by. Then, concentrating hard, he said thank you to the short man. 'Thank you for saving our lives.' Rasci said with his mind. 'I hope we can repay you some day.'

With that, he looked at Roxana and, without another word passing from his lips or from his mind, he strode off across the clearing and down the side of the mountain.

'They were creepy!' Roxana said as she caught up to Rasci.

'Rather men I have never learned to trust than a wolf that would betray me in a blink.' he said to her as he quickened his stride. 'We were trapped inside that tomb together. It didn't change anything. You are a treacherous snake and now we are out of there, you can go where you like so long as it is as far away from me as possible. I will honour Rhamin's pledge. You are free to go despite your venomous plan.'

'Oh don't be like that! I thought we'd mended our relationship!'

'Relationship? Don't be stupid. We never had a relationship.' Then he added, 'Thanks to you and your evil friends.'

'But I was wrong…' Roxana began to say when, suddenly, she heard a ferocious roar. She spun around at the same time as Rasci. The noise had come from further up the mountain. It had come from where they had left the two men. She looked at Rasci and then glanced back up the mountain. 'What do you reckon that was?' she asked.

'I know exactly what it was,' Rasci shouted as he took off at full pace back to where they had left the men.

Within seconds, Rasci was back in the clearing. There, he watched as the man with the bar swung it wildly at the snarling snout of Bortag. His companion was lying on the floor behind him, struggling to get back on his feet. But Bortag had killing in mind and he went for the standing man again.

'Bortag!' Rasci shouted over the huge animal's growls. 'Bortag!'

Suddenly hearing his name, the bear swung around and faced Rasci. Roxana stood beside him, waiting to see what

Rasci was going to do and say. 'You! What do you want?' the bear snarled. 'These are the people who killed Molem. Now I've got them! So mind your own business,' he growled as he turned back to his task.

'No they are not,' Rasci shouted to keep the bear distracted. They are unarmed. They are not the ones who killed your mate. I saw it happen.'

The big bear turned again and looked at Rasci. 'You're that old wolf's protégé, aren't you?' he said, tilting his head on one side.

'You mean Zelda,' Rasci informed Bortag. 'Yes, she's my old wolf. I'm her young apprentice.'

'I know what happened.' The bear said, calmly now. 'I was told that she saved Brunus my bear cub.'

'Who told you that?''

'That weightless friend of yours,' Bortag replied, referring to Corvak. 'He was concerned that I might think that because Molem died near your den that I might presume that you and your wolves had killed her. I went to see for myself. Molem had not been killed by wolves. That I could tell.'

'It was Rhamin that saved her cub,' Rasci explained. 'All Zelda did was calm the little thing down.'

The bear turned his head towards the two men. The taller of the two had got back to his feet and, with his brother, they were standing with their backs against the camouflaged containers. They were watching the animals exchange strange noises.

'So who are these?' Bortag demanded. 'They are the same species that kill harmless animals.

'I'd hardly describe you or Molem as harmless Bortag.'

'You know what I mean.'

'The men who killed Molem were armed with guns.'

'Guns?'

'Fire sticks that sent many invisible teeth into your mate's body. It was the armed men who killed her. We, the Rhamin pack were all there. We saw it happen. And these men had nothing to do with it. I promise.'

'Armed with fire sticks, heh,' Bortag murmured to himself. He was still angry. He turned his head back to the two men and shook it at them wildly. With a blood freezing growl he stood up on his hind legs, leaving the two men in no doubt who was the king of the forest around here. He gave the men one last glance, then spun on his heel and bounded off towards the trees.

A moment or two later, Rasci looked at the two men. They read his mannerisms even if they couldn't read his mind. 'Thank you again,' Rasci said and turned to leave.

'So we're friends with bears now,' Roxana said as she trailed behind Rasci.

'At least he has honour,' Rasci snapped as he glanced at her. 'Are you still here?'

Roxana stopped and watched as Rasci continued to wend his way past the trees and through the undergrowth. Soon he had disappeared from sight. She bent her head and sniffed the ground. She could follow him, she thought. Even with her badly inflamed nasal passages, she could still pick up his scent. But there was no point. He had made his position perfectly clear. Silently, she turned to the east and loped off to where she last camped with Solin's wolves.

It would be strange without Solin and Rhiana.

CHAPTER SIXTY

When Sally arrived mid-morning, it was without any warning. Smokey barked. A car drew up outside in the farm yard and, watched from the door by Raymond and the rest of his family, Sally climbed out of her car, went around to the rear and lifted the boot lid, took out a suitcase and looked at the greeting party. She smiled with her mouth but her eyes didn't show any pleasure. In fact, Raymond thought Sally looked totally preoccupied. It was as if her mind was somewhere else and she was going through the physical motions of being there.

'Surprise surprise,' Raymond called to her as she walked towards the door.

Elsie grunted a grudging welcome. 'Hello mother,' she said with a loud sigh. Then she added, 'What have you come for?'

Her mother raised one eyebrow. 'I'd expected a warmer welcome than that, at least from my daughter,' she replied.

'Didn't have time to get all excited,' Elsie struck back. 'You should have told us you were coming.'

'Would it have made any difference?' her mother asked and then went on without waiting for a reply. 'Sounds like you've settled in then. That's not what I had been led to believe.'

'Huh.' Elsie grunted.

Raymond and Maria just stood by the open doorway and let them get their quarrelsome greeting over with. It was clear that they loved each other. There was a spark in Sally's eyes as she bantered with her daughter. And Elsie would have been bereft if her mother had turned and left. The problem was that they had both loved Elsie's father. They had lost him. And they had blamed each other.

'Room for one more?' Sally said, now smiling a more genuine smile as she tilted her head at Raymond.

'You know you are always welcome, Sally,' Maria put in. 'We were just a bit surprised you didn't come with Elsie, instead of sending her on by herself.'

'She's a grown girl. She can look after herself.'

Maria was going to say that *for goodness sake, Elsie is only thirteen and you dispatched her like a parcel*. She was surprised Sally hadn't put a label on Elsie's lapel, but Elsie, who was standing slightly in front of her mother, shot an apprehensive glance at her aunt. With an almost indiscernible shake of her head she pleaded with Maria not to say anything or get into a discussion about the last few days' events.

'We know that very well,' Raymond stated, seeing Elsie's signal and not wishing to relate just what had been going on in Sally's absence.

'Well, come on in,' Maria said congenially. She gave Sally a cheery smile and stood back from the doorway to let her pass. 'We'll soon make a bed up for you.'

Ben and Margo had watched with undivided attention. This was Elsie's mother. This was the woman that their cousin had said she had hated more than anyone in the world, but it was the same woman who had taught Elsie self defence! What sort of lady was this aunty of theirs they wondered? Margo thought she could feel Elsie's sense of relief at seeing her mother. In fact, she thought Elsie had needed her mother despite saying things to the contrary.

'I'm Ben and this is my sister Margo,' Ben announced as Sally looked down at their upturned faces. 'We've so much to tell you,' he exclaimed excitedly.

Elsie gave him the same slight shake of the head that she had given Ben's mother and, with a wide eyed glance, she waylaid any further discussion. 'It's been fairly quiet here compared with the city,' she announced.

Sally looked at the way Raymond was standing favouring one leg and leaning heavily on the side dresser. 'Hunting accident Ray?' she asked innocently.

'Something like that,' he replied, not wanting to state that it was he and his family who had been the ones that had been hunted.

'We'll talk later,' she said to him, quite clearly indicating that the conversation was only being put on hold and that it had, by no stretch of the imagination, come anywhere near being finished.

Raymond and Maria were happy with that. All they wanted to do was to rest and get the children back to some kind of normal life. Normal! Raymond studied the faces of the three children as they looked at his sister. Elsie was gazing at her mother with an inquisitive expression on her face. Ben was looking at Sally wide eyed, in awe of the mother of this wonderful new cousin, a girl they had discovered had the courage of a wolf. Margo was sitting on a dining chair, her feet up on the seat and her arms around her legs. No doubt she knew what Sally was thinking, Raymond surmised, but he didn't prompt his little daughter to talk.

It had taken a real effort to induce Elsie to believe their crazy tales. He had no appetite to start all over again with his sister Sally.

But Elsie broke the silence. 'Why have you come here mother?' she asked. 'You could have telephoned me if you were wondering how I was getting on.'

Sally scowled. She began to say something but Margo broke in.

'She knows.' It was a simple statement.

All eyes turned to the little child on the chair. They waited for her to speak again.

'The police have kept her informed,' Margo stated.

As she scowled and gave Margo a curious look, all eyes turned to Sally.

'They told you?' Raymond asked. 'I didn't know they knew Elsie was not our child. How did they…?'

'It's complicated,' Sally interrupted.

'Complicated?'

Sally looked furtively around the kitchen trying to avoid eye contact with anybody. 'Well,' she began, 'there's something I haven't told you.' She looked at her daughter who was standing with her hands on her hips. Elsie had tilted her head slightly in a way to indicate that she was waiting for the full briefing.

'Perhaps we should all sit down and talk about it nice and calmly,' Maria appeased, sensing a tension in the air. 'After all, we have all day.'

With that, Sally seemed to relax a little. She pulled out a chair and sat at the table next to Margo. Everyone else sat down as well, except Maria who had busied herself getting out some mugs and making a pot of hot tea. She got out some cake and cut it into slices. Then, completing her task, she placed the plate and the mugs of tea on the table and sat down beside Sally.

The break seemed to clear the atmosphere. Sally had relaxed a little. After all, she'd had a long journey. Maria was feeling a little guilty at the reception they had all given Raymond's little sister. Raymond would have preferred to just let Sally have something to eat and then they could all sit down and get to know each other but, clearly, that wasn't going to happen.

'So,' Sally began. 'Tell me what you've been up to.' Her voice seemed relaxed. 'Tell me about the wolves on the mountain.'

'You know about the wolves?' Elsie gasped.

Her mother nodded. 'And the car crash.'

'Crash?' Elsie had tried hard to blot the burned out station wagon from her memory. It hadn't worked. 'Oh, the station wagon?' she said, her voice rising at the end of the word. 'We all got out safely,' Elsie explained.

'Obviously,' Sally responded. 'But how did it happen? How come your uncle Raymond wasn't driving? How come you were left alone on a mountain full of wild and dangerous animals?'

So she knew that Elsie had taken the vehicle. 'How do you know about… about any of this?' Elsie gasped.

'Because I have spies watching you,' Sally jested.

'Right,' Elsie said with a sigh of relief. Her mother was at least taking it all rather well.'

'The wolves aren't dangerous,' Ben came in. 'They are our friends.'

Here we go again, thought Raymond.

'Let's not bother your aunty Sally with that at the moment,' Maria said, steering the conversation away from the fantastic and incredible to the merely totally unbelievable.

'She's thirteen, Maria,' Sally said firmly. 'Doesn't that mean anything to you country folk?'

'Elsie is quite grown up and we...' Raymond began, but was cut off by Sally's withering glare and Maria's firm grip on his forearm.

Maria thought it best that she continued to do the explaining. 'The children are fine,' she broke in. 'There was an accident and they are safe,' she insisted. She looked at Elsie rather quizzically. Up till now, even Maria and Raymond had been given no details of the car chase or the ordeal in the mouth of the cave. Perhaps Elsie would like to tell the story in full.

Elsie just remained seated, sipping at her mug of tea, quietly letting the story unfold in its own dishevelled way.

Then suddenly it was out. 'You've had trouble with some people watching you?' Sally asked. 'Have they bothered you?'

'Bothered us?' Maria almost shouted, but controlled it to a gruff bark. 'They damn near killed your brother. They came close to killing them all!'

'Just what do you know about these people?' Raymond asked, now convinced that Sally knew more than just what the police had told her.

'So they have been after her?' Sally countered.

'After her? You mean they have been watching Elsie?'

'Were they just watching though? Or was the accident something to do with them?'

Raymond swung his head to Elsie but before she could speak, Margo piped in.

'She knows who they are daddy. She knows these nasty people.'

Unaware of Margo's gift, Sally just ignored the child. To her, Margo's little chants were just a young girl's apprehension from not knowing the facts. 'Have they tried to get at her?' Sally pushed on.

Raymond thought for a moment, working out all the questions and answers in his mind. 'Right,' he said, raising his voice. 'I want to know exactly what all this is about, Sally.' He was shouting now. 'You sent Elsie here and we took her in willingly, but you said nothing about people watching or attacking the girl. You didn't even warn us that we, that's me, Maria , Ben and Margo would be in danger. You clearly have some explaining of your own to do before we go explaining how your wonderful daughter helped save *our* little children.' When he'd finished speaking his voice was dry with anger. He picked up his mug and drank his tea down in one gulp.

'Did they do that?' Sally asked, nodding at Raymond's wounded leg.

Raymond glared at her. 'Stop changing the subject,' he grated. 'Who are these people and why have they come here?'

Sally glance at Elsie uncomfortably. 'I… I'd rather explain in private,' she said, suddenly avoiding Elsie's stare.

'Why mother?' Elsie demanded crossly. 'Afraid I'll discover what you are really like?' She paused only for a second, just enough time to see a reaction from her mother but before Sally could respond. 'I have news for you. I know!'

Sally's eyes swung to her daughter. 'You know? You know what?'

'I know that you are involved in some shady business. I know you never had time to bother with me even when Daddy died. I know you never cared for him and I know you never cared much for me either.'

Sally's face paled. 'That's just not true. Your father was…' She stopped in mid sentence and quietly contemplated what she was going to say.

'My father was more of a family to me than you ever were.'

Sally just carried on, ignoring her daughter's anguish. 'You had to find out some day. The problem is; I work *with* the police.' Then she added, 'But I work undercover.'

'And I suppose you are going to tell me that my father was the same. He was a secret agent or something.'

'No, your father was a librarian. But he made enemies.'

'Yes, I know he was a librarian, mother. He took me to school he picked me up. The rest of the time he worked all his life stacking books.'

Sally shook her head.

Raymond and Maria and their children just listened, transfixed by the conversation.

'You were too young for us to explain,' Sally fought on. 'Your father was writing an article about our town and the local businessmen. His research uncovered some things that happened long ago, before you were born, but things that, if they came to light, would upset the balance of power amongst the people who, supposedly, run the town for the benefit of the community. He uncovered a possible murder.'

'And you? What about you?'

'When I started my profession,' Sally began, 'if you want to call it that, I had no children. Then I met your father. He and I worked on an operation together although he was not from the same department as me.'

'What? Now you're telling me my father was an undercover agent?' Elsie shook her head. 'Never!'

Sally ploughed on regardless of Elsie's protests. 'We got married and when I had you, your father and I decided that I would continue with my career and that he would be the one to look after you. He left the force and, because he had a lot of experience in internet technology, he got a good job in the local library. We decided you should never know what I did, simply because as a youngster, teachers and school friends ask you what your parents do, and to save you having to lie to them, we lied to you.'

'I still don't believe you. You are lying now.'

Sally shook her head. 'When your father died, I sent you here because I thought you'd be safe.'

'Safe from what? What has any of this to do with me?'

'The people who your father was going to expose… it was a man called Alfred Avon and some thugs that worked for him. Well, they wanted to get rid of the evidence he had gathered. They wanted to make sure that any research he had done was destroyed. They offered him money, but he refused to be bought off by them. He just told them that the truth would come out sooner or later and he was going to do it sooner.'

'And? What are you saying here, mother?'

'And they killed him. They ransacked his office at the library. They even broke into the house, *our* house. But despite taking the computer, they couldn't find out where he kept his back-up files.'

'So that's why you said that you'd sold the computer.'

'They wanted him to talk. We suspected that they were going to abduct you to achieve that. He was determined to stop any such event and went after them on his own. He got himself killed.'

'Daddy died in a car crash.'

'That's the official version.' Sally shook her head. 'The problem was, they knew you and your father were very close. They must have thought that he may have talked to you about them, or had given you something that you could keep for him.'

'He did,' Elsie whispered sadly. 'He did give me the back up of his work. It's on a data stick. But I didn't know what was on it. I thought he was writing a book on the history of our home town, not a thesis on the local mafia.' She put her hand down the neck of her sweater and pulled out a thin gold necklace. On a clasp that fitted around the chain, was a small pink data stick. 'And my father died for this?' Elsie growled, looking at it with all the disdain she could muster. She reached behind her neck, unfastened the necklace and detached the memory device. 'It wasn't worth it,' she sobbed, as she slapped it down on the table.

'Even after they had killed him they were still watching the house,' Elsie's mother went on. 'That's why I decided to send you away.'

'And you never thought to mention that our children and our lives might be put in danger!' Maria said quietly.

'Calm down, Maria,' Raymond soothed. 'What's done is done. The children are safe now.'

'No thanks to your sister,' Maria snapped. 'No thanks at all.'

'So do I get to stay the night?' Sally asked in a conciliatory manner.

'Of course,' Maria said with a shrug. Her voice was sharp with anger. 'You are still family. And anyway,' she added,' Elsie will no doubt want to talk to you before you take her back.'

'Take her…? Oh no, I haven't come to take her back!'

'As if she would,' Elsie cracked.

'I've come to help get the men who killed her father.'

Eventually Sally was able to extract the full story from her brother. Raymond had no reservations about letting his sister know the details of the last few days. He told Sally about the cut telephone wires and about the mystery vehicle in the night which Elsie had investigated. He even told her about the men who had shot at him and his family from the black SUV.

But he didn't talk about the chase and the overturned station wagon. That was Elsie's story and she had gone out after the debacle in the kitchen. She wasn't speaking to her mother. If Sally wanted to know about the children's adventure, then she would have to wait. Deliberately, Elsie gathered Ben and Margo, made sure they were wrapped up well against the blustery wind, and took them outside for some air.

CHAPTER SIXTY ONE

Whatever it was that Sally did, she seemed to have the influence to get information from the police. But that's as far as it went. She had arrived a couple of thousand miles from her own patch. She had no authority here. No one was taking any of her complaints seriously now that the children had been found. The local policemen who had helped Raymond and Maria were unable to fathom just what had been going on up in the forests. As far as they were concerned, Elsie had gone off and got herself and the children lost. And now they had been found safe and sound.

'We can presume that the men we are after had something to do with the overturned station wagon,' Sally instructed the police officer in charge. 'There were four men in the SUV. One was the man who killed my husband. One was the man whose past life Bill had uncovered.'

'Are the children safe?' the officer asked.

'Yes.'

'Are they prepared to come in and make a statement? Have they alleged that the men caused the accident?'

'Well no but I…'

'And you don't know where these men you *think* have

been chasing them are?'

Well of course she didn't! She had just arrived there. She sighed and slammed down the phone.

'So what are you going to do now?' Raymond asked, as he reclined in his rocking chair with his injured leg on a stool.

Sally shrugged and lifted her arms up in a resigned action of despair. 'Where I live and work, we would have had three police cars and a helicopter waiting in the farmyard by now.'

'Yes, but there you have jurisdiction. Here you are just a visitor. What I suggest,' Raymond said, easing himself up and limping off the veranda and through the door towards the kitchen table, 'is that we have a good breakfast and then go look for them ourselves.'

'Over my dead body!' Maria shouted. She slammed a plate of toast down on the table so forcefully that Raymond thought it should have smashed into a thousand pieces. It remained intact but the contents bounced all over the table top. 'Scoop it up yourself,' she said gruffly as she marched out of the kitchen.

Raymond looked at Sally and shrugged. 'Without any idea where they are, then it's a waste of time anyway,' he said loud enough for his wife to hear.

'Then I'll look myself,' Sally snapped and, picking up a couple of slices of toast, walked out onto the veranda. She sat on the rocking chair, all the time gazing out into the distance. From there she could see the green forests rising up out of the plain, even though they were many miles away.

Raymond watched her from the kitchen. Trying to relax, he and his family had their breakfast. Sally was still gazing out onto the plain and beyond when he looked her way again.

He pushed himself up off his chair and limped outside. Standing next to Sally, and gazing across his land and over to the mountains beyond, he said, 'Of course, there might be a way we can find them,' he said casually.

Sally's head whipped around. 'You think so?'

Raymond nodded. 'It's a bit of a long shot. But I think I could find them.'

'It's been raining Raymond. I know you are a fabulous tracker, but you can't track them now.'

Raymond shook his head. 'No I can't. But I think I know who can.'

'Who?' he had Sally's full attention.

'I'm not going to say yet,' Raymond said evasively. 'What I need to know is, what do we do if we do find them? They are armed and dangerous.'

'You are a crack shot,' Sally replied. 'What have you got to worry about?'

'And I have no doubt you are, too,' Raymond answered back. 'But you have no jurisdiction here. The local police have already told you that. You can't just deputise me or anyone else you like and then go and round them up.' He shrugged. 'And besides, I'm crippled.'

'Then, tell me how to find them and I'll go myself.'

'You always were strong headed. No wonder Elsie is a hand full.'

Sally chuckled. 'Isn't she just,' she whispered proudly.

'We'll be looking for that black SUV,' Sally stated. She had followed Raymond up stairs and into Ben's bedroom. 'Who are you going to ring?'

'I'm not going to ring anybody,' Raymond answered crossly. 'Please, Sally, let me have a word with my son in private.'

Sally shrugged and, closing the door behind her, she trotted lightly down the stairs.

'Ben...' Raymond began.

'I know, Dad. Margo has told me what you want.'

'Margo? Oh, of course!' He shrugged and smiled at his little daughter who was sitting beside Ben on his bed. She smiled back at her father.

'But it's Rasci who contacts me. Not the other way round,' Ben went on. 'The last time he helped us he said he was no longer in this world. I think he's dead, Daddy.'

'Yet he still guided you up the mountain?'

Ben nodded. A small tear appeared in the corner of one eye. 'I don't know if I can live without Rasci,' he said sadly.

'We can have a go at contacting him,' Margo said, more to comfort Ben than with any expectation that they could actually talk to their wolf friend. But her words seemed to reassure her father and Ben a little.

'So is there any way you can get in touch...?' their father asked.

Ben shrugged. 'I'll let you know,' he said.

With that, Ben watched as his father turned and silently left the room. When the door was closed, Margo said, 'We'll try together.'

Rasci had just left the tree line behind and was heading across the plain towards the Darin when he stopped and concentrated. Something was niggling away in his mind. Before he could work out if it was something he had forgotten or something he needed to do, a thought sprang into his mind.

Hello Rasci. This is Margo. Ben needs to talk to you.

It was as simple as that. Or so it seemed. Margo had never tried to communicate with a mind that wasn't in the same room or near to her. Today she had no idea where Rasci was, but he was certainly many miles away.

'Hello Ben,' Rasci said, minutes later as he appeared in front of Ben. 'Do you need my help?'

'Hello Rasci! Gosh, you really are still alive?'

'I've been very lucky, Ben. But some of our pack have perished. For a while I thought I was one of them.' He paused and then asked, 'So how can I help you? You know I will if I can.'

Ben explained that they needed to know where the black vehicle was, the one that had chased the station wagon.

Rasci shook his head. 'They are bad news Ben. You really need to leave them alone. They have tried to kill us all once. Believe me, they'll try again.' He thought for a moment and then continued. 'Whatever their motive for chasing us, they must know that they have not succeeded. They didn't catch us and they got nothing from you, Margo or Elsie. At this very moment they will be working out another evil plan.'

'Elsie's mum says she can sort them out.'

'You don't believe that any more that I do Ben. Seriously, you don't want to find them.'

'I think it better she finds them than they come here looking for us,' Ben replied.

Rasci sighed. 'Okay, I'll let you know if I can find out. But even if I can see them in my mind, it doesn't mean that I'll know where they are.'

'But you'll try Rasci. You'll try won't you?'

Rasci nodded as he faded from Ben's sight. He had serious doubts about helping his young friend with this, but Ben had done everything in his power to help Rasci save Rhamin. Could he refuse to return the debt? Resigned to whatever fate might cast upon them, Rasci decided he would do what Ben and his family asked of him. But he would be there when anyone caught up with the men in the SUV. He wasn't going to let any of his friends face such danger alone.

Quietly he lay down and concentrated on the sinister black vehicle. Sure enough, he could see it in his mind. It was parked under an overhanging rock ledge in some sort of dry river valley. Next to it was a bigger vehicle with long white sides and windows, and steps at the back which led up on to its roof.

But try as he may, he couldn't tell Ben where the site was. He had never seen it before and there were no other wolves from the pack around to ask if they knew of it.

Ben, however, was delighted with the news. He thanked Rasci and told him that he would tell his father and aunty Sally. They would know what to do.

When Raymond described to Sally the place where the SUV was concealed, she scowled. 'And you know this because?'

'Because I have ways of finding these things out,' Raymond stated, not wishing to go into any detail that would provoke the very same response from Sally that he and Ben had got from her daughter. 'We can look at the maps and see where, within twenty or thirty miles of here, there are any small canyons or gorges.' He sat at the table and drank off some coffee. 'We still have no idea how we are going to bring these people to justice even if we do catch up with them.'

'We can make citizens arrests,' Sally explained, not at all reassuringly.

'A little woman like you plus a cripple like me? Sounds a great adventure. I can't wait to get out of the door!'

'I'm working on it,' Sally snapped back. 'The local police will respond if we call them for help.'

'Once we have found them?'

'Once we have confronted them.'

'And just what happened to your husband when he tried that? Remind me again.'

Sally threw her arms in the air. 'All right. It's a foolish idea. Bill and I were obviously a good match.'

'They've killed your husband, Sally. I'm not prepared to let them do the same to my little sister.'

Sally gave him an affectionate pat on the hand. 'Oh, I love you too big brother.' She smiled at him fondly, stood up and looked out of the window. 'But they won't have given up yet I don't think. For all we know, they could have been watching everything you have done; the drive out to the caves; the trek up the mountain; even the drive back home with the children. No, if they had given up, they would have gone back home. But they are still around here according to you, and we can't just leave it like that.'

CHAPTER SIXTY TWO

By morning the storm clouds had cleared. The sky was still dull but now, where there had been stacks of relentless black thundery nimbus clouds, the sky was filled with white fluffy cumulous vapour clouds that told the world beneath them that the really stormy weather had passed.

As weary as they had been, with some food brought by Powla and Vela, they had all rested well. Rhamin and his wolves had recovered and were still assessing what their next move should be. Should they remain at the Darin or should they move away from the caves and never return again. The memories of what had happened when they fled into the caverns would cast a shadow over their home forever, but the caves were not to blame.

Rhamin was still contemplating the loss of Rowan, Fatz, Jual and Rasci. Although he had followed the Jeep to where they located Margo, Elsie and Zelda, he had no way of knowing that it had been Rasci who had led the child up through the forest. As yet, Rasci was one of the casualties of war. And war it was.

The pack would always have casualties, of course. But those that had died were always going to be missed. Especially

Rasci. He was the wolf who had taken on leadership just to save Rhamin. He was the wolf closest to Rhamin next to Yeltsa his mate.

But Rasci had been Zelda's wolf as well. The old wolf was fading since Solin had told her of the loss. Lexa and Silvah were trying their best to lift the old wolf's spirits, but Zelda had had enough. She'd had enough of the needless killing that men kind spill out upon the rest of the world. She'd had enough of trying to keep her frail old body mobile. She had had enough of living. She lay in the corner of the Darin and refused any food. She wanted to die. When the wolves went out hunting, she was determined, she would creep silently away and go to a secluded hollow in which to curl up and die. She had already found a spot, a clump of rocks that formed a hole. She would be away from the scavenging beaks of vultures. The rest of nature could take her remains.

Refusing any help or comfort from her companions, Zelda thought about her life and what sort of impression it had made on her world. She was proud of the way the young cubs had always grown up to have the decent moral code of fine, well bred wolves. Except for Solin, that was, but then she had nothing to do with the rearing of Solin. He had been nurtured and taught by his mother, Rhiana. An evil wolf, Zelda thought. Given the right circumstances, Rhiana's son, Solin could have been a fine member of the pack. She was proud of the fact that something good had seemed to seep into Solin's character. Somehow, despite his mother, Solin had, at the final moments of Zelda's life, shown the dominant traits of good moral fibre and even leadership. He had shown strength when they, Elsie, Margo, Smokey and Zelda had needed it most, he had shown cunning in using the strength of their biggest predator to help them escape the deadly rising waters. And he had shown compassion, the biggest gift of all character traits.

She thought about Rasci. The loss was almost too much to bear. He would have been twice the wolf she ever was. He was strong, he had courage and, most of all, he had the powers that Zelda had once had, but stronger and sharper and more intense. He had been truly gifted.

As the day progressed, Rhamin gathered his pack and went to the mouth of the cave. 'I'll leave Silvah and Lexa with you,' he said to Zelda. But before he had instructed them, Zelda had retorted.

'I'll be fine,' she snapped, knowing that she needed to be alone. 'They deserve to have the chance to get out in the open and enjoy being free to enjoy the hunt and the kill. Let them go with you Rhamin. They have earned it. They'll be better for it.'

But she knew nothing of Rhamin's plan. Or so he thought.

Taking one last glance at Zelda, Rhamin shrugged. 'You sure you'll be okay?' he asked finally.

'I was when those renegades came after me. I can look after myself. Just go for goodness sake.'

As worried as he was about her, he honoured her wishes. Deep down he had a feeling that she had come to the end of her days. And secretly, he was glad that Zelda wouldn't see what he had to do. 'We'll be back by nightfall,' he said, a sad note in his voice. He didn't know if he or any of his wolves would return. They were setting out on the most dangerous mission in their lives, one that would have repercussions that would possibly mean the extermination of the Rhamin pack. He was sad for old Zelda, but he was sad for what he had still to do. Just as he turned to go, Zelda spoke.

'Rhamin.'

'Yes.'

Zelda paused for a few seconds and then, with her sightless eyes on Rhamin, she said, 'Thank you for all you've done for me Rhamin. You are a true leader.'

'And you say this because?' Rhamin asked, knowing full well what the old wolf meant.

'Try and live a peaceful life,' she answered, drawing worried looks from all the wolves around her.

'Are you sure you want to be left alone Zelda?' Lexa asked, worried now by the tone in Zelda's voice. 'I could stay if you wanted.' With a tear in her eye, she licked the old wolf on her ear. 'You mean the world to all of us. You do know that, don't you?'

Zelda nodded wearily. 'And you all mean the world to me. Just remember everything I have told you and you'll be fine.' She licked Lexa on her nose. 'Now, I would prefer to be alone, young wolf dog.' She sniffed and turned her face up to Lexa. 'You are a credit to the pack. You are a true wolf.'

Silently, with a leaden heart, Rhamin turned and led his pack out of the Darin and into the open air. 'Come,' he said, to break the lingering melancholy. His resolve was unbending. He was still determined to end the threat that hung over Raymond and his children. The farmer and his family had done so much for Rhamin and his wolves that they had become part of the Rhamin pack. Despite the rapidly fading old wolf, now was not the time to have doubts about his mission. Now it was time to hunt the hunters.

It was just the way things had worked out that Rasci arrived back at the Darin after Rhamin had left. He wasn't really hungry. He'd caught a small rabbit on his way down to the plain and that was enough for him at the moment. His appetite was not what it usually was. Something was niggling at his mind but he wasn't able to quantify it. Was it the way Roxana had behaved? He didn't think so. He hated her now, so she couldn't have an affect on him in any way. But he had no idea what it was that was preying on his mind.

He went inside the cave and looked at the blackness that covered the rear passages in which they had all been trapped. There was still the sound of water forging somewhere along potholes and through caves. He'd heard it before, but it had never been something he had ever visualised. Now, however, he knew what the sound was. Whenever he heard it again, he would remember…

A shiver went down his spine. Would he ever venture into those caves again? He thought not. There was something about them that was positively unsettling. Was it the way the water rose so quickly? He thought not. It would go down with the same speed it had risen, now the rains had stopped. Was it Blue Tooth, that incredible tribute to all wolf kind? Perhaps. There was certainly a mystery as to who built it and why. It could only have been men kind of course. Only they had the ability to carve images out of rock and paint pictures on the walls. It reminded him of the way Ben had explained their use of writing. But that didn't unsettle him. That just made him envy the ability he knew Ben would have.

No, what was disturbing about the caves was the way they turned from natural phenomena to man-made tunnels. Men kind had excavated their way through to the caves but he didn't know why. It wasn't those men who had carved

Blue Tooth. And the tunnels were not the path that the builders of the monument had travelled to and from their art. There was another route, an easy way to get into the Blue Tooth cavern. What was most unsettling, he realized now, was that some of his wolves had died because, with him and his leader, they had followed the wrong route to freedom. How could he have lived with that if his mistake had cost the lives of the children?

The pack must have gone out hunting. Even Zelda was absent. But he knew she was in no physical state to go running after prey. He wondered where she was, and began to sniff at the ground to find her scent. Surely, she hadn't ventured back into the cave complex again on her own. She said she had done it before when the rest of the wolves were out and about their hunting business. But he didn't think she would go there again. He sniffed around for several minutes, trying to pick up Zelda's scent trail. He felt he needed to find her. But try as he may, he found no trace of his Gran.

Right, he thought to himself. I'll have a wash in Silvah's water hole and then I'll go and find old Zelda. I'll keep her company, he mused. After all, that was what he and Silva and Lexa did most of the time when they were home.

He took his time washing and soaking his thick coat. It was thick and heavy with dirt and dust. Eventually, he climbed out of the water-filled hollow and shook himself. The water sprayed off him in all directions, leaving his coat damp but not soaking wet. The undercoat was thick and usually impenetrable, but he had soaked long enough to let the water do its job. He felt clean and refreshed.

It was mid-day when he went to the cave entrance. As he looked out into the daylight, he got a strange feeling. It was weird. Suddenly, even though he had searched before, he picked up Zelda's scent instantly. The rain had stopped quite a while ago and in fact the wet ground actually held the scent of her footprints better than if it were dry and dusty. It was strange that for a while she had followed in Rhamin's tracks, but then, with his nose still close to the ground, her trail veered off to the left. He lifted his head and looked to see what the landscape was like. Straight ahead, where Rhamin had taken his pack, was the rising tree line that ran into the foothills and up to the mountains. To the left were outbreaks of rocky protrusions, remains of the same escarpment that also ran towards the foothills, the backbone of the formation in which they had all travelled underground. It was the line of the caves and it led back up to the place where Zelda, Elsie, Margo, Solin and Smokey had eventually escaped. Rasci wasn't sure what was drawing the old wolf back in that direction. He had only been there in his mind when he helped Ben find them and, in real daylight, rather than in his head and at night, it was hard to bring the two worlds together as one. The remote view had been real at the time. But, somehow, it didn't seem the same in its physical form now.

He wandered slowly at first. Something in his mind told him that there seemed no great urgency. Zelda must have eaten well before venturing out on her own so she would be enjoying the day and the freedom after being, like Rasci, a prisoner underground. But then he became puzzled. Zelda rarely ventured out alone. She was old and frail and always vulnerable if predators were anywhere around. Wolves hunt the weak and vulnerable and the same applied to other predators, eagles, bears, other wolves from other territories who were venturing into an opponent's land. He quickened his pace. He was worried now.

Zelda had made good progress, turning gradually to follow a path eastwards along the base of the foothills. For another good hour, Rasci loped on at a pace that he knew Zelda could not have maintained. And still, her trail led on with no sign of the old wolf. Another hour passed as he ran now, panting wildly, and still he didn't catch up to his Gran.

But then, suddenly, as if the time was right for him to find her, Zelda's scent became much stronger.

Soon he would find her and she would be safe.

CHAPTER SIXTY THREE

The black SUV and its occupants would have had to have a base somewhere. There were four men, according to Raymond, and they would be staying nearby. Unable to be dissuaded by Maria, Raymond had insisted on accompanying his sister in her search for her husband's killers. But they found nothing. No SUV, no camp site, no sign of the men who had terrorised Raymond and his family. As the day passed, Raymond and Sally drew their search to a close.

Rhamin had watched the search from the slopes on the foothills. He had seen Raymond's Jeep tracking backwards and forwards. A woman was driving the vehicle, a woman Rhamin had never seen before, but she reminded him of the farmer. Raymond sat upright in the passenger seat with one of his fire sticks in his hand, the wooden stock on his knee and the fire ejecting end pointing up to the sky.

Rhamin knew what Raymond and his driver were looking for, but they had no chance of finding the men in the black SUV without direction from someone. There were no trails after the torrential rain and furthermore, their quarry was nowhere near the search site. And even if Raymond and Sally had been near the people they were hunting, the bad men were so well hidden that they were unlikely to see them.

Rhamin had a good idea where the men were, the ones who had attacked him and Raymond, the ones who had chased him and young Elsie. At first he had set out to find them where Powla had last seen them when she and Vela had taken Brunus and the young wolf cubs away to safety. Powla had led him to a remote but heavily wooded area that lay at the base of the mountains. But the men had been moving at the time that Powla had been there and they were no longer in the area. From the rise on the hillside, however, Rhamin could watch and see Raymond tracking phantoms in the same area, in and out of the tree line at the base of the mountains.

It wasn't until Silvah talked to Corvak that she could tell Rhamin just where the men were. Corvak had told her that he had seen the SUV. He knew where the vehicle was hidden but he also knew that the men had got another vehicle, one in which they could sleep and eat. It was parked in the forest but under a high ledge that protruded over the dry rocky floor of what had once, in ancient times, been a small river canyon. Apart from a little clearing which had been part of the old river bed, there were trees up to the overhanging ledge and trees on top of it. Even the man-made, metal hovering machines they call helicopters could not have seen them from the air. From above, all that could be seen was trees and a bare sandy hollow. The overhang was totally invisible from above. Only Corvak had been able to fly below the canopy of tall trees, low enough to see beneath the huge ledge. The men had been there but they ignored the black raven. No doubt the bird was a local inhabitant.

And Corvak had told Silvah.

No, Rhamin knew who and what he was hunting today. Realizing that Rhamin no longer had a tracking device implanted under his skin, Petersen's men, unable to locate him, had long gone. They were probably back at the safari park from where they had no doubt come. The men in the black SUV, however, were still around and Rhamin was going to deal with them once and for all.

But now nightfall had come, Corvak had to wait to lead Rhamin to his quarry. It would take a couple of hours to get to the place where the bad men were camped. They would set off at first light.

CHAPTER SIXTY FOUR

Nightfall had already arrived when Rasci found Zelda. She looked so peaceful, curled up with her tail around her face, in the bottom of a rock-covered hollow. It could have been a natural den for a mother and her young cubs. Rasci wondered if it had been used for that in the past. Perhaps Zelda had used it herself when she had been an alpha female. He didn't realize at that moment that he would never get the chance to know. He nudged her with his nose, but she didn't move.

'Gran,' he said gently. 'Gran.'

He poked her again with his nose. Her coat felt very soft and sleek. He licked her nose but she felt cold.

'Gran,' he said again gently. 'Gran, it's me.'

The old wolf stirred. Slowly, and with great effort, she lifted her head. Her blind eyes stared sightlessly towards the shadow that had cut off the light from the opening of the hollow. 'Rasci! Is that really you?' She sighed. 'Oh Rasci, you know, until you arrived at the Darin, I thought I was going to join you on the other side.'

'No, I'm here Gran, in the hollow with you. I'm alive. Honest.'

Zelda moved her lips into a wolfish smile. At first it looked like really hard work but then, in the shadow of the hollow, her whole face seemed to regain its energy. Even her eyes seemed brighter and less opaque. She sighed again deeply. It was a sound of relief as much as fatigue. 'I'm so glad it worked out. It's a happy ending after all. I thought… Solin said you had died.'

'Solin! What does he know Gran? He's never been right once in his life.'

'Oh yes he has my young wolf. He has been right.' She shuffled a little to ease the weight on her hips. 'He saved the two young girls, you know.'

'What, Margo and Elsie?'

'Yes, Margo and Elsie.'

'How?'

Zelda wrapped her tail around her face again. 'Oh it's a long story. Perhaps Smokey will tell you,' she whispered. 'She was there too.' She rested her chin back on her front paws.

'But I want you to tell me Gran… Gran?'

For a long while Rasci talked to the old wolf, unable to get any response.

'You must go now Rasci,' Zelda snapped suddenly. She lifted her head and looked directly at Rasci, her eyes washing over him as if she were really looking at him for the first time.

'Gran?' Rasci said, wondering why she was being so peculiar.

'You really are a fine young wolf,' she said proudly. She regarded him for several more moments and then, as if struck by the urgency of what she had to say, she barked, 'But you must go and find Rhamin.' When she continued, she lowered her voice to a whisper. 'He has gone after the evil men. He didn't think I knew where he was going. He didn't tell me because he was afraid I would talk him out of it. But I've seen the men. In my head I have seen them and they are not where Rhamin thinks they are. Rhamin is relying on Corvak to show him where they are in the morning. But they are not where Corvak saw them,' she warned urgently.

'Where are they then, Gran?'

Again, the old wolf fell silent. Her breathing seemed shallow and she seemed to be having difficulty staying awake. She closed her eyes. 'The bad men have been watching the farmer drive around looking for them.'

Rasci shook his head. 'Oh no! I was afraid he would do that.'

'You were afraid he'd do that? What do you mean?'

'Ben asked me to try and tell them where the bad men were. I didn't want to tell him but I owe them so much. We all do. But I could only describe their camp site. I didn't know where it was.'

'That's why you must go, Rasci. Go to Rhamin. Tell him that the bad men are heading back to Ben's home. They are heading towards the farm.'

'When?'

'During the darkest part of the night when the world is at its quietest.'

Rasci knew what she meant. She expected that the men would strike the farm about four hours before dawn.

'But where is Rhamin now?'

'He has been watching the farmer as well. But the pack is resting for the night, waiting for Corvak to wake from his sleep. You must get to the pack and warn them before the bad men get to the farm, do you hear?'

'I hear Gran. But what about you?'

'I'm fine. Now that I know that you are all right I'll be able to sleep and rest peacefully again.'

Rasci gave her a doubting look. 'Are you sure you'll be okay?'

Zelda nodded. 'Go now young wolf. Go and warn our friends.'

'I don't like leaving you here alone,' Rasci muttered but Zelda seemed to have gone back to sleep.

'Gran? Gran?'

But Zelda didn't answer.

Warn them? Of course! I can warn them. Realizing that he could get to Ben before anybody had the chance to go to the farm, Rasci went outside the hollow and lay down to meditate. Some stars twinkled through the broken cloud as he gazed into the distance. He concentrated for a few moments as his mind travelled across the plain faster than a bolt of lightning, travelling over the steaming rock-strewn land and past the water-filled gulleys and over the post and rail fencing that surrounded the Rozalski farmstead.

'Hello Ben,' he said as his form sat next to Ben's bed. 'Wake up Ben. Ben!'

Ben stirred in his sleep and stretched as he opened his eyes. It took a minute or so for him to wake up. And then he saw Rasci.

'Rasci! You've come to see me again!' he said excitedly.

'Yes, Ben. But I have come to warn you. You must tell your father that the bad men are on their way. They watched your father and the female searching for them. Now they are going to come to the farm tonight when you and your family are all asleep. You must warn your father. Tell him!'

'Daddy,' Ben shouted, his heart beating wildly in panic as he ran down the stairs. 'Daddy, Rasci says that the bad men are on their way to our farm. He says…'

'Rasci?' Sally asked, frowning.

'It's true Daddy. He came to warn us. He says that the men saw you today.'

'I knew it was a mistake to go looking for them,' Raymond said crossly. 'Now *they* are looking for us!'

'How on earth does a child know this?' Sally asked angrily. 'He's just making it up. He's been having a bad dream or something.'

'I am not in the mood to start explaining to you,' Raymond responded. 'If Ben says the men are on their way, then they are on their way.'

He stood up and put his hand on Ben's shoulder. 'You did good Ben. Now what I want you to do is go to your room, close the shutters on your window and then do the same for Margo and Elsie. Do you hear? It's important that I know that you are all safe. Then I can face the danger without any worries.'

'I'll see to the shutters,' Maria said with a quiet determination. She stood up and, taking Ben's hand, she walked him back up the stairs. She turned on the top step and said, 'They wouldn't have left us in peace even if you hadn't gone looking for them Ray. It's nobody's fault.' Then, watched by Sally who had gone very quiet, she turned and continued to Ben's bedroom door.

It took at least four hours for Rasci to locate Rhamin. First he went back to the trail he had left where Zelda had branched off. He knew where it was but there was no scent of Zelda when he got there; just Rhamin's trail and that of his pack. Then, after sniffing around for a few moments, Rasci set off into the dark, still night.

It was cool after all the rain. The ground was still damp, and steamy condensation was beginning to form a mist that hid his feet and legs, making him appear to be floating over the earth. The scent he was following hung to the damp soil beneath the blanket like a long snail's trail over a cold grass pasture.

CHAPTER SIXTY FIVE

Never before had Raymond ever felt that he or his family were under siege. But tonight, he felt totally isolated. The telephone wires were still down, and although, this time, Sally had a mobile phone, there were no transmitting stations in the area for her to pick up a signal. The old radio was the device of last resort and Maria sat at the kitchen table turning the dial and trying to get a response from any listener. Unfortunately, there was no direct radio link to the nearest police station.

Raymond had opened his gun cabinet and taken out two of his hunting rifles again. Because of the children, he never left his weapons lying about in the house, but now the children were safely in bed, his guns were out, loaded and propped by the locked door. He didn't know if what Ben had said was true, but he knew and trusted his son's abilities and for that reason he was taking no chances.

Sally on the other hand thought that Raymond was being rather paranoid. He was jumping at shadows.

Smokey could sense that her master's nerves were on edge and that made her edgy. Every time she heard a noise, her ears would prick up, she would give out a short, low bark and that would set off the same chain of events. Raymond would spring out of his chair, bound over to the door, he'd pick up his rifle, slide the bolt of the weapon forward and, easing the curtains to one side, he would peer out of the window.

It was going to be a long night.

And what for? On the say-so of a young child who, it seemed, was in the habit of having seriously bad dreams. No, as far as Sally was concerned, the men in the SUV wouldn't risk turning up at the farm.

Elsie knew why the bad men were coming. It wasn't just for the data stick that she had given to her mother. When he had researched the death of a local politician that occurred twenty or so years ago, her father had uncovered a motive for murder and as a result he had been murdered. The men they were up against were killers. Every time they failed to find what they were after, more and more people became embroiled in their clean-up plan. Now, the whole Rozalski family had been drawn into their grubby world. When Ben told his father that the bad men were on their way, Elsie knew what it would mean.

Quietly and carefully she opened her window shutters and lifted the casement window. The tree outside the window was still brushing its leafy branches against the roof of the farmhouse in the gentle wind that followed the rain storm. It wasn't an old tree, perhaps fifteen years old or so, but it was strong and flexible. Maria had scolded her for hanging upside down in a nearby oak tree. But Elsie loved climbing trees. Now all she had to do was reach out to the nearest branch of this one, step onto it and climb down.

The tree flexed and bent sideways as she gripped the top leafy branch. She stepped onto the thicker branch below and realized that the tree was just a sapling compared with the trees she had climbed before. With her weight on one side of its trunk, it bent towards the window. Her back crashed against the jamb and then, as she rebounded, the tree sprang the other way, bending like an archer's bow, bending, bending and then, just as she thought it was going to snap, she realized she had stopped descending. The treeling was bent over to the ground. She jumped off it quickly, as it whipped back up to near vertical. She didn't think that she would be able to climb back into her room that way, but then, if things panned out like she expected then everybody would soon be outside the farmhouse.

With both feet on firm ground, quickly, she ran across to the big barn.

CHAPTER SIXTY SIX

When he caught up with the pack, none were more surprised to see Rasci than Rhamin himself.

'We thought you were dead,' Rhamin exclaimed as he and the rest of the wolves ran around Rasci, tails in the air, greeting him ecstatically. Their number two leader had returned from the grave and none could have been happier than Rhamin.

Rasci was surprised how far he had travelled. Rhamin and the pack was less than an hour's travel from the farm. The greeting had been inevitable of course. Wolves would always make time to greet pack members especially those that had been lost and presumed dead. And Rasci was always one to enjoy meeting up with friends and family with light hearted banter and wolf cub behaviour. But only minutes into the greeting, Rasci suddenly had a sense of urgency about him that broke through the elation of the pack.

'What is it?' Rhamin asked as his brother became very serious.

'The bad men are on their way to the farm. They are going to kill the farmer and his family.'

It was a simple statement and one that sent a new tremor of rage down Rhamin's spine. He had set out on a mission to end this once and for all, and now the bad men had somehow pre-empted Rhamin's intention.

'They are going there tonight,' Rasci repeated.

All the pack heard. Every single one, the cubs and even Brunus the bear cub began to mill about their leader, waiting, ready to do whatever Rhamin commanded. He looked at them all, the rage and frustration of being beaten once again by these men, etched clearly on his face.

'We go now,' he said very quietly. 'We go now and we don't stop until our task is finished.'

CHAPTER SIXTY SEVEN

Why Raymond would think that Alfred Avon and his men would just turn up at the door, dumbfounded Sally. If her brother's paranoia was substantiated then she suspected that they would be more devious than that.

And they were.

The men had parked their SUV at the bottom of the farm lane. For the last three miles or so they had driven without lights, intent on avoiding any chance of being seen. They had no intention of forewarning the Rozalski family that they were coming.

But they hadn't banked on Zelda. They knew now, after the chase in the station wagon and the pursuit through the caves that Raymond and his family were friendly with the wolves that lived in the area, but Alfred Avon had no idea just how close the farmer and the pack were, and he and his men had no idea what connection the children had with the pack. All he knew was that, by watching the farm from a distance for the last two days, it had become quite obvious that the children, in particular the daughter of Bill Hendon, had survived. For two days he and his men had waited to see if their mission was over. Now they knew it had only just begun.

Quietly, and only using the light from the cloud-masked moon, they walked down the dark farm road. They were heading into a slight breeze that carried any sound they made away from the farm as they reached the gate to the yard. But they were careful not to speak. They knew that the farmer had a dog and they wanted to give the man no warning. Their plan had already been devised and they all knew what they were to do.

Each carried a bag containing explosives, detonators and timers. They would only take five minutes to plant the four bags, one at each side of the farmhouse. They would retreat to a safe distance and watch the obliteration of their problem. Alfred Avon did not intend chasing after Elsie or her family any longer. He was heading back home once his mission had been accomplished. He had a commercial empire to run and messing about in the countryside did nothing for him or his business. Tonight his problems must end once and for all.

CHAPTER SIXTY EIGHT

The farm gate squeaked.

Smokey barked.

Elsie jumped. She had been waiting in the big barn, but the night had been long and she had wrapped herself in her thick jumper and had begun to doze. It was a chilly night and the clear sky and light breeze cooled the air even more. But she hadn't felt the wind. She had been well sheltered from all the weather in the cab of Uncle Raymond's big tractor.

She saw a movement by the gate. It couldn't be Uncle Raymond. There was more than just one person stealthily heading across the yard. It had to be the bad men. They were the hunters again tonight. But not for long.

Suddenly the engine of the tractor roared into action. A thick plume of diesel fumes pushed the weather cap back off the top of vertical exhaust pipe and belched black smoke up into the roof of the building. Two huge headlights flooded light out of the front of the building and into the entire yard. Like rabbits caught in the headlights of a car, the four men stood, dazzled and bewildered. But their astonishment only lasted for a couple of seconds. Dropping the bags, they ran back the way they had come. They could see clearly now where they were going. The headlights of the tractor lit their path as it lurched forward and accelerated through its automatic gears.

The tractor was fitted with a large front-end loader. Powered by hydraulic pressure, a huge bucket moved up and down at the end of two thick arms. It was used mainly for lifting grain and one-ton bags of fertilizer. Tonight it was going to be used for scooping up men.

The men were running, but Alfred Avon was in no condition to run, so he yelled to his men and they stopped and turned towards the advancing machine. They were all carrying guns and took little time pulling them from their belts and aiming them at the driver in the cab.

Rhamin saw the lights of the tractor. He and the pack were still half a mile away from the farm strung out as the faster wolves pulled ahead and the younger wolves and Brunus gradually dropped behind. They had run at full speed to get there before the men, but they were too late. They heard the roar of the tractor as it accelerated towards the intruders. The tractor lights suddenly went out as shots blasted from the men's weapons and shattered the headlights. With their keen eyes the wolves could still see clearly what was happening. The tractor still surged forward towards the men, but it seemed out of control. Suddenly its front end bucket hit the massive gate post. With an earth quaking thud, the tractor bounced up in the air and landed again on its massive tyres. Its engine had stalled and it had come to a standstill.

Avon ordered his men back towards the tractor. They were on a mission and, despite the uproar, they still had their guns and explosives. As they rounded the shattered gate post, the farmhouse door swung open and two rifle shots rang out.

Neither Raymond nor Sally had a torch in their hand, but the light from the open doorway was just enough to enable them to see the shadows of the advancing men. They fired their rifles again as the dark and sinister outlines of the men merged into the night. One of the men fell backwards into the darkness of the lane, clutching his shoulder. Firing his rifle from his hip, Raymond ran, limping, towards his tractor as more shots from Sally's rifle went past him into the darkness of the farm lane.

But being fired on by high velocity rifles had changed Avon's plan. One of his men was wounded and, disregarding any further orders from their leader, the other three had already disappeared back down the long farm lane and into the blackness of the night. Avon panted after them.

By the time Raymond reached the shattered, leaning gate post there was no sign of the attackers. Dropping his rifle, he grabbed the tractor hand rail and swinging himself up beside the tractor cab, he flung open the door. Elsie lay slumped over the steering wheel.

Rasci reached the men first. Two were only five or six paces from the SUV, but one seemed to be staggering, clutching at his shoulder. Another man was helping him and, as he got to the SUV, he opened the vehicle's door with his free hand and helped the wounded man inside. Two others were close behind, both carrying weapons. Appearing suddenly out of the night, Rasci bounded forward and grabbed the nearest one by the arm and, with his weight, brought the man down. Smokey had charged through the farmhouse door. She was suddenly there by Rasci's side, her teeth sunk deep into the other hand that held a gun. The fingers were crushed and the hand gun fell harmlessly to the floor.

Gasping for air, Avon had caught up to the rest of the men, he passed the one that was struggling with the dog and the wolf, and had made it safely into the driver's seat of the SUV. Its doors slammed closed and its engine fired and boomed as he gunned the accelerator. The headlights exploded into life. Suddenly, the machine lurched forward, its wheels spinning wildly as Avon twisted on the steering wheel to turn the vehicle around.

Rasci and Smokey bounced out of the way as the big, wide wheels of the SUV careered towards them. Rhamin and six more wolves had reached the SUV. They milled around the closed vehicle, jumping at its blackened windows but to no avail. The men inside were safe from the pack this time.

Whether it was intentional, none of the pack knew, but the spinning wheels of the SUV cut across the body of the fallen man, bouncing him over the ground like a twig on a raging river. Swerving violently as it corrected its trajectory, the SUV sped off into the night, leaving the carnage behind.

The pack watched and minutes passed as the headlights dimmed and gradually disappeared into the distance.

CHAPTER SIXTY NINE

The tractor cab was dark. Fumbling above his head Raymond reached for the switch that worked the courtesy light. When it came on, he eased Elsie back into the seat. Sally appeared at his shoulder as she pulled herself up the steps to the cab and shone her torch inside.

'How is she?' she asked in a trembling voice. She was on the verge of bursting into tears; tears of anguish, tears of pride. 'Elsie!' she called softly. 'Elsie?'

Raymond took the torch from Sally's hand and shone it on Elsie's face and chest. There was no sign of blood. He looked at the windscreen. It was crazed with fractures spreading out like spiders webs from small holes that had splintered the glass. None of the holes looked to be directly in front of the driver.

'Come on, Elsie.' he whispered to her as he put one arm under her knees and the other around her shoulder blades. Gently, he lifted her up and stepped carefully backwards down the metal tractor steps to the ground. With Sally stroking Elsie's head, and Smokey trailing him at his side, he carried Elsie across the yard and into the farmhouse.

'Oh my God!' Maria shouted. 'What have we done?'

'*We've* done nothing,' Raymond retorted. 'It's those evil

men that are responsible for what has happened. Believe you me, they will get more than they bargained for!'

Lying Elsie on the sofa in the front room, he examined her carefully. She had a lump on her forehead the size of an egg. 'She's hit her head when the tractor collided with the gate post,' he explained. 'She's unconscious but she's breathing all right.'

Sally brought a cold wet cloth from the kitchen. Carefully she wiped Elsie's face and brow, talking to her gently.

'I'm so proud of you,' she whispered to Elsie. 'You are definitely your father's daughter.'

'And her mother's,' Raymond added. 'She has the heart of a lion. I remember what you were like when we were kids. Even though you were four years younger than me you never liked being beaten at anything.'

'But we were brought up on a farm. Elsie's a townie. She reads books and writes silly stories. We've never heard her say so much as boo to a goose!'

'I heard that you taught her to look after herself. She's not one to back down any more than you were. That I do know.'

'I didn't know she was so brave.'

She hasn't told us her story of what happened with the wolves yet, Maria thought, peering over their shoulders. 'Come on Elsie,' she said as she pushed past Raymond's shoulder. Carefully, she took the lid off a small bottle and passed it under Elsie's nose.

Elsie jerked her head away as the smelling salts did their job. Her eyes sprang open and, after taking a moment to get her bearings, she asked, 'Did we get them then?'

'One is lying in the lane' Sally explained. 'The others got away. But they left their bags behind.'

'Bags?' Elsie frowned. 'Oh yes. What was in them?'

'They had no intention of leaving anyone alive,' her mother said with a clenched jaw. 'They were going to kill us all.' She shook her head and frowned. 'But with you and… and those wolves…' She glanced up at Maria as she mentioned the wolves. 'I don't know where they came from but Avon and his men were the ones who ran off with their tails between their legs.'

'Wolves?' Elsie asked. 'They were here? Tonight?'

'A whole pack of them by the looks of it,' Sally responded, relieved that Elsie was conversing after her injury. 'Disappeared; chasing after our visitors. Not before one of them and your Uncle Raymond's dog had brought one of the men down though.' Remarkably, neither Raymond nor Maria had even thought to mention the unusual phenomena. A pack of wolves turn up at the farm in the middle of the foray and join Smokey in seeing off the raiders. Then, they disappear like phantoms in the night and Smokey returns to the kitchen panting as if she'd had a really good and enjoyable night out hunting rabbits! She looked at Raymond for an explanation, but Elsie spoke first.

'Those men will still come back,' she said, fixing Raymond and Maria with her eyes and giving them a barely perceptible shake of her head. She couldn't remember just where she'd heard about information being released on a need to know basis, but right now, her mother really didn't need to know anything about the wolves. She sighed heavily. 'Those men won't give up until we are all out of the way. You do realize that, don't you?'

'We'll go after them tomorrow,' Sally said to reassure her.

'The police will go after them,' Maria said firmly. 'And I mean it this time! After what has just happened and with what those men left behind, including a body, the police will have no choice but to do something about Avon now.'

'If we can get hold of the police,' Raymond said.

Maria smiled. 'The radio still works for some people. A farmer at the other side of the town picked up my SOS. He has rung the police. He called me back to tell me that they are on their way.'

CHAPTER SEVENTY

The pilot of the police helicopter knew what he was looking for. The black SUV and its occupants would have had to have a base somewhere, and it was somewhere close. To appear and disappear as they had been doing meant they were within twenty or thirty miles of the farm.

Now one man was dead, Avon would be either getting ready to leave or getting ready to make one last attempt to suppress the knowledge that he presumed Elsie had brought with her. There were three men left, according to Raymond, and they had not been seen leaving the area.

But they found nothing. No SUV, no camp site, no sign of the men who had terrorised Raymond and his family. A fierce breeze during the early morning had obliterated the tracks made by the vehicle. Despite the day being calmer, the stormy weather had not ended. The hunt was fruitless and as the daylight faded, a fresh, strong wind began to blast everything and everybody with sand, dust and grit as it hammered from the sky. Winding up their windows and switching on their headlights, the team of police cars drew their search to a close and drove away.

Once again, Rhamin had watched the search from the

slopes on the foothills. He had seen the police helicopter. He had seen the police cars. The men in the police cars had little chance of finding what they were looking for, however, without direction from the flying machine and, once again, the SUV had been invisible to anything passing in the sky.

This time, however, Rhamin knew for sure where the SUV was parked. He and the wolves had no difficulty following it from the farm. It was not easy to drive at speed over the rough terrain in the depths of the night even with bright shiny headlights. The men had returned to their big camping vehicle beneath the overhanging cliff where Corvak had seen them. They were lying low, waiting for the police presence to dissipate. They would wait another day before returning to their unfinished business.

CHAPTER SEVENTY ONE

As they approached, Rhamin told his wolves to be on their guard and to make no sound. He knew that what he was going to do would have severe repercussions, but it had to be done. These men that he was now hunting were armed, dangerous and had a deadly intent. He knew, that whatever any men kind thought, whatever retribution they brought on the Rhamin Pack, he had to do what he had planned for the sake of the farmer and his family, the farmer who, with his children risked everything to save him and his mate Yeltsa.

As he moved forward silently and slowly, he spotted the creamy-white form of the camping vehicle that the men had been using. As he padded closer, it looked a little out of kilter, sloping down to one side. One door was open, clinging to the side of the vehicle because of the slope of its body. There were no men around. At first, there was no sound. Or at least, there was no sound of men kind. From behind the camper vehicle, the wolves could clearly hear a shuffling noise. It seemed familiar, but Rhamin couldn't place it. He had heard it before, but what was it now?

Slowly, he led his wolves along the front of the camper and peered around. There, the black SUV was on its side, scraped and battered. All the windows were broken and various contents from within it were scattered over the ground.

Still they could hear the shuffling sound. Rhamin quietly ordered his wolves to spread out. They were still in attack mode and if there was any trouble then they were instructed to defend themselves and all other wolves to the death. It meant that they were not going to leave without finishing their mission.

The shuffling sound moved. Whatever it was, something was going to appear around the stricken camper and very soon. Then they saw him.

Bortag had no mind to be watching or listening for any other predators. He was king of the forests wherever he chose to be. So it came as a bit of a shock to him when he looked up and saw that he was being watched by Rhamin and his pack of wolves. He looked at all the onlooking faces. There were the wolves he knew and there were some he didn't recognise. Further back, well out of danger, there were several younger wolves, obviously from this year's batch, but then he saw another youngster. It was Brunus. Like all the other wolves, she stood alert and ready. Bortag couldn't help feeling proud of the little bear cub, despite wondering if she was ready to fight or ready to run. But there she was, ears forward, on her front toes, facing the potential enemy just like the rest of Rhamin's wolves.

'Well well,' Bortag growled. 'This is a surprise!'

'No more than it is to us,' Lexa barked. 'Where are they?'

'Where are…? Oh the men kind!' Bortag couldn't help giving out a wicked chortle. 'They have paid. I told the old wolf they would. These creatures with weapons that kill indiscriminately, they have paid!'

He lifted his huge head in the air, stood on his hind legs

to his fullest height and roared. The sound echoed off the rocky cliff face, through the trees and bounced its way down to the plain.

Rhamin and his wolves just stood and watched, neither aggressive nor afraid. The bear landed back on all fours and turned to face Rhamin, his blind eye eerily staring at the leader of the wolves. 'Go,' he shouted. 'Go and don't come back. I know what men kind are like. They will hunt all the wolves in the land if they think you are responsible. But me? They won't touch me. I'm a bear. Bears kill men and there is never any retribution. They say that it was the men kind's fault for crossing the bears' path. Not so with wolves, and you know that. If a wolf kills a man kind then all the world sets against wolves, whether they were the ones to perpetrate the deed or not... so go, Rhamin and take your pack with you. You were never here.'

He rolled the SUV in front of him like a child with a big ball, and as he did, it spun on its side further out into the open clearing from under the overhanging cliff. He pushed once again and it landed once more upon its roof. Now seemingly engrossed in what he was doing once again, Bortag added, 'Take my cub and look after her, for you know that male bears do not rear cubs well.' Then, as he turned towards the debris that lay behind him, he added, 'Don't forget, we bears sleep in winter. Feed her well. Keep her safe.'

With that Bortag turned back to the SUV, leaned inside through one of its glassless windows and began to rip out more of its insides. 'They will only guess what happened of course,' he growled as he went about his dreadful task. 'But wolves can't do such damage. Wolves are puny compared with a full grown bear. Yes, you can attack and bite and sting like hornets, but you haven't the might of Bortag.' He pushed the dead SUV over again so that it landed on its side. Then standing on all fours again he growled, 'Go Rhamin before I change my mind.'

CHAPTER SEVENTY TWO

It was two days later that the police helicopter found the remains of the camp site. The SUV had been battered beyond recognition and had been dragged out from beneath the ledge that had been concealing it. It had been ripped apart, looking like something from a salvage yard. The camper was torn to shreds as well. They are made of soft aluminium metal and Bortag had ripped and folded and crumpled every single piece, every single panel. The twisted frame lay on its side. The fibre glass insulation had been torn out and shredded and was wafting about in big tufts by the breeze. The inside of the cab had been shredded. A slick of oil, the machine's blood life-force had drained into the ancient river bed and dispersed in a muddy puddle, leaving a black-brown iridescent stain that would eventually wash away with the heavy rains. It was hard to believe that either vehicle had been used in the last ten years. Neither the machinery nor the occupants would be long remembered.

The contents of the stricken vehicles were strewn over the forest floor, but apart from some scattered clothes and two odd boots, there was no sign of the men who had gone there.

Various utensils and their guns were discarded in the sludgy, gravelly sand. It didn't appear that any of the weapons had been fired. The whole existence of these people, it seemed, had been erased from the pages of the book that told the life story of the forest, the plains and the mountains.

The police report concluded that the men may have left the area, but the vehicles had been rented in false names and there was little evidence to be able to trace, or pin an identity on, any of the people who had been there.

A second theory, but not one put in the report, was that the men had been killed by a sloth of marauding bears, but without any bodies, no great effort was expended to look for the animals. They would be long gone, and bears were natural killers anyway. Men should either know how to avoid them or know how to defend themselves against them. Or they should keep out of woodlands and wild country if they haven't any idea how to survive there.

No doubt the men had gone home.

CHAPTER SEVENTY THREE

Sally left the Rozalski ranch later that week. She waved goodbye to her brother, his wife and two children. Then she gave Elsie a big hug, kissed her on the cheek and said. 'Let me know if you change your mind.'

'I won't,' Elsie answered, kissing her mother back on her cheek. 'I like it here and besides, if I came home I'd miss Dad too much, especially if you are going to be away all the time.'

'I've told you, I'll take a desk job,' Sally responded.

'And you'd hate every minute of it. I've watched you over the past days, and the work you do sparks a light in your eyes. You'd hate leaving it and you'd come to hate me. I'd rather we loved each other as we are.' She looked her mother straight in the eyes as they pushed each other gently away. 'I love you Mum.'

Without a further word, Sally turned and walked away to the departure lounge. Raymond, Maria, Ben, Margo and Elsie waved as she turned to go through the gate. Then she was gone.

CHAPTER SEVENTY FOUR

When the pack left Bortag, Rasci couldn't help feeling that there was a dire sense of urgency to find old Zelda. Explaining what had happened when he returned to the Darin, he led Rhamin and the pack back to where he had left his Gran. It took several hours, but when they got there, the hollow beneath the rock was empty apart from some old dry leaves that had blown in before the rains came.

'But I left her here. She was asleep!'

Rhamin licked Rasci's face. 'She was dying Rasci my brother. She hadn't eaten since Smokey, Solin and the children had reached safety. It was as if she had to stay focussed until the farmer's children were safe. And when she heard you had died, she just gave up. She no longer had the will to live.'

'But she knew I was alive. I talked to her. She was right here.'

Rhamin shook his head again. 'No Rasci. This is the hollow where she raised her first litter of cubs. She showed it to me when we were out hunting one day. She said it was a sad place. It held sad memories. She wouldn't have come here.'

'What memories?' Lexa asked, coming into the opening of the hole.

'I don't think we will ever know now,' Rhamin stated forlornly.

Rasci scowled and glared at Rhamin. 'I tracked her here.' he insisted.

'When I left her in the Darin she was so weak she couldn't walk. There's no way she could have travelled even part of the way to this place.' Rhamin sighed and licked his brother's face. 'She was dying, Rasci. I'm sorry.'

'It's true,' Yeltsa confirmed. 'We left her by herself because she wanted to be alone to think about her life and all she had done in it. She had no reason to travel this far. She loved the Darin and she wanted to be there at the end.'

'But I'm telling you, I tracked her!'

'There's no sign that she has ever been here,' Lexa said, anxiously. 'We've all scouted around. There are no tracks. There is no scent. She wasn't here Rasci.'

'And at the speed she could walk you would have caught up to her much sooner,' Yeltsa added.

Rasci didn't understand why the pack was so adamant that he didn't go out to find Zelda. 'I'm heading back to the Darin. She might have gone home.'

The rest of the pack just nodded. They could see how distressed Rasci had become. Leaving the rocky hollow, and without a single word passing between them, they set off behind Rasci at a fast lope towards home.

Rhamin was happy to let Rasci be the first to reach the Darin. He climbed up the escarpment, and watched as Rasci bounded over the crest and down to the cave.

'Zelda! Gran?' he shouted.

There was no answer to Rasci's calls apart from the echo of his own voice rattling through the dark passages at the rear of the cave. He sniffed at the floor. Zelda's scent would still be there. It would confirm what he said. Her trail would lead out of the Darin.

But it didn't. Zelda's Scent was there, to be sure, but, as he picked up the strongest scent, he realized that Zelda had never gone from the Darin. Instead, she had gone to the back of the cave and returned to the black and haunted passages that led to Blue Tooth.

Silently, Rasci turned and went to the opening of the cave. Dawn was breaking and a grey light was beginning to lift the dark curtain off the night sky. Perhaps it was going to be a better day. Raising his head high, he heaved a deep sobbing sigh and looked out onto the plain. A numbing weight seemed to be getting heavier inside his chest. He sniffed loudly as a small tear trailed down the fur on his cheek and dropped onto the ground by his feet. He had no energy left to go on searching.

As the tiny droplet splashed into the dirt, he lifted his nose into the air and wailed a soft and tender howl.

CHAPTER SEVENTY FIVE

It wasn't until after Sally had gone that Elsie told her Uncle Raymond about Blue Tooth. It was a secret that she, Margo and Ben had kept to themselves because Elsie had insisted that her mother should not know how close they had all come to being killed - and not just once! But Elsie realized that the children would at some time end up telling their father and mother, so, reluctantly, she released her two young cousins from their oaths of silence and let Ben and Margo tell their parents the full story.

Each child had a different story, of course.

Ben told how they had all been chased by bad men into a cavern with a mouth like a wolf; how he had swum under a lake with Rhamin to try and go to get help. And he explained how he had been saved by Rhamin who had carried him out of the ancient, collapsing mine shafts, in his jaws just like a wolf cub.

Margo explained how, because she couldn't swim, Elsie stayed with her; and she told how Elsie had never once shown despair and that she actually told Margo one of her wonderful stories to pass the time. She told of how the bad wolf Solin had suddenly made good and found them a way out of the Blue Tooth cavern. They had all been trapped beneath a rock grid, and Solin had called a big bear called Bortag and the huge creature had come and set them free and then said *goodbye* and just walked off through the trees.

Elsie told how she had stayed behind in the caves with Margo and old Zelda and Smokey and how they had examined the Blue Tooth cavern. It had been some kind of arena with entrances and writing on the walls. She told how it was lit by some kind of living bacteria or insect life high in the cavern roof, but she couldn't reach high enough to examine the source of light closely. She told of the wolf sculpture having stalagmites and stalactites as its long canine teeth and she described how they had been encrusted in blue crystals. And finally, she explained how one of the blue teeth acted as a lever to let down a floor from above and that Solin had appeared and led them to the stone grill and ultimately to safety.

Of course, her mother, Sally, would never have believed any of that. Even Uncle Raymond and Aunt Maria were a bit sceptical, at these amazing versions of what happened, so it would definitely have been no good telling Sally of any of these things.

So no one would ever know about the story of their adventures with the wolves of the Rhamin pack in the caves of Blue Tooth and The Arena of the Wolf.

Unless, one day, Elsie showed them the large, uncut, blue diamond that she kept under her pillow.

— THE END —

Also by Bryce Thomas

Lucy Lockhart

After being in a coma and undergoing a surgical operation, Lucy Lockhart discovers that she has certain knowledge and skills that, she is told, she didn't have before her accident.

Her new found friend Loanne, on the other hand, was born gifted with certain paranormal abilities, but as a result of bullying at school, developed a dark side to her character where she could use her abilities against people if she was frightened or angry.

When the two thirteen year old girls wind up in critical danger, they use a mix and match of their abilities to extricate themselves from the situation. But things get far worse before they get better and the shockwaves propel Lucy and Loanne into a journey of exploration and discovery so full of danger, excitement, fear and drama that it will change their lives and that of their parents for ever.

Coming soon by Bryce Thomas

The Last Spell

A fortune hunter, a witch, a mad scientist, a homicidal ship's captain and a megalomaniac. Not much in common except that, in 1854, as each one tries to control their own destiny, they will all permanently alter the lives of the others. Unfortunately each one's future depends on possessing The Seal, and all of their futures depend on one or more of their adversaries dying.

EXCERPT

The air was becoming chilled, but Henri dared not pick up his coat. For what seemed like forever, he watched and waited as the men prowled the dockside, chatting and laughing, looking for nothing in particular, but moving on only slowly.

Henri cursed under his breath. He couldn't stay in the country any longer, but neither could he risk confrontation with these men. Already there were signs of movement along the quayside. *The Arinosta* was getting ready to sail and still the men were wandering about in the shadows. But eventually, after what seemed like a long time to Henri as he stood and waited, the men started moving away at last. But he still waited and watched them for several more precious minutes before daring to slip out of the shadows and step lightly towards the quayside.

He had to move or he would miss the boat. Dragging his heavy great coat behind him, very slowly, he picked it up and pulled it on. He fastened it with a cord around his waist, glancing back constantly as he manoeuvred carefully past hanging nets and stacks of crates, towards the steps that led down to the water's edge. With a sigh of relief he found the small rowing boat still moored under a shabby tarpaulin where he had left it. He pulled back the sheet, climbed into it, checked that his own canvas bag of clean clothes was still stowed safely in the bottom, pulled the tie rope to release it, sat down and picked up the oars.

The sound of activity got louder as orders were called, preparing the ship to sail. The order was given to raise the gangplank and more voices broke into the night as the soldiers on watch gave up their vigil and, with no sense of urgency, began to walk back towards the inn.

Henri kept the boat close into the sea wall. Slowly and silently he rowed towards *The Arinosta*. But he feared he might have left his escape too late. A bell sounded, a final command was given and the crew began to rig the sails. The brig would begin to move any time now. He knew he had but a few more remaining minutes to get on board the ship. Desperate and determined to leave the port for ever, he began to row in earnest. He pulled and pulled again as his oars began to plash and make a noise, but the sound of activity on *The Arinosta* was now deadening any sound he made.

To get alongside the ship, he had to move away from the wall of the dock to row into clear water where the moon was trying its best to light up the sea like a new morning sun. Cursing the fine weather, he headed straight for the bow of the ship. *The Arinosta* was beginning to sway with the movement of the wind in its sails. Soon the anchor would be hauled in, the mooring ropes would be unlashed and his chance to escape would disappear with that wind. As the mooring ropes were being detached, he realized that he was still a hundred yards or more from the vessel. He rowed as fast as he could, pulling on each stroke with all the strength in his body. Despite the chill in the air, his back began to prickle with sweat. His arms began to ache with the sheer effort of getting to the ship, now without any regard to being seen. Twenty yards to go and the anchor was being weighed in. He was so close now that he could see every glistening link.

Then an outcry barked from the dockside. A soldier had seen his little rowboat and was calling for the ship to haul to and re-dock. But the captain was watching over the side. He too had seen Henri rowing towards the ship. And he too had no love or respect for the mercenaries of Abraham Drach. While in dock he would let them search his ship and pilfer apples from the stores, but now he was in command once again. The ship was twenty feet from the dockside and moving away slowly. Twenty five feet. The calls from the soldiers were now raising the alarm. Alerted by the calls, more soldiers were running down to join them. 'Haul to!' a voice demanded, but the captain shrugged and lifted his hands in a gesture of impotence against the strength of the wind now carrying the brig, yard by yard, on its way out to sea.

A shot rang out in the air. A musket ball passed over Henri's left shoulder. Another sank into the side of his rowing boat. Yet more shots were fired and desperately Henri pulled at his oars with the last of his strength. His arms burned with fatigue. Sweat poured down his face, streaking through the dirt he had rubbed on it to age his features. He had missed the chance to sail with *The Arinosta*.

More shots rang past his head as the ship moved towards him. And then the bow of the ship hit his rowing boat at an angle and, almost upending it, threw it to one side. In his effort to keep the boat upright, Henri let go of the oars and grabbed the sides of the boat with both hands. The sway of the little boat almost tossed him overboard. The oars disappeared into the dark water as the ship somehow drew the little boat around the bow. The boat was being washed along the starboard side.

The Anchor was lifting out of the water only feet away from Henri's head. Now, out of sight of the soldiers and out of reach of their shot, he had but one chance. Desperately he stood up in the rocking boat and, placing one foot on the side, he pushed and jumped at the point of the anchor. The boat gave, rocking sideways beneath the pressure of his feet. His effort seemed to have little effect on his attempt to propel himself upward as the boat dipped down. When the tips of his fingers grabbed at the anchor, it was wet and slippery. No amount of strength would have enabled him to grab a hold of it. Helplessly, he realized he was falling into the black water. He hit it, landing on his side as the boat disappeared from beneath his feet.

Now he found himself caught in the wash of the ship; he was being carried alongside it like a cork, as *The Arinosta*'s weight and speed gained momentum. The heavy great coat began to weigh Henri down as it soaked in the water. Should he discard it? He knew it would kill him to keep it around his body. But then he knew that if he survived he would be caught by Drach's men and his fate was sealed in that direction.

And what about his possessions? The few he had were deep within the inside pockets of that coat and his remaining gold was sewn into the lining. His bag of clothes had already disappeared to the black murky depths of the dock with the rowing boat.

He began to sink. Kicking wildly with his feet, and gulping at the air as he went under the water, he managed to get his head above the surface. But his head cracked against the ship's bow as the thrust of the rushing bore dragged him under once again. In the black murky depths all he could see was a glistening ball that had been the moon, ripped to pieces by the rushing foam way above his head, and a solid, shadowy hull glancing past his shoulder. He swallowed water as he struggled to stay conscious. Frantically he pulled at the chord around his waist, desperate to free himself from his coat but something was caught against his hand and was pulling his arm away from his body and the string. The other hand alone could not loosen it. Struggling and kicking, and not knowing how, he rose once more to the surface. He took another gulp of air, knowing it would be his last one, for he knew he would not have the strength left to kick himself and the weight of his clothes back from the deep watery grave that awaited him.

But the thing that had tangled about his arm seemed to be pulling him now. Grasping at it, suddenly he found his head free of the water. His arm was outstretched above him. A dragging rope had somehow washed up against him and had wrapped around his wrist. No longer was he being washed alongside the ship, he was being carried along with it, the tension of the rope was lifting his shoulders out of the spume as the ship gained speed. As the angle of the rope increased he was lifted higher again. His legs were now skipping over the foam. He looked up at the side of the ship and could see the rigging towering above, but there was nobody that he could see on the deck. He had only himself and his own determination to help and save him. For a short while he just clung to the rope. The sheer exertion of rowing and then jumping and then half drowning had taken all his energy. He was safe for a while, dangling there. He could tell the ship was turning now, heading straight out to sea. He looked back along the ship towards the stern, and slowly the dockside and its occupants came into sight, now too far away to be able to see him or shoot at him. Their lanterns flickered in the darkness as they gathered at the water's edge looking for the body of the man who they were sure they had killed. Henri watched, for what seemed like ages, as the flickering lights and the land slowly but surely receded into the darkness of the night.

Henri didn't know how long he had clung to the rope. If it hadn't been wrapped around his wrist he would never have had the strength to hold onto it, but as it was, and with the sheer and utter feeling of relief of having escaped from Yemara, and watching the moonlight glinting like stardust on the rolling waves, he felt he could have clung there forever, skimming over the surface of the water as the ship ploughed on into the darkness and out into the open sea. Eventually, though, his strength returned. Slowly at first, he began to bend his arm and pull himself upwards. With his free hand he grabbed the rope a little higher and with that he pulled himself completely clear of the water. Now, still leaving the rope wrapped around the wrist of his right hand, he let go with his left hand and reached a little higher. Inch by inch, and dragging his heavy drenched coat, he hauled himself upwards, stopping every few feet to regain his strength.

Eventually he came to the top of the rope where it hung through the base of the rail that edged the wooden deck. The gap beneath the rail was too small to pull himself through. With the rope still firmly wrapped around his right wrist, he gripped it with the same hand, and then with his left hand he grasped at the loose rope below his arm and wrapped that part of the rope around his wrist once more to ensure he could not fall. He rested there for some considerable time, breathing in the cool night air and contemplating his next move. Somehow he had to get over the rail and when his strength had returned a little, once more he hauled himself upwards. Slowly, he managed to get his fingers onto one of the rail posts. Now he loosened the rope that had secured him and, gripping it in his right fist, he grabbed the post with his left hand and, with all his strength, pulled himself up to the top rail. As he tried to get his arm over it, he kicked with his legs, trying to get his feet onto the ridge beneath the rail. But with the weight of his clothes, and now having lost all his strength, he dangled helplessly from the side of the ship as, slowly, his arm began to slide back off the rail. With panic coursing through his whole body, he heaved again but his efforts seemed futile now. At some point he knew he would have to give up his struggle. His will to survive had pushed him so far, but he could do no more. He looked down, wondering if he could dangle there high above the water until his strength returned. He let his arm relax and began to slide down the outside of the rail when, suddenly, from out of the dark night air, a pale, thin hand brushed past his face and grabbed the collar of his coat. He kicked frantically again as another hand heaved at his sleeve, and with his last grains of energy, he pulled at the rail one last time as he was hauled over it onto the deck.

About Bryce Thomas

Bryce graduated from Leeds University with a degree in Law, but hankered after the life he remembered as a boy growing up in the North of England on his father's farm. These memories drove him to follow in his fathers footsteps, and he began making a living off the land as a farmer.

This vocation inevitably fosters close links between man and nature, and Bryce developed a profound fascination with these relationships. It is this deep-seated interest and Bryce's love of nature, coupled with the vivid recollection of family tales told to him as a child, which led eventually to his first novel *Rhamin* being released in July 2010. It went straight to number one in the Welsh Books Council's *Top Ten Bestselling Children's Books List* and won the WBC *2012 Bestselling Children's Novel* award for its UK and international sales.

His second novel, *Lucy Lockhart - The Awakening* was published in October 2011, whilst *Blue Tooth,* his third published title, continues the compelling *Rhamin* trilogy.

Bryce's novels have turned out to be as popular with adults as they are with youngsters. This coupled with critical acclaim, has led to him now being recognised as one of the best, new authors based in Wales today.